CHASING

DREAMS

Dear Mollie & Tom:

[signature]

JAHED RAHMAN

STRATTON
—PRESS—
Publishing Life

CHASING DREAMS
Copyright © 2021 **Jahed Rahman**

Stratton Press Publishing
831 N Tatnall Street Suite M #188,
Wilmington, DE 19801
www.stratton-press.com
1-888-323-7009

ISBN (Paperback): 978-1-64895-464-1
ISBN (Ebook): 978-1-64895-465-8

Printed in the United States of America

To my in-laws,
Rahela Abedin and Zainul Abedin

CONTENTS

Previous publications by the author:

Bends and Shades (2014)
Indu (2015)
House of Twenty-Two Buffalos (2017)
Passion and Pathos (2019)

Backdrop

The tail end of my life amusingly appears to have a lot of similarity with my growing-up phase, stamped by indeterminate interests in matters of abstract virtuosity. Besides academic engagements, my principal focus was acting and writing while growing up.

As a class six student, I was selected by the local patrons of Sonapur to portray the role of the second son of *Tipu Sultan of Mysore* (*The Tiger of Kingdom of Mysore of India*) in a drama play so titled. My quasi involvement with dramatics continued throughout until I joined civil service. In between, and due to social compulsions, I had to walk out, with dismay, of an opportunity to join the nascent film industry of Dhaka as an actor.

During my growing-up, akin to a middle school phase, I very much liked history as a subject and used to sketch my disjointed thinking about presumed kings and queens and invincible heroes of made-up detective stories. I even had a pseudo name of *Kuasha* (Mist). As it came to my knowledge that someone from Dhaka was already writing with the same name, I changed that to *Jhapsha* (Fuzzy) at the behest of my immediate younger sister, Bilkis (died a few months back).

My writing took a more structured shape during my high school rung, when I started writing essays for schoolwide and interschool competitions on various occasions of social relevance. In my early youth coinciding with intermediate level (akin to the eleventh and twelfth grade of the American system) educational pursuits, I started writing one- and two-act plays, staged them at the local community level during vacations, and acted in some of them as well. The most embarrassing experience I sustained, while portraying a drunkard young man, was when I found my father adorning the chair of the chief guest as a replacement of the deputy commissioner of the district who could not make it.

As I moved to Dhaka for my intermediate education, I was bewildered. Even the then limited span and extent of Dhaka city, nothing compared to present Dhaka metropolitan, baffled me. I was at a loss in the new setting, but I also soon realized that focus and competence are pertinent but not all-embracing equations for access in pursuits of life, more extra-academic ones. One like me from a subdued social setting of Sonapur needs contact and support.

Armed with that realization, I made efforts to be visible when I got into the Dhaka University. I consciously bade adieu to my writing craving and happily got into acting in plays staged by the residential halls and the Dhaka University Central Students' Union. I started enjoying portraying characters, mostly lead roles, scripted by more celebrated theater enthusiasts. That continued even when I was teaching in colleges. It logically came to an end as I joined government service.

The initial few years of my retirement in the serene and picturesque setting of Vancouver went merrily in the warm care and love of a few relatively young Bangladeshi couples. That was my most intimate relationship with Bangladeshis since leaving Dhaka in early 1980 to join the Asian Development Bank in Manila.

Destiny eventually ordained my relocation to Chicago, a place I never wanted to be. The irony is that since living in Evanston City, one of the contiguous suburb, I love genially living in Greater Chicago.

In the initial few months of living in Chicago, I realized, absolutely my personal prognosis, an apparent variance among the Bangladeshi-origin immigrated populace of Vancouver and Chicago. Those of Vancouver are mostly immigrants since early 1990s, with no typified prejudice about life and related professional competence, and most of them have had reasonable higher level of educational attainments. Chicago settlements, mostly beginning late 1950s and early 1960s, were of professionals, followed by hosts of new young arrivals since the early 1980s for studies and in search of jobs. Evidently, there were abrasions initially. That has since mostly been defused, but the elements of that subsumed feelings are still there. Thus, our full integration in the Bangladeshi community of Chicago took a relatively longer time. Once that phase was over, we were enthusiastically accepted by both sets of warm and friendly Bangladeshis of Chicago.

The interim period was a challenging one for me. I had no contact. Not many were aware of our presence in this large metropolis having about a third of Canada's population.

Taking advantage of this situation, I decided to leave behind something in writing about our root and background for our progeny, if one is interested, since we as a family happily opted for a cross-cultural family setup. That took the shape of a biography titled *Bends and Shades*. That attainment recommenced and propelled my interest in writing anew. Subsequent publications are the logical outcome of that.

As I presented my last book titled *Passion and Pathos*, published in late 2019, to some friends and well-wishers happily coinciding with my eightieth year, I decided to retire from writing. Then the most devastating worldwide pandemic of COVID-19 took the whole humanity by shock and nervousness, with infections, ailment, hospitalization, and death becoming unpredictable and pervasive. Occupational pursuits, educational attendance, social interactions, and travel all became constrained, and continued through 2020.

Many obviously used this space in productive pursuits. I do not have that privilege, being a retired individual and being unfamiliar with most technological advancements of today, so I opted for writing to avoid tedium, and used my constricted existence within my home using illimitable, and equally exasperating, time. Writing is an endeavor for which I do not have a natural proficiency but blessed with boundless alacrity. *Chasing Dreams* is the outcome of that in the prevalent constraining situation.

—Jahed Rahman

CONTEXT

That was a joyful evening in the Bilkhana official residence of Major Fazal Abbas of the Bangladesh paramilitary force, officially known as the Bangladesh Border Rifles (BBR). As in many countries, the BBR is an auxiliary force between the army and the police establishments of Bangladesh and manned by regular infantry with deputed army personnel at senior positions (officers' level) on a rotation basis.

The residence of Major Abbas was full of friends and relations on the eve of his being promoted as a lieutenant colonel the following day in annual *Durbar* (akin to an annual general assembly), where discussions are held and guidance articulated as to the state of setting and affairs of the BBR. The event, because of its relevance as an annual event of distinction, had all the planning and preparation for excellence. It was divided into two segments. The first segment in the morning was to be presided over by the commandant in chief of the BBR. The second segment, commencing at noon, was to be graced by the president of the country in awarding recognitions to recommended officers, besides delivering his ceremonial presidential address. That was to be followed by *Bara Khana* (big feast).

The joyousness and exuberance of that evening in the abode of Major Abbas were predicated on the frustrations of his late father, Major Azeem, and the ardent hopefulness of mother, Rukiya Azeem.

Father Azeem had been a student of Dhaka University during 1965 war between Pakistan and India. The war between the numerically and materially superior forces of India and tinier equivalence of Pakistan was projected to be at par even though the actuality

12

remained undetermined. The physical reality at the end of the seventeen-day war and the media hype in Pakistan galvanized the mindset of Pakistanis at large. That ethos mirrored into the minds of younger East Pakistanis even though the war was fought in the western front of Pakistan only.

The other backup factor was the heroic performances of East Bengal regiments in a number of war fronts in West Pakistan, a performance that surprised many as East Pakistanis were always looked down on as a martial race. Simultaneously, the performance, both on the ground and in the air, of East Pakistani airmen and pilots astounded many. One squadron leader, Amal, became a household name all over Pakistan.

The ubiquitous psyche influenced many young people. Azeem, being a regular member of Dhaka University Officers Training Corps, popularly known by the acronym UOTC, was no exception. That background and emerging hype propelled a strong yearning within Azeem, and he joined the Pakistan army as a second lieutenant under the recruitment policy commonly known as "short-course." On his completion of mandatory training requirement, Azeem became a lieutenant and was assigned to the Sixth Baluch Regiment, stationed at that time in Muzaffarabad of Azad Jammu and Kashmir. In carrying out regular reconnaissance work in challenging situations and occasional skirmishes with opposing Indian forces across the Line of Control—an artificial demarcation line agreed, under the auspicious UN at the end of battle of 1948 with respect to the accession of Kashmir—Azeem exhibited both valor and leadership. He soon was promoted as a captain and was posted in Lahore Garrison in the late sixties.

Life for Azeem was beautiful and rewarding. The reputation he earned and the attainment of quick progression made his superiors and colleagues happy, and him challenged and exuberant. He harbored a sublime impression of positivity with respect to his future in the Pakistan army.

He was neutral, as part of the army conduct and values, with respect to the prevalent political upheavals that was swarming the nation. It was not that he was insensitive to the larger stream of political developments, but he always concluded that politicians would eventually address those with magnanimity and cohesion while his duty was to protect the country, as per the army code of conduct.

Back home, Azeem's family and his well-wishers were equally pleased knowing his career progression. A decision was taken to get him married soon, more at the behest of his loving grandfather, addressed as *Dada-ji*. After intensive scouting, Dada-ji, in consultation with the family elders, decided to get Azeem married with the daughter of late Father's childhood friend, Sikendar Gulshan, who most of the time worked for the central government, both in Karachi and Islamabad. His only daughter, Rukiya Gulshan. was born in Karachi and grew up in Islamabad.

In a long affectionate letter, his eldest uncle informed Azeem about Dada-ji and his family's decision, with the full family background of his future in-laws. It was simultaneously emphasized that Rukiya's familiarity with the environment of West Pakistan would ensure a smooth family life in the future while he and his offspring would have the piquancy and cultural orientation of East Pakistan. Azeem, who had always been a very obedient and considerate family offshoot and grandson, agreed and applied for leave.

On his arrival in Dhaka, Azeem was surprised to observe the smack and focus of political campaigning and cautiously evaluated the demands being agitated. He optimistically hoped that the final agreement on the demands, some of which were legitimate in view of the exceptional nature of the state's geographical structure, could be negotiated within the framework of Pakistan. Azeem further concluded that whatever might be the results of the election, the political process and forces in play and the interim federal authorities would definitely be able to work out solutions acceptable to the majority, ensuring a sustainable Pakistan.

Azeem's other deduction was that, being an army man, he should not unnecessarily be preoccupied with and burdened by such thoughts. He had full confidence in the political process and the wisdom of politicians and federal policy makers. He focused on renewing his contacts and relationships with kith and kin and associates, randomly participating in marriage-related discussions and preparations.

The wedding took place matching the euphoria of the prevailing national election. Though an arranged marriage and though he had neither seen nor had any interactions with the bride before, Azeem was pleased to have Rukiya as a life partner based on what he was told by those who interacted with her informally.

Traditionally, Bangladeshi urban weddings take place in the evening, and the wedding first night is a very long and late one as relations spend time and energy in welcoming and ushering the bride in her new home, performing a number of rituals and hilarious exchanges. For the groom, the time for acquaintance and intimacy is further delayed due to the bride's passive approach to intimacy, more as a symbol of modesty and the dictate of traditions.

That, however, was not the case of Azeem. Rukiya was open and smart and surprised Azeem with sporadic short exchanges in the Urdu language and broken Punjabi (the dialect of Punjab province of West Pakistan), besides fluent Bangla. That made Azeem very happy. That happiness multiplied observing the lean frame, fair complexion, and long straight hair of Rukiya. He was beguiled by her well-shaped and penetrating black eyes, with long eyelashes. Azeem experienced a fulfilling first married night.

His upbeat approach to life, ambition pertaining to his army career, and perception about the future of his family life made him a very optimistic and satisfied individual in the following days. In Rukiya, Azeem found a very supportive life partner in a would-be setting far away from East Pakistan. Azeem quickly concluded that Rukiya's ability to converse functionally in various languages would enable her to mix and interact with the families of colleagues and friends with confidence and competence. His innate ambition for a very rewarding progression within the army structure burgeoned, and he saw in Rukiya as a causative partner.

As the focus and excitement pertaining to the wedding of Azeem mellowed gradually at the family level, new excitement started manifesting at the national level, centering on the political scenario. The election was over. The Awami League won a landslide victory by win-ning the majority of the 160 national assembly seats and 298 of the 310 provincial assembly seats in East Pakistan. The major winner in West Pakistan was Zulfiqar Ali Bhutto's Pakistan People's Party (PPP), which won only 81 seats in the national assembly, with majority seats in two (Punjab and Sindh) provincial assemblies out of four.

Political movements started heating up. Azeem's family and his in-laws were concerned. Azeem, maintaining his faith in the political process, assured everyone, stating that while the heightened political hype is a natural corollary of unforeseen election outcomes, politicians have the inexplicable acumen for maneuvering, compromising, and moving on in challenging situations. Thus, he did not see any reason for concern relating to the statehood of Pakistan. The family reluctantly consented for their journey back to Lahore.

Though optimism pervaded his outward expressions and avowals, Azeem was conscious of an inward anxiety within himself. He kept that private to minimize the afflictions of others. His dream of attaining an elevated position in the Pakistan army persisted, notwithstanding the negativities on the horizon.

Rukiya resorted to consoling Azeem, aligning herself with his stated positions, and further assured him of her unconditional commitment to be with him and by his side in any adverse situation. She did not hide her own longing to reconnect with her childhood friends in Islamabad.

On the appointed day and time, the couple boarded their vehicle to go to Dhaka airport (known as Kurmitola airport) in the company of the family elders. That was ordinarily to be a happy occasion, but the expressions and utterances on that journey had all the somberness and visible anxiety.

Azeem, dressed in formal military uniform, and Rukiya, in a light yellow chiffon saree without formal wedding ornaments, an exception for a new bride, took slow and steady steps toward the parked Pakistan International Airlines (PIA) flight bound for Karachi via Colombo. As they were negotiating the awaiting aircraft, both of them looked back a number of times to have a glimpse of awaiting family members. That was normal for one like

Rukiya but an exception for Azeem, who was always an optimistic individual.

As the plane crossed the East Pakistan border, Azeem exchanged a look with Rukiya, apologizing for suggesting simplicity in her outfit without ornaments. It was the families' decision also to keep her wedding jewelry back in East Pakistan in view of the prevailing uncertainty. Rukiya surprised Azeem when she said, "You are my jewelry. I am happy to be with you and by your side. InshaAllah, we all have a lot of them in future. At the moment, let us relax and enjoy our time together."

Azeem was overwhelmed. He responded, observing that, "You are looking extremely adorable in this simple saree, normal gold chain, and bangles." He then cautiously, in view of all types of fellow passengers, took possession of the hand of Rukiya and pressed it, signifying his agreement with what Rukiya earlier stipulated and confirming what he just stated.

Azeem, being assured, then opened up, saying, "We are going to Lahore in a delicate situation. Unexpected things can happen. We should be prepared to handle those with understanding and grace." Instead of further talking, they exchanged looks frequently, expressing emotions more in silence than in words.

Reaching Karachi after a long six-hour flight with a stopover in Colombo, the couple boarded the connecting PIA flight for Lahore. The detour through Colombo was the offshoot of India's decision not to allow Pakistani aircrafts to fly over its national territory.

Once in Pakistan soil and during the Lahore flight, Azeem was much relaxed and at ease with himself. Rukiya concluded within herself that perhaps the change in places helped Azeem to reorient himself and be confident about the milieus.

As the aircraft alighted at the Lahore International Airport, Azeem apparently was in a rush to get down, expecting a very warm and friendly welcome by friends and colleagues whom he informed earlier about the date and time of their arrival.

The exuberant quick steps of Azeem slowed down suddenly as he approached the reception area. To his utter dismay, he noticed only one colleague with his spouse and one common friend against the expected welcome by many. Rukiya noticed and remained calm.

The inner thoughts of Azeem cogently were premised on the possible impulses centering the outcome of the just-held election. He was more worried about the immediate repercussions of that, his future in terms of his career, and the family life he dreamt of since getting married.

Azeem kept his cool, parked his anxiety in the inner cabal of his mind, shelved it for the time being, and reacted graciously, as if the absence of expected friends and colleagues had no bearing. He enthusiastically embraced the colleague and the friend present while thanking the spouse of the colleague for taking the trouble of coming to the airport, hiding his inner frustration.

Zubaida, the spouse of the colleague, went out of her stance in welcoming Rukiya, hugged her warmly, and complimented Azeem for having such a sublime and graceful lady as life partner. Zubaida did not fail, in line with the army's open and frank way of interacting with spouses of colleagues, to comment that, "Azeem Bhai (brother), you won the lottery. She is so attractive and poised. I envy you."

Having said those words, she picked up the hand of Rukiya and said, *"Khush Amdid"* (welcome).

In a prompt nonchalant reaction, Rukiya responded, saying, *"Shukriya"* (thanks).

The ease with which Rukiya responded, and in Urdu too, with her tone and accent very local, amazed Zubaida, but what she encountered subsequently made Zubaida very exultant.

Rukiya thanked Zubaida in effortless Urdu for being present at the airport, saying, *"Bhabi* (sister-in-law), when you embraced me a while back, I felt the touch and warmth of my sisters in Dhaka. I am so thankful to you."

Zubaida was astounded, and the colleague and friend were pleasantly surprised. Azeem stepped in to elucidate and told them about Rukiya's birth in Karachi and growing up in Islamabad till her family's return to Dhaka four years back upon the retirement of her father.

Zubaida smiled, drew Rukiya close, and said, "From now on, I am not your *Bhabi*. I am your *Appa* (elder sister)." Saying those with all emotions and warmth, Zubaida drew Rukiya close and hugged her for a second time.

All of them then boarded the parked microbus of the friend, with the colleague taking the front seat, Rukiya and Zubaida the middle seats, and Azeem along with the friend occupying the rear ones.

As the travel commenced, taking the new bride to her destined place of living, Zubaida continued to talk to Rukiya. The Urdu language proficiency of Rukiya was an added incentive, even though part of the conversation was undertaken in English. As Zubaida told Rukiya that she hailed from a place called Multan, Rukiya promptly interjected, stating that she also understood and spoke a little Punjabi. That enthralled Zubaida, and the follow-up conversation by her on varied issues was prolific.

The exuberance of Zubaida evidently annoyed her husband, sitting in the front seat. He looked back a number of times, trying to draw the attention of his wife, and occasionally passed signals for restraint.

That was noticed by Azeem, who apparently did not like that. Being happy with the easy mingling of the two ladies, he was concerned about his colleague's possible attempts to hide something. His thought once again linked that to the overall political syndrome and was concerned about plausible upshots.

As the vehicle stopped in front of the small abode of Azeem, the entry door suddenly opened, and his colleagues and their spouses came out with sweets, flowers, and garlands to say welcome to the new addition. That was too much for Azeem to absorb. His eyes soaked. Happiness in gestures and expressions were ubiquitous.

Azeem was taken aback when he entered his abode. The small dining table and still smaller side table were full of food and fruits, prepared and bought by families of his colleagues. All of them shared and enjoyed the food, and they had a sumptuous lunch together. That was possible, being a Sunday. Everyone enjoyed talking and sharing jokes with Rukiya, more to entice her. Her openness and ability to communicate with unknown fellows impressed everyone. That was a wonderful initiation for Rukiya, who was living far away from home and immediate family members for the first time.

The lodging was small. The number of attendees was relatively many. Everyone was in a joyous mood and talking. Consistent with the local custom, the ladies clustered at the rear end and the men occupied the space between the entry and the dining table. While quick comments and laughter dominated the ladies' section, the men's one was noisy and loud, traversing varied issues.

The issue of election outcome was, however, more subtle. But the outcome of the exchange pleased and relieved Azeem simultaneously. The consensus was the election is one thing, and going to power is another. Politicians, being shrewd and experts in maneuvering, will find their way out as power, by connotation, has its own attractions for reaching which both principles and positions are often compromised with justifications either way.

Having settled down in their own place and while sipping hot tea, Azeem requested Rukiya to give up the immediate household errands and sit by his side. Rukiya immediately complied, sensing a likely romantic interaction. That excited her. Since getting married, they were always surrounded in Dhaka by friends and relations and never had private moments together. To most of them, the new couple had no other onus but to give company to others, and that was more as the couple would soon leave for Lahore. In spite of longing for escape, they had to comply with the wishes of well-wishers, even until late hours. Thus, the call for taking a seat by his side triggered a sudden dashing up of amorous feelings in the mind of Rukiya.

She took her seat by the side of Azeem, but the expected romantic expressions from Azeem were missing. Rukiya looked at Azeem, reminiscing that they never had such private moment since their marriage due to the overarching enthusiasm of relations and friends. She moved closer to Azeem with naivety, but the follow-on reaction, in the deep-voiced utterances of Azeem, was the least she expected.

Without any dithering, Azeem started his soliloquy, saying, "Since our arrival, I have been under an emotional burden and would like to unleash that. I want to share it with you so that both of us can shape our future life learning from that."

After a pause, he continued, saying, "I had inside an inkling about a grand welcome for you at the airport by colleagues and friends. Having noticed the presence of only two and a spouse, I instantly lost faith and confidence in my colleagues and friends. I fleetingly concluded that perhaps the election outcome and resultant political quagmire caused an erosion in their feelings and warmth. That was aggravated when my colleague was trying to restrain his wife by passing on indicative signals to her during the travel from airport. I was speechless when I saw most of them coming out our abode with all the welcoming preparations. Internally, I sustained a major quiver for prejudging the sincerity of friends based symbolic experience.

I felt equally ashamed a second time in succession when Riaz explained the backdrop of his repeated passing of silent signals to Zubaida Bhabi in the vehicle. During our exchanges dominantly pertaining to army argots and jokes, Riaz diverted the focus to narrate his own contribution to this hilarious noon.

He said, 'Being worried about the constant chattering of Zubaida, I was trying to caution her so that she does not unwittingly divulge anything about the reception arrangements here. I soon realized that Azeem noted that and was feeling edgy. I quickly thought of a strategy to make him more nervous and resorted to passing frequent signals. Azeem's face reflected his dismay and confusion—I enjoyed that.'"

Everybody thanked Riaz for doing that and giggled at Azeem. His embarrassment swelled as his negative thoughts, mainly regarding the election outcome and what he thought were Riaz's attempt to hide it, were exposed.

He was honest enough to admit, "I learned my lesson from these two incidents."

Azeem positioned one hand of Rukiya in his lap, pressed it, and drew her closer than before, saying, "The major vulnerability of human social contact is our tendency to quickly prejudge persons and positions without giving them the benefit of the doubt or the required time for clarification. Once such prejudgment is made, man's thinking ability is shrouded by a deep band of cloud. Subsequent thinking is impaired by defending prejudged positions, or closing the mind to new information. Both the incidents of today taught me these. Please always have these in mind in our life together moving forward."

He continued, saying, "Another point I would like to share with you is that there is no permanent right or wrong thing. Time elapses. Facts change. New information and dynamics emerge. So what is right at a given moment may not be so after some time. That does not mean that one should not have opinion, but that it should not be absolute for all time to come as subsequent reckonings may change the scenery."

Saying those words in soft but profound lingoes, Azeem hugged her warmly and maneuvered to place the inert physical frame of Rukiya on the bed decorated earlier by the spouses of his colleagues as a gesture of welcoming the new bride. Azeem rolled on her upper body with his left hand across and his right hand gently caressing her hair while rotating his face around her neck in a passionate way. Rukiya, with her eyes closed, refrained from swiveling.

Sensing that it was early evening and anyone could drop any time to welcome Rukiya, Azeem indolently got out of that transient romantic feeling and straightened himself. Continuing in a soft and loving tone, Azeem stated, "I am conscious of the fact that when initially you sat by my side and moved closer, you had expectations of adoring words and acts. Instead, you had my deep voice and heavy librettos about the emotional burden I sought to share with you sooner. That was my priority at that moment. We do not have a separate pathway anymore. Our life is tied together. We should have uniformity in our thinking frame even though our opinions may differ. So I wanted to share that with you at the earliest time."

MUDDLE

---

*T*he couple settled down in their abode with confidence and aspirations, even though the mixed signals about the political dialogue in Dhaka were multiplying and confusing. That was depressing as the couple could not converse on the telephone in East Pakistan freely anymore. Both Pakistan Television (PTV) and the radios' coverages were always optimistic and positive. Azeem and Rukiya, being in an army location, could not tune in to All India Radio or BBC, and for that matter most of international news and televisions sources, as they were locally leveled as biased and pro-Indian.

Apparently, the political situation relegated to chaos, confusion, and fear as the establishment, under pressure from Bhutto of PPP, refused to summon the national assembly and hand over power to the majority political party, Awami League, under the coalesced leadership of Sheikh Mujibur Rahman. He was adorably crowned as *Bongo Bondhu* (friend of Bengal) during the initial phase of the movement, having the hallmark of the Six Point Movement, demanding self-rule for East Pakistan.

In the midst of such a scenario, a bewildering bombshell dominated the late night news of PTV on March 25, 1971. It reported army action in East Pakistan to quash political movement. It also reported about the president's unannounced abrupt departure from Dhaka along with prominent political leaders from West Pakistan, cancelling the much-valued ongoing political dialogue.

The prevalent psyche of the establishment and among many of the West Pakistan politicians was manifested when the newspapers of the following morning appeared with Bhutto's cynical statement: "Allah has saved Pakistan."

Having a sensitive mindset, deep thinking prowess, and perhaps due to living in the milieu of East Pakistan for about four years since their relocation from Islamabad, Rukiya reacted more intensely than Azeem expected. Both the nature and intensity were blurred. Rukiya instantly became worried about the safety and well-being of her family having residence in the Mirpur enclave of Dhaka and started sobbing. Azeem was sympathetic and consoled her, saying that it might be a limited operation centering on the political hotbeds of Dhaka, which mostly, as he noticed during a recent stay, was the university area. He took pains in assuring her that things would settle down within a short while, but Rukiya was not convinced.

As detailed news about the military operations in Beelkhana Rifles (the predecessor of BBR) and that of the Rajarbagh Police Line, the blazing photographs of them and other establishments, appeared in the newspapers, Rukiya became more nervous. The news of the arrest of Sheikh Mujibur Rahman, the undisputed leader of the ongoing political movement for self-rule, and his prompt relocation to Rawalpindi of West Pakistan were taken by Rukiya as ominous indications. Azeem mostly kept quiet and focused on extending emotional support.

On his part, Azeem slowly, and quite naively, got used to a dual behavior pattern. Still having faith in a possible negotiated resolution, he carried on his official duty and assignment without dithering. Back at home, he opted for a quiet life, apprehensive of possible surveillance. They talked about East Pakistan–related issues in bed only, and that too in low pitch. This became all the more pertinent as the student leaderships of East Pakistan renamed the province as the new independent country, Bangladesh. A new interim exile government took oath in a parcel of land adjacent to the West Bengal border of India. Politically, the setting became complicated locally while Indian leadership and its military establishment were euphonious.

As Pakistan military spread out to areas beyond Dhaka to establish its authority and control, two specific things happened. One relates to random commitment of mayhem, and the second one pertains to magnified reporting of those by All India Radio. It was compounded by the policy of organizing pro-right civilian organizations, like Al-Badr and Razakars, to help the army in its objective to maintain law and order in areas cleared by them from actions and moves of so-called secessionist elements.

Consequently, and motivated by the call that Bongo Bondhu made on March 7, 1971, as well as to escape from the uncertain and whimsical actions of the army, young people, students, politicians, and activists from urban and rural locations of Bangladesh silently left for various friendly territories in both Assam and West Bengal states of India. They were soon organized as *Mukti Bahini* (liberation force) and successfully undertook guerrilla operations within Bangladesh. That received wide international coverage and visibly unsettled the Pakistan army of about 90,000 stationed in Bangladesh.

The other thing that happened, due to sustained and heightened Indian propaganda, was the creation of panic among people's mind based on stories of atrocities by the army and its support militias flown from Pakistan. Ordinary people living in the border areas and a large section of the minority Hindu population started crossing the border and taking refuge in sanctuaries within India.

The last one was the singular most negative development. Images of millions crossing the border on foot and the sustained Indian diplomatic and propaganda efforts drew international attention. Western media, liberal politicians, especially from France, UK, and the USA, as well as artists and liberal activists, openly opposed the atrocities and aligned themselves in support of the Bangladesh movement. Among others, the high-profile visit of Senator Kennedy to refugee camps in India, the elderly French intellectual's well-publicized readiness to fight for the cause of Bangladesh, and the Beatles' guitarist George Harrison's concert with the famous Indian sitar player, Ravi Shankar, at Madison Square Garden of New York galvanized the world's opinion.

All these had little impact on the thinking, policy, and operational strategy of the Islamabad-based power elite controlled by army. The added factor was the secrecy pertaining to Henry Kissinger's maiden clandestine visit to Peking using Pakistan as a conduit. Having diplomatic contact and eventual relationship with the People's Republic of China was a very high priority of the US policy agenda of the time. Nixon was very eager to have functional and sustainable China contact for the immediate growth of trade and business. That became his cherished foreign policy vision.

During the related contact and dialogue, US policy makers assured Pakistan about their diplomatic pressure on India to ensure Pakistan's territorial integrity. Henry Kissinger even stipulated that US would deploy its Seventh Fleet to neutralize India's war capacity, if so warranted.

These impudently emboldened the senior hierarchy of the Pakistan army. Assured of US position, they were oblivious of the international reaction and support for the cause of Bangladesh.

The people of West Pakistan had no clue of the on-the-ground reality in Bangladesh. Radio Pakistan and PTV continued projecting the heroic performance of its forces, broadcasting imaginary stories of success in attaining stability and peace in East Pakistan. Both the entities were competing with each other in telling people about US support and commitment.

Against that setting, the Pakistan army command decided on a strategic option to position an army company level outpost near the most significant and sensitive entry corridor (border outpost), popularly known as Wagah, located on the international border of Punjab, to avert an unnoticed Indian army advance. This was not to be a deterrent but a precautionary initiative based on their experience of the 1965 war, when the Indian army, without notice and resistance, advanced up to Jutanagar, at the periphery of Lahore city.

Consistent with that decision, the Lahore Garrison Command promptly set up a company-level outpost after Jutanagar, a hub of industrial and commercial activities between main Lahore city and the international border corridor of Wagah. Being very close to the border and being a city of pride and tradition, Lahore was always important to Pakistan's identity, and equally vulnerable to a possible Indian invasion. Thus, Lahore has always been a very prized city for Pakistan to shield and for India to seize.

Unexpectedly, Captain Azeem was put in charge. The main job was reconnaissance and, if needed, to confront any advance by the enemy, giving time for the main force to move from Lahore cantonment.

On the other side of the border, India, with the unqualified support of the USSR, continued its diplomatic efforts to corner Pakistan, and its military started preparations for a possible engagement with Pakistan. The Indian army determinedly took a posture of belligerence in its western front.

The news of Azeem's posting in the front camp off Jutanagar, a very vulnerable and super sensitive entry point, caused concerns in Rukiya's mind. She did not hesitate to open up bluntly, saying that, "The command has posted you, a Bengali officer, as being sparable one in the face of all risk and vulnerability." She did not hesitate to say, "Your *shadaat* (martyrdom) is written on the wall. I did not marry to lose you so soon."

Azeem drew her close on the bed and said, "I understand your worries and concerns and respect your feeling. I took the oath to protect the territorial integrity of Pakistan. The day I took that oath, I opted for death, as all my comrades did. You married me knowing fully well that I am an army officer and must always respond to the call of duty irrespective of the risks inherent. None of us can now walk back. Also, understand that I will not be alone. There will be a whole company unit with me. They all are sons of this soil. If I die, many of them will also die. So individual risk is of no consequence."

He took a pause and continued, saying, "I have a slightly different perspective about the decision to post me there. The policy makers perhaps are trying to send a signal to other Bengali officers that they are still being trusted irrespective of the ongoing East Pakistan situation."

Having said those words, he drew her still close and embraced her warmly as a prelude to physical intimacy, which happened to be constrained in the immediate past. Rukiya, however, was on the reverse side of that feeling, sniveling irresistibly with her head on the chest of Azeem.

The following day, Captain Azeem left his abode to join his new post.

The civic surrounding of Jutanagar was both normal and calm; however, its military proximates were just the opposite on both sides of the international border. All actions and motivations were spotlighted on ensuring the territorial integrity of Pakistan. Similar was the situation on the other side of the border. The resultant focus was on increased training and effective preparedness, with recce being the most effective tool. That ambience had no space for personal feeling and experiences.

Life has its own rhythm in its passage forward. Leaving his new wife in a relatively unfavorable situation and taking command of a position akin to a death sentence were very unsettling for Captain Azeem. In the viscosity of the insurmountable emotional backlash, Captain Azeem received a message that evening about the sudden demise of his mother in Bangladesh. Consolation visits and words were few, in view of the size of the personnel under his command, the duty commitments inherent in deployment, and with Rukiya being in a separate location.

There is a saying in Bangladesh that misfortune never travels alone. If that could be extended, it can also be said that a bad time never occurs in isolation. That is what precisely happened in Captain Azeem's life. In an unexpected scenario, the patrolling army unit of Pakistan was challenged that evening by the Indian army within the territory of Pakistan. The resultant skirmish was fierce and brutal.

The Pakistan army unit, under the courageous and committed leadership of Captain Azeem, fought back vehemently and pushed the numerically superior Indian army back to its border. In the process, he was injured.

With immediate medical attention and care, Azeem slowly recovered and was allowed one month's medical leave to recuperate.

The leave period was very helpful for the new couple to understand each other better and to tie up more solidly, but the apprehensive mind of Rukiya was never at ease. The type, tone, and length of communications from Dhaka were causing anguish in her thinking.

The letters in terms mailing schedule were regular but increasingly became shorter, conveying less and less about the actual situation in East Pakistan, possibly fearing censorship and to ensure safety of all concerned.

Rukiya's perception about the ongoing situation was in marked variance with that of Azeem's. While absorbing that feeling for the peace of mind of her dear husband and a warm connubial relationship, she always kept quiet. More so, she outwardly made an effort, to the delight of Azeem, to remain friendly and have increased contact with the spouses of fellow officers.

Azeem had an additional emotional burden. Part of this was premised on his despondency pertaining to the loss of his mother, whom he'd seldom seen in life. He had reminisced on hearing the sad news. His reaction was neither loud outwardly, nor dense internally as his emotional association and physical involvement with her were minimal. To him, she was like a surrogate giving birth to him. Though, somewhat strange, his immediate focus at that time was handling the limited but fierce confrontation with the Indian patrol team.

While recuperating from the injury, he was rethinking the whole episode. His blaming of his mother was lessened significantly as he realized that both himself and his mother were victims of the decisions of the family elders, who did not care for or value the bond between a mother and her son.

Azeem thought it to be obligatory for him to be by the side of her grave and pray for her soul's peaceful eternal journey. However, it was neither possible to travel to Dhaka at that time, nor were the political and security situation conducive for such a travel. He was saddened but drew consolation that death, no matter how cruel it is, possibly spared her from probable recurring emotional pain and physical discomfort. Against the backdrop of the reality that she carried him for months in her womb, Azeem commenced praying for her soul even though he had never enjoyed motherly care and love.

His maternal grandfather and his kin, who came on hearing the news of the death of Azeem's father, weighed more about their widowed young daughter and less about her progeny. So the decision was taken to leave the toddler behind alone in the care of Dada-ji and his clan. The chapter was closed.

His trepidation was manifold as he observed marked changes in Rukiya's attitude, interaction, and responses with the passage of time. Azeem, by choice, refrained from asking her about such changes, specially within months of the recent avowal. He rapidly concluded that young women step into marital life with all dreams and high hopes. In her case, all these were shattered too soon, with the future remaining bleak. So the behavioral changes are normal, and there is no sense in bringing that to the surface as a talking point.

Then came the most unexpected news. In the last week of November, military command, based on the recommendation of Lahore Garrison, made a decision for the out-of-turn promotion of Azeem to the rank of major. That was the recognition for his leadership, commitment, and valor in the most adverse situation. His friends, colleagues, and command were ecstatic. Sweets and bouquets overflowed the abode of Azeem and Rukiya.

Soon after that happy milieu, the news highlighting the preemptive assault of the Pakistan Air Force (PAF) to cripple Indian air capability was in the air. The whole strategy was to repeat the 1967 Israel-Egypt war experience, when, by launching a coordinated preemptive air attack, Israel literally grounded Egypt's mighty air fighting power.

It soon dawned that the Indians were smarter and thought through such possibility earlier. They relocated their operational aircrafts from bordering airfields to deep in the middle of the country and substituted those with replicas. PAF, naively but merrily, bombed those and returned to their bases.

Soon thereafter, the Indian Air Force (IAF) roared back and pounded the sensitive establishments in Pakistan, including their war-related civilian facilities. The thick cloud emanating from the oil refinery in Karachi visibly juddered people and establishment.

An all-out war between India and Pakistan broke out. The symbolic PAF presence in Dhaka was defused at the beginning of the war, and IAF warplanes roared on the sky of East Pakistan blithely, including undertaking frequent low-level sorties over the provincial Governor's House, the symbol of Pakistan's power, control, and authority. Within a few days, soldiers of the Eastern Command of Indian Army reached Dhaka, with the help and support of *Mukti Bahini*, and supervised the surrender of about 90,000 East Pakistan-based Pakistan army. Bangladesh came into its physical existence on December 16, 1971.

The subsequent history in Bangladesh was one of unabated joy for achieving the most unlikely reality in the shape of a real and new legal country and regaining bygone pride and identity. Ecstasy, in divergent forms and shapes, pervaded all around.

This response was the opposite in pared Pakistan, mostly focusing on the reshaping of its truncated identity and laying strategies to get back its soldiers, who were being held as war prisoners in the custody of the India-Bangladesh joint military command.

The world at large enthusiastically embraced Bangladesh, promptly according diplomatic recognitions and unhesitatingly extending the needed support and assistance to the war-ravaged new country. Internally, the political leadership successfully organized the government soon, to the sheer surprise of some.

Back in their abode, both Rukiya and Azeem were fraught, struggling emotionally and thinking through uncertain ways forward. Reacting to the expected trauma and more to have temporary escape from the current undefined and dampening situation, Rukiya, with pause and prudence, started saying, "You have all the reasons to be depressed and disconsolate. My exposure to your life and professional zeal is brief. Still I embraced the both with all earnestness, conducted myself accordingly, and I assure you that I will be by your side and with you all through irrespective of decision you take."

As Rukiya was finishing her aphorism, she was worried, observing the nonchalant antiphon of Azeem, who kept his face static and down focused. She instantly decided to open up and unleash what she had been harboring for a few days.

She continued, saying, "Look, Bangladesh is a reality, and our root and families are there. Though Pakistan was our country, it is no more. We are now aliens. The government's decision last night to disarm Bengali Regiments and house them in secured camps are definite indications of how we will be treated in future. Your dream is to be a professional army officer. It does not matter that it would no more be the Pakistan Army. We will go back to Bangladesh. Officers of your mettle will be needed to build up the army of the new country. You will not be losing anything. You will still be in the armed forces instead of being a mercenary here. Even if things do not work out that way, you may have other scopes and options in our new country with opportunities likely to be limitless. Let us decide accordingly without any inhibition."

Azeem gleefully looked at Rukiya, drew her closer, and said, "I am so blessed in having you as my life partner. I was motionless and very inert during your oration as I was listening very carefully to what you articulated. I had exactly the same line of thinking but was hesitant to share those as I was unsure as how a fresh bride like you, with expectations, desire, and dreams of a new life, would take that. I am amazed by your thinking probity. Can you tell me how you were able to think so intensely at such a young age and so soon after our marriage?"

That sort of observation enthralled the lives of both. Instead of responding immediately, she withdrew to prepare coffee for them both. Perhaps she deliberately took herself off from the scene to organize her thoughts for articulating a proper response.

With a hiatus, Rukiya took a revisit of her life so far, framed a line of response, and came back. Sitting by the side of the electric heater and sharing coffee, she softly said, "Your query warrants a rather long response. My initial fifteen years in Pakistan were conditioned by local social imperatives focusing on restrained communal behavior requirements, with emphasis on orthodox religious practices and adherence to varied restrictive norms. Relocating in Dhaka, I suddenly discovered myself in a setting and environment of social openness, ensuring, nevertheless, the compliance with relatively relaxed religious requirements.

My last two high school and two college years life in Dhaka, the latter being a coeducation one, allowed me to reorient myself with confidence, competence, and conviviality. The role played by my history professor in that transition of life had all pervasive impact. For reasons unclear, she liked and loved me. In our general conversations, Professor Rashida Anjum generally talked to me very slowly and softly, with emphasis on each of her words and opinions. Through that process, she guided, and I discovered myself with a greater awareness of society and a better understanding for social communications. Her oft-repeated advise focused on how to handle the startling events or occurrences in the journey of life. She always said, 'It is not advisable and prudent to conclude too quickly or to act hurriedly on anything. Once one does that, the related thinking process is constrained by rigidity. In that situation, the frame of mind is covered by a band of thick cloud. That impacts considering options beyond the conditioned frame of mind. In the event of distressing experiences, always try to assess what more damaging thing could have happened, or are happening in cases of others. That will console and equally enable you to pursue life's journey with positivity. Life's varied episodes do not take place in isolation. Most such events have inherent options to minimize the pain, helping life to move forward.'

Occasionally, she used to refer to my crying at the time of leaving Islamabad, the place of my growing up encompassing entire childhood and early teens period. She often used to remark, 'What I said to you now and before in this regard aptly applies to your life. You see what you got in terms of growing up as an individual in Dhaka and the happiness you now enjoy here compared to social rigidity of the place you grew up, and for leaving which you shaded tears. This is the cycle of life.'"

Rukiya than continued, saying, "Her those thoughts and advices are imbedded within me and swayed my personality and thinking. I happily consented to our marriage proposition fully conscious of the inevitable relocation to West Pakistan, leaving my elder parents and siblings back home. The pragmatism that evolved within me due to Professor Rashida Anjum's guidance enabled me to accept your stationing in the advance outpost facing the most direct and vulnerable border position without dithering. My worries were multifarious, but I could keep my cool, giving you peace of mind.

From letters back home, even though brief and indirect, I had hazy impressions as to how things are moving but did not open up to you. With Bangladesh being a reality, I had a clear vision about our future and thought of ways to mitigate your worries and frustrations. So what I said to you was not an off-the-cuff opinion. I thought through the entire episode and came to the conclusion that going back to our root is our best bet."

The time passed. Both Rukiya and Azeem had quiet living, stepping out of their home only when needed, with a decline in the frequency of visits by previous colleagues. While anguish was piercing, that space provided them with options and alternatives to think through and plan for their future life in Bangladesh. Azeem used to be encaustic while thinking about his position in the Bangladesh army and his likely opportunity and role. Rukiya kept her feeling within and limited her optimism, centering reunion with families.

Both were having breakfast, and Rukiya was toadying Azeem for being able to make a perfect omelet in his maiden effort. Right at the moment, a knock on their entry door surprised them as that is not normally the hour for anybody to show up. Azeem opened the door and was startled at seeing two noncommissioned officers (NCOs) of his battalion with an order to hand over his Pakistani army uniform and other paraphernalia.

Azeem had a concoction of feeling within him and was shell-shocked by the encounter. He had always thought that even though not in the Pakistan army anymore, he, and others like him, would be treated with the honor and dignity that they deserve. Instead, he was now to deal with NCOs, and of his own battalion too, in handing over his proud sets of uniform, including badges and stripes.

Once they left, finishing the instructed errand, Azeem went to deep musings with a visible signage of desolation. Rukiya, sensing what was going on within Azeem, came close to him, put both hands on his shoulders and passionately said, "It is okay. It is expected."

In his dejected response, Azeem said, "I also understand this. But what pained me is that being on medical leave at the material time, I did not have chance even to wear my uniform for a day with the insignia of a major on my shoulder, salute my superiors, and accept salutation of juniors."

While saying so, Azeem had soaked eyes. To give him time alone in that emotive setting, Rukiya excused herself to make fresh tea for them both.

By the time she came back with smoke-emitting tea, Azeem remarkably recovered from his earlier emotional gloom. He said, "I had clarity about the likely outcome but never had an inkling that it will be like this. One is valued and recognized so long he wears the uniform and has stripes and bars on his chest and insignia on the shoulders. Without them, one is just a trash."

Rukiya responded by saying, "That is perhaps the norm of the society we live in. My father enjoyed unreserved prestige and recognition in his official circle. His social standing was also very high in our locale of Islamabad. But soon after retirement, those prestige and prominence evaporated. Many will recognize him casually, though a few continued to greet him. In either situation, the warmth was missing. My family's relocation to Dhaka speedily freed us from that familiarity. Rest assured that once we are in Bangladesh, all these backlash will disappear."

Azeem stood up, lifted Rukiya from chair, and positioned her opposite him in a standing stance. He then, in an emotion-laden voice, said, "I told you about my feelings for you and my adoration for your intelligence and sense of understanding many a times before in different contexts. Standing today on the crossroad of life, together in the most uncertain backdrop, I would like to restate them as my avowal seeking your continued love, care, and support in uncertain good and bad times ahead."

Instead of responding orally, Rukiya moved close to Azeem and surrendered herself on his chest, affirming in silence what more than a thousand words would not transmit, and conveyed her commitment.

Azeem was momentarily relieved and assured. But his inner self was concerned about her ability to adhere to what she conveyed now in silence as the future is possibly full of uncertainty, frustration, and probable hindrance in pursuing a more structured, but not necessarily an affluent, normal life. During the last many months, Azeem made specific efforts to convey to Rukiya what his military training and orientation imbedded within him about pursuing a meaningful life.

Azeem was wondering within himself, with nihilism beholding all around, what would be the future like? His such thought was deepened considering the impact on Rukiya, especially in the context of the life both of them dreamt of during the months after their wedding. *Her married life is too short, and she is too young to absorb the sudden uncertainty.*

Soon thereafter, Azeem and Rukiya, like other Bangladeshi-origin Pakistani soldiers, were interned in guarded camps at various locations. The same also happened to civil servants and other civilian Bengalees.

The couple was moved to such a detention center near a place called Charsharda. With movement restrictions and other written and unwritten impositions, their life was a constrained one.

Earlier friends disappeared from their life. New contacts with fellow disarmed Bangladeshis were slow to start, and suffered from his military psyche. Each one of them was conscious of his rank, and he expected salutation from juniors. The difference was that in place of formal saluting, no more an option in the absence of uniform and rank badges, they unconsciously continued the army practice of straightening the chest when crossing or meeting a senior wearing civil attire.

Their common anxiety as to their future and the possible induction decision and process of Bangladesh government preoccupied the thoughts and actions of disarmed Pakistani soldiers of Bangladesh origin. That heightened with the lapse of time. It was basically premised on reported elements of expressed distrust and resentment in Dhaka against stranded soldiers for their voluntary lack of support and contribution during the war of liberation.

It soon became clear to many stranded ex-soldiers that the manning of the new Bangladesh army by major segments of *Mukti Bahini* and ardent followers of Sheikh Mujib was the stumbling chock on the path to eventual induction.

The opinions of soldiers and officers in camps in Pakistan were varied in the absence of compacted information. With the passage of time, such mindset became focused and sharp. That emotionally drained many. The main desire at that time was to return to their homeland.

Azeem, besides an elderly major, was the senior-most officer in that camps. Most other officers were junior to him in ranks, and the main constituents of the camp were noncommissioned officers and ordinary soldiers.

Azeem was distressed in observing most of the male inhabitants of the camp spending time without any activity, and were mostly engaged in hearsay.

Sharing his observation with the senior major, he organized a gathering in the small playground. The senior major, in his address, said, "What Major Azeem would say has my consent, and you all should not only adhere to that but also pass on the message to your known comrades."

In his brief but thought-provoking address, Azeem stated, "All of us are in the same situation, with future being uncertain, but there is an imperative need for us to remain mentally alert and physically active and fit. So I propose to have two slots of a physical exercise event every day: the first one being a one-hour physical exercise after *Fazar namaj* (early morning Muslim prayer) and the second one being games, sports, running, etc., for two hours in the evening after *Asar* (afternoon) prayer. In this inactive life, what we are proposing is your three hours' time so that in the event of eventual repatriation, we can show up as fit and committed individuals for likely induction. This is voluntary, and it starts tomorrow. The venue is this field. As many have not joined this gathering, you all are requested to pass this message on to your colleagues and friends. I will supervise both events every day and will join you all in every activity."

The following morning had the presence of more people. Every day it went on increasing. Everyone was happy, though the prevalent situation was gloomy.

As the days passed, confusion goaded and frustration accentuated.

With relevant thoughts occupying his mind, a very common phenomena in the recent past, Azeem returned from an afternoon's exercise engagement and was stunned to observe an unusually happy and smiling Rukiya. Attired in the beautiful Jamdani saree (Bangladeshi saree of feather-light and sheer material with motifs woven all over, providing a luxurious finish), with dark violet overlays against white backdrop, that his grandmother had presented when Rukiya first performed formal salam (touching elder's feet seeking blessings) at the time of wedding. Rukiya was looking not only beautiful but equally contented. Besides that, she'd put on light makeup, enriched her lips with bright lipstick, and combed and arranged her long hair in classy Bangladeshi way.

Observing him entering their camp accommodation, she smilingly went to prepare coffee for them, avoiding eye contact.

Azeem continued to have mixed thoughts dominating his yearnings and to his antipathy, unusually sat on the bed instead of chairs and kept quiet.

Rukiya positioned the lone small service table in front of him, placed coffee cups on it, and sat close to him in spite of his body still having the wetness consequent of earlier physical activities. She drew herself close to Azeem and with mixed feelings of shyness and joy, whispered in the ear of Azeem, saying, "You are going to be a father."

Stunned and euphoric, he lifted her and started dancing in a circular manner. Rukiya managed to free herself from that entrapped situation, and returned to her earlier sitting position. Azeem followed her full of glee and excitement. He apparently had follow-on trepidation concerning the accuracy of the good news. Without spending any time, he asked her, "How you are sure about your pregnancy without the needed medical test?"

Rukiya gave a detailed answer, saying, "I missed my two consecutive periods. I was having uneasy physical syndrome, lost appetite, and recently vomited twice. I was also feeling nostalgic, longing for my mother. I was equally conscious of an increased waning of warmth in our conjugal relationship. I did not like to burden you as you have many other major worries. So I opted to consult Major Bhabi (the wife of the senior major) as she is of my mother's age, besides being an experienced and intelligent lady. I went to her this afternoon and explained my condition.

She looked at me and put her right hand on my belly. She then hilariously said, '*Betty* (daughter), why are you so worried? You have a good news. You are going to be a mother. I am a mother of four and grandmother of two, so I am certain about my finding. Had your mother been here, she would have said exactly the same thing. From now on, think positively and be happy in the embrace of your husband.'

I came back happily, took a shower, and performed a few *rakats* (single unit of Muslim prayer consisting of prescribed movements and words) of *nafal namaj* (voluntary/optional prayer) thanking Allahpak and seeking His blessings for our progeny. I also made submissions for a healthy and intelligent baby having the attributes of Father. I then dressed up and was waiting for your return."

Azeem was mesmerized and momentarily lost words to express his full feeling. Rukiya continued, saying, "Probably, you do not recall this saree. It was given by your grandmother desiring that on any happiest moment of my life, I should wear it as symbolically seeking her blessings. So that is it."

Azeem enthusiastically drew her still closer but released her, soon recounting his body still had a tangy whiff from the games and exercise and left immediately to take a shower and freshen up.

Surprisingly, the subsequent expressions of joy and exhilaration were subdued and mute. Most expressions were in taciturnity, communicating respective happiness in an exchange of looks and gestures. Quietness permeated that small camp accommodation, culminating in a heartfelt embrace in bed at night when Azeem frequently put his palm on the belly of Rukiya, more to convey feelings in silence than anything else.

All that night and the following morning, the couple was having thoughts of wholly divergent nature in the backdrop of exhilaration: Azeem's fretfulness centered around his new obligations in the context of the uncertain future. Rukiya was preoccupied about the handling of the prized pregnancy in the absence of needed medical care and family support.

In early afternoon of that day, the senior major and his wife showed up with fruits and sweets to celebrate the happy occasion in the despondent life of interned camp. Both Azeem and Rukiya welcomed them happily. The senior major congratulated the couple, and his wife said, "Had you been in your normal life, your family and friends would have celebrated the good news with a lot of merriment. In this camp, we cannot have that, so we thought of celebrating it with sweets and fruits that we could have from outside."

The senior major injected, saying, "I have quietly informed some of your acquaintances here and desired that they should be at your place also so that we can have real ambiance of celebration."

Slowly, those acquaintances, accompanied by spouses, appeared with various types of snacks. Congratulatory handshakes and embraces dominated the greeting process. The one-and-a-half room camp accommodation of Azeem and Rukiya was full of fellow Bangladeshis, and for a short while, everyone was laughing and enjoying, forgetting for a time the harshness and frustration of interned life and their uncertain future.

While departing, most of them, especially the spouses, assured Rukiya and Azeem of all-out support and care at any time and in any event. That relieved both of them and helped them shed their earlier anxieties.

Rukiya thoughtfully observed, saying, "Life is a strange journey. While problems and uncertainties are parts of life, it is fascinating to note that each problem has its own options. I firmly believe in the oft-repeated saying that if one door in life's journey is closed, Allahpak opens up many more. You see, I did not know any of them. In a constrained interned camp life, and at our times of need, they showed up as a family. I am relieved."

Rukiya unhesitatingly continued, saying, "That many wives present inquired from me as to what type of food and eatables I developed craving for recently and promised to bring those in future. I was overwhelmed."

As the time passed, the routine life of the camp became boring and arduous. The only exception was the pregnancy of Rukiya, and that premised the minimal joy in their life.

In that setting and at noontime, there was a knock on his door. Azeem opened the door and was greeted by an uniformed staff from the camp commandant's office with request to accompany him. Azeem was both confused and nervous as it never happened before. He even did not know the commander.

After advising Rukiya, he started following the staff. The only reason he could envisage was his initiative to organize physical activities of the detainees without informing the commandant's office. During the walk, he was framing his probable response.

As he entered the office, he was stunned at seeing Captain Riaz sitting in front of the commander. By straightening his chest, he shook hands with the commander, and surprisingly Captain Riaz stood up and embraced Azeem. Spending a few minutes' time in the presence of the commander, Riaz said, "I was always thinking about you and Bhabi, so at the behest of Zubaida, I contacted the commander of the camp and sought his help for a brief meeting with you. I am happy to see that you are well, so I assume Rukiya Bhabi is. Now I can go back happily and report it to Zubaida."

Azeem thanked him profusely and also acknowledged, saying, "Though the camp life is tedious, we all are relatively happy as it is being run efficiently under wise leadership of the commandant."

Azeem took leave of the commandant and extended his hand as a prelude to shaking hands.

Riaz spontaneously said, "If I have the endorsement of the commandant, then let me see you off as perhaps this is our last meeting."

The commandant nodded affirmatively with a smiling face, enjoying the bond of two friends.

Stepping out of the camp office, Riaz took Azeem's right hand as a gesture to shake hands, but kept on clutching. He looked around, and in choked voice with visible wet eyes, he started saying, "You know that I am from Nowshera and have no brother. From the first day of our life in PMA (Pakistan Military Academy), I developed a liking for you. My parents and family know about it. Also, incidentally both of us were assigned to the same battalion. So while reflecting on that since you were located in the camp and at the behest of Zubaida, I thought of a way out to help you. I know very well a tribal *sardar* (chief). He can help to smuggle you out. It entails no risk for me. I thought of this option as the dialogue process concerning the repatriation of you and other related fellows of Bangladesh origin has been stalled due to a lack of diplomatic recognition. It is, at this stage, quite uncertain too."

It was Azeem's turn to be emotional. He said, "Under normal circumstances, perhaps there was merit to have further discussions, but Rukiya has conceived. The delivery is expected in March. It is not advisable to take a rough and agonizing journey at this stage of her first pregnancy."

Before Azeem could say anything, Riaz intervened, saying, "Zubaida will be very happy. I agree with you and take that option out. I am now adjutant (a staff assignment assisting the commanding officer of an army unit, also known as regiment) to the CO (commanding officer) of our reorganized regiment. I will endeavor to propose to my CO for submitting a proposal to the higher authorities for your air repatriation, considering your past service and the pregnancy of Bhabi and maybe that of newborn child."

He then released his hand, embraced warmly, saying *Khoda Hafeez* (seeking Allah's blessings and protection), and took steps toward the camp office.

A few days thereafter, another good news spread out within the camp. That related to the UN involvement in the dialogue process for repatriating the Bangladesh-origin ex-Pakistan soldiers and civilians detained in Pakistan. An agreement was reached soon, and preparations were underway to smoothly implement that. But time was needed for gradual repatriation, and hence all kept on awaiting the final date.

In the meanwhile, Rukiya gave birth to a healthy baby boy. Senior major's wife supervised the delivery, and three ladies of the camp, having experience and natural ability, successfully carried out the process. Everyone was relieved and happy. The couple was over-joyed and devoted all their time to take care of the baby boy.

In his excitement, Azeem proclaimed that he would like to see his son also join the army and fulfill his currently stalled dream of becoming a senior officer in due course. He then saluted his newborn son. Rukiya could not hide her hilarious riposte.

During those initial days, they referred to the baby as *Babu* (a common Bangladeshi address for a newly born son). Then there was the imperative need to name him to obtain a birth certificate. Without pretention, Azeem proposed the name of Fazal Abbas: *Fazal* being the name of the most famous internationally recognized Pakistani cricket bowler of the sixties whom he liked the most, and *Abbas* being the abbreviation of his grandfather's name, Abbasuddin, whom he adored most. Rukiya readily agreed.

Communication received from the authorities indicated the date and time for the couple's repatriation. That was about ten days from the date of the letter. It was the month May, 1973.

The couple hurriedly packed up the remnants of their belongings. Most of the camp's inhabitants, being from different regiments and locations, had separate schedules.

Meanwhile, like others that preceded them, Rukiya and Azeem continued taking leave from their new friends of the camp with the promise to reunite once in Bangladesh. Emotionally and physically, the couple was all set to leave Pakistan forever, with dreams and hopes centering on toddler Fazal.

ANXIETY

O n the basis of earlier intimation, a few family members of both Rukiya and Azeem were at Dhaka airport on the scheduled day to receive the couple. There was some initial confusion at the Dhaka airport about the arrival of Azeem and his family as the passenger manifest did not have the name of Ziyauddin Abbassuddin Azeem. There was anxiety prevalent; however, the family decided to stay put.

The plane carrying Azeem and his family landed at the Dhaka International airport, known as Kurmitola airport. Rukiya, slowly and watchfully, stepped out of the aircraft with Fazal in her lap and the right hand of Azeem providing the necessary shield for both. They carefully negotiated the rolling access platform, also called ramp stairs, and proceeded to the special counter of Customs and Immigration meant for returnees from Pakistan.

The few NCOs of new Bangladesh army handling them at the immigration counter were both apathetic and nonchalant. Azeem had the impression that they were being treated as unwelcome arrivals due to their lack of participation in the liberation war. That unexpected lackadaisical interaction at the immigration counter disturbed Azeem, but he kept his cool. He, however, could not get out of that adverse feeling the more he thought that it happened in his own soil, and that too from his own people.

On coming out after fulfilling requirements, the couple and baby Abbas were warmly greeted by both families of the couple. Representation of Azeem's family was minimal due to the deaths of his parents earlier and the lack of regular contact. In the melee, the parents of Rukiya literally snatched baby Abbas from her and started hugging and kissing him. Joy and happiness were all around in the airport reunion, and it appeared that most present, for a short while, were oblivious of the uncertain future of the couple's life.

That was not the case of Azeem. In spite of being sober outside and sustained efforts to remain normal, he was visibly worried. He made intermittent efforts and epigrammatic avowals to convey his enjoyment in celebrating the reunion.

Contrarily, Rukiya was enjoying her time with family members, mostly on her aisle of relationships. She kept on talking about the warm way she was welcomed in Lahore and their short conjugal living in Lahore, with the overwhelming love and care of Azeem's colleagues and friends. All of them not only loved Azeem but were equally vocal about his professional competence. That was unique against the emerging tension and uncertainty enveloping the political panorama.

With a concoction of doubt and despair overwhelming his inner self, Azeem reported to the Bangladesh Army HQ the morning following the day of arrival. Pleasantly, he was poised, noticing the decency and decorum shown by officers in handling his case, including the verification of his service documents and related correspondences. Though the outcome would be communicated in due course, Azeem consoled himself for being treated well.

On his way back, and the subsequent time, he intently tried to rein apparent negative musings that were bothering him since the decision to return to Bangladesh and his encounter at the immigration counter of Dhaka airport. He was happy recalling the universal saying that "even the darkest cloud has its silver lining."

Visiting the army HQ often thereafter, he developed an in-depth sense of sulk and spasms the army, rated to be an organized and disciplined organ of the government, was transiting through. His anxiety and dismay, nevertheless, multiplied with the fresh deleterious information trickling in each discourse. Emanated facts caused more alarm about the future.

The despondency and incoherent reflections in Azeem's personality traits did not escape Rukiya's notice. Prior to retiring to bed after dinner, she stepped in with a cup of broiling coffee, a liking of Azeem she was used to since living in Lahore but discontinued after their arrival in Dhaka. Rukiya spent most of her time taking care of the families and numerous visitors from the extended families and was exhausted at the end of the day. Hence, the after-dinner coffee service had not been much of a priority.

Azeem was pleasantly surprised, and had an impish exchange of looks with Rukiya. Handing over the coffee, Rukiya instinctively said, "Even though mother is taking care of Fazal, I remain busy in performing diverse chores and get exhausted at the end of the day. I am doing those willingly to convey my love and care for the families. The ritual of coffee service after dinner slipped out of my mind. I assure you that it will not happen again."

With Fazal being asleep by the side of his grandma with a bottle of draped milk nearby, the setting of the couple's room had ideal ambience for romanticism and ecstasy. Rukiya moved fleetingly to change into her negligée as she used to do both in Lahore and the detention camp. She combed her hair, applied moisture defense lotion on her face, put on light lipstick, and treaded forward with expectation. Normally and in such a setting, Azeem used to jump up, hold her intensely, and caress her body, with expressions some audible and some not, but that was not the case that evening. He looked at her and quietly put the empty coffee cup on the side table of the bed he was lounging.

Rukiya refrained from conveying her frustration and annoyance. She sat quietly, took the hand of Azeem, and positioned that on her lap, slowly massaging his lone hand. Azeem was nonresponsive even then.

She then lifted his hand, tightening her grip, and said, "What happened to you? All your expressed enthusiasm for being a part of the new Bangladesh Army while in Pakistan as well during our flight appears to have withered away. Every day you return from your reporting chores with rambling gestures and in a mood. I opted to allow you to sail as you think fit. Also, because of family errands, I did not have the mindset for inquiring, and always hoped that you would open up. It has now become unbearable. My preparatory dressing up of minutes back to make you aflame did not work, so I want to know your predicaments. Please share with me frankly. I would not like to repeat the vow to be with you and by your side under all duress and happiness pronounced in Lahore during the initial phase of our conjugal life. For me that is a lifetime pledge. I will not deviate from that come what may."

Azeem thoughtfully made the space available to enable Rukiya to unleash her fretfulness. He listened minutely to what Rukiya painstakingly and candidly dealt with in her unusual oration. As an immediate reaction, he took both her hands in his grip and held that intently as if communicating not only his concomitance but also refurbishing his feeling and adoration.

He opened up, saying, "I have no doubt about your rumination of what I said since our wedding about who I am, my thinking and priorities in life. I grew up with all my focus on conviction, clarity, and acquiescence in charting my life. All these were reinforced when I joined the army with the main mantra of command, loyalty, and dedication irrespective of the risks inherent. I was sad but not surprised when three of my soldiers gave their life at my command in confronting the superior Indian army in their incursion near Wagah border point. That is how I was trained. That is what guided me in dreaming of a new life and role in the new Bangladesh army. I always parked those values in the earnest corner of my heart.

I stepped into the soil of motherland Bangladesh with no high hopes of a warm welcome. But I also did not expect the expressed and hushed hostility that greeted me in the special immigration counter for returnees from Pakistan. I did not nurture that experience and considered those as being individual behavior. Leaving that behind, I happily went to army HQ for reporting. During the reporting process, I visited army HQ frequently and came into contact with many. One of them was Major Khalil, who was the brigade major (BM) of the main garrison stationed in Dhaka.

Noting the internal stress I was having with the respect of command, obedience, and unity per se as a singular fighting force, Major

Khalil took pains to apprise me the background and current situation of the inchoate Bangladesh army. He, during intermittent discourses, said, 'If one gives a deprived child a toy, the latter would definitely enjoy it. If a bunch of toys are given at the same time, the child would lose focus. Exactly that is happening in case of Bangladesh Army. In the process of being composed of various groups, there is inner friction and mistrust. So what you experienced at the airport and what you are observing now are an outcome of that. The quick and unplanned political decision to create Jatiya Rakkhi Bahini (National Security Force) in early 1972 accentuated the problem.'

He continued, saying, 'The decision to create JRB had its root in the perceived political need to have an elite paramilitary force absolutely loyal to the government and the party. As the government was new and various factions were competing with each other for power and position, the authorities felt shaky. Unfortunate lack of clarity in thinking as to relevance, manning, and role of Bangladesh Army in future was another contributing factor. Eventually, JRB took the shape and role of de-facto military wing of the party in power.

This qualms within the army was aggravated by the systematic induction of various fractions/groups collectively called *Mukti Bahini* (freedom fighters). The principal constituents are the erstwhile East Bengal Regiments, East Pakistan Rifles, Police Force, and civilian volunteers, mostly youths and students that actively participated in the War of Liberation. The pressure from other subgroups like Mujib Bahini, Maderia Bahini, etc., was all-pervading. The situation was inflamed due to absorption of repatriated soldiers from Pakistan. All these caused unexpected but inevitable stress on what otherwise would have been a structured and disciplined institution. The unforeseen factionalism within the army, even at its infancy, caused concerns in the political leadership of the new nation too.

If looked negatively, one has copious reasons to be disheartened. Another option is to have a positive outlook considering that we, as a group of people, got our independence and identity sooner than expected. So the initial confusion is expected. In this setting all of us have a fecund role to play with patience and understanding.'"

Azeem was convinced by the statements and the rationale put forward by Major Khalil and reasonably relieved, hoping for a new dawn sooner. That mindset was burgeoned when he received a call from *the* army HQ advising about his induction in Bangladesh Army with his present rank of major. He was told that formal assignment to a specific battalion and posting per se would take little time. In the meanwhile, he was instructed to report to army HQ immediately.

Dressed in new uniform and with a major's emblem of Bangladesh army on his shoulder, Azeem reported for duty. He was assigned to a staff position in GHQ overseeing the organizational matters of the army.

During his formal call on the adjutant general (senior-most administrative position reporting to the commander-in-chief (C-in-C) of the army, responsible, among others for the personal administration, welfare, rehabilitation, etc. The position was commonly referred to as AG. Azeem was being advised by the AG, saying, "With the army still in a seminal stage due to the lack of clarity on many matters and decisions changing frequently, we are urgently in need of drawing a vision statement for the army with an identification of the rungs and supporting actions. This has become imperative because of the formation of JRB.

The proposed vision statement, besides policy articulation, should have the indicative numbers for a well-organized defense force in the geopolitical context of Bangladesh, the establishment of new cantonments, and their possible locations. Further details can be worked out later on. We should proceed step-by-step, with urgency nevertheless driving our efforts."

As the AG was about to continue, a message came that the C-in-C would like to see him. He stepped out of his office room, leaving Azeem alone. That forlorn setting was impelled by the sudden arrival of a support staff of the AG's office with tea tray. The staff put the tray on the table, saluted Azeem, and served the tea quietly, nevertheless having a motley smile. Azeem was intrigued but ignored that and concentrated in having the tea.

Soon the AG returned and resumed his unfinished opinion, saying, "From the perspective of Bangladesh Army, this is a major task. I know that as a young officer, your priority is for field posting. But this assignment is for about two years. On completion, you will be assigned to field duty. In the meantime, try to do this astutely without publicity. Because of the latter priority, you will work in my office, and the staff concerned has been instructed to identify the needed logistic support in consultation with you and make necessary arrangements. Your unit is being envisaged as a camouflaged core unit, and you are to remember that in conducting yourself in all matters and situations."

Azeem's induction and posting made everyone in the family exuberant and delighted. Most exultant was, of course, Rukiya. Though not a command position, he gradually started enjoying the assignment. It enabled him to get meaningfully involved in shaping the army and having interactions with different segments and varied staffs.

While sitting by the side of Azeem prior to retiring for the night, Rukiya repeated her opt-repeated axiom that "if one door in life's journey is closed, Allahpak (the Creator) opens up hundred others." She emphasized that, "One should always have faith that whatever happens in life perhaps happen for a reason. As mortal beings, we can't always handle that. All your agonies since the creation of Bangladesh were possibly normal reactions, but the end results are definitely indicative of new challenges and prospects."

Saying those words, Rukiya, to the taciturn surprise of Azeem, went to the shower room, performed the Muslim ways of ablution, opened the *jai namaz* (prayer mat, a small rug used by Muslims for performing devotional prayers), and started performing *nafal namaj* (optional prayers).

That night, for both, was a euphoric one, repositioning themselves against future prospects, compared to postdinner times of the evening.

Azeem was very happy with his new assignment, though it was far different from the usual job responsibilities of an army major.

He was pleased within himself for having the opportunity to make a contribution in shaping the Bangladesh army in terms of policy, planning, and direction. He continued to maintain a low profile, both in his professional life and personal dealings.

Another good news surprised him. Azeem was told that in view of the nature of his assignment and to ensure the prompt access to his superiors' call, he was allotted a small two-room quarter within the cantonment. That made all, especially Rukiya, blissful even though the free access for friends and relations would be constrained.

The couple soon moved to their new accommodation and settled down promptly with the help of her mother and her sisters. Their departing scene, after all the settlement-related chores were completed, was a sad one. The grandma was particularly depressed at leaving Fazal Abbas behind, but accepted the reality of life.

Life moved on, leaving all anxieties behind. In a low-profile life pattern, both in their official and private lives, contrary to Azeem's liking, the couple rediscovered themselves, centering all their attention on the toddler Abbas.

In his professional work, Azeem was preoccupied in manning his core unit, reading about the command structure and the formation of various armies of pertinent countries, especially those of Indonesia, Malaysia, and Thailand. He was engrossed in having the initial draft of the vision statement, but his enthusiasm was impacted by the emerging uncertainties shrouding the army as a whole. In the context of a low-profile official and personal life, Azeem often shared emerging anxieties with Rukiya, who was overly concerned.

In one of such exchanges, Azeem wanted to share his assessment pertaining to prevailing irritants with Rukiya, but that was not to be inside the quarter. He proposed to have a walk in the garden after dinner, and that surprised Rukiya since Azeem always preferred to sit before the TV after dinner to listen to Bangladesh TV's (BTV) national news of 9:00 p.m.

While strolling in the small garden with minimal traffic around, Azeem said, "What I am going to share with you is nothing portentous but just my assessment at this stage. I could as well tell you in our living area, but I am uncertain and increasingly feeling nervous. My nervousness predicates on the suspicion of possible wiretapping and surveillance.

Having interactions with divergent segments of the armed forces in connection with official matters and lending my ears to the whispers that are rampant all around, I have a feeling that factionalism within the army heightened to a dodgy smudge to cause a real worry to all. That warranted the cautionary need to talk in an open space."

After a pause, Azeem continued, saying, "As you are aware, I have had been experiencing anxiety since the dismemberment of Pakistan. I have, without hesitation and with your encouragement, opted to be in Bangladesh, and proudly associate myself with Bangladesh army and its well-being. With that mindset, I have cheerfully accepted my present assignment and have no complain and regret.

What is presently fretting me, however, is the visibility of an emerging factionalism within the army. Suspicions in actions and dealings surfaced to the discomfort of many." After saying those, Azeem suddenly kept quiet.

Rukiya, besides carefully paying attention to the tone of Azeem's deliberations so far and the related facial expressions even in the shady hours of early night, was convinced that the problem was much larger than what he had shared so far. She was certain that the emerging anxieties had more far-reaching implications than what he was telling her. Possibly, the pressures of what was going on in the army impacted on his belief and confidence. All the emerging negative developments are affecting him, and such developments and new anxieties astounded him often. He had to share some of such anxieties with his wife to unleash his straining worries. But she was certain that it was not all.

Rukiya clutched the hand of Azeem, kept on holding it for some time, and then pressed it, saying, "Our married life is not that long. It has so far experienced unexpected jiggles and jerks. But whatever time we have lived together so far, particularly those trials and experiences, have given me a complete sense of who you are. Now be candid and tell me unwaveringly what you wanted to, and I assure you, come what may, I will always be by your side. This is a firm and conscious renewal of my earlier pledges on challenging circumstances."

Azeem opened up, saying, "What I have in mind and what I wanted to tell you are my perceptions based on some facts. So I was wondering what to tell and how much to tell."

Having said so, Azeem drew Rukiya close, stating, "My problem is I do not know very well any one of my colleagues here to unburden myself occasionally. Also, my current responsibility is not conducive to socializing, so you are the only one for me to unbridle my concerns and anxieties, big or small.

There is a rising tension, even at the senior levels of the army and JRB, on every dimension of relationships—the role, influence, responsibility, and propinquity to power base, besides manpower and resource allocation.

All these are aggravated by a rumored political perception to dismantle the established central command structure and put segments of the army under the control of the newly planned district governors. That caused disarray among the senior commands of the army.

These developments and irritants make me disconsolate, perhaps driving me back to previous mindset. I feel dejected thinking that all my work pertaining to the vision statement and the policy framework of about a year will be a waste."

As they were strolling, both of them were quiet. After a while, Azeem asked Rukiya whether she had anything to say in light of the issues just articulated.

Rukiya smiled and softly said, "You know that I do not always respond to the matters of life instantaneously. I was digesting what you said and thinking how best to enunciate my response that would suggestively help to lighten your present worries.

I am neither concerned about the factionalism that presently is besetting the army, nor bothered by the JRB factor in the light of what Major Khalil said to you initially. But I am really apprehensive of the long-term fallout of the political priority to place army units at the district level. That may be a precursor to relegate the army into the elite police force at district level and for JRB to assume the role and functions of the army.

In this regard, two points are worth keeping in view: first, there are senior functionaries to handle the issue of the possible role of JRB vis-à-vis army. Staff of your level can't address that issue without worsening the situation, so put that to rest. Second, whatever happens, the proposed vision statement and policy framework will remain relevant, even if JRB assumes the role of the army. Your work will thus not be a waste. Being visibly neutral, you should carry on your work. You should not be disheartened just based on feelings."

In that shady scenario, Azeem spontaneously drew Rukiya close and cuddled her, observing, "As always, I am so thankful to you for your candid opinion. In the melee of the divergent developments and free-floating rumors, I lost track of systematic thinking. Some trivia resurfaced in my thinking. After listening to what you observed, I assure you that I will be guided accordingly. But tell me one thing honestly: being a housewife, how could you organize your thoughts so succinctly even though my pessimistic observations had imminent impressions of turbulence impacting our life immediately?"

Without dithering, Rukiya instinctively said, "My life during the growing-up phase was conditioned by my school and home at Islamabad, specially Mother. I did not learn much in school about social interaction. Whatever I learnt was by observing Mother. She was a friend and guide to many Bangladeshi ladies and some Pakistanis too. Her long stay both in Karachi and Islamabad made her an icon of the local social milieu. She used to listen to others minutely, always took time, and gave her suggestion and opinion later. But that was not the end. She would ponder on issues, revisit what she communicated, and on some occasions, inversed her earlier observations. Noting that, I gradually picked up that particular attribute of hers. But my real transformation was during my college life in Dhaka under the guidance of my dear professor Rashida Anjum. For some odd reasons, she developed a liking for me. We used to have frequent discussions. I minutely listened to her and stored in my inner self her observations and advice. On a particular occasion, she said, 'Rukiya, you are definitely a good student, besides being intelligent and smart. But please bear in mind that there are different ways in harvesting benefits from those. In the case of success in life, never be contented. Think seriously of other ways to perform still better. While confronting a problem or a depressing situation, think of the worse that could have happened as well as delineate relevant scenarios enabling you to take a right decision.' Those words are ingrained in my mind and thoughts. I try to, instead of giving up or harboring frustration, always look for a better response. That is what I did during our conjugal life and the walk of this evening."

Azeem expressed thanks and gratitude to Rukiya, and the relaxed couple slowly returned to their room, noticing the naughty Fazal Abbas in deep sleep, being symbolic of innocence and relaxation. Prickling his hand, Rukiya observed, "Learn from your son too."

ANGST

Based on such deliberations and exchange of opinions, Azeem gradually was making determined efforts to disassociate himself from trivial paroxysms, and made specific determination to focus on his job. But the preferred journey was not as easy as Rukiya envisaged.

Azeem's much-preferred constructive approach was thwarted many a times by clandestine tensions visible among the sundries of army personnel, many of whom frequented AG's office for support and help. The related element of tension was goaded further as he was required, being staff of the AG, to regularly attend the conference of senior HQ officers and field commanders.

His attending of such conferences was premised on ensuring a better perception about the role, responsibility, and functions of army in the immediate and long-term futures in the context of tasks on hand. He continued to be dismayed.

In an unplanned discourse with Rukiya, Azeem shared this portent with her. As on earlier occasions, Rukiya found positivity in that setting comparative to negative musings of Azeem.

Lifting herself from the frame of angst reflections of Azeem, Rukiya lovingly observed, "I agree that sustaining that sort of setting day in and day out is emotionally stressful, but see the other side of the outcome. Even though a major, you are new in Bangladesh army. The occasional exchanges of looks and salutations make you familiar to many soldiers, NCOs, and officers whom otherwise you would not have known. This makes your assimilation process smooth with a better footing.

"Being required to attend the meetings of commanding officers, you are likely to be noted by many. Occasional but brief discourses with HQ and field commanders, assumedly during breaks, make you known to them, and equally you know them. This definitely is an upbeat passage for your future progression."

Azeem's response, as on the past occasions, was one of adoration.

Time passed, and Azeem was engrossed with his task, parking the end result to opacity. Even the unanticipated political decision to have a single political party in the country with shrunken number newspapers did not unnerve Azeem anymore.

Then the most startling, wretched, and improbable thing beleaguered the whole nation: the bewildering military intervention by a group of midlevel officers. In the early morning of mid-August of 1975, they assassinated the Father of the Nation and his family, except two daughters, being abroad.

That abrupt and catastrophic national tragedy dumbfounded the infant nation, but what surprised Azeem, and nonpartisan fellows like him, was the absolute absence of remonstration anywhere in the country. The millions of hands that went up, responding affirmatively to the historic speech of Sheikh Mujib on January 7, 1971 shockingly were all folded in mid-1975.

Mega confusion, beset by looming uncertainty, prevailed. The senior staffs of army were all running around with puzzlement overshadowing their thinking and actions.

As the sun was setting on that fateful day, another news stunned the people. His one-time colleagues in the cabinet, except the senior four taken to custody earlier, took the oath of office as members of a new Cabinet under the presidency of another senior-most leader and confidant of the assassinated Father of the Nation.

Sitting in his office chair alone in the midst of bedlam and ambiguities, Azeem was deeply engrossed, wondering about the emotive and psychosomatic mindset of the populace at large. Within that short time, he summarized that as being possibly due to the economic downturn being experienced since the independence and the socio-political irritants besetting the nation.

A sudden positive reflection vibrated within the thinking of Azeem. He took formation of the new government, so soon and by same party people, as a much desired symbol of stability. With such thought negating his earlier pessimistic assessment, Azeem happily returned home.

Rukiya was dazed seeing a relaxed Azeem, recalling her earlier telephone discourses of the day with him soon after the news of the national catastrophe was aired. She never expected to meet a smiling Azeem returning home.

Without giving Rukiya an opportunity to verbalize her thoughts, Azeem sat on one of their dining chairs, placed his cap on the table, and relaxingly desired to have a cup of coffee. Those were not the norms as he meticulously always changed into civvies, washed his face and hands, and then only would be at the dining table for evening snacks and coffee before playing with Fazal.

While sipping coffee, Azeem opened up, saying, "What happened this early morning is horrific for any country, more particularly for Bangladesh, a country in its infancy. There is no expression to convey the feeling of despondency. Whatever may possibly be the limitations, one does not kill his father. The assassination of the Father of the Nation with his family in his own country, by his own people, and at his own residence is too appalling. However, my happiness is premised on the ability to form a government so soon and by his own people. The other silver lining is likely the reversal of earlier political decisions, particularly the one related to fragmenting the armed forces at district level. None in the present political leadership has the charisma of the late leader to carry out such decisions. We feasibly would have a breathing space to frame a more sustainable option."

Rukiya kept quiet to shorten the discussion in the midst of swamping ambiguities. She had qualms about the buoyancy that swept the feeling of Azeem. Rukiya obviously was not very familiar with political syndromes, but she had been blessed with the uncanny ability to analyze events from a wider perspective. That premised her misgivings shrouding the events of the day. In her inner self, she concluded that Azeem's sunniness was grounded on short-term implications. She was concerned about the long-term fall-out. The sudden absence of the prominent leader from the scene could well be a precursor to political jealousy for power and position, and the armed forces would likely not be immune from that. But she kept that within herself so that Azeem could relax in spite of overbearing sadness of the day.

Rukiya's assessment unexpectedly was proven to be more on line sooner than she thought, and surprisingly correlated to the armed forces while the political sideline remained unstable and confusing. Rumors of mini coups within the army, though mute, were in circulation. That was aggravated by the killing of the four senior political leaders in custody in the central jail.

A senior army officer who had actively participated in war of liberation staged a coup, deposed the political government, and arrested the most prominent general who, in 1971, declared the independence of Bangladesh on behalf of the Father of Nation.

The puzzlement and vagueness prevailed for about three days when *shipahie-janata* (ordinary soldiers and public) revolted at the middle of the night, freed the other general while the one that toppled the latest civilian government was killed while fleeing with some of his associates.

The army took charge of the country. Martial law was imposed. The Chief Justice of the Supreme Court was inducted as the president, and concurrently the Chief Martial Law Administrator (CMLA) and the freed general assumed the charge of finance alongside being the Deputy CMLA.

Major policy decisions related to the disbanding of JRB, abandoning the planned politico-administrative decisions for the introduction of a district governorship, and logical turnaround concerning the decision to locate the army at the district level were promptly taken. Stability returned, but frictions among divergent groups of army continued. That was encountered firmly.

These decisions and developments had a promising impact all around. More was in the mindset of Azeem. He devoted his time and energy in finalizing the draft vision statement. That draft was circulated to a limited few. Concerned high level functionaries of the armed forces endorsed most of the first draft for refocusing and reorganizing the army, including the gradual absorption of JRB personnel.

As earlier indicated by the AG, and in recognition of his loyalty and meritorious work thus far, Azeem was posted at the outpost of 15 Bengal Regiment located at Rangamati Headquarters, the only hilly district of Bangladesh, officially known as Chittagong Hill Tracts (CHT). He was to be given, upon reporting, his specific command assignment in the headquarter-based battalion as a company (a company in army usually is a military unit of about 100–250 soldiers under the command of a captain or major) commander.

That made Azeem ecstatic. The family was particularly very happy. But Rukiya was not. Her main concern was related to the safety and security of Azeem based on media reports and what she came to know from others. The other anxiety pertained to the educational needs and priorities of six-years-old Fazal, already enrolled in the cantonment school.

The security concern was grounded and heightened on the prevalent insurgency in CHT—an area roughly accounting for about 10 percent of the total area of Bangladesh inhabited by about five hundred thousand tribal people. They, unlike majority of the Muslim population, are followers of Buddhism even though fragmented into different tribes. They are racially more close to Mongolians, speak the local dialect, dress differently, and have their own of life and living practices.

People of tribal ethnicity vehemently resisted being grouped with Bengalees and had been adamant in protecting and nurturing their own identity, faith, culture, and dialect. The situation worsened with the voluntary migration and settlement of plain land people in CHT. That served as a warning bell to various tribes. Their earlier concerns soon turned into looming fears. They took up arms against the government, forming a resurgence armed group named *Shanti Bahini* (force for peace). *Shanti Bahini*, within a short time and with help and support from sympathetic neighboring countries, created a major law-and-order situation. Hence, more competent officers were being posted in CHT. Azeem's posting was consistent with that policy of the government. Another attraction was the additional perks with the posting.

The family setting was a pretentious one, Azeem being enthusiastic and Rukiya relatively disconcerted.

In that sort of unusual family milieu, Azeem opened up during lunch of a weekend holiday in the presence of Fazal, being engrossed in eating. Slowly but firmly, he detailed his position, outlining, "Look, during the last few years of our tumultuous married life, you have had been a very compassionate and understanding life partner, helping me to remain steady in life with a reflection of positivity under every dreary situation. Our present condition is no different.

As a member of professional army, challenges and risks are always ubiquitous. My call for duty at the Jutanagar advance camp near Wagah border point and confrontation with the Indian army intruders were one of those. Bangladesh is facing a major insurgency problem in CHT. If we do not contain that, it could result into a serious catastrophe. Also, my posting there will be in a command position and will be a major step in my assimilation process and progression objective. As you are aware, I always liked and looked for field posting. That precisely is the reason for my enthusiasm.

But that does not mean that I am oblivious to your taciturn concerns. We are not moving as a family. At my request, the AG's administration will allow me to retain our present accommodation, so Fazal will be able to pursue his education and grow up in a preferred military ambience. All my objective is to orient him right from the beginning to be a part of Bangladesh army in future. I will be with you both as time permits. Further, both of you will be in Rangamati during school holidays. As on previous occasions, I need your support."

There was a pause, a period of lull with minor noise emanating from empty plate of Fazal as he was indulgently playing a war game with the residue of his lunch eatables. Azeem was relieved after off-loading what he wanted to convey, more as his decision. Rukiya was dejected but nevertheless maintained her outward equanimity.

Her ever-vigilant and thoughtful mind, while preparing post-lunch tea, soon found a spot to park anxieties beholding her and to move forward in conjugal life. She thanked Allahpak silently for giving her initial years of normal life with the needed emotional support during period of crises. That also enabled a firm bonding between father and son. She also thought that such a posting could even happen immediately after the induction with no options on the horizon.

While having such thoughts, another common but mostly unnoticed phenomena of life dawned in her mind. That related to the vicissitudes of a life's journey. Seldom does life follow the trajectory of its journey as appears to be evident. Neither does it adhere to the desired or planned trails. These are the vagaries of life one learns to live with, success being premised on individual competence and unanticipated failures or shortcomings being parked to destiny.

Premised on such thoughts and self-examination, Rukiya happily reconciled with Azeem's stipulations.

Freeing herself from her recent cheerless feeling, pragmatic and self-assured Rukiya stepped in and served tea to Azeem, who was enjoying Fazal's pseudo war game. There was no acknowledgment from Azeem. The usual exchange of happy look after every such service was mislaid.

Rukiya noted those exceptions but did not feel bad. She realized that her lack of enthusiasm was hurting Azeem. He was cogitating that as a likely obstruction to his career progression.

Rukiya kept quiet. She cleared and cleaned the dining table except that of Abbas's, allowing him to play his war game, and Azeem's continuance of enjoying that.

Premised on earlier thinking and conclusion, Rukiya took slow steps out of the kitchen, stood behind Azeem's chair, put both her hands on the shoulders of Azeem, and with all the expression of happiness, conveyed her full agreement with what he had in mind.

That impulsively changed the setting of the house. Both of them were exultant and continued playing with Abbas, contrary to the normal practice of having quiet time after lunch. There was a resurgence of the upbeat feeling in that minuscular family. In between, they decided to visit Rukiya's parents in the Mirpur township of Dhaka to apprise them about his posting and other arrangements that were being finalized, or contemplated.

Making arrangements for the secure living and safety of his minuscular family, Azeem boarded the Chittagong-bound night train. After disembarking at the Chittagong railway station and changing into a bus for a hilly road travel of about fifty miles to Rangamati, he reported to the HQ of Garrison Commander (GC) around noontime.

Azeem was received by the staff of GC following the standard protocol but had to keep on waiting for a formal call on the GC. While awaiting, he was surprised, observing the flurry of unusual traffic to and from the GC's office which were significantly at variance with what he experienced in the AG's office.

Finally, the clock clicked. The staff of the GC's office escorted Azeem in and then left.

Azeem saluted the GC and introduced himself as part of reporting decorum.

The GC unwittingly, and beyond expectations of Azeem, was somewhat apologetic for keeping Azeem waiting. He equally was prompt enough to dismiss Azeem, saying, "There will soon be lunch break. We will have lunch together as I have very important things to tell you. So please sit in the reception area. You will be called in due course."

That call came sooner than expected by Azeem. After brief exchanges as to family details and arrangements made in Dhaka for their living, the GC quickly shifted, while munching lunch eatables, to professional matters, stating, "Your posting at Rangamati command outpost of 15 Bengal Regiment and related arrangements were all completed before your arrival. In any well-established army setup, these are nominal and routine matters. But our case is not like that. In the backdrop irritants within the rank and file of forces, the army was called upon to counter insurgency movement launched in 1977 by *Parbatya Chattagram Jana Shanghati Samity* (United People's Party of the Chittagong Hill Tracts) through its armed wing, the *Santi*

63

Bahini. We are still in unsettled conditions, having the noble task of protecting our territories with inimical natives opposing us.

We have the sacred task of safeguarding the territorial integrity of Bangladesh, ensuring government authority within the CHT. But our resources, both manpower and material, considering the size, topography, and accessibility issue in many of the hinterland areas, are perilously inadequate to meet the challenge from fretful and calamitous tribal natives.

In the midst these constraints, a bolt out of blue landed in my piazza about an hour before your reporting. Our commanding officer of Bandarban was injured badly in a skirmish with a band of gun smugglers. As Bandarban is a pivotal topography linking Burma with seven sister states of eastern India, its geographical location is of overriding relevance to varied bands having divergent objectives. We need to replace the officer-in-charge soon. There we landed into the problem.

Recently, we underwent a structured redeployment of men and materials in the context subtle assessment of law-and-order situation. Any sudden change in that arrangement may affect the deployment plan's efficacy and success. So based on careful deliberations, it was decided to send you to Bandarban as the replacement commandant of the company while urgent arrangements have been finalized to airlift the injured commander to Combined Military Hospital (CMH) of Chittagong.

This is an order. There is no need to explain the reasoning. Still, in view of the precipitous nature of the decision soon after your arrival, I decided to informally convey the rationale of the decision.

More significantly, this is an important and challenging assignment. Many of your colleagues would love to be in Bandarban. Just to avoid disruption and keep that at minuscular level as well as sending loud signal of our preparedness, we decided to post you there. You can relax this evening, and tomorrow early morning you are to leave. I will instruct my brigade major (BM) to get you in touch with your wife. You can take time to explain this sudden change and relieve her of any unwarranted trepidation."

The road travel of about fifty miles commenced in the early hours of the following morning in a military jeep, with armed escort behind. Wearing the standard military uniform with a swagger stick (usually carried by uniformed persons as a symbol of authority) and befitting Ray-Ban Highstreet Phantos Aviator sunglass, a parting gift from Captain Riaz of Pakistan, he unknowingly carried with him all the attributes of a hardened military personnel.

The unceasing hilly terrain with occasional bends reminded Azeem his PMA days in Abbottabad. However, noticeable differences did not escape his attention and admiration. Generally, the Bandarban setting comprised of thick greeneries, with the occasional savannas and frequent bush vegetation along with majestic presence of medium-sized trees compared to the dry landscape, sparse presence of vegetation, and some tall trees of Abbottabad.

The other feature, as told by the army driver of the jeep during a stopover, is the flow of the Sangu River from the north to the south, almost dividing Bandarban equally from east to west. The other notable river of CHT, known as Matamuhuri, is also in Bandarban territory.

As Azeem was engrossed in experiencing the beauty unveiled by nature, one thought suddenly started fretting him. He was certain that the garrison commander had something in mind to tell him but refrained for reasons known to him. Azeem was wondering what that could be! In his assumed thought, Azeem made a quick decision to devote his first two to three days in going through records and in reading about Bandarban—its history, the ethnicities, local practices and way of life, and the changes in the recent past and their impact on social, political, and religious perspectives. His inner priority was to have facts based on evidence rather than hearsay and opinions.

The jeep carrying Azeem stopped in front of company commandant's office. Instead of getting down, Azeem surveyed the setting and the surroundings of the camp. That was very brief but sufficient for his staff to line up to receive the new boss.

Azeem got down from the jeep with all the whiff of a commander, slowly moved forward with the rear end of his prestigious swagger stick positioned under his left armpit while holding the front end by his left palm. He responded to salutations and shook hands with all in the line and followed the sergeant-at-arms to his office.

In a brief conversation, he desired to have records of all incidents, both law and order related and socio-religious conflicts, with their final reports. On his query about the hundreds-of-years-old ethnic and religious chronicle, the agreed position was that the district public library had good collections in this regard, and it would be better to reconnoiter that source.

Azeem devoted the next three days in reviewing related documents and reading the historical perspective of CHT, more particularly that of Bandarban. To him that was both interesting and illuminating, but what astounded him in the process was some of the details he came to know about Bengal (mostly present Bangladesh).

Azeem was pondering how the education board–approved history syllabus of the high school years could be so deficient, focusing mainly on battles and conquests, bypassing other valued information pertaining to history, culture, literature, economy, and standing in the trade rapports of the emerging world.

Unknown to many, and contrary to perception of recent past as being a poor country ravaged by natural disasters, Bengal was at its zenith during the reigns of the Buddhist Pala and the Hindu Sena dynasties.

Beginning in the times of the Buddhist Pala dynasty (eighth to eleventh centuries) and the Hindu Sena dynasty (eleventh to twelfth centuries), Bengal came into prominence. They mostly ruled entire northeastern India and extended for a while up to Kannauj (modern time Kabul). It was, however, during Mughal rule, and as a result of enhanced international trade relationships, that Bengal drew the attention of emerging developed countries of Europe like England, France, Portugal, and the Netherlands.

That far, part of history was okay for Azeem. He was thrilled and felt robust in knowing that Bengal Subah (akin to Province in the Mughal empire), contrary to its present perception, was the most prosperous of all the Subhas, and accounted for 50 percent of the GDP of the Empire. That was about 12 percent of the world's GDP during the period. Bengal's wages for labor were higher than

European economies of the time. People enjoyed better standard of living.

Because of these, most trading nations of Europe had trade-related settlements in Bengal. Their initial focus was on business priorities within and with India. The items in high demand were grains, fine cotton muslins, silk, liquors and wines, salt, ornaments, fruits, and metals.

The other accompanying advantage was the location of the maritime port at Chittagong. That was most prominent port of the time, having regular sails to ports like Akyab, Ayuthya, Ache, Malaka, Johore, Ceylon, Bandar Abbas, and so on.

Among such trading settlements, the earliest one was that of the Portuguese (1528–1666). They were followed by the Dutch (1610–1824). The early English settlement of the 1600s was followed by the French and the Danish.

The local scene of the time was conducive for business operations by foreign entities. The Mughal rule was weakening in peripheral territories, and related revenue collection declined. The foreign traders were ruthless in that regard, both trading in and with India. They generated more than expected revenue. The increased revenue enhanced the inflow of funds to local rulers, and that made them happy and laidback. They got engaged in unproductive tryst of squabbles with neighboring rulers.

That paved the way for a grand change in objectives of operations by foreign trading companies. The priorities shifted from trading to territory, from profit to politics, and from traditional farm practices of locals to home country's need.

In that game play for power and politics, the British government succeeded through its East India Company, established its authority all over India, and landed into consecutive armed conflicts with neighboring Burma. This was the offshoot of the quest for power, resources, and influence, both in trade and territory. That brought the Arakan territory of northwest Burma, particularly Akyab, both its capital and seaport of eminence, into greater contact with Bengal anew as control and contacts with British India and Burma experienced a convoluted pattern.

Arakan was ceded to the British India Administration as the settlement of the first Anglo-Burmese war of 1824–26. It was reverted back as part of Province of Burma of British India after the occupation of Burma. When Burma was split off from the British India administration in 1937, Arakan was made a part of Burma.

There was a lattice contacts and varied subdued relationship between Chittagong of Bengal (as Bangladesh and West Bengal state of India was known before 1947) and Arakan of Burma. Chittagong's (for that matter Bengal's) topography notably changes as it borders Arakan in south-west and partially other parts of Burma in its remaining southern territory.

Arakan, being surrounded by the Arakan mountain ranges on its east, south, and northern sides, had access through water of Bay of Bengal in the west.

For the greater part of the earliest history, Arakan was mostly an isolated territory. The earlier populace, who were dark skinned, are believed to be of Indian origin as they resembled Bengalees.

Burmese from the south, mostly Buddhists with Mongolian features, started settling in Arakan at about tenth century. These Burmese settlers in Arakan have had been known as Rakhines, and they all through maintained their ethnicity. The earlier dark-skinned populace of Arakan had Hindu and Buddhist roots possibly originating from India, but successive generations had a mix of Arab, Portuguese, and other Muslim warriors and settlers' blood, faith and cultures through settlement and intermarriages beginning in the fifteenth century. They primarily live in the northern Arakan with close proximity to Chittagong's southern border. They are the Rohingyas claiming pedigree of Arakan.

With power and forces to back up from predominant south, Rakhine settlers systematically pressed Rohingyas, who increasingly moved north bordering Bandarban.

This historical conflict with roots in both demography and ethnicity reflects the dominance of nationalist Rakhine. The resultant oppression and deprivation had been opposed by Rohingya minority, and they started resisting. The consequent exodus of Rohingyas to the north, and more particularly to Bandarban area, became the norm. The available sanctuaries in Bandarban paved the way for better organizing, relatively improved planning, and the efficient execution of resistance by Rohingyas.

Azeem was pleased to have an indicative insight about one of the puzzles he had in mind.

Apart from the proximity to Bengal, a silent transformation in Arkan itself was in progress due to settlement by Arab traders, vassalage of Arakan to Bengal Sultanate for a long time, prolonged British hegemony with control in Bengal, the settlement of plain land people of Chittagong, and the sustained exodus of Rohingyas.

To Azeem, the influence of Arakan in general and the above-mentioned amalgamation factors on Chittagong turf per se, specifically CHT, was quite fascinating. That equally enchanted him.

The Arakan mountain ranges have had six semi-mountain ranges in Bandarban area. They account for all the high peaks of Bangladesh.

Besides topographical changes, there has had been an equally significant transformation in the life and living practices of southern and eastern Chittagong. They embraced social interactions, religious practices, cultural exchanges, food arrays, etc. But the most significant one related to the dialect of the area. That dialect, even though it had roots in Bangla, was less similar to that language. Commonly known as Chittagonian, the dialect spoken was premised on Bangla language, with the strong influence and heavy mix and match of Sanskrit, Pali, Arabic, Farsi, and Portuguese. Thus, to ordinary Bangla-speaking people, Chittagonian dialect often sounds Greek, and was a matter of jokes and hilarity. The Chittagonian dialect, as spoken, sounds rough and loud, but quite interestingly its lyrics are often sweet and soft. That makes this particular dialect interesting to many.

Simultaneously, Azeem reviewed all reports pertaining to social issues and incidents. In summation, he identified peripheral involvement of people on the ground in deciphering and coming to conclusions about social incidents and issues. The process was mostly confined to consultation with or involvement of a few elites to the exclusion of aggrieved people.

Azeem continued his search and reading. He soon came to the realization that perhaps the initial perceptions he needed were already in place. While additional interest and research may be relevant, the need of the hour was action on the ground. He decided to have an open *durbar* (assembly) with his battalion and then have a consultative meeting with representative local people consisting of elites, teachers, priests, imams, settlers, and students. Those were acted upon promptly.

In his durbar deliberations outlining the operational objectives and guidelines, Major Azeem firmly stated, "This is Bangladesh territory, but the land belongs to the local people. It is with them and with their help, we are to ensure territorial integrity, peace, and development. Any excess on our part most certainly will backfire with unyielding consequences. In all our future operational engagements, we should remember this. Under no provocation, should we repeat the mistakes of the Pakistan army in Bangladesh, treating local inhabitants as sort of aliens in their own land. Our strategic goal will be to scout for optimizing local support in all eventualities."

After a pause, Major Azeem, recalling what he learned during his assignment in the AG's office, laid out a strategy in dealing with the prevalent insurgency challenges in his area of command. He delineated his thought, strategy, and approach, stating, "All our operations should have priority and focus on people, both indigenous and settlers. Keeping that in view, it would be our endeavor to follow two strategies: first, we should always be conscious of the realities on the ground. That, in essence and most importantly, is premised on the nature and type of the insurgency problems in CHT. Being generally complex issues like land utilization, land ownership, culture, faith, settlement and autonomy, they are premised on intratribe commonality involving emotions, pride, and sentiments and are vulnerable to exploitation by baleful groups. Second, such complexities involving an area of 10 percent of the national territory with a population of less than 1 percent of this tiny country inhabited by about hundred and thirty million have been compounded due to presence of and operations by a number of extraterritorial insurgent groups. Among them, prominent ones are the Rohingya Liberation Front, the Arakan Muslim Movement, the Mizo National Front, and the Nagaland Independent Movement, besides smaller ones. This configuration of local and extraterritorial elements have inadvertently paved the way for smuggling—arms and weapons being the prominent one."

Taking advantage of a short breather, Commander Azeem browsed the facial reactions of the attendees and, being satisfied of being able to convey aforesaid communication intent, resumed his oration with conviction and authority, saying, "As you are aware, being a new country, our army's present capacity is constrained in terms of both men and materials, so we need to have a strategy to optimize the impact of our presence and effectiveness. We should not be engaged in confronting all insurgent groups at the same time. Our best strategy would be to keep extraterritorial groups apart to minimize their contact and coordination. The twin element of that strategy is to have a simultaneous supportive social approach to minimize misunderstandings and the misgivings of indigenous tribes. The resolution of the complex issues mentioned earlier are the responsibilities of higher authorities, but we can help in laying a soft landing cushion for that process.

The other related strategy, significantly more important in terms of relevance and impact, is not to repeat mistakes that the Pakistan army committed in Bangladesh. We should always remember that killing a shanti bahini is easy, but eventually that would result in creating ten more shanti bahinis. The preferred objective would be to capture, treat well, counsel, and imbibe a sense of national pride side by side while respecting tribe heritage to make them one of us. Even if we succeed in 30 percent of the cases, the multiplier impact of that in the long run may be manifold.

The other germane emphasis should be on avoiding race, faith, social, and opportunity related abuses and injustices. Experiences corroborate that these cut a deep mark in the mind of aggrieved people, with subsequent negative and hatred-based responses for a long time. We need not only to have patience but make it a visible face of our regular dealings. The long-term benefit is always manifold."

In concluding, the commander stated, "These statements were not made by me as casual observations. They are meant to be operational guidelines for every day and for every action. Compliance is mandatory and will be monitored."

The battalion commander organized a subsequent civic gathering of varied constituencies with the support and participation of the civil authorities. In order to minimize undue trepidation and ensure a sense of comfort, that gathering was organized in the local football field. In his short but equally to-the-point deliberations, the commander emphasized, among others, the following: "This land is yours. There is no dispute about that. But it is equally true that it had been part and parcel of Bangladesh, and its previous geographical identities, from time immemorial. Taking care of this land and ensuring its development are your responsibilities. Protecting territorial integrity and minimizing external incursions are our obligations. We are partners in the same game with different objectives. We can't achieve the objectives alone and by sheer force. As you need us in your efforts to achieve your objectives, we also need you by our side. As civic groups, you will receive equal and fair treatment under my command. For the prompt registration of major grievances and to channel propositions for the betterment of peace and order, we will have a social council, to be known as Bandarban Social Council (BSC). This will have representations from all segments and will meet on the first working Monday of the month. Besides, council members will have direct access to me any time of their choice."

After exchanging affirmative looks with the Marma chief and the subdivisional officer, the commander continued, saying, "I have articulated the changes in the games rules at the field level. You will soon enjoy the flavor of the new fragrance. Its sustainability, however, depends on your cooperation and affirmative response. The ball is in your court. This is the time for action. Do not keep your hands folded. Extend them. Embrace the changes in the offing. With joint efforts and trust, we will have a new beginning to the joy and merriment of all in Bandarban, and eventually in CHT."

During a postdinner chitchat in the setting of mini officers' mess of the battalion, Azeem voluntarily opened up, saying, "I am somewhat taken aback for not having any suggestive comments from any of you regarding the deliberations in the durbar and the subsequent interactions with the social gentries, including youths and students. That is okay with me. I have done what I considered to be the best in handling the causable rise in security situation. I have my own doubts about the efficacy of that but considered it worth the try, learning from what the Pakistan army did."

Sipping his cup of tea, Azeem continued, saying, "My objective of saying those had four specific goals: one, containing, and not necessarily controlling, the present inclination of the people towards insurgency; two, to involve and treat the general populace as part of redressing the current distrust; three, to create conditions for the better appreciation of the grievances of the locals in working out related solutions; and four, to minimize challenges predicated on the presence of extraterritorial insurgents to help smoothen the tensions with neighboring countries.

It is my conviction that anyone having love for Bangladesh would disagree with these objectives. Moreover, our recent past is a horrendously tragic and a palpably sad one. We are presently the tittering subject of other people's opinions and comments without cognizance of our potential. It is time for us to avoid military engagements of any type and magnitude and concentrate on building the economy exploring our potential and acumen.

Right or wrong, these are imbibed within me. I want to ensure the battalion's and my small contribution to those noble objectives. The rest is with you and your commitment."

As Azeem stood up to walk back to his quarters, his fellow officers also followed suit. Senior among them, Captain Bashar, interposed momentarily, drawing the attention of the commander, and said, "Sir, thank you for your postdinner additional clarifications with respect to what you articulated in Darbar speech. We unhesitatingly agreed with those at the time of deliberations, but tonight's clarifications will help us in motivating the troops better. You have our unabated commitment, rest assured about that."

The following days and weeks were spent by Azeem in implementing what he articulated both to troops and civilians and in assessing impacts. The progress was patently slow but steady. Besides visits to Rangamati for briefings and command conferences, he spent most of his time with troops at different locations, visiting mosques, temples and pagodas, schools, medical centers, and sports fields. The lushness of the greens in the backdrop of the hilly topography, the majestically flowing rivers and lakes, and the sparseness of population enchanted him. All through these preoccupations, Azeem was yearning to bring Rukiya and Fazal to this beautiful location of Bangladesh. But he was waiting for a good time, from the perspective of the local security situation, the weather, and the conformity with Fazal's school holidays. By design, Azeem restrained from divulging the enchanting natural beauty and charm of Bandarban to give a surprise to Rukiya. In their occasional telephone discussions, they mostly talked about family and Fazal.

Bandarban's uniqueness is not only confined to nature's gluts. Its importance is heightened manifold due to its strategic geographical location. On its eastern side, Bangladesh has a common border with Burma of about 120 miles, and the rest, about 1,000 miles, are shared with four of the seven eastern sister states of India. In view of the insurgencies going on in some of those eastern states and in bordering Burma, Bandarban, and for that matter CHT at large, got prominence as a safe shelter for various rebel groups. Bandarban soon became the main gateway and prominent pathway for transporting smuggled arms and ammunitions, both needed by Burmese and seven states insurgents. These provided the ideal backdrop for tribal insurgency in CHT, beginning early seventies. The combination of all these elements made military operations more problematic and challenging in the quest for safety and security. It generally applies to CHT, and specifically to Badarban, in view of geopolitical realities.

Azeem took the challenge with full determination. His continuing motivation was to pursue the path with patience and to carry on and chase the objective of participation by the civil society with trust and openness. It was a mission for him—a war of a different brand and enormity. It was a new love for him, fleetingly deflecting him from family and relations.

Intensive discourse at ground level and in-depth evaluation of cases and reports of earlier incidents convinced Azeem about the dynamics that caused the origin and now sustaining the multi-pronged insurgencies in CHT. Extraterritorial insurgent groups from India and Burma had been using sparsely populated CHT as a safe haven for quite a while. At variable times and reflecting variegated facial of bilateral relationships, such presence has had the blessings of the authorities. That soon paved the way for arms trading and smuggling. The resultant easy money easily swapped the initial ideological prominence of those insurgencies. Not only that. It carved out space for drug trafficking from Burma.

Azeem was convinced that the twin factors of illegal arms and drug trades, having insurgency as a pseudo cover, constituted the main elements of the law and order problems in CHT. Initially, funds generated by such activities were solely used to finance insurgency movements. With the increase in trade and the inflow of unexpected returns, Bandarban, with common borders with Burma and India, was playing a strategic role in this regard. The importance of Bandarban increased manifold due to a surge in demand for drug in Bangladesh itself. Officials and functionaries were increasingly being influenced and manipulated by such soft funds increasingly flowing in to their pockets. That caused additional worries to Azeem as it is akin to cancer in human body. His conviction as to the approach he had charted remained firm. His determination to confront the menace increased manifold.

In further deliberating the issue, both formally and informally, with colleagues, subordinates, and civil society, and drawing on his experience with his Jutanagar outpost assignment of Lahore, Azeem was convinced about the apparent inadequacy of necessary physical presence along the trails of illegal trafficking. As Bandarban's administrative locations are at the tip of its northwestern territorial limit, there has always been a time lag between request for support based on the intelligence report and the physical presence. To obviate that, Azeem, in consultation with colleagues and approval of GC at Rangamati, positioned a small unit of his battalion at Ruma. The unit, though small by nature, proved to be very effective because of location at the midpoint of the areas of conflict as well as that of illegal trafficking. Ruma is situated between longish geographical area of Thanchi to south and Rwangchori to north, all three being parallel to the Burma border.

The impact was immediate. The upshot was spectacular. Arms and weapons seized in the first two weeks were more than the last six months. The drugs impounded were much more than ever envisaged. Insurgency-related incidents, however, continued unabated. That reinforced in Azeem's thought about participation of civil society in addressing such issues. But he also realized that security-related insurrection and illegal activities generally thrived in the areas of conflict. It is thus necessary for the authorities at varied levels to strive for political, economic, and social inclusion of the aggrieved populace through development and social initiatives. That most likely to propel the desired objective of community participation in addressing the prevalent insurgency. Azeem also concluded that the principle-based objectives that ushered related movements years back have largely been eroded due to the dominance of smuggling and illegal trafficking, coupled with inflow of soft money.

Armed with such thinking and assessment, and bolstered by the significant trapping of arms and drugs, Azeem went to Garrison HQ meeting and in reporting the status and progress, highlighted the elements of his experiences and evaluations.

During the meeting deliberations, the GC, mostly by nodding head, took note of the advancement and insinuated pathway in tackling insurgency as emanated from Major Azeem's submissions. During the predinner drink homily on the occasion of the meeting, the GC took Major Azeem to an isolated corner of the dining space and slowly told him, "You achieved good progress and made good points. Make efforts to sustain that so that we can prepare a sound and tested document based on the outcomes of your efforts in Bandarban. That document envelope should be a well-tested one to withstand examination and scrutiny by higher authorities."

On indication from the GC about the end of that short talk, Azeem, being in civilian outfit, stood straight, bracing up. Being an army personnel, this reflex was ingrained in his system from day one of induction.

While he turned back in a blissful mood to join the gathering of colleagues, he was called back by the GC. Even though alert and poised as he has always been, Azeem for a while was also nervous. As he approached, the GC, while sipping his drink, casually stated, "I am scheduled to go to Dhaka the day after tomorrow to attend an urgent command briefing. I have some other garrison-related errands to be sorted out, so I will stay for three days. Except my ADC (aide-de-camp), there will be none in the chopper. Since you came at short notice and did not visit the family at all, you can, if you like, join us the day after tomorrow at about noontime and return with me on schedule. If your inclination is affirmative, then submit a leave application before your return to Bandarban. I will be expecting you around noontime of the appointed date."

During the chopper flight to Dhaka, Azeem observed that the GC, though not necessarily a reserved superior and person, was definitely a less talkative individual. He was always engrossed within himself with varied thoughts and ideas, both sensitive and trivial. That was proven when the GC, while getting down in the porch of the army club cum mess, instructed the jeep driver to drop Azeem to his abode.

Back home, Rukiya was ready to step out in her routine walk to school to fetch Fazal. She opened the main door, took a step out, and suddenly recalled that she forgot to take out meat from the freezer so that she could heat it up easily when back from school with Fazal.

Azeem was surprised observing main door of the house open. He took cautious steps and saw Rukiya fixing eatable food containers and vegetables in their mini refrigerator while planning to take out the meat dish. Azeem looked around, took small steps, and embraced Rukiya from her back with one hand put on her mouth. As Rukiya was struggling to unleash herself as well as scream, Azeem said that it was him and released her happily.

Instantly, Rukiya lost control of her physical balance and stamina, and she, with tears of happiness rolling down cheeks, surrendered herself on the chest of Azeem. He embraced her warmly, kissed her a number of times, and continued to hug her. In that moment of bliss, Rukiya looked at wall clock and hastily said, "I am getting late for picking up Fazal. I need to leave now."

Azeem glanced at her observing he too would accompany her to experience the sporadic antiphon of a son seeing his father unexpectedly.

As they were negotiating the trail toward the school, Rukiya, in a motley tone, stated that, "You could tell me in advance instead of the surprise." Azeem explained the backdrop in a nutshell, observing, "It was not my idea in normal course. Unexpectedly, the proposition was mooted by the GC, and acted upon quickly. In the current army setting of CHT, more akin to a war-like situation, everything is uncertain. I therefore opted not to inform you until I am in your embrace."

Listening carefully, Rukiya observed, saying, "It is too much for me to absorb."

Responding with love and care, Azeem countered, saying, "It is too little from me to share for all your understanding and support that made me happy and proud in rebooting myself in my military career after the Bangladesh-Pakistan episode."

They reached the school compound, and Azeem intentionally positioned himself slightly behind Rukiya in an angular locus.

As usual, Fazal came out, saw his mom, and started walking toward her with his backpack sliding and water bottle dangling. After his initial steps, he suddenly stopped, had an intense look, exchanged eye contact with his father, and started running, offloading his frills. Azeem was overwhelmed. He instantaneously positioned himself, bending his knees on the ground and extending two arms to embrace his dearest progeny. That unexpected simple union was more emotion laden and adoration premised than any formal or prearranged event could ensure.

During the walk back, and while holding the finger of his dad, Fazal was engaged in narrating his school experiences, some details about his class fellows, and full details about his teacher, Ms. Kohinoor. Azeem admirably and intently listen to those without interruption except the occasional happy exchanges of looks with Rukiya.

Since schooling started, Fazal had gotten used to having sandwiches for lunch with a supplement of milk. That practice of Fazal became very handy for Rukiya to serve food to Azeem too, who merrily opted for a sandwich following the preference of son. During that casual lunch and to convey a feeling of oneness, Azeem inquired whether he knew what is meant by *Kohinoor*, the name of his teacher. Fazal nodded sidewise, indicating a negative response.

Taking advantage of that opening and as a demonstration of paternal wisdom, Azeem, in simple terms, detailed the historical background of the name Kohinoor. In explaining, he said, "This is a Persian word meaning, 'Mountain of Light.' As the world's largest known diamond piece, mined in India, it was given the name of 'Kohinoor.' After changing many hands and dynasties, it now adores the crown of Queen Elizabeth as part of British Crown Jewels."

Observing Azeem in his oratorical mood, Rukiya quipped, saying, "You are talking in a fashion as if Fazal has grown up. All you are saying is definitely beyond his comprehension at this tender age. Also, among the many things he said, why have you become interested in his teacher?" With a mischievous smile shrouding her startling inner happiness, she served a sandwich and tea to Azeem and got engaged in preparing some nominal eatables for herself.

Relishing the inner hints in queries paused by Rukiya, Azeem merrily responded, saying, "You have two questions. With respect to the first and from lessons I learnt so far, a father-son relationship is bonded strongly by such exchanges during the growing phase of life. I am conscious of the age of Fazal and his likely inability to absorb them fully of what I said about Kohinoor. This will be in the storage of his brain. As he grows up, he might revisit them, think about those, and understand it. With respect to your second observation, I find you traditional women of our society always fearful and suspicious. I do not envy the Queen for having Kohinoor in her crown. She can neither see it, nor feel it. Conversely, you are my Kohinoor, who is always within my reach and touch, giving me enormous sensation and satisfaction. You are beyond the reach of anyone, and much more adorable than the lady teacher about whom I do not know anything. So, lady, please relax. Allow me to enjoy my Kohinoor as I wish."

They exchanged impish looks to the happiness of both.

Azeem took Fazal out of their home to play a rudimentary cricket game with a mini bat and tennis ball. But most of the time, Azeem was talking about Bandarban and life there as well as how much he missed him and his mother.

In the midst of that, Rukiya called Fazal to finish his home assignment while she got engaged, along with lady part-time help, in preparing a sumptuous dinner with the available provisions. Azeem picked up the telephone and informed families and friends about his sudden short presence in Dhaka.

That was enough. By the time Rukiya came out of kitchen area with a steaming coffee cup, leaving the remaining preparations to the care of the household help, Azeem concurred with relations and friends about propositions for lunch and dinner covering his entire stay period. On being told, Rukiya had mixed feelings. Nevertheless, she happily handed over the coffee cup to Azeem.

A sudden bizarre realization engulfed her. She was wondering about the palpable change in their conjugal life practices and stances. With the passage of time, inevitable changes in their life's arrays are increasingly becoming the norm. It was no more the early days of living after the wedding, life in Lahore cantonment, and the period of stay in the repatriation camp of Charsharda when Azeem used to consult her on every issue for discussion and concurrence. But it is no more now. He had contacted relations and friends and accepted invitations without feeling the need to tell her. For a brief while, she felt disjointed.

The guidance and teachings of her history professor at college, Ms. Rashida Anjum, inadvertently came to her rescue at that hour of agony. Rukiya revisited the other aspect of her thinking, resolving that this could as well be the result of his adoration for and trust in her with the passage of time. She also concluded that this may be the beginning of a convoluted pattern of their married life, with shades and imprints of romanticism being gradually overtaken by the realities of life, premised on years of bonding and living together. Without further dithering, she reconciled with the present, resolving to be alert and participatory in the future to avoid shock and surprise.

After finishing his coffee, Azeem focused on putting Fazal asleep, but he was not in that mood at all. Fazal was too excited, enjoying the sudden presence of Dad. As a way out, he opted for an alternative, saying, "*Betta* (son), it has been a long day for me. I am tired. Let us go to your bed and lie down." Enthused by that proposition, both father and son went to the designated bed, and Azeem pretended to be asleep. After a while, Fazal followed the suit.

When the father-son game of hide-and-seek related to sleeping was being played, Rukiya nonchalantly returned to her room, brought both horizontal parts of the traditional door in a semiclosed position, shred off her usual wears, graced herself in a sleeveless silk nightie, combed her hair, removed her earrings, put on light moisturizer with special emphasis on her cheeks, and adorned her lips with a creamy matte color lipstick. Awaiting a romantic encounter with the love of her life, Rukiya started singing, with closed eyes and in a murmur, a popular Bangla movie song "*Tumi Ashbe Boley, Kache Dakbey Boley* (that you would come, would call upon me to be close)."

Right at the moment, Azeem slowly pushed the twin sections of the door, took hushed steps in, positioned himself behind Rukiya, and embraced her from the back. Rukiya, as if she had the inkling, though her eyes were closed, unflappably conceded to the silent ingenuity of Azeem.

Lifting Rukiya with his two hands, the left one positioned at her upper back and the right below her hips, with the lower portions of nightie impishly misplaced, Azeem pressed her against his chest and placed her on the bed. He hurriedly approached the door to secure it from inside as a precaution against the sudden presence of Fazal.

During the entire process, Rukiya kept her eyes closed. Nevertheless, she was alert to feel each move and action of Azeem, her inner self bulging with emotions and excitement. As Azeem lounged by her side, Rukiya hopped on him, kissed him copiously, and scratched his back. Azeem responded with equal intensity and emotional rage. They experienced an intense physical outburst to their mutual satisfaction.

Both of them had a pleasing and fulfilling night tryst. The subtle follow-on exchanges mostly related to tribal girls, their physique and attractiveness, with a quip from Rukiya as to how much he missed her! Instead of orally responding to her query, Azeem started to caress her, and unleashed series of loving kisses all over her upper body, specially the upper back, neck, and ears. As Rukiya started squeaking, Azeem took full charge of her bared body and got engaged afresh in robust strokes. The first follow-on thing Azeem did was to remove the security gadget of the door for the possible unhindered entrance by Fazal.

The following three days just passed without any track. Lunch, dinner, and Abbas's school dominated the schedules. Divergent updates and queries on matters of varied subjects shadowed most of the social interactions. In between, Azeem piloted a proposition for a summer visit to Bandarban by both Rukiya and Fazal. It was agreed that both mother and son would visit Bandarban during the ensuing school summer break. Though the planned visit would relatively be a short one, it would definitely be rewarding living together in the beguiling and serene landscape of Bandarban. It may orient Fazal to army life at field level as well, forming a favorable impression at childhood. Rukiya, being familiar with Azeem's dream to have their son enlisted in the army, consented promptly. Her hidden agenda was to have an interactive and engaged family life as much as possible under the current configuration.

Azeem's preoccupations with command-related office and field work increased manifold suddenly. Part of that was due to the GC's guidance during the preceding Rangamati meeting to document the progression of his priorities and actions pertaining to ground operations in the effort to contain insurgency. Those, of course, predominantly were ensure that extraterritorial insurgent groups have minimal contact with each other; a better and more humane treatment of captured *Shanti Bahini* members; the tolerance of their faith and culture; a social platform for mitigating grievances; better interactions among tribal people and settlers; and the formulation and initiation of community-endorsed development work initiatives.

In spite of that, he kept his focus, though intermittently, in planning the arrangements for the visit of his son and wife. That included the logistics of receiving and bidding them farewell at the Chittagong railway station upon arrival and at departure, besides escorting them in their road journey by civilian bus from and to Chittagong. He did not spend much time in planning the desired outings within Bandarban as he would like to give way to their choices and preferences.

Time passed. Fazal and Rukiya arrived in Bandarban to the mutual happiness and joy of all concerned. Fazal soon bonded very well with the batman of Azeem. He was often out with him in the periphery of the camp, unwittingly giving his mother time to ponder. That was stress-free as most of the household chores, including cooking, were being taken care of by the camp personnel.

After pulling the curtains and opening the window of the bedroom, Rukiya looked far to the east and the south and was thrilled to observe from the hilltop residence's undulating landscape of lush green vegetation and dense forests. For a while, she traveled back to her growing-up place of Islamabad on the lap of Margalla Hills. Even though those hills were in length and height much bigger than what she could see from the window, the magnificence and beauty of the Bandarban forestation outshines dry and mostly barren Margalla in many respects. An unforeseen composite happiness amazed Rukiya.

During casual exchanges, mostly at the time of evening tea and predinner discourses, Azeem gradually unveiled to the family matters of general interests and specific relevance about Bandarban. Most of that description was aimed at creating interest in Fazal and Rukiya, and outline a probable plan to visit the sites in due course. But in every such proposition concerning the plan, he stressed one point: visits being planned are always tentative until acted upon because of security concern and alertness.

Within that limitation, Azeem managed to take Fazal and Rukiya to the places of interests he had in mind. Those included: Chimbuk Hill, located at a height of 2,500 feet from sea level, the third highest peak of Bangladesh, and located about 25 km away from the Bandarban township. That was a drive of an hour through a meandering road navigating between sporadic tribal settlements. Both Fazal and Rukiya liked the entire jeep journey, specially the sections of the drive where one had the feeling of floating above the clouds. The zigzag nature of the road reminded them some of the scenes of thriller movies as seen occasionally in TV. The reflexes of both, in expression and excitement, was an unrestrained one seeing the lone Buddhist temple and an observatory at the peak. While Rukiya focused on the temple, the visible excitement of Fazal was related to the observatory. Azeem enjoyed the happiness and bliss palpably visible in the face and body languages of both his son and his wife.

The other memorable visit was to Boga Lake. The lake is located at a distance of about 15 km from Ruma Township, which signifies a distance of about 60 km from the Bandarban administrative area. The family's road journey to Lake Boga in a military vehicle was memorable for two reasons: the ruggedness of the road and the accompanying jerks and bumps. The jeep journey was naturally both very uncomfortable and exhausting, especially the span after Ruma.

Situated at an altitude of about 1,200 feet, Lake Boga is the highest elevated lake in Bangladesh with an area coverage of about 18 acres. Surrounded by semi mountain peaks on all sides, the source of water is summer rainwater. Dense forestation, mostly consisting of thick bamboo growths, induces heavy rain in the lake vicinity. The greenness of the peripheral peaks, especially during and after rainy season, brings out nature at its best. It is simply beguiling.

The lake water mostly has a tint of green due to presence of abundant algae. However, that color occasionally changes depending on sunlight, humidity, and cloud formation.

This and other related orations of Azeem worked as a stress-relieving factor, and Fazal started to take interest about the lake. The family had a strenuous but relatively enjoyable drive while Azeem shared what he had in mind, Fazal queried, and Rukiya looked around, absorbing the scenic excellence. Soon the family was in the compound of an army makeshift camp, and both Fazal and Rukiya were astounded to see Azeem's batman with surprise arrangements for food services, though basic and as per standard army menu. Even then, that was of great relief to both son and mother, who were hungry due to jerks and bumps on their way. Father, as the initiator of present arrangement, was at ease and smiling, being used to such travel and meal. When son and mother went inside to freshen up, Azeem went out and talked to camp in charge. He was told about the unscheduled departure of a military vehicle for Ruma. Pleased, though somewhat surprised, he returned to their temporary retiring place, called the batman, and instructed him to quickly hand over the food service arrangements to the designated substitute of the camp, and for him to leave for Bandarban by the unscheduled military vehicle going to Ruma.

The family enjoyed their army's standard lunch with some trappings, like a few local fruits, some cookies, and two chicken sandwiches for each, thoughtfully brought by the batman. So over all, it was a good lunch for all. Hot tea served by the camp guy made Rukiya happy while Fazal was relishing the most unexpected service of cookies in the setting of an army camp. But he silently enjoyed one thing more: everyone in the camp saluting his father. He saw that in Bandarban but never observed something so repetitive in official interactions. Some sort of pride inhabited his thought process.

The return journey was as wearying and unnerving as the first one. The only positive thought in the minds of both the son and the mother was they were going back to temporary accommodations.

Azeem had a different thought. He was looking at his wrist watch frequently whenever they passed a roadside mile post as he was to return to the base camp before sunset due to security concerns.

The following morning, family chat at the time of breakfast was very encouraging. Rukiya opened up, saying, "Whatever the nature of discomfort, I really enjoyed every bit of yesterday's travel. It exposed me to a very different brand of Bangladesh topography which words can neither describe nor convey. It is more a matter of feeling nature's enthrallment, and one needs to experience it. It is not to be portrayed."

Azeem was delighted, and quickly redirected the conversation toward Fazal, inquiring about his reaction.

Fazal hesitantly responded, saying, "I too liked it, but I missed batman *bhai* (brother) as I thought of having a stroll with him in the nearby areas of the lake and camp."

Azeem looked at Rukiya and quipped happily, saying, "See, our infantile son is learning to think and formulate his opinion." Looking at Fazal, he continued, "I really appreciate your comment. Because of my concern about the journey, I sent him back sooner than planned so that both of you do not feel any pressure and frustration on your return. Happily things worked out on the desired lines, and we had warm food and vapor-emitting rice for our dinner last night after out exhausting trip."

Everyone concurred and laughed.

As the time passed, the family started to explore nearby places of interest. Walking along the traversable bank of Sangu River, which in any case was rather a few, Azeem shared with the family basic information about the river. He said, "The uniqueness of Sangu is its being the only river originating in Bangladesh." He continued, saying, "In addition, evergreen forests, sporadic waterfalls, and irregular peaks make the banks of the river and walks by its passable acres a thrilling experience."

In carrying out related conversations in a series of such walks, Azeem endeavored to create excitement and interest in Fazal's mind.

Casually brandishing his makeshift walking stick, Azeem said, "In my excitement of having you both, I forgot to tell you that the name Bandarban stands for expression "the dam of monkeys."

Having said so and observing the giggling face of Fazal, Azeem unleashed his plan to take the family to Nilgiri, the highest-altitude resort place in Bangladesh. It is located at a distance of about 33 km from Bandarban, enfolded by unique geographical settings. It is often ascribed as the "queen peak" and equally adored for its unspoiled natural beauty. Located at Thanchi thana, the lowest administrative unit in Bangladesh, Nilgiri is one of the tallest peaks, with a height of about 2,400 feet. It is popular for being associated with beautiful hilly natural views with the presence of clouds most of the time. In otherwise a flat land, it is termed as most esthetic panorama for enjoying quietude with unbounded relaxation.

Nilgiri's location is the home of two other highest peaks of Bangladesh—Tahjindong (also known as "bijoy," the highest peak) and Keokradong. These three peaks together represent a unique setting with rolling hills all around and the omnipresence of natural lush green vegetation. The presence of all of these peaks is distinctive in their own beauty and nature, yet the location of Nilgiri, even with a height of about 2,400 feet, has been attracting immense popular attention of late.

If properly developed, Bandarban-Cox's Bazar axis could be a popular tourist package and destination with the world's longest unbroken sea beach (a sandy beach with a gentle slope having an unbroken length of 155km/96 miles) of the latter at negotiable distance. What is of utmost importance is, however, to ensure security, peace, and infrastructure.

As Azeem was portraying his idea to create interest in the minds of Fazal and Rukiya for the visit to Nilgiri, they were about to cross a small bridge with side rails. Noticing a local intelligence contact person standing on the other side of the bridge passageway, Azeem paused, held the bridge rails, looked at opposite direction, and started talking to the intelligence guy discreetly. Soon thereafter, he decided to return to the base camp.

While having cold indigenous drink of lemon and sugar on their return, with Dad wearing a grim mien, Fazal could not hide his inquisitiveness anymore. He straightaway asked Dad the backdrop of talking to a stranger without any eye or physical contact, as well as the reason to abandon the walk planned thoroughly earlier.

Azeem happily looked at Fazal, gazed at Rukiya, and for the first time in a relaxed mood smilingly responded, saying, "I need to go to the camp office now. We will talk about your query at dinnertime."

Rukiya drew the head of Fazal to her chest, kissed his forehead, and started talking to herself, saying, *This is perhaps another bend of our conjugal life. A direct question like this from the wife during a period of stress would possibly have caused some irritation. As this one was from his son, the father reacted differently.* That was a lesson of life for her.

Azeem returned from the camp office demonstrably self-assured and happy. The family composedly sat for a slightly delayed dinner. Fazal was in a cozy mood and focused more on the food, enjoying his favorite semigrilled bird meat with roasted potato. Rukiya, as usual, was engaged in monitoring the food intake of Azeem with the intermittent serving of curry items while mindful of her own eating. Both the mother and son forgot about Azeem's pledge to update them on the query of Fazal about the former's monologue while pausing on the bridge. But Azeem did not forget. He deliberately gave them time so that everyone could take care of their immediate priority of eating, realizing that an empty stomach is never conducive to a better absorption of information.

In explaining the rationale for the soliloquy on the bridge and to make the backdrop clear to both his son and his wife, Azeem deliberately touched upon stuff beyond a straight and short response. He said, "Contrary to general perception, wars are not necessarily won by only a uniformed army. It has always been a mix and match of morale, fighting power, ground intelligence, and coordination. In this game plan and as far as ground intelligence is concerned, civilian intelligence frame plays a crucial role. In the hierarchy of defense establishments, it does not have any identity. They are locally recruited and managed by civilians belonging to local populace but under close monitoring and guidance of contact army hierarchy.

Their role is keeping their ears and eyes open for sensitive information and to pass that on to their local coordinator. They are more relevant in confronting civil disobedience and insurgency.

"Since joining my present position, I have focused on this and strengthened their field presence. The gentleman on the bridge looking opposite direction was one of our civilian contacts. He was advised earlier about our walk plan with the responsibility of monitoring local conditions. He became aware of the presence of some insurgents belonging to a Tripura tribe sympathetic to the aspirations and demands of the Tripura people of greater Assam in India. His advice was not to pursue our walk plan. That is the reason why I resorted to soliloquy. This is the most effective way to have updated information as well as protecting the identity of the informant. Another feature of such a monologue is brevity, just pass on the information."

The following few days were passed in having activities around the camp, except a three -our boat trip in Kaptai Lake from its Bandarban side. The man-made lake, with a catchment area of about 4,300 square miles, ordinarily is an ideal and relaxing tour destination with its crystal clear blue water surrounded by lush green hills. But the prevailing security situation was not conducive for many. That exactly was the distress of Rukiya, which she had to yield to the penchant and enthusiasm of Azeem.

The boat carrying Azeem's family was shadowed by a few army personnel in civvies. That made the trip uncomfortable for Rukiya as she had the hunch of the inherent security concerns. All along that three-hour boat ride, Rukiya was unmindful of the background of this man-made lake as being succinctly narrated by Azeem. She was preoccupied trying to cover Fazal against any unforeseen surprises. Azeem enjoyed the time of having playful exchanges with Fazal while Rukiya was emerged in inaudibly reciting verses from the Holy Quran.

All three happily returned to the base camp and relaxed. Azeem was happy as he could make the boat trip without any incident. His very solid position was that even though the present trip was just a recreational outing for Fazal, it would have indelible print in his mind and thought as he grows up. He, however, was conscious of the anxiety sustained by Rukiya all through and decided to discuss with her later. Fazal was happy for having the trip, and that happiness was conveyed in a simple expression, "It is so beautiful." Rukiya's happiness was due to the safe return of the family.

During the follow-on after dinner parley, Azeem thought through this facet of happiness, and concluded that, unlike his earlier stance, it was the outcome of variable acuities. The variance depends on who the individual is and from what angle he is looking at it. On being explained the related implications later in a congenial setting, it was an eye opener in a sense for Rukiya, and she unhesitatingly decided to preserve that in her future life.

Azeem was more vocal when he raised the issue of the boat trip at the time both were about to retire to bed after a hectic day. He straightaway said, "Whatever was the nature of your tolerance, I am certain that you did not enjoy it. But I expected you to have greater trust in my decisions. I am not only your husband, but more so I am the father of our offspring. I am equally concerned about you both, and only being satisfied about security imperatives decided to have the boat trip. Today is *Buddha Purnima*. Insurgents throughout CHT, like the greater Buddhist world of most Asia, are respectful to the solemnity of the day and naturally refrain from any violent acts. Because of this and the security briefing, I decided to expose both of you to the atypical magnificence of Bangladesh. I always thought that you have trust in my judgment, so I did not discuss the plan of boat ride beforehand."

Rukiya, both embarrassed and emotional, surrendered on the chest of Azeem, and whispered, saying, "I am so sorry. For a moment, I was oblivious of guidance of my mentor in college, Ms. Rashida Anjum, and uncertainty and doubt crept in my mind without exploring other possible reasons. Perhaps it was due to the worry of a mother about the safety of her son."

As a testament of her genuine regret, Rukiya slowly started caressing the partly bare chest of Azeem with her soggy lips. The emotions were built up immediately. Excitement overwhelmed both.

That resulted in intense physical contact and a fulfillment of eventual erotic yearnings.

Assured and fulfilled, both were relaxing in postsex milieu when Rukiya wanted to know the exact import and implication of the term *Buddha Purnima*. She said, "Once relocated in Dhaka, I became familiar with the day more as a school and college holiday. As Father is retired, I did not have any idea whether this was a government holiday too. But one thing is certain. I never realized that it has so much relevance in the life of many and carries so much esteem in the thoughts and prayers of people. I really do not know what exactly *Buddha Purnima* means and implies."

Meandering to the side of Rukiya, Azeem started softly playing with her messy long hair after preceding a physical bout. He started saying, "*Buddha Purnima* means 'Buddha Full Moon,' signifying the date of the three main events of Lord Buddha's life: birth, attainment of enlightenment, and death. It is believed to be the same day coincidentally. It is the most revered date of Buddhism. Like most east and south Asian countries, Buddha Purnima is a public holiday in Bangladesh too."

After taking a break, he continued, saying, "There are a few Buddhist temples in Bandarban too. In local language, they are called *Kyang*. We will visit one of them before you return to Dhaka."

Saying that and perceptibly relaxed after off-loading his thoughts, Azeem went to sleep. Rukiya, composed by both preceding action and discussion, followed him.

The important remaining item for the family to visit was the much talked about Nilgiri hill resort. After careful assessment with his colleagues, Azeem decided not to try that this time. Instead the consensus was to explore nearby spots of interests, some of which have both the attractions of being rural, rugged, and still shining in terms history, culture, and current relevance as well as being rated safe from a security perspective. One of them is known as Prantik Lake, located about fifteen miles from Bandarban *sadar* with a volume coverage of about thirty acres. The other one, a waterfall locally known as *Shoilo Propat*, is nearly two and a half miles from Bandarban sadar on the road to Thanchi.

The nearby small markets along these sites, besides trading in local handicrafts, handloom products, and food, also symbolically provide a firsthand impression about the hardships of life of the indigenous people around.

The family agreed with the proposition to defer the visit to Nilgiri for some other time. Rukiya, referring to the looming schedule to leave for Dhaka, observed, "We have so far enjoyed our time and stay in Bandarban. As, InshaAllah, we will be coming more often in future, there is no need to rush our sightseeing program. We will do whatever we can. Our priority for the next few days is to spend quality time with you as much as possible and to hold your hand as dotingly as we can. So far, and frankly speaking, that is short of our expectation. You go in the morning and come back late afternoon or in the early evening. In between tea, prayers, and dinner, we have little time to interact. That is due more to the need for Fazal to go to sleep, ensuring adherence to his normal schedule."

Azeem was pleased in noting the candid avowal of Rukiya regarding expectation and reality with respect to quality time, feeling, and love during the sojourn. He waggishly looked at Rukiya and drew Fazal close, amenably enquiring whether he misses Abbu's (Daddy's) closeness and love? The content of that query was definitely not clear to Fazal in terms of implications, but he somehow had a bouncy expression alluding to its intent, possibly from the body language of Mother. He replied affirmatively and drew himself close to Father. Soon thereafter, Fazal left the scene to spend some jolly time with his favorite batman-bhai before going to bed.

Azeem was emotionally heightened, thought through multiple insinuations of what Rukiya just said, and decided to be candid and direct in articulating a response. He purposely took a breather, and then started his oration, saying, "Please, take cognizance of the fact that besides being a major in army, I am a husband and a father too. I do love you and feel for you as intensely as you do. But life, in its progression phase and as is common with most human beings, changes due to the challenges being faced. In that scenario, reflections and responses do undergo perceptible changes without being noticed by one, but the extent of feeling and love, by no chance, is impaired at all. That happened in my case. And that happened in your case too. Previously you used to eagerly await for my return from an errand. Now that eagerness is palpably missing, and you possibly take my return as a natural thing. But that does not mean that you love me less. It perhaps is the natural offshoot of other priorities and obligations in life surfacing, and keeps you challenged and engaged."

Rukiya kept quiet. Azeem enjoyed the respite, but soon continued saying what he wanted to make his point completely, "Look, my life so far was a blessed one, more by having you as a life partner. But my professional life, contrary to the focus that I maintain with full sincerity, has been a serrated one. Being of recent occurrences, you are mostly aware of that. Life having thick shadow of doubt about allegiance and commitment was part of our initial conjugal life in Pakistan. My induction to the Bangladesh army is being haunted by variable perceptions about my commitment and devotion contrary to the unconditional allegiance to the oath I have taken. Frictions within varied groups of the army, constant suspicion, and uncertainty related to that haunt me, so I am always to be ahead of that challenge and must perform very well under all circumstances. Moreover, this is my first major command assignment in handling an unfortunate and divergent insurgency with the presence, sometimes the dominance, of extraterritorial armed groups. I spend more time to be ahead of occurrences and to lead and to be demonstratively proactive in the greater interest of the army and that of Bangladesh. I do not have any other objective in life."

Saying those words, Azeem passionately looked at Rukiya, held her hands, and said, "Your love for me and my love for you are unreserved under all settings, even though some elements and expressions are not always voiced. As in the business-related accounting world, a 'reserve for bad debt' is always made, so unspoken feelings and argots of our youth are reserves for our old days when physical attractions will naturally be quiescent." Azeem merrily smiled with a feeling of accomplishment in conveying what he wanted to.

Rukiya was, however, not to be outshined so easily. She moved closer to Azeem and positioned her head partly on his chest. She than started playing with the chest hair of Azeem, a specific activity Rukiya undertakes at the height of her passion at an emotionally susceptible moment. She then initiated her avowal, saying, "I am conscious of all that you said. You would perhaps recall that I did not talk much on our wedding night but just listened to and absorbed what you were saying. With my own intuition proficiency, and as guided by revered Professor Anjum, I discovered you on the first night of our wedding. Emotionally and in practical life preferences and choices, you, based on that night's words and utterances, appeared before me just the type of a person I had always thought to be my life partner. Based on that, I committed myself to you and your life journey on that night without hesitation. I do not regret. But think for a while. I am not a decoration item in your life as most household things are. I am also a person. Like all individuals blessed with specific passions and yearnings, I too need some expressions, some recognition, some tolerance, and some understanding in my journey path. To my assessment, that is the way to build up the reserve you alluded to. For me, conjugal reserve is not a matter of a bookkeeping entry at the end of the year or on the anniversary date. It is an ongoing process in the journey path to be carefully nurtured by both wife and husband. That is all from me."

Spellbound, Azeem repositioned Rukiya in front of his physical self, put both his hands on her shoulders, and drew her close, muttering repeatedly "I am so lucky. I am so blessed."

Emotion laden, Rukiya responded warmly, surrendering herself totally to Azeem's embrace. That was disrupted as Fazal unexpectedly showed up complaining about a scary dream. Azeem took him to bed for a second round of sleep.

Even though Azeem was late in coming back, he was amazed at observing Rukiya still awake, going through a Bangla daily newspaper published in Chittagong. Azeem did not miss a minute to join her in the bed, only to be alerted by Rukiya about the door being open. Azeem hurriedly closed the door and engaged in a tempestuous interplay. Both had a wonderful and gratifying time together.

On the following day, Azeem returned from his office relatively early. The family had tea/drink and snack together in the cozy but small open space adjunct to the accommodation, a setting Rukiya always preferred to have afternoon snacks in if Azeem returned relatively early. It was that sort of afternoon. After finishing his drink, Fazal wanted to have a stroll around. Rukiya drew the attention of the batman as he was about to retrieve the tea paraphernalia, and requested him to accompany Fazal while she would take care of the stuff. Both wife and husband continued to sit in their respective places.

Azeem was adoringly having frequent looks at Rukiya but maintained his taciturnity. Rukiya kept her pause but could also not help looking at Azeem occasionally. Finally, she gave in and asked Azeem straightaway, "Do you want to talk something, romantic or practical, because, to my mind, you are presently having an edgy mindset. If not romantic, is it something we discussed last night? Whatever it may be, please open up. I want to have a relaxed husband by my side. Life is too short to be spent only in agonizing thoughts. Please open up and share. Both of our emotional burdens will be lessened."

Azeem leisurely responded, saying, "Let us be clear. What we discussed last night is final and absolute for our life's journey together. There is no sense in resurrecting those predicaments as that would only enhance our stress level, causing anxiety of multiple magnitudes. So for the time being, it is a closed matter.

I definitely have something in mind that has been bothering me for quite a while. I do not have any perception for peace of mind. It is my thinking that perhaps sharing with you will lessen the agony, and more so, you might have other discernments to give me the needed peace of mind."

Making those statements, Azeem took a break, more to have some initial reactions or comments from Rukiya. But Rukiya kept quiet, not being the type of making quick comments. She continued to look passionately to Azeem and then quipped, saying, "So what next? Man, open up before me fully. That will only enable me to oxidize meaningfully."

Azeem continued his avowal, saying, "Of late, I am having a frenzied thought about our future life. It is having an undiluted impression within me. I am stressed and fretted. The more I look back to our immediate past, the greater are the antagonistic musings. As a happy and contended couple, we landed at Lahore airport. Then came the order to be in charge of the Jutanagar advance camp confronting the aggressive posture of India, a posting generally meant for a more experienced officer. I had to prove my commitment to protect the territorial integrity of the country. That was traumatic for me, though I put up a calm face before you with the rationale of security and national interests as determining factors. You handled that with sobriety and poise. But what bothered me during that challenging period was martyrdom, so likely and so soon, after the wedding, and your future. Against the resultant glory and the very positive outcome of that assignment, and as I was dreaming a bright future, we landed in the repatriation camp of Charsharda as pseudo detainees. Then the Dhaka saga started. At every step, I had to prove my commitment as a professional soldier under variable settings. Suspicion and the resultant disquiet became an internal segment of my thinking and daily existence. That brings me here. I do not have any positive presentiment about my future. That quandary disturbs my mental peace and impacts on my confidence level. That is what I wanted to share with you."

Rukiya, who listened to each word of Azeem warily and riveted emotional expressions emanating from those, took the usual strategy of thinking through a proper response that, even if would not mitigate his anxiety, could at least console him and pave the way to move forward. She stepped out to make a second cup of tea for them both.

Returning with tea, Rukiya, wearing shade of casual stance in physical expressions, gently commenced her simple and short response, having profound life-related implications. She started, saying, "What you are going through and what you said are, in a larger perspective, very normal. Life is not a highway like the Islamabad-Lahore one. Unexpected twists and turns are poignantly customary rudiments of life. Those happen with each individual. With every unexpected turn changing the course of life, one usually feels despondent. But time, which is the ultimate healer, helps one. The journey of life continues with happiness and sadness, as relevant, being integral segments of twisted life. Most others take this as normal. You are feeling anguished as you are blessed with an inquisitorial mind. But please do not allow such thinking to prejudice your life as you see currently. We can only think about our future and put up our best efforts. The outcome is not necessarily in our hands. Pursue your journey as you deem appropriate.

I am conscious of the reality that the army at this moment has a number of groups, each representing a respective vested interest. It's reeling, at this moment, is a predictable consequence of the War of Liberation. But as a product of the armed forces, you are aware that the inherent strength of any army is its organizational structure with the highest commitment to command, control and devotion. Things are bound to be all right soon. No individual or action is to be blamed.

And finally I would like to repeat for the last time that whatever happens to your army career, whatever the nature of any turn in your life, and whatever the challenges are, you are, and will continue to be, my husband for all time to come. My love, my feeling, and my support for our joint life will not be impaired at all.

As you know, I grew up around the bounds of Margalla Hills. Internally I have both the ruggedness and resilience of that hilly topography. I give you my word, once and for all time, to swim and sink together, in either case happily, as you would expect."

Both Rukiya and Fazal returned to Dhaka by train as scheduled earlier, and resumed their normal life, but predictably it was less normal for Fazal. He went out of his way to narrate to his relations and friends, disjointedly though, many features of the swelled and natural topography of Bandarban. But the most enjoyable ones, to his grandparents, were the ways his father was saluted by most of the battalion personnel, whether in uniform or civvies, and Father's taking salutes in a march-past ceremony attended by him in the company of batman *bhai* (brother). At that formative age and imbibed by what he experienced, Fazal developed an earnestness to join the army when he grew up. Rukiya did not fail to communicate the same to Azeem, who was both happy and proud.

In between, both mother and son had two short visits to Bandarban, with Azeem visiting them in Dhaka as occasions permitted. The focus of the subsequent visits was on other parts of CHT, more particularly Rangamati and its periphery, including a visit to the earth-filled Kaptai Dam, with its magnificent spillways. Fazal enjoyed that even though only one gate was open and three others were closed.

In between, four years passed. Azeem felt exultant, having perceived the recognition of accomplishing unquestioned assimilation in the Bangladesh Army. With each passing day, his confidence burgeoned, his dedication reinforced, and his commitment multiplied. He once again started floating in the happy dream of a positive career progression in the Bangladesh Army.

During latest visit to Dhaka for official work, Azeem met his previous boss, the AG, who by this time was promoted and posted as quarter master general (QMG) in charge of administration and supplies. Over a cup of tea, the QMG expressed happiness for his work earlier in the AG's office and now for his leadership in leading forces in the turbulent Bandarban area. Azeem was aware of QMG's favorable disposition toward him, but what he had up in his slips astounded him. The QMG continued, saying, "Your previous work in the AG's office was appreciated by the hierarchy of the senior army establishment. Part of it is being implemented already. An all-catered cantonment with medical and educational facilities is being planned about ten miles away from Bogra civil city headquarters. Besides catering the need of a full-fledged Infantry Division, that campus will also be the locations of the Armoured Corps Center & School (ACC&S) and the induction and training academy for noncommissioned officers (NCOA)."

He then continued, saying, "Your significant success in containing illegal arms and drug trades, better interactions with local communities, and sustained general improvement in the local security situation are all well documented in current official records. But I would like to add one more from my side. Your ability to keep the morale high of the forces under your command and in adverse situations is noted by me. We will work soon to post you out in a still demanding assignment, possibly the implementation of some your recommendations. I will retire soon, but will take care of you before I retire."

Azeem was awed. He started feeling shaky as both the tenor and texture of the current discourse were contrary to defense force's much cherished practices and decorum focusing on brevity in communication. Azeem was in a quandary within himself. The QMG could read the predicament of Azeem and volunteered, "I can read your mind. During the Liberation War, I was posted in Gujranwala of the Punjab province as second in command (2 IC) of the seventeenth Punjab Battalion. My dearest friend, more than a brother and a dedicated officer, Major Haseen, was transferred as 2 IC of the Sixth East Bengal Regiment, stationed at Moinamoti Cantonment of Comilla. The day he and his family were to leave Lahore for Dhaka, we, as a family went to Lahore, had food together in a traditional Lahore eatery at an eating place popularly known as *Goalmandi*, one of the offshoot lane having numerous traditional eateries, and had to our hearts' content Lahorie food items like mutton *karahi, chanay* (gram pulse), *nihari* (stewed beef), and chicken *jalfrezi* (special preparation, mostly popular in the Punjab province). Haseen was thrilled as he was going back to his birth place after many years of postings in West Pakistan. The other reason for his happiness was the opportunity this posting provides for his three daughters, in their mid-to-early teens, to assimilate Bengali values, cultures, and practices as well as enjoying interactions and connecting with a larger segment of the family.

I too was very happy as I concluded my posting in Bangladesh only a year back before taking over my present assignment in Gujranwala. I fully could fathom the rationale of his elation.

As our eldest son finished his last year of high school and two years of intermediate years in Bangladesh, he opted to stay back in Dhaka under the care of my younger brother and study electrical engineering at the now well-known Bangladesh University of Engineering and Technology (BUET). We readily agreed with the proposition.

Our son, Massud, received the news of Major Hassen's posting in Comilla, visited the family in the midst of the political upheaval, and wrote back to me. I was happy to know about the family's comfort and well-being. Then the liberation war broke out. We were physically away, but the mental torture suffered by us were manifold more than any physical ones. Our silence and emotional suffering at that time were our participation. You are exposed to this part of history, so I need not elaborate on that with caution that those silences will haunt us all through as it all depends as to who is looking at it and from what perspective. But the fact remains that we are the sons of this soil.

In the midst of all these, a group of soldiers showed up in Major Hassen's official residence of Moinamoti one fine evening and took him to custody. He, along with some others of Bangladesh origin, were shot point-blank and killed. The family was devastated. Far from the scene, we were shattered. Doubts penetrated in our minds about our real identity, compounded by burden of the family's presence and obligations. We were all in a quandary, but our son could not take that. He was in the right place at the right time and took right decision. He joined *Mukti_Bahini*. In an assignment to create havoc in the principal financial center of the Motijheel commercial area of Dhaka, he succumbed accidentally to the blast of his own bomb in hand while hurriedly retreating from the aggressive advance of patrolling army. We were informed by our brother in due course. The most tragic part of it was that we could not talk about it in public or show our grief. And we were not alone. There were other families too who suffered tragic incidents of divergent natures. That emotional backlash sustained by us, more me and my family, could not either be acknowledged or recognized by anyone else.

In the euphoria of Bangladesh reality, war-related participation and recognition, like other criteria for progression, swiftly underwent a drastic change, focusing on physical, real or pseudo, participation in the Liberation War. That was mostly used in promoting self-interest or group objectives. Pronounced efforts were noticeable to demean us once we landed in Bangladesh. I, among some lucky others, managed to swim, and for me, I surfed on the dead body of our dearest one.

The first time I read your service record as the AG, I developed empathy for you without knowing you. When I saw you first, it appeared to me that my son Massud was approaching me. You might recall my flopping with the tea cup, least expected from an army general.

I will try to place you nicely in recognition of your services and leadership in Bandarban. And the rest is your destiny. But your further headway may not be that easy, as I notice that you have some real good friends who are out to stall your progression. That was all I wanted to say, and keep it personal. Now, go to your work."

Since the CHT posting was an insurgency areas related assignment, the personnel policy was designed, as in the case of most countries having similar problems, for a short-term assignment period. However, because of field necessities and his success, the earlier envisaged two-year assignment rolled to be one of four years. With an expectation of immediate transfer, Azeem happily returned to Bandarban, briefly and privately appraising Rukiya of the points discussed with the QMG, including a likely transfer soon.

TWISTS

With befitting farewells in Bandarban and Rangamati, and a friendly welcome at the newly established Bogra Cantonment, to be the headquarters of the Ninth Infantry Division, Azeem, accompanied by family, joined his new assignment and moved in to his new abode. His specific assignment was being in charge of implementing the Bogra Cantonment Development Project (BCDP) as the 2 IC under the division commander.

The envisaged public school for the cantonment and its surrounding areas, modeled in line with a cadet college, was in an embryonic stage, so following the footsteps of other colleagues, Rukiya and Azeem, in consultation with the principal designate, decided for the available best option of enrolling Fazal in the district (*Zella*) government school, traditionally a government run and supervised educational entity of eminence in each civil district with a better faculty and exact discipline practices. Logically, their own accommodation was a modest one in the upscale location of the town. Rukiya expressed happiness as, after a gap of about four years, the family is living together. Nothing else mattered to her.

The blueprint of the planned cantonment setting impressed Azeem, but inner happiness burgeoned as he was reading the introduction section of the project document. In enunciating the vision, objectives, and focus of the proposed cantonment, most of the articulations repeated his thinking and words in his final report to the AG. In essence, the Bogra Cantonment, is to be designed as the more integrated and least costly plan, with efficiency in land management, future extension, and coordination needs, minimizing time for the movement and transport and other logistics.

Azeem was pleasantly surprised as it was being planned both as a standard cantonment-cum-training and induction center for NCOs besides being the location of the critical armored corps center and school. Azeem envisaged it as the future comprehensive and viable center of excellence for the Bangladesh Army, and he felt proud of being associated in its planning, though indirectly, and in having the opportunity for implementing it unswervingly. Azeem committed himself to his assignment and started working resolutely with full understanding and support from Rukiya.

The intrinsic backup of such commitment and dedication of Azeem were premised on his last major sharing of views about life in the serene setting of Bandarban. He agreed with what Rukiya stipulated about the inevitable quirks in life. That can impact one's life both positively or negatively. Taking each bend of life as a challenge and seeing that challenge as an opportunity is the sine qua non of life and its progression. This sort of assertion by Rukiya has had profound impact on Azeem's life philosophy and its journey.

Time passed. The Bogra cantonment started to take shape consistent with the architectural blueprint and design, increasingly giving in to bricks, cement, and mortar, to the happiness of all concerned. Major Azeem received kudos from varied stakeholders.

It was time for the top hierarchy's decision for the promotion of identified majors to the rank and position of lieutenant colonels. The initial selection process endorsed Azeem for promotion, but that was not approved by the selection board. Azeem was distraught but continued to work with the same commitment and zeal. Likewise, and contrary to what she earlier philosophized a number of times, Rukiya was flustered too but kept quiet.

After some time, a new opportunity was on the threshold. In view of the increase in demand, the United Nations decided to take peacekeepers from Bangladesh. Major Azeem saw this as an opportunity for him, with additional income, which by local standard was significant, being the principal motivating factor. Azeem's game plan was returning to Bangladesh with savings and seeking voluntary retirement from the armed forces, but that also was denied to him.

Azeem, frantic and frustrated with two successive denials, decided to go on voluntary retirement and met the general officer commanding (GOC) of the Ninth Division located at Bogra Cantonment, his immediate supervisor. He had good rapport with the GOC, slightly senior in age but much higher in rank, who gave him a patient hearing. During the entire conversation, Azeem premised his irritation on emotional expressions, maintaining, however, the coolness and decency expected from an officer in uniform. The GOC was equally compassionate, maintaining a sort of supportive mien, nevertheless highlighting the protocols of decision-making. His apparent aim was to console the frustrated junior colleague as well as upholding the inviolability of the decision-making process at the higher level.

What the GOC articulated later conveyed more the personal aspect of that discourse. He said, "Major, please understand that as both a division commander and your supervisor, my opinion matters and my recommendation has significance. Same applies to the recommendations of the AG and the QMG you previously worked with, so I was certain of your getting promoted. It went through the process smoothly until it reached the level of the top political authority. At that level, your political affiliation issue was raised due to sustained anonymous representations concerning your fighting the Indian army valiantly near the Wagah border post in 1971 and your getting an out-of-turn promotion. In submitting those representations, your friends in uniform were relentless. That was the genesis of the negative decision concerning your promotion.

That decision now haunts you, but it is not all. It will continue to impact on your career so long you are in the army. This is the reality of life."

It reminded Azeem of his last discussion with the QMG. The greater portion of what the GOC just said mostly echoed what the QMG expressed in their departing meeting months back. Azeem concluded that two different supervisors mostly said identical words casting a shadow of doubt on his future career in the army. The current decision echoed that possibility. Azeem's immediate thought soon fixated on the uncertain probability of early retirement.

While returning to his office, he faced his office quarter master sergeant (a noncommissioned staff) who instantly and smartly saluted him. It soon flashed in his mind that being a stalled major, he would have to salute tomorrow many juniors of today in his remaining life in the army. He was flummoxed. His initial thought about early retirement was reinforced. He soon left for home, expecting some time out with Rukiya before Fazal returned from school after his usual passion of playing football game. The school's sprawling game field had drawn instant fondness when Fazal saw it first.

Azeem entered the home laden with the frustration and worries he suffered since knowing about latest decision negating his aspiration to work as a UN peacekeeper. This and his unusual return timing struck the thought process of Rukiya, who right from the time of the denial of his professional progression, was preparing herself to face the eventuality while keeping a normal facade in day-to-day conversation and dealings.

Azeem, fortified by a sense of self--assurance, tried to be extra nice and forthcoming in interactions with Rukiya. She kept quiet, maintained her cool, and served Azeem tea without any snack as they waited for Fazal to return from school. The practice in their home was to have evening snacks together as a family as dinner had variable scenarios, more commonly invitations.

Knowing Rukiya well and observing her present taciturn approach, Azeem took shelter in his poise. He quietly concentrated in sipping his tea.

Rukiya voluntarily took her seat on the opposite side chair of their mini dining table, looked straight at Azeem, and queried, "What happened? Is there another bad news for us?"

Azeem momentarily stumbled, and then managed to say, "I have decided to opt for early retirement. I just can't bear the burden of saluting my juniors as they make progression in their professional life."

He then continued, saying, "The world is much bigger. There are many opportunities outside army life. You said in the past that if

Allahpak closes one door, He opens a hundred more. So possibly this is my time. This is my opportunity. You are aware that I have good relationships with contractors, suppliers, and enlisted manufacturers. Most of them were eager to do any favor for me. So with their help and cooperation, I plan to do business."

Rukiya steadily listened to what Azeem articulated and then bluntly asked, "What happened to your plan for peacekeeping work? Has there been any development on that front? Is that negative too?" Those unpretentious queries hit the rock bottom of the discourse which Azeem wanted to bypass for the present. He just nodded his head and said, "We will discuss that at night. I can see Fazal is entering our premise."

That was a brief discussion at night, but it signified the beginning of an unknowing monumental change pertaining to the family decision-taking matters. It was Rukiya who was slowly taking over the driver's seat, with the exhausted and frustrated Azeem taking a backseat.

The envisioned voluntary retirement question was decided promptly that night, but what astounded Azeem was the strong sense of alertness, pragmatism in approach, and understanding as well as uncanny ability to organize thoughts and foresee the future with confidence and clarity as demonstrated by Rukiya all through their conjugal life, and more particularly that night. There was no two different opinions, or for that matter any "ifs" and "buts." Rukiya promptly and firmly interlined by saying, "I married you to live honorably as a couple. Your position, status, and power are apposite but do not matter to me so long you are happy in the given situation and we have a decent life within our competence and capital. I would not be happy to be your spouse while you are needed to keep your head low, so this is final for us. You will opt for voluntary retirement."

Rukiya, more signifying conclusive nature of that discourse, repositioned her pillow and turned herself opposite to the body position of Azeem and lazed motionless. Hesitant as well as downcast, Azeem softly and slowly put his hand on her body and started touching the upper portion of her back just below her neck, knowing that the particular section of her body was one of the most sensory part of

Rukiya's physique. The whole effort was to smoothen Rukiya from the possible suddenness and shock of the pertinent discourse and resultant decision and help her in managing emotions.

Some sort of calmness beguiled Rukiya. She started revisiting each of her steps right from the time of their wedding. Though she harbored a hardened stance outwardly, she felt miserable for what Azeem was going through. Army life was the focus of his world. It was his dream. It was the sine qua non of his existence. The emergence of Bangladesh after a bloody breakup was the first shock. That, however, was overcome by relatively smooth induction in the emerging new army of Bangladesh. In all subsequent assignments, he worked diligently, earning official recognition and social kudos from his superiors. That became his problem and burden.

The Bangladesh Army had treated him, like most others from various groups and of previous identity, with fairness within the frame of law. As an organization, the army lived up to its motto and vision. It was some colleagues and so-called friends who were jealous of Azeem's emerging profile as an officer with a combination of professional competence and intellectual aptitude. It was that set of colleagues who opted to highlight his heroic Wagah encounter against India in 1971 as symbolically portraying him as being one with an anti-Bangladesh mindset. Those sustained efforts and actions easily created a sense of doubt in the minds of higher level political leaderships, and Azeem was just a victim of that.

With that sort of realization, Rukiya softened her stance and gradually started responding to Azeem's caress with moaning. To his bafflement, Rukiya turned toward Azeem, held him to her warm embrace, placed herself on the top of Azeem's body, and started playing with his nipples, occasionally pecking those with her wet lips.

That gameplay was just the opposite of the emotional stress both suffered the entire evening and even a while back. Azeem was bemused. In that bewilderment, he unexpectedly recalled a piece of comment a guest in his wedding gathering sarcastically made.

With side cuts and sideburns having the stint of gray, with the top full of black hair, and smartly dressed with a matching tie and hankie, he followed the stream of guests to congratulate Azeem.

Unlike most others, he did not just congratulate him but also made a brief joking observation, saying, "Young man, you do not know where you landed. You just bonded with a creation of Allahpak whom perhaps the Creator Himself does not understand. Women are emotionally sensitive and unpredictable and act and react with impulses which ordinarily are beyond the compression of ordinary mind. You will enjoy it."

Even in the present disparaging surrounding and current state of his mind and reality, Azeem recalled those joking thoughts and words of attentiveness after many years and laughed at himself. Notwithstanding what had been said jokingly by that guest, Azeem appreciated the antiphon against the backdrop of all the negative things in life. He felt relaxed for the time being and positioned himself to fall asleep.

Right at that moment, Rukiya, whom Azeem thought to be falling asleep, firmly said, "You are not going to office tomorrow. We will have a new beginning starting tomorrow and celebrate that with a sumptuous lunch. We would also endeavor to communicate with Fazal carefully and systematically so that sudden anguish does not overwhelm him."

Azeem went deep in comprehending the inner undertone inherent in Rukiya's statement. He soon realized a prominent change in his life concerning decision-making. Discussions on possible decisions and actions in matters of family relevance had been mostly initiated and spelled out by him so far. He, nevertheless, always allowed Rukiya's to spell out comments. While she generally agreed, Rukiya, most such times, exhibited sagacity and acumen in articulating more credible aspects and options. That was liked and appreciated by Azeem unwaveringly.

But the pronouncement she made just before falling asleep was something exceptional and encroached on his professional and decision-making competence. Instead of responding immediately, he kept quiet. Two successive negations with respect to promotion and deputation, premised on the observations of the GOC, had shattered his confidence level. Had that not been the case, probably he would himself decide to stay back home for the needed time to manage the related frustration. Azeem looked at the inert physique of Rukiya deep in sleep and thanked her silently. That signified his voluntary withdrawal from his decision-making prowess. The process of a new beginning in the family domain was initiated much before its celebration during the sumptuous lunch as envisaged by Rukiya.

The following morning was a quiet one. Rukiya had the physical ambience of calmness, and concentrated in making the postulated sumptuous lunch as well attending to other household chores as if nothing of concern was happening in their life. Azeem was deeply absorbed in envisioning his life to be as an ex-army major.

That managed quietness was too tenacious for Azeem. During lunch, he opened up, saying, "I am thinking of doing business in my post-army life. You know that I have many admirers among suppliers, contractors, engineers, and so on. They are always eager to help me in any way, and expressed that number of times. My current savings and separation money will be enough for a start-up. As demand increases, I may approach my admirers for accommodation. So I see that to be a very feasible proposition."

After finishing that self-assured statement, he looked at Rukiya with confidence and conceit. But the long response from Rukiya flabbergasted him.

With innate affirmative response, Rukiya started saying, "If doing business is an option, I won't oppose that proposition. But please bear in mind that the business world, where the prime motive is to maximize returns, is, by connotation, a very cruel place to be in. There is no friend. The only loyalty is to money and to the power base that facilitates the flow of that money.

As you would recall, my father was a senior support staff for a very long time in the Office of Chief Controller of Imports and Exports (CCIE). His seniority, his reputation, and long stay in the same office made him privy to many aspects of policy initiatives and changes. He was well known to many businessmen and industrialists.

Father, being a person believing firmly in the well-known dictum of 'unguarded spoken words are one's worst enemies,' has had been a relatively reserved individual. Even in the case of agreement on contentious issues, his response would be a silent nodding of head. Our mother always complained about that, saying, 'Allah sent him to this world with the instruction to talk less, and with the family minimal. We seldom had conversations even on family matters.' In the case of such provocative comments from his spouse, he would respond by nodding head with a tender smile. He never talked with us about his office matters or, for that matter, the reputation he enjoyed in the work setting. But his enthusiasm to talk with us never lacked passion when matters were concerning with study, schools, book stalls, or social issues.

We came to know about his office-related reputation when important business people or their senior staff would drop in to our modest abode of G-6/4 of Ramna in Islamabad on pretentious excuses. Most of those were like, 'Was just passing and wanted to know your well-being as you did not go to office today,' or 'Our boss was so appreciative of you for clearing our license-related documents without dithering at a critical time and instructed me to convey his sincere thanks,' or 'I am always very appreciative of your efficiency and rectitude. I understand you have a relatively young family, with retirement due in about two to three years. Please treat me as a brother and let me know whether I can do anything to help you in terms of extension and/or postretirement settlement.' Those were the norms.

My young sister and myself had the habit of peeping by slightly manipulating the door curtain and often merrily enjoyed the visitors eulogizing our cloistered father to his embarrassment. As we understood later, that embarrassment was for two reasons: first, the simplicity inherent in the décor of our seating area with the odd presence of a bed, one reading table, and three wooden chairs of mundane design and finishing. And the second one was the inability to entertain these VIP guests. Our standard service items for these occasional guests were *lebu* (lemon) sherbet during summer and milk and sugar-based dark tea and *Nabisco* wrapped biscuit during winter. As a family of six (parents, two elder sons, and two daughters), we seldom could have cookies and other enticing products of the famous United Bakery of Sector F-6/2 of Islamabad.

But there was no innate regret for that from us. Most of those guests would seldom take more than one or two seeps of sherbet or tea. We merrily took care of the residue without bothering about societal and hygiene related advice and impositions.

Father was not a smoker in traditional sense, but used to enjoy *hookah* smoking, more so after dinner. Also known as '*narghile*' or '*shisha*' smoking, the event provided us the opportunity to have an intimate and frank discourse with him. In one of such discussions, he opened up, saying, 'I know them. I know their motives. All the niceties towards me were designed to get advance information, more about importable items to be in the new list or deletion from the existing list. This is very important for importers and traders. They were just looking for hints to plan their business priorities and actions. Ours is a closed economy. Most of the business opportunities hinge on government decisions. Hence, that advance information is so important.'

What he observed as a follow-up was more relevant and far reaching. Reading in class seven, I took note of that and could mostly assimilate the inherent inference only as I grew up. He continued, saying, 'In business, four Cs are critical. These are: capital, commitment, contact, and clue (signifying advance information). Though the first three are usually personal attributes, the last one is critical for succeeding and remaining ahead. It is more relevant as our economic system is relatively closed.'

One my brother's query was what he means by 'closed economy' and how he came to know the term. Father, without dithering, explained by saying, 'Our economic policies are not market-based. It is decided by the government. That is what is meant by *closed economy*. With respect to your second query, please recall that my basic education was a bachelor of commerce degree, with sufficient insight of basic economics-related terms and issues. Right from my service career in CCIE, I had regular interactions with trade and business people and their senior staff. When more than one such people were in my table, they, possibly sheer due to coincidence or by design, would start taking about controls, regulations, market-based system, and so on. I gradually picked up some ideas and terms too, and appropriately used them in official noting or conversation. Remember one thing: there is no end to learning, and there is no specific source to learn. Diversity in learning sources is perhaps the best germinal the society has for its sustained progression.'"

Rukiya continued, saying, "Yes, that was the most relaxed conversation with our otherwise reticent father that I could recall. Perhaps, his impending retirement thought was having an impact on his behavior pattern. I could not conclude precisely as both my age and exposure were not attuned to understand or analyze such factors of life. Besides, I grew up in the sheltered social vibe of Islamabad, which, at our level and related social backdrop, did not encourage thinking by girls beyond religion, family, and marriage. My discerning faculty got its needed boost when I came into contact with a person like Professor Anjum. I developed a habit of visiting important experiences in bed before falling asleep and thought about their ramifications in my evolving life. That is how I remember every bit of parental intervention, advice, and observations.

As I was told, there were very few East Pakistanis of Bangladesh origin in Islamabad when our family moved from Karachi. But when it was the turn of the family to leave that beautiful place for Dhaka, about one-third of the Islamabad population was from Bangladesh (East Pakistan). But our, especially the youngsters, dealings and involvement were mostly focused on close relations, parental friends, and neighbors. Our life and world thus evolved around our official residence, more specifically House#10E, Street #58, Sector G-6/4. Unlike many Bangladeshi residents of Islamabad, our relations were very few. That comprised of Mother's young cousin with her husband in the foreign office, and Father's young nephew working in the Central Board of Revenue. With fewer places for socializing and their limited liquidity, our common places of visit as a family, and sometimes at the behest of those two relations, was Rawal Dam and a market known Aabpara, a combination Bangladeshi-style *bazaar* (biweekly market) with a row of pseudo cement-concrete stores open all through week. One of such stores was very popular for its *lembu* sherbet and freshly roasted potato with chili powder.

As per the rules for public servants for superannuation, Father went on leave preparatory to retirement. In our growing-up process, we never saw him at home during the weekdays, so that was not only a problem but unknowingly caused uneasiness in our home. We liked his presence but did not feel comfortable for his observing everything we do. His partaking of huqqa increased noticeably, causing frequent irritating exchanges with Mother.

Possibly Father soon realized that his presence at home twenty-four seven and unwelcome interferences with repellent homely chores were causing strains in the family. The family was also under emotional pressure for the scheduled return to East Pakistan after about twenty-eight years of living in dry and sandy Karachi as well as the hot and very cool weather of Islamabad.

During a lunchtime side talk, Father unexpectedly proposed the idea of the family's going to the AbPara market surroundings next Friday afternoon for a stroll, capping that with *lembu* sherbet and freshly fried potatoes in the famous outlet. We enthusiastically responded while Mother objected. She saw it as a waste of money which the family needs most because of the impending resettlement in Dhaka. But she was overtaken by the overwhelming enthusiasm of all others.

As we were cosseted around two small tables placed together and readily enjoyed our bites of spiced fries and sips of sherbet, *Janab* (akin to *mister*) Sher Mohammed Haroon, the senior employee of a renowned import trader, was traversing to the opposite direction of father's seat. If that was the case a few days back, Mr. Haroon would have jumped at seeing Father and would have created a scene for making the payment while kissing and hugging all of us, being a regular visitor to our home.

Father was apparently awaiting for him to say '*salam*' (a Muslim greeting) as per past practice, and a brief social chat. But that appeared not to be. As he was about to cross Father, who was still under impression that Mr. Harron perhaps did not see him, drew his attention by saying, 'Salam, Mr. Haroon.' Embarrassed, Mr. Haroon turned back loudly, saying sorry for not noticing him and the family, shook hands, and quickly took paces promising an early visit.

All of us were confused, with accompanying sadness. Father kept quiet, perhaps lost in thought about the reality of life. He released a long breath and said a most exceptional riposte that could be mastered by him at the time. He, with an elfin smile adoring his frustrated face, took a sip of sherbet from his glass and said, 'I was aware of this reality but never expected so quick a reversal of face in public dealing. Most business people—for that matter, rich people, being wedded to money—are generally deferential to power and position with ever pressing priority to make more money. They equally orient their senior staff in dealing with the concerned government functionaries accordingly. The more one is up in the ladder of the business progression, the less is his/her sensitivity about basic social decorum and fairness. What Mr. Haroon just exhibited is a rude manifestation of that practice. All of you are logically disturbed by Mr. Haroon's action. But it would perhaps be appropriate to evaluate the whole experience from a different perspective. He is not alone in this game. None of my previous admirers ever contacted me or visited us since my retirement. All such people are worshipers of money and power. So instead of being sad, learn this lesson as you would too encounter this in your future life.'

Even though our that joyous evening had the sting of foiling, Father was in a relatively blissful disposition. Mother later raised this issue in a lamenting tone, emphasizing the goodness in leaving Islamabad sooner than scheduled to escape a repeat of such incidents. Father, after having taken two successive gulping through his *huqqa* pipe, observed, saying, 'I see a lot of positivity in today's experience. Even if I would have lectured for hours, I am not sure whether I could convey to my children the essence of this experience having life-related relevance. This particular human behavior is not Islamabad or Pakistan specific. It is universal. Clarity about it helps an individual to shape up social relationships without suffering emotional duress.'

All these I have detailed for you to take cognizance of my opinions and views in proper context. All those were based on what I have experienced so far and what I learned. The final decision is yours, of course, and I will be with you all through in that journey."

She apparently concluded her long oration but then continued, saying, "If you decide to do business with the fond hope of help and support from your acquaintances, then do it. But prepare yourself not to be downcast by their response and behavior. Second, think about your ability to transform yourself from a disciplined, dedicated, and decision-oriented organization's personnel to be a cunning and multifaceted businessman always competing with equally clever competitors. To my mind, this transformation is fundamental. Third, our capital base is modest. That perhaps is sufficient to carry us as a family through for some years, but we can't navigate life all through with that. The rough and uncertain waters of business are intrinsically very much a part of that scenario."

Having said those and after having a doting look at Azeem to roughly get an impression of his immediate reaction as manifested by physical expressions, Rukiya got up, lifted dry plates and other service bowls, and put them in the washbasin. She moved quickly to prepare tea, and returned to the dining table, eager to have the response of Azeem. But there was no response from him. He was deep in thought, more visibly perturbed as well as unsure.

After serving the tea, Rukiya initiated the follow-on discussion by politely inquiring whether he had any observations about her life experiences, what she detailed, or on any other matters related to those. Azeem maintained his quietness as if something innate was bothering him. Rukiya became concerned as she was never exposed to such taciturnity. Under duress, and to initiate a response, she asked Azeem directly, "Is something portentous bothering you?"

The response of Azeem took her aback. Since their wedding she knew him as a determined, single-track individual. He would normally take time in taking decisions. But once taken, it was final for him unless material equations invalidated that.

His short response was, "Perhaps my impromptu decision for early retirement was more emotion laden and less sensible. At that spark of the moment, I was derailed from reality and reacted to the whole episode from the perspective of my pride and prestige, to the exclusion of my family obligations and future challenges. For a short while following the obvious thwarting, I was oblivious of its practicality and inherent challenges as it relates to you and our son. Will my dream to get him in the commission rank of the army remain unfulfilled?"

Rukiya was sad. She repositioned the teacup, more to induce its sipping by Azeem as a relaxing approach. To hide her real feelings, she looked outside, got up, and went to washbasin to clean up used crockeries of lunch. That was her way to buy time to think through any pressing issue.

She returned to her seat and started talking without any eye contact with Azeem. This time her voice tone was quite firm. She said, "Perhaps your decision and my concurrence with respect to opting for early retirement was a hasty one, but the rationale for that are still valid. With both position and prestige at stake for no wrongdoing on your part, I am very much inclined to go through challenges and sufferings in our future life rather than live with the injustices handed down. So from my side, the very firm position is, there is no going back. Reversal of that decision is not an option in our life anymore."

Fazal was slowly and carefully initiated to the family's impending relocation to Dhaka and the decision of Dad's early retirement from the army. He was about twelve years of age when he received the message and was too young to understand its insinuations. Aware of the tension his parents were feeling and the gloominess suffusing their recent life, Fazal kept quiet, and then responded by articulating one wish and one despair. The first was his desire to finish his schooling in Bogra until the present school year ends. And the second one was how much he would miss the *Zilla* school's sprawling play field. But the follow-on additional comments of Fazal made his parents both happy and enchanted. Fazal observed that the lush green play field surrounded by very big and mature trees all around imbibed within him a compelling desire to love and excel in sports, especially football.

Rukiya moved out of her sitting place, embraced Fazal very warmly, and blessed him profusely by kissing his brow. Unexpectedly, Fazal felt shyness and left the place.

Azeem quipped by saying, "Our son is growing up. He started appreciating nature and the environment. Also, he is showing signs of sensuality. We need to be careful in handling him in the future."

That evening was an exceptional one, and the positive vibe of the afternoon was even noticeable in the dinner table. Azeem, referring to Fazal's afternoon observations, said, "Yes, I am conscious of your school year. I thus timed my voluntary retirement in July next, sufficient time to move to Dhaka on time to complete preparatory arrangements for your admission in your old school. I have already talked to the principal of your previous Dhaka school in this regard. With respect to your missing the sprawling play field of Bogra *Zilla* School, the principal advised me that the school management, in coordination with the Office of Military Land and Cantonment Services (a civilian outfit within the army command managing, among others, land development including housing and other civil facilities like markets, entertainment and sports facilities) got more adjacent land, and the school now has a very nice and big play field."

That made Fazal very happy. His parents, likewise, were relaxed, observing the flexibility being shown by Fazal in handling this unexpected reality.

That happiness had its own twists, depending on approximation of the concerned family member. Hiding from his parents and in a lonely setting, Fazal was always pensive in thinking about the reasons for his dad's decision to go for early retirement. He was unable to make sense of it. Dad enjoyed irrefutable reputation as a hardworking officer all along. It was only weeks before that Dad envisaged a longer stay in the supportive milieu of Bogra, more to help him growing up and cementing their bond as a family.

Fazal was at his wit's end to find a feasible rationale but was unsuccessful. He then concluded that there must be something fundamentally wrong to upset his parents, and there was no sense in trying to unearth that. The process could as well be a traumatic one. So he decided to do what he could do easily for the happiness of the family. Fazal decided to make conscious efforts to be close to Dad to understand him better and to have glimpse of his hushed desires. That gradually had its favorable impact on their family life.

Azeem started enjoying the newfound closeness with the son while Mother was delighted, noting son's closeness and warmth.

Both started to eagerly await for Fazal's daily return from school with stories of how the school day ended.

Rukiya was busy preparing snacks for the family's afternoon snack and tea service. Azeem, having persistent worries about his future and the way forward for the family, stood before the kitchen shank and was looking outside casually. He insouciantly focused his attention to a boy in khaki uniform of Fazal's frame at a distance and instantly drew the attention of Rukiya.

She had a concentrated look and amusingly commented, "What happened to you? You even do not recognize your son!"

Azeem responded, "What is my fault? First, it is not yet time for Fazal's usual return from school. Second, he never came back from school in a khaki outfit, their school dress being gray pant and white shirt."

As he was about to continue additional supporting comments, the entry door opened, and Fazal entered the house, greeting his father with a smart salute, saying, "Scout of the year is reporting to you, sir."

Baffled, Azeem remained motionless for a while, took a slothful step forward, recovered from the surprise, and bent significantly to bless Fazal with a warm hug, conveying his happiness and pride. Tears started rolling down his cheeks. Azeem maintained that physical posture for quite a while as Rukiya, standing nearby, turned her face to wipe her tears of joy composedly.

Fazal was confused when drops of his dad's tears started dripping on his neck. At that age, he was exposed to and aware of tears more as an outburst of sorrow. Slowly disengaging himself from the clutch of his father, he frankly inquired the reasons for the sniffling by both.

Azeem once again hugged Fazal and warmly said, "These are not the tears of sorrow. They are tears of joy for us. You really made us happy today. We fervently look forward to the day when you would receive your commission in the army, and made us proud and fulfilled with a similar private salute."

That was the time for young Fazal to be overwhelmed with emotions. As a spontaneous response to the soaked eyes of his parents,

Fazal embraced Dad and said, "I promise that I will do everything to pursue and fulfill your dreams, including crossing the successive steps of a career as a commissioned officer. You could not be a lieutenant colonel, but I promise that you would have pleasure and joy of being the father of one."

After saying those unexpected words to the joy of his parents, Fazal moved to Mother and hugged her warmly too, saying, "You too would have the same bliss and conceit."

That was a very ecstatic and gratifying evening for the family. Mother hurriedly prepared a nice dinner to celebrate the achievement of the son. The dinner was served with all the love and care of Mother at the appointed time. Both Father and Son occupied two opposite chairs, with Mother's plate positioned by the side of Fazal and other chair by the side of Father being empty. Things have changed tonight, and the sitting arrangement is exceptional. Fazal always used to sit on the chair by the side of Father. For unknown reasons, he took his seat opposed to Father as if to convey a silent but game-changing message that he was not only the scout of the year but also a growing-up son of the family. Observing a satiated mother's facial expressions, Azeem repeated his favorite philosophical dictum, "This evening's experiences are so absorbing that I have the mindset to accept, leaving all inhibitions, the golden saying that 'even the darkest cloud has its silver lining.'"

Everyone had a participatory laugh, but the follow-on observation of Fazal stumped his parents. Fazal said, "There is no doubt that our family is under a very thick dark cloud. We will have to work hard and determinedly to see the silver lining. So no more dithering. No more lamenting. Let us move forward as a family. Let us do our respective parts as diligently as we can."

Saying those words with all veneration, Fazal stood up, saying, "I have a lot schoolwork to do, so I need to go." He then hugged Mother and took leave from Father by saying "salam," a practice he'd developed since moving to Bogra.

As Fazal left, his parents were in a state of trance. Both, in their own way and without any exchange of words, were incredibly preoccupied with the same thought premised on what Fazal stipulated for moving forward. Finally, while serving steaming coffee, Rukiya opened up, saying, "We always tried to keep agonizing family matters away from Fazal. It now appears that he has not only been aware of all those but also thought through them. I am more than certain that he has outgrown himself."

Azeem took a pause and said perceptively, "What a pleasant surprise for us. He has not only outgrown but grown up wisely. That makes me happy and assured. Anything unforeseen happening to me, you will be in the safe care and love of our conscientious son."

Rukiya was distressed and anguished by the last few words uttered by Azeem. She retorted by saying, "You started talking like an elderly person. It is just not the time to talk such negative things. It is such a beautiful and fulfilling day for us. Our son has told us clearly to shun dithering, so we should think positively and act prudently. We should never be oblivious of the golden saying to 'hit the iron when it is hot.' We should act accordingly."

She continued, saying, "Thinking and planning alone would not take us to destination of our postretirement life. We need to prepare in advance and adequately. I was thinking about it for a while. Though my parents would love to accommodate us in this hour of need, you, and for that matter any individual of your attributes, would not perhaps relish it for an indefinite duration in the face of challenges, failings, obstacles, and success in establishing ourselves in a new life and a new setting. So I suggest, based on immediate past rumination, that you take about ten days' leave, go to Dhaka, and discuss with Father and other relations the efficient way forward for immediately building our modest home on the plot of land allocated by the Cantonment Board some years back. We need not go for completing the house. The foundation of the complete house just has to be laid now, while the present construction can be limited to two bedrooms, one washroom, and the kitchen. That will give us the needed space for the time being, and we can finish it gradually. That will be a solid use of a part of our current liquidity, ensuring a reverential identity. This is more applicable for Fazal, to minimize any depressed feeling on his part. He will be with us perhaps another two or three years before leaving for higher level challenges, so we owe it to him too. What I told you is not an off-the-cuff opinion. I thought through it during the last few days and had it in mind. I was awaiting for the moment. It is now up to you."

Azeem did not have an immediate response but continued looking at Rukiya absorbedly. He was engulfed by the thought of the unexpected turn his life was taking. In his mind, he was asking himself whether with the decision of voluntary retirement, he was also under an unforeseen abdication process of life-related decisions!

He had no qualms with what Rukiya just stipulated with logic, backed by additional justifications of family prestige and the related happiness of the only son at a critical transition phase of his life. But he was wondering why he did not say those things earlier as he had had similar thoughts too. Was it because as life was taking its unexpected turn, he was unknowingly relegating his living domain to his relatively alert and smart life partner? He was happy to note that and relaxed.

The life of Azeem and his family thereafter moved as per the suggested line. After visiting Dhaka, Azeem happily briefed his family about the progress made in consultation and coordination with the larger segments of their family about the construction of their abode, including their temporary stay for a few months in their in-laws' house. He also made it a point to visit Fazal's previous school to ensure his son's smooth readmission upon relocation.

This period between action pertaining to early retirement and the preparations to leave for Dhaka unobtrusively brought out a quality of Azeem's innate personality trait which made Rukiya happy and proud in the midst of uncertainty and despair. Against the expected human impulse of getting slowly disconnected from routine current responsibility on the eve of retirement, Azeem doubled down his commitment and energy to the assigned work of his position.

In a dinner table chitchat, Rukiya thoughtfully enquired as to why Azeem still was so committed to his work since the family would get delinked from the army life soon and would leave for Dhaka immediately. Azeem, after swapping an adoring glance with son and wife, replied with ease and confidence, saying, "So long as I am on the payroll of the army, the assigned project is my baby. I should be diligent to hand it over to my successor in good order. This is how I grew up. This is how I was trained. This is the work ethics I would like to transmit to our son. Those are the reasons."

TRIGGER

*T*he family moved back as per their plan. Rukiya and Fazal were ostensibly happy from their own limited perspectives, but what surprised Rukiya was the evident and expressed recent happiness of Azeem, which was unexpected. She was always apprehensive of the emotional backlash that Azeem might suffer once in Dhaka because of being totally delinked from his passion, the army. The initial few weeks had a mix of excitement related to the house construction and that of anxiety caused by lack of any progression in identifying a steady and productive engagement in life. Though the status of a new professional engagement remained unchanged, for some odd reasons, Azeem demonstrated a relaxed and happy behavioral pattern during the last few days, especially in the company of Rabia, the loving younger sister of Rukiya. Even then, Rukiya could not stop worrying, and started thinking of dreary alternatives.

Rukiya could not hold it to herself for long. In a light family exchange after brunch of that day, she prudently referred to it in a subtle way, saying, "I am so happy to see you so relaxed and enjoying every bit of your retirement time."

Azeem looked at her in an impish manner and said, "I can respond to your query both casually and seriously, and that all depends on your preference."

Rukiya was not to be outsmarted. She responded, saying, "I want to know what you mean by both 'casually' and 'seriously.' I will then make my choice."

Azeem said that he needed some time to think through both, and that would be hastened if he could have a second cup of steaming coffee. Rukiya stood up and with a mischievous quip said, "You have now mastered very well the art of asking for coffee on diverse excuses."

She soon returned with the much-preferred coffee. Azeem promptly took his first sip, picked up a pillow from the bed, put that on his lap, and was about to make an advance for the second sip.

Rukiya's quick riposte to that gesture was, "Sir, this coffee is very warm, so take it slowly. In any case, this is your last sip before you articulate your response to at least the first one. This coffee should last until you finish your response of the second one. There will be no more service of coffee before lunch of today."

Azeem noted and obliged by saying, "In Bangladesh, there is a very waggish saying with reference to the in-laws' house of any son-in-law. Since you grew up in the sullen social setting of Islamabad, you may not be familiar with that. It stipulates, '*Shoshur barri modhur harri*' (in-law house is akin to a honey pot), and that refers to entertainment and indulgence specific to the son-in-law. My current happiness may as well be due to the fact that I did not spend any informal time in your parental home since our wedding to enjoy a life of indulgence as a son-in-law. I am now availing that in the happy company of my only budding sister-in-law.

On the other note, I am convinced that I have played my innings in the army, spanning about eighteen years, with experiences of one step forward and two steps backward. My decision for an early retirement is obviously a practical and pragmatic one. For any commissioned officer, as also generally applicable in other cases, the door to professional progression is mostly thwarted or closed once one encounters successive hitches in the career path, so it was the right time for me to retire and pursue other initiatives in life when I am still young.

That took me to explore my inner ambition to start a business not because I have any experience but because I have had supportive contacts based on the Bogra assignment. Besides, the occupation of business allows me to be by the side of Fazal as he is growing up, and to be with you at the prime of your youth. I had in my mind what your aphorism once articulated about the rapport between power and esteem based on your experience in AbPara market while having *lembu sherbet* with the family. I have had no skepticism about your inferences but wanted to test that in my life and with the people about whom I always have had upbeat feelings. Frankly speaking, and fortunately so, it did not take much time to experience the reality. My soreness was minimal primarily due to your earlier sharing with me of what you experienced and what your father told you about cogency of life in terms of power and veneration. As the reality of my life was known to all around, many of those whom I met just became impulsively my well-wishers instead of being aficionadas. Warm, with both palms clasped, handshakes, heartfelt embraces with pious and caring words were instinctively substituted by soft *salams* from a distance and casual good wishes. I recalled each word of that oration as you were avowing your viewpoints. Those words provided me with the much-needed cushion to absorb the most unexpected shock due to human quirk of those whom I once considered as friends and admirers. I learned the lesson of life. I thanked you silently without being anguished by my current experiences. I closed the door of the much-preferred option of doing business as an alternative to army life, permanently.

Frustrated as I was during that process, I availed of an escape by visiting last week an upscale restaurant in Bongobondhu Avenue (previously Jinnah Avenue). Besides having tea and snacks, I spent a lot of time solitarily thinking of a probable way forward for me with happiness and dignity. I was in total doldrums and stepped out of the restaurant in abhorrence mixed with self-pity.

And then, what a turn of events for me, even though it was not anything specific. I bumped into my much younger but loving cousin, Shafiq. Having most of the attributes of a semirural mindset, the ecstasy of Shafiq was much more physical and vocal. He embraced me very warmly saying, 'What a coincidence! I was just thinking of you, lamenting simultaneously that your location at Bogra precludes a meeting with you sooner that I so fondly hoped for a long time.'

I was also happy, but my military background, training, and urban lifestyle were evident hurdles to match my cousin's exuberance. But I sensed that Shafiq had many things to tell me or share with me, so we entered the Capital restaurant in the stadium area and took our seats in a corner. In munching a funny mix of *nimakpara* (slightly salt-based mini fried eateries of flour) and fruit cake with intervening sips of *garam chai* (dark hot tea with heavy milk and sugar), Shafiq relentlessly narrated most of the family events and happenings since my wedding of 1971. The most pertinent ones were related to our *Dada-ji* (revered parental grandfather).

Among his numerous grandchildren, Dada-ji had a particular affinity for me and Shafiq. For reasons unknown to all of us, Dada-ji was of the view that my two hands have blessed operating sensitivity with land, and my future is tied to land. Dada-ji equally liked and loved his relatively younger grandson, Shafiq, for his steadfastness, truthfulness, and sense of responsibility at that stage of growing up. Once I left our ancestral home for higher studies in Dhaka, Shafiq became very close to Grandpa. Though endowed with many practical and social qualities, Shafiq had no passion for learning and did not pursue higher education beyond an intermediate level in our local college. That made our grandpa very happy as in Shafiq, he saw someone to be smart enough taking care of significant landed property among contending inheritors. Conversely, as confessed to Shafiq later on, Dada-ji did not emotionally approve of my joining the army. He was of the firm view that my potential and opulence are tied to any calling related to land.

Shafiq then said, 'As Dada-ji's health was failing before his demise, I was by his side almost twenty-four hours of every day. Various uncles also took care of him but in an uncoordinated manner due to perhaps their own family needs and compulsions. I thus became privy to many family secrets and Dada-ji's hidden desires. I am also carrying the burden of a promise that I made to him. The time today is short for sharing some of those emotional experiences. I also need some support papers, but, in any case, I would like to do so at the earliest. Some of those details are more pertinent from your perspective as he died when you were in prison camp in Pakistan. I need to go now but look forward to spending some time with you soon.'

As he was about to make his move, I instinctively invited Shafiq to visit us anytime beginning the end of next week, and shared with him our address. I had been delighted to meet him and enjoyed the renewed link and nascent updates with some family details. That was very satisfying for me as I had a subdued longing within me to be updated about the family. Even though I had no chance of visiting home due to the recurrent anxieties pertaining to a settled position in an unsettled army life, the family has always been very dear to me, more because of Dada-ji's role and care in grooming me up. I do not regret my getting delinked from the family during the intervening period due to the unforeseen and nonenvisioned political developments and my professional focus. But since, and quite coincidentally, I could link with Shafiq, trusted by Dada-ji as well as liked by me, I would fully emerge from the unintended darkness spanning about thirteen years. That is the palpable reason of my current happiness. In Shafiq, and as I have the opportunity to undertake my planned colloquy with him, I will definitely rediscover myself. I have the hunch that this effort of mine will also make you happy."

Rukiya's unprompted riposte stunned Azeem. In a tone typified by both regret and reverence, she intently commenced, saying, "I do remember *Dada-ji* vividly even though our interaction was brief and formal. When I bent myself to perform *salam* by touching his feet, he very lovingly raised my physique and said, 'Azeem is a gem. You are the shining crown befitting his persona. Always take care of him. I am putting both of you under the care and love of Allahpak. I am happy to have you as the wife of my most loving *nati* (grandson). My happiness will be multiplied the day you will step in our ancestral home of Massumpur.'"

She continued saying, "In the midst of the excitement of the wedding, the preparations pertaining our immediate departure for Lahore in the most unstable mindset due to the raging liberation war, your getting wounded in the encounter with the Indian army, the emergence of sovereign Bangladesh, our camp life, and the birth of our son, Fazal, those loving gestures and words of blessings of

Dada-ji were eclipsed from my thoughts without any design. I am so sorry about that.

Once we are in Dhaka, we normally would have occasions to talk about your ancestral place and Dada-ji, but did not do so. That happened in spite of our permanent relocation in Bangladesh. Observing that failure on our part from a wider perspective, one can argue that not a single day of our life in Bangladesh was stress free. You had to struggle to prove yourself on a routine basis. That was aggravated beyond expectation as the Bangladesh Army was going through unparalleled fractional mayhem in its formation stage. Navigating through that bedlam was a challenging task. But the worst for you, and some others like you, was proving your commitment and loyalty to Bangladesh on a sustained basis, being an absorbed ex-Pakistan army personnel. The end result was most apathetic one."

Having articulated the known facts in a succinct manner, Rukiya was very happy with herself. That unknowingly was a step forward for her in having influence on future family matters.

She concluded her speech by authoritatively saying, "Thanks to Allahpak that even though fortuitously, and partly by sheer quirk, you had your chance encounter with Shafiq *Bhai* (brother). Make sure when he comes, he should stay with us for a few days."

Surprisingly, Azeem expressed some hesitation in having Shafiq as house guest. His predicament related to a lack of accommodation, but what Rukiya said made Azeem both surprised and exultant.

In her retort, Rukiya said, "Fazal will be told to share his room with Shafiq Bhai. I will talk to Fazal. He should have knowledge about his family, but more importantly, he should learn to share what he has. Sharing makes one happy, as it connotes sacrifice and accommodation. But it is also equally blissful as that gesture contributes to mental peace and makes an individual a compassionate person.

In this regard, I always recall my two relatives in Islamabad, mother's cousin and father's nephew. In spite of limited liquidity, they still visited us regularly and shared whatever they had to make us happy, including outings and entertaining us with *lembu* sherbet. Father always alerted Mother to take care of them.

That sort of understanding and feeling our son should have. We need to orient him accordingly."

Shafiq showed up on the Friday of the week indicated by Azeem during their last meeting. He was warmly received by Azeem and conducted to their very ordinary living space. The excitement of both was irresistible. They were engaged in a disjointed discourse. In his eagerness to explain his current status, Azeem even forgot to ask Shafiq to be seated. Both were in a standing status.

Right at the moment, Rukiya entered the space with a serving tray having drinking water, tea, and a very common dessert item of *dud shemai* (milk-based vermicelli).

Seeing her entering, Shafiq instantly pushed sidewise the carry-on bag hanging from his left shoulder in an attempt to deflect Rukiya's attention and promptly said, "*Salamu-alaykum*" (local salutation of formal Muslim hailing '*Assalamu Alaikum*'), *Bhabi* (how the wife of an elder brother is addressed in the Muslim society of Bangladesh). This is your *debar* (younger brother-in-law), Shafiq."

Placing the tray on the modest table nonchalantly, she wondered the reason for his being in a standing stance so long, so she did not leave anything to chance. Requesting Shafiq to be seated, she served the glass of water to an apparently thirsty brother-in-law. Then serving him *dud shemai*, she politely but quite resolutely said, "We are so delighted to have you among us. You are to stay a few days with us. There is no formality. There is no *if* and *but*. And I believe you have a duty to our son, Fazal. He should know about Massumpur. He should have clarity about the family, more importantly Dada-ji's avowed love for your brother, Azeem. There is no better person than you to communicate with him about the family details.

We are sorry for our current inability to provide you with proper space. As perhaps you have already been told, we are in the state of resettlement in quest for a new life, so you will have to readily accept what we can offer. Based on the expectation of having you in our abode, I have already discussed with Fazal about sharing his room with you for a few days. He readily agreed. I hope it is okay with you too."

As Rukiya retreated to attend to dinner preparation related chores, Azeem gleefully engaged in updating himself about Massumpur surroundings and the family. Azeem was enjoying every bit of that update. Unintentionally, Shafiq referred to cousin Julaikha *Bibi* (an elder sister is so addressed in the formal rural setting of Bangladesh. *Bibi's* most informal expression is *Bu*). Julaikha-Bu was also marginally elder to Azeem, but local custom dictated that she be addressed as Bu. With a tall frame, slim physique, fair complexion, hazel-shaded eyes, and an adorable nasal voice, she was an exceptional girl in the rural setting of Massumpur, growing up with prominence and endearment. For those makings and specifics as well as her accompanying wit and intelligence, she was known in the vicinity as well as loved and liked by most. She was most amorous granddaughter of our revered Dada-ji.

Right from the early growing-up phase, Azeem was attracted to Julaikha, was fond of her, and very innocently had a crush on her. That was stimulated and fostered due to the supportive but innocent physical gestures and oral responses of Julaikha. Azeem was too young to comprehend the inner implications of those reactions, specially communications by eye movement, in which she had a gifted ability and which Azeem used to enjoy.

As he was growing up, the symptoms of youth and the related emotions and feelings started to dominate Azeem's private actions and antiphons. Whenever the occasion permitted, Azeem would position himself before the small hanging mirror in the room of Dada-ji, look intently at his emerging mustache and move his finger on them to feel the firmness. Occasionally while seated in his room alone, Azeem used to have special feel in touching his genetalic organ, more as an offshoot of thought pertaining to Julaikha-Bu. Azeem was alert and smart not to encourage that particular thought process and minimized occurrences. He was happy with his life with limited focus and paid less attention to the words and actions of Julaikha-Bu.

That comforting attitude received an unexpected jolt. At around the end of the academic year of his ninth class, Azeem accompanied his class fellows to the most notable tea stall of Massumpur bazar, popularly identified as *Manik Miar Chaer Dhokan* (tea stall of Manik

Mia). There was the coincidental presence of a few young locals too, who had been in that tea stall earlier. They were loudly and randomly exchanging views on varied matters, from sports to movies, and from social issues and the upcoming Union Council election. Though the youngsters were mostly aligned to secular politics, there was an unexpected division among them. That related to Haji Ahmed Ali, uncle of Azeem and father of Julaikha-Bu. His candidacy for the Union Council chairmanship was at the center of the resultant discussions. He was an independent candidate but backed by rightist religious political setups.

As most of the youngsters agreed to oppose Haji Ahmed Ali, the leader among them backed off. When pressed, his frank admission related to his liking of Julaikha, and her affirmative casual gestures based on situations came into surface. That opened up the emotional box of many in that gathering. Some of them affirmed almost similar experiences, which, as a personal secret, they never shared with others. The obvious consensus of the gathering was either she was playing with all she had access to, or, very innocently, that was reflective of the inner element of her persona and all those frustrated fellows in that gathering duped themselves only.

While his class fellows were engaged in talking about their subject-specific teachers and probable questions, Azeem paid rapt attention to what the group of youngsters were loudly discussing about Julaikha-Bu.

Azeem did not buy the first proposition leveling her alleged gestures as designed choices of Julaikha-Bu to fool others. As a family offspring, he had the chance to observe her in daily exchanges with family members of both sex and varied ages and never encountered anything suspicious or pretentious. Nor had any family member ever questioned her negatively. Contrarily, perhaps because of that, she was adored by most, more specifically Dada-ji. He readily identified himself as one as who perhaps fooled himself too.

At that phase of life and with a mindset overly influenced by and predicated on immature emotions, Azeem was unable to unearth the real implications what was meant by the "inner element of persona." But one point impulsively became clear to him. He realized that there are many suites of grown-ups in the neighborhood seeking her hand, and he had no place in that. Azeem was very clear on that awareness and took a firm decision to distance himself from any mental pressure premised on inner emotional feelings for Julaikha-Bu. He also quickly realized that his sublime desire of a possible relationship with Julaikha-Bu directly conflicted with his dreams in life premised on higher education and better learning.

Azeem rejoined the discourse with his class fellows. He decided to focus on learning, with the secondary school board examination in about fourteen months. He was determined to pursue his way forward by excelling in the board examination.

Something happened unwittingly around the following hot and humid month of *choitra* of the Bangla calendar (akin to mid-March to mid-April). It was a quiet afternoon of a Friday. Azeem was preoccupied in preparing well ahead for the upcoming board-conducted Secondary School Certificate Examination. Both the heat and humidity made that preparation a discomforting one. To get relief, Azeem stepped out and suddenly decided to climb the mango tree at the northeast corner of the family's private pond. That particular tree was known for bearing very sweet mangos. Because of the feature, that mango tree was known among children as *chini am gass* (sugar mango tree). Azeem managed to have one mango easily and was striving to have the second one to share with Dada-ji. Coincidentally his focus was diverted to the opposite end of the pond, where he saw Julaikha-Bu getting into the water for a routine bathing.

As a matter of normal practice, household ladies mostly finished their bathing around early noon after finishing cooking-related errands and before the return of the male members from their usual occupational engagements. Because of the heat and humidity, the late afternoon of *choitra* is normally the time for the male folk to enjoy a siesta after lunch and for the ladies to chew *paan* (betel leaf) and/or do the needle or embroidery work. It was a most unlikely time for bathing.

That specific situation is opposed to practices and decency followed by his traditional family. Unsure about what to do, Azeem was dazed in his safe position of the mango tree observing Julaikha-Bu, standing in waist-deep water, effortlessly removing her wrapped *anchal* (tail end of the saree), getting it soaked, and applying that gently on her bulging breast, more to cleanse. Azeem was astounded but started intensely viewing the bare physical features of his adorable Julaikha-Bu.

As she got out of the water at the end of bathing, Julaikha-Bu was changing her wet saree to the replacement dry one, keeping her focus on the unlikely movement of unforeseen traffic. As she unconfined her wet saree before wrapping with the dry one, the whole back view of her bare physique was unveiled momentarily to both the admiration and delight of Azeem. He was enthused but equally nervous due to the dictates of family values, and started shivering. Precipitously, one of the mangoes fell into water, making a slight noise. But to Azeem, that appeared to be a loud one. He almost froze in his particular posture on the mango tree's support turnoffs until Julaikha-Bu disappeared.

For the few following days and nights, Azeem experienced an inner excitement and compulsion as the scenes of the bubbly bulging breasts and the bare back of Julaikha-Bu flashed in his thoughts.

By nature, Azeem had a reticent personality right from his growing-up phase. That was accentuated in youth for varied reasons. He grew up as a lonely individual in, at that time, a small family with no particular feeling for his immediate clans. For Azeem, the relative exception was while he used to have occasional discourses with Dada-ji with a wall of eminence and reverence in between. But his real bonding in early childhood was with Firoza Dadi-Amma, with one exception. Whenever Azeem raised the issue about his parents, Dadi-Amma used to divert the subject. Once when Azeem insisted, she finally shared with him, with a caveat, about their accidental death. In closing that discussion, she cautioned Azeem never to raise this issue with Dada-ji ever as that pained him.

He followed that meticulously.

While growing up, Azeem always enjoyed both oral and facial communications with Julaikha-bu within the limits of decency and restraint. That discreet mindset unexpectedly gave in to the attractions and attachment related to Julaikha-Bu's recent bare body exposure in the pond. He equally realized that it was impacting his academic preparations. Azeem talked about this with his most revered well-wisher, Dada-ji.

While initiating that discourse, Azeem wisely took a very watchful route in mentioning his own emotional quandary. He was also respectful to the status the family icon enjoyed and the constituent of his very loving and frank relationship with him, featured by respect and dignity.

Azeem had sort of a disagreement with Dada-ji, within the bounds of respect, about the former's preferred plan to move to Dhaka for higher college level studies. Availing that avenue, and without divulging details pertaining to the family pond event linked to Julaikha-Bu's bathing, Azeem raised the issue of suffering emotional distractions due to the constant presence of Julaikha-Bu in the family setting.

He frankly said, "Dada-ji, my earlier admiration for Julaikha-Bu is increasingly taking an emotional stress as I am growing up. That sort of feeling is a major distraction for me in prudently pursuing my studies. I continue to have priority on learning and higher education to live up to your expectation and to do justice to your trust and love. That possibly is the only way to pay my indebtedness to you for loving me so passionately and wishing me well in all respects. So I seek your early understanding and permission to pursue my college-level education in Dhaka. That will put me at ease."

Dada-ji listened intently to what his loving grandson just said. He looked at him passionately and asked him to be seated next to him on the bed. While lounging on his bed, Dada-ji took the hand of Azeem and softly kneaded that before mellifluously saying, "Your father's premature death lumbered me with a solemn responsibility to look after you. That was the promise I made to him on his death bed. You made that easy for me due to the all-round caring qualities you demonstrated while growing up. You made my life so easy, so I too owe you something."

Dada-ji closed his eyes, and for a moment it appeared that he was lost in deep evaluation. He opened his eyes, looked at Azeem once more, resumed rubbing Azeem's palm, and said, "Look, *Nati* (grandson), your old Dada-ji was also young once, with the associated preferences and emotions. So I could read your mind much earlier than your current opening up. As in your case, I too love Julaikha dearly. I repeatedly thought through the possibility of a union of you both, but I did not have a positive inner response endorsing that proposition. That was not due to the social parameters of the age issue and her father's controversial political leaning. It was because of its impact on your future progression in the greater landscape of the country. That was the disablement. My soul will only rest when I will be referred to as the grandfather of Azeem of Massumpur. As I am rubbing your palm, I could feel a transmission of the real agony you are internally suffering in making the proposition of pursuing further education in Dhaka, far away from Julaikha. In giving my unqualified consent, I have an almost similar pain. You are liberated to decide the course of your life without precincts and impediments. Remember, nothing in life takes place as we want them to be. Changes in the course of life are a part of life. We should learn to accept those, though not necessarily to our liking or choice. This decision of mine is predicated on my trust in your very solid practical senses and the preservation of our family and my good name. I have only one request: do not forget Julaikha. Like you, she too grew up without the love and care of a mother from early childhood, so she has been a special gem in my thoughts and prayers."

As Azeem was about to get up, Dada-ji asked him to continue sitting for a while. Expressing that desire, he once again closed his eyes and appeared to be lost in in endless thoughts. Those few moments were very agonizing for Azeem. He was worried, lest Dada-ji changed his mind or invocated new impositions.

What Dada-ji pronounced after intense thought overwhelmed Azeem. It dawned on him that Dada-ji's closed-eye meditation was his way to see the future.

Dada-ji smiled, exchanged looks with Azeem, and then affectionately said, "My earlier consent for you to pursue college and higher education in Dhaka pained me. Still I did so to make you happy. This separation will be the beginning of the erosion in the

135

warmth of our relationship and feelings for each other. None of us are to be blamed for that. It is the outcome of physical separation and the element of time. I also left my father in Moulvibazar subdivision at my youth in search of a better life. I did not forget him at all, but the warmth of expressed feeling suffered a taciturn plunge. I am certain of a similar outcome with you too.

My consolation is your cousin Shafiq. Though very young, I find in him one in the family who would possibly stay back in Massumpur and who could be trusted in preserving the family name and to take care of Julaikha in my absence. I am grooming him accordingly.

In the event of my demise, please be in touch with Shafiq. I will keep him advised about my wishes and desires concerning you and your future. You are to give me your word."

DAZING

B ecause of such interrelated predicaments, there was a lull in the discourse. Shafiq kept quiet, obviously taking the time before verbalizing his oration, as the likely expressions would have an emotional load so far Azeem was concerned.

Shafiq resumed his discourse with a soft query about the lack of any communication from him after the death of their dear Dada-ji. He said, "We tried our best to reach you in Pakistan. The emergence of Bangladesh and being a prisoner were insurmountable obstacles. We gave up hope. Information about your repatriation was vague and mostly confusing. Everyone was surprised, but the shock suffered by Julaikha-Bu was beyond words. In the tragic setting of Dada-ji's *chollisha* (prayers and mass feeding for the salvation of the departed soul on an uneven date before the expiration of the fortieth day), all family members were present. The absence of any communication from you was the center of inquisitions.

The most startling one was from Julaikha-Bu. She took me to a side corner of the sprawling home and inquired about your silence as continuous drops of tears rolled down her cheeks. I explained your status, including being in the so-called repatriation camp, a civilized identity to old prisoners' camp, somewhere in Pakistan. She did not have any word of anguish or accusation but silently lamented, saying, 'Why all these are to happen to me? I had such a nice growing up life experience. Then everything appears to be falling apart.'"

That discussion did not make further progress at that time. Azeem was immersed in thoughts related to the unfinished oration of Shafiq. What happened to Julaikha-Bu? Why did Shafiq suddenly withdraw from the discourse? Shafiq was very polite during the whole process and did not cross the boundary of decency in conveying what he wanted to, or was tasked with. The lingering question in Azeem's mind was, what else could have happened to Julaikha-Bu? He deliberately kept quiet, giving time to Shafiq to open up.

In the midst of the quietness, Rukiya smilingly stepped in while scraping her face with the tail end of her saree. Requesting both to join the dinner, she apologized to Shafiq for the mundane nature of their dinner as she was unprepared for a visitor like him.

Shafiq, for the first time, had a loud laugh, and responded, saying, "*Bhabi* (sister-in-law), why you are embarrassing me? We are from the same homestead. We have the same blood flowing through our body. Moreover, for varied family-related issues, about which I am promise-bound to the late Dada-ji, I have had been mostly out of my own abode and have almost forgotten the taste and ambience of a family dinner. You are giving me back that pleasure. And the company of Azeem Bhai and our loving nephew, Fazal, is an unexpected bonus. I am thankful to you for all these, and have something to share with you after dinner. By the by, I had a little chat with Fazal before his study time and was amazed by his love, care, and feeling for his ancestral heritage as expressed in words and gestures. His lively passion to know about the family, especially Dada-ji, overwhelmed me. I would request for Fazal's limited presence in our postdinner discourse."

Both Azeem and Rukiya, putting their logical inquisitions to rest for such a request, nodded their heads. But the response of Fazal was loud and clear, conveying his willing participation in the discourse as it relates to the family. He stated, "My homework is almost complete, and thus I have time. Moreover, in my limited conversation of this evening, I found in Shafiq Chacha a knowledgeable, honest, and sincere person. That is my added interest."

The partaking of dinner had all the normal attributes, including the hostess urging additional helpings and the guest quietly acceding with what he could have. Azeem was unusually subtle. It was Fazal who was sharing his mini family's desires and despairs including his own game plan, so he suddenly made a reflective statement to the discomfort of parents. He said, very innocently, "Chacha, please pray for me. InshaAllah, I hope to join the army after my intermediate level and will strive hard to become at least a colonel. Once I achieve that, I will come home to salute you, beside my parents, in full uniform as my repayment for telling and sharing with me family details. I had a lingering desire to know about my ancestors, and you appeared as a God-sent apostle for me. Looking forward to hear more from you. I will value those very much."

Azeem had mixed reactions, but kept quiet. He did not like to dampen the enthusiasm of Fazal by commenting contrarily. Rukiya, by repeated facial expressions, tried to convey to Fazal to slow down. But Fazal's endearing Shafiq Chacha, the center of all these, was exuberant. He lovingly said, "Yes. I will do that matching your interest. Once you come home as a colonel, I will take you to our revered Dada-ji's grave. You could salute him, and I am more than certain he would be happy in acknowledging your love and respect from the other world."

Rukiya placidly commented, "Fazal need not have to await till getting to the rank of colonel to visit the revered Dada-ji. We hope to make a trip sooner for Fazal to be blessed by his pedigrees, more specifically by the late Dada-ji."

Shafiq said, "I will look forward to the day."

Azeem was visibly happy.

Rukiya excused herself to make tea before continuing the dialogue earlier proposed by Shafiq. She soon returned with *dud shemai* and tea. The setting was perfect for Shafiq to commence.

Instead of saying anything, Shafiq took custody of the bag hanging from his shoulder, an item he had been very careful to take care of since stepping into Azeem's home. Everybody observed that particular attention, but refrained from making a query, lest it embarrass him. Azeem first took that as a common rural practice of demonstrating alertness by focusing on minimal possessions. But observing Shafiq in terms of manners, speaking ethics, his sense of prudence with words and expressions, and his cautious approach in the discourse participation made Azeem curious. He joined wife and son in monitoring Shafiq's drills in unpacking his treasured hanging bag.

Shafiq, as a matter of abundant precaution, moved all teacups at a safe distance, and placed a paper-wrapped flat possession on the table. He opened his mouth only after placing the draped packet properly, saying, "It has now been many years since I made a promise to Dada-ji before his death. To explain the backdrop in its proper context, as well as to the adequate understanding of my nephew in terms of his inquisitiveness, I need to step back slightly.

Dada-ji came back from Dhaka as a very happy person after your wedding, more due to interactions he had with *Bhabi-shaeba* (elder brother's wife with respect). In sharing your wedding experience with me, as I was unable to go due to my sudden illness, he was ecstatic.

Dada-ji said, 'Though the conversation was limited and short due to the salam rituals a Muslim bride needs to perform as per custom, I observed in her eyes and expressions a living and caring damsel blessed by intelligence. After blessing, I told her that I would look forward to the day she would step in our abode of Massumpur. In responding, she was prompt and confident. She exchanged a look with me and confirmed certainty by saying, "InshaAllah, I will fulfill your wish soon."' That made him very happy.

Upon return from your wedding, his persistent passion was to finish two tasks before he breathed his last: one was getting Julaikha-bu married, and the second one was division of his vast farming property and land among his inheritors.

The first one was accomplished in a small scale due to the liberation war, and the groom was from a family aligned to a conservative political leaning. That family was not active in politics. However, under the circumstances prevalent at the time, earned undue repute as being a supporter of Razakars (right-wing militias supporting Pakistan establishments). Dada-ji was not concerned about that. The family was a traditional one with lot of property and influence around, and a good number of highly educated people gracing that family's identity. Also, the groom to-be was well admired by all and was finishing his second year of law education in Dhaka.

Under his direction, I made all arrangements for the division of property. In the process of related consultation, he suddenly said to all present that the single largest track of farmland in between the triangular location at the periphery of the main district road and its branched subdivision road towards Netrakona that passes through Massumpur would not be up for distribution. 'Since I am still alive, that will remain in my name for my own support. Other properties are to be distributed equally among my children and those grand-children who prematurely lost their father/mother. All of you need to have agreement within the week about the distribution. I will then ask Shafiq to arrange a visit by subregistrar for preparing and regis-tering the proper documents in the presence of you all. I would not have any qualms as to what you would do with your inherited prop-erty. Each one of you has the freedom to use or dispose of it as you deem appropriate.' Giving those specific directives, Dada-ji reclined in his favorite easy chair, and, as indication of the end of meeting, closed his eyes. All vacated, and so I did."

With what he was supposed to say still unfinished, Shafiq took a pause and then filched a document from the paper wrapping and rechecked that before continuing his unfinished oration, saying, "I found Dada-ji to be quite relaxed and contented after that family meeting. However, I was bothered in my inner self with a query. But due to my age and status, I was hesitant to open up. Dada-ji proved his sagacity once again. He directly asked me whether something was bothering me. In my response, I asked him why he decided to hold on that piece of land while giving away everything that he acquired with so much hard effort. Dada-ji affectionately asked me to take a seat on the lonely stool by the side of his easy chair and loving held my right hand while saying, 'That piece of land is very dear to me. That is not just a parcel of land. That represents all what I am today. After finishing my *Fazil* level Arabic education in the local Madrassa of my native place, Sunamganj, at the behest of my poor father, I was in an emotional imbalance about my life and living. I unknowingly started looking for the direction of my life and moved from place to place, sometimes without food. I eventually landed in that plot of land owned by a local Hindu family. They were in the mood to migrate to India and were awaiting to work out an assured arrange-ment about this parcel of land.

To begin with, I started working with them as a sharecropper. The day I first started working, I smelled a supportive aroma from that soil, as if it was communicating with me. My inner self was vibrating with each shuffle of the soil. That was a huge success in year one, and I saved a good amount of money. The Hindu landlord was very happy. I continued working with them and eventually bought that piece of land on an installment payment arrangement. Whenever I was in a mood to buy additional land, I made it a point to visit the particular site, had the feel of land by having stirring interactions with the involved soil, and only bought it after having an affirmative mental indication. That was the beginning of my success story so far as land was concerned. Whatever I touched in and around Massumpur, it was a winner story. In between I bought this piece of land which became my homestead. This is factual.

But there is another facet. In between unabated successes, there was a brief period of uncertainty and concern due to an unforeseen drought in and around our area. I was in a state of distress and wariness: first, due to sudden demise of my son, the father of Azeem, and the second one was due to the prevalent drought. As a diversion, I took seven-year-old Azeem with me to my golden parcel of land in that triangle. We were accompanied by a few day laborers and carried with us the needed seasonal seeds for plantation. The inhabitants of that locality, most of whom knew me very well, discouraged seed planting as the outcome would be negative, and, more so, it would amount to the wasting of valuable seeds. After some thought, I, nevertheless, decided to plant the seeds and initiated the process by asking Azeem to lead in planting along with the daily laborers. He enthusiastically participated, more perhaps as a fun. After a few days, there was a most unexpected but much desired rain. We not only had a bumper crop but were well ahead of the other farmers in terms of marketing the produce. That was a great success. I had the feeling that like me, Azeem has the golden connection with land, and his future life and success are attuned to land, irrespective of his preference otherwise. I have not changed my opinion even though he joined the army.

I kept that parcel in my name publicly to help the distribution process move smoothly, but in separate sittings, I talked to subregistrar privately to register that land in the name of two of my grandchildren: one is Azeem obviously, and the other one,' with a silenced pause in between and a wink in expression, he said, 'it is you.'

What he said later enthralled me. He said that 'the division is not equal. Azeem gets two-thirds of the land adjacent to the district road, and your share is one-third at the rear end bordering *Upo Zilla Shorak* (the subdistrict road). That was my best judgment. That was my preference.'

He then continued, saying, 'This information should be kept private until I divulge it. So far as Azeem's title deed is concerned, you are my designated custodian. You are to hold that as *amanath* (trust/ keepsake) on my behalf and until he returns. All other related obligations I leave to your discretion, in which I have enormous confidence. I have given you a share from my most valued land to help you make a progression in life. I have full faith in your trustfulness, faithfulness, honesty, sincerity, and capability, but the apportioned land is not in recognition of those. It is simple. It is straight. It is symbolic of my love for you. And I hope that come what may happen to me, you will be always by the side of Azeem and his family.'

Having said those, Dada-ji took out from the drawer of his lone table and handed over these two inheritance deeds—one related to you and the other one for me. I have had been bearing the burden of that trust for the last many years and am happy tonight to be able to live up to the trust of Dada-ji.

I do not have much to say except a clarification. The reason I requested my nephew's presence was to convey to him our family values and the love so eminently nurtured by Dada-ji. By listening to the just finished discourse, I am certain that he would have clarity about the whole gamut of our relationships. My isolated statements and solo references could not have been able to convey the essence of Dada-ji's love and care for you and your family. I am happy that he patiently participated."

Rukiya responded lovingly by recalling their short exchanges at the wedding night and reiterated her promise to visit the ancestral home of Massumpur earliest. She was prudent enough to take the space to thank Shafiq bhai for taking care of the inheritance deed and for holding it in trust so long without the knowledge of others. She concluded her manifestation by saying, "Thanks Allahpak for blessing you with a beautiful mind." She continued to have look full of inquisitiveness in the lull prevailing.

Shafiq inquired by saying, "Bhabi, would you like to know anything else?"

Rukiya exchanged looks with Azeem, who nodded his head. She then inquired about how he was managing the ownership of the land as the deeds were not public among the offspring of Dada-ji.

Shafiq responded, "Dada-ji was just not a wise person. He was equally a farsighted individual. As his health was giving in, he told me to communicate with my uncles and aunts, urging all of them to celebrate next Eid-ul Adha with him, pointedly mentioning that he might not have the second chance in life to share such happiness with the family.

The family was gradually spreading out of Masumpur by that time due to the professional and occupational compulsions of the next generation. But most of them complied.

The day following the Eid day, Dada-ji called all the elders of the family for a discussion. Among others, he made two points: One, he has not restricted their lives in any way by pronouncements or any impositions. He was fair, to his best judgment, in distributing the properties. Then he solemnly said, 'My health is giving in. My days are limited. I thus would like to inform you all that the parcel of land I have in the triangle of the district road in my own name has been given by me to Azeem and Shafiq, with the latter having the additional burden of taking care of Julaikha Bibi in my absence. I hope I have your concurrence. If you have disagreement, please pardon me. But the arrangement is final and absolute from my side.' Happily everyone concurred, some vocally and others by keeping quiet. The irrepressible tears of Julaikha overshadowed expressions and feelings of others."

Shafiq then said, "Bhabi, perhaps I have answered your query. But I have one more information to share with all. Dada-ji passed away after a few weeks. Soon thereafter, we had a great tragedy. Julaikha-Bu's husband was brutally killed by so-called *Mukti Senas* (soldiers of freedom). The pregnant Julaikha-Bu was shattered. I rushed to be by her side. In a family discourse, the seniors opined that though the family has different political views, it did not do anything or act in any manner which was provocative during the war of liberation. The consensus was the murderers were not from *Mukti Bahini*. Most of them are *Razakars*, making an about turn to become *Mukti Senas* (Army for Liberation) overnight. They are responsible for the present chaotic social conditions in an effort to prove loyalty. Julaikha-Bu's husband was a victim of that.

I proposed her relocation to our ancestral home, but she declined saying, 'I am carrying my husband's progeny, and I want him to be born and grow up in his/her ancestral environment.' She was firm and steel faced. I did not prolong that discussion, but continued visiting her periodically, and send her gifts and presents as a daughter in our culture is normally taken care of after wedding."

Shafiq then said, "I had no idea that I would be talking so long and in such detail, but I wanted to place all facts and emotions on the table for your better understanding and appreciation. There remains the last part of my statement yet untold. You might have a query in mind as to how I used the income generated from our common land at the triangle of the district road.

At the end of every farming season, I divided our net return into three equal shares, and I took my one-third and credited your two-thirds in a savings account in my name, with Bhai as beneficiary. All local taxes and *jakat* (levy on wealth as per Islamic injunctions) were paid out of this account. The same is related to farming-related annual expenses and investment. You have now about four hundred sixty-five thousand taka as savings in that account. And here is the bank and cheque (as 'check' is spelled in Bangladesh) books in support of that. I was always nervous of the possibility of losing them, so I frequently touched my main paper packet and shoulder bag."

Having said that, Shafiq slowly handed over the bank papers and land-related deeds to Rukiya with a profound sense of relief. He jokingly quipped, "I observed Bhabi Shaeba's frequent monitoring my constant checking of the contents of the paper sachet. That was symbolic of my associated nervousness. I am now free and would like to thank you all for your time and patience. I would now enjoy a fresh cup of hot tea."

Leaving the just-handed-over valued documents on the table as they were, Rukiya hurriedly went to kitchen to prepare tea. Fazal got himself excused and went back to his room for study. The other two relevant persons continued sitting silently in the dining space.

In the isolated setting of the kitchen, with the water in the kettle emitting a vaporous sneeze, Rukiya was lost in thoughts of the incomparable humane qualities of Shafiq Bhai, even though hailing from the rural setting of Massumpur. In stirring tea with warm milk and sugar, she recalled her mother's opt-repeated opinion, "In spite of the proliferation of bad experiences that one encounters in daily life, the social system is still blessed by some remarkable good people, and the society sustains because of them." Shafiq Bhai epitomized that.

In his separated space, Fazal started reading his social science textbook to prepare for the assigned lessons for tomorrow's class but could not concentrate. His omnipotent thinking was how a person of a narrow upbringing and constrained knowledge could be so upright and sincere? He instantly developed an enormous amity for his new uncle.

While Shafiq was in a happy mood for being able to fulfill most of the promises made to Dada-ji, he had a persistent anxiety as how to fulfill the former's desire for him to be beside of Azeem and his family. That appeared to him more arduous, as most of that stipulation was not within his rheostat. He stopped navigating through the undefined way forward, preferring to make the best use of the present positivity.

That was, however, not the case with Azeem. He was scanning through family-related association, incidents, and events, more specifically pertaining to Dada-ji. Among others, he recalled Dada-ji's avowal that he was grooming Shafiq to be the future warden of the family's homestead and his trusted person.

Azeem marveled within himself, thinking about the sagacity Dada-ji embodied all through his life, right from linking with the land, judging individuals, and foreseeing the future of his loved ones. He was wondering about how Dada-ji's guidance and influence shaped up Shafiq, even though he had grown up and lived in a rural setting. Shafiq's words and deeds since they had reconnected spoke a volume in this regard.

Keeping quiet in that hegemony of the emotional paradigm concerning Dada-ji and Julaikha-Bu, Azeem was in deep thought concerning Shafiq and what he'd learned so far.

While placing the second service of tea on the table for all three, Rukiya spotted the doldrums. To enliven that locale, Rukiya simply threw in a topic of discussion on the family life of Shafiq. The enthusiastic response of Shafiq was ephemeral and evenly explicit. He responded, saying, "The fun point is that in the absence of Dada-ji, all my uncles became my guardians. Suddenly, and without prior consultation, my marriage was arranged with the daughter of my second aunt. They were living quite far away by local standard, and thus I had little chance to know her. As my destiny was tied with the ancestral home, more importantly as spelled out by Dada-ji, I reluctantly agreed. We got married about three years back, and she is *Bokul*. We have unwittingly two successive daughters by this time. One good thing about Bokul is her very understanding, supportive, and noninterfering approach to our conjugal life."

Rukiya's rejoinder was both emotional and pragmatic. She said, "I was about to propose a visit by us to Massumpur to fulfill my promise to Dada-ji. Now we have an additional reason—to meet your very nice wife and our budding two nieces."

It was finally the turn of Azeem to participate in the discourse laden with passions and reminiscences. While opening up, the hardboiled soldier and retired army major could not help but succumb to his inner feelings and could not hold back the tears from rolling down his cheeks. Smearing those involuntary tears, Azeem promptly came out of that emotive pressure by delinking himself from unpredicted wails, and quite unhesitatingly conveyed his covert desire too to visit Massumpur with family soon, concurring with next school holiday schedule.

He continued, saying, "That will be wonderful exposure for Fazal too, besides enabling Rukiya to fulfill her pledge to Dada-ji and enabling me as well to comply with my solemn undertaking given to him in the sprightly moment of the wedding following completion of *salam* ritual by the new daughter-in-law of the abode."

Having those specific stipulations, Azeem abruptly confronted a poignant backlash involving two persons but for different reasons: Dada-ji, for all his concerns and thoughts about Azeem and his future, having the intuitive reflexes about his future being tied to land; and Shafiq, for demonstrating commitment, sincerity, and honesty in handling the responsibility reposed in him by the former. Both these in combination will perhaps pave Azeem in overcoming the current impediments and usher a new life. He considered himself extremely blessed.

While getting ready to retire for the night, the urbanized persona of Azeem took steps forward toward Shafiq, lowered his head, and embraced his rural, much younger cousin with unspoken words of love and appreciativeness.

In their bedroom, both Azeem and Rukiya were relaxing and enjoying their moments of tranquility from apparently different perspectives: Azeem being pleasantly preoccupied with the best way to move forward to capitalize the opening unveiled by Dada-ji's sagacity. Rukiya, on the other hand, had a feeling of relief and security in navigating through life with the support from Azeem's family, more specifically that from Shafiq Bhai.

To break that silence of coherence, Rukiya could not help but to pun, saying, "I hope you would now concur my repeated universal saying that 'if one door of opportunity is closed, Allahpak opens up hundreds,' about which you always taunted me."

Azeem charmingly beamed, held the hand of the passing Rukiya, with a hand towel in hand, drew her close, and placed his head on the front belly of her lower physique. He whispered, "Most of my negativity and open dissonance are meant to enliven you and sharpen your thinking and prudence. Moreover, I enjoy doing that, observing how easily you get upset with me. I have no disagreement with that saying of 'opening many doors.' My life so far is a living testimony of that."

Saying that, Azeem pulled Rukiya by his side of the bed and started slowly caressing her with passions overwhelming his follow-on actions and her responsive groaning overridden by uncontrolled argot. They had a mutually pleasant and satisfying stress-free night after a long time.

The following few days were dominated by the unabated contentment in Rukiya's abode. Shafiq not only was enjoying the care and love of this mini family but was equally focused on discovering the peripheries around the home of Azeem.

Fazal unexpectedly exhibited unbounded care and love for his ancestors and that of Massumpur in his short exchanges with Shafiq. Rukiya was dazzled by the sudden turn of events in her family's domain, and opening up of the future with promise and prospect. She was happy within her own thinking, observing that in many years there appears to be an emblem in her life aligning passion with perspective of steady progress, both in terms of Fazal's growing up and a most unexpected financial stability. She was engrossed in thinking of Dada-ji's unrestrained love and good wishes and the divine intervention in her life. She involuntarily started following religious edicts gradually The manifestation of that was evident in her new commitment to adhere to performing the daily ritual of *namaz* (prayer) five times a day, and the traditional placement of her saree's tail end (commonly called *anchal* in Bangla) covering most part of head.

Azeem was on another pole of thinking. Among the varied past experiences and events, the only one humming in mind was the judgment and forecast of Dada-ji. He washed off all other setbacks, particularly those related to professional life. His current unrelenting preoccupation was with respect to thoughts about the viability of the potential alternative openings the current developments unwrapped.

The more he thought through it, the more he was getting confused. Azeem decided to keep such thoughts pending till he and family had the chance of visiting Massumpur, having implicit feelings about the parcel of land Dada-ji gifted to him and Shafiq, and to be appraised of any unforeseen stipulation made by Dada-ji which Shafiq did not share as yet. This last position was premised on the observed communication pattern Shafiq exhibited so far withholding relevant discussion until the setting is apposite to his judgment.

Being relieved of the immediate burden of life and the related challenges, Azeem was in an indulgent mood about a planning visit to Massumpur. That was contrary to what Shafiq had in mind. He wanted a definite schedule so that he can invite close relatives for a visit coinciding with Azeem and his family's planned presence.

Shafiq had, of course, another unexpressed pressing priority. There is a very lucrative proposition from a reliable party who was interested to buy that entire parcel of land. Even if the entire parcel couldn't be sold currently, the party was willing even to buy presently the parcel Shafiq owns. He withheld any discussion on this until Azeem visited the site and opened up.

Shafiq's current priority was fixing the date for the visit by Azeem and his family to Massumpur before leaving for home the following morning. Having been blessed with a practical nous and upbeat acumen, he was planning to pilot the related discourse through his most trusted Rukiya Bhabi. But that was not necessary.

Fazal came back from school with the most unexpected news of the suspension of classes for about a week in early May to repair a number of exigent constructional deficiencies and leakages from the roofs before the full monsoon rainy season set in. Those came to the notice of the school authorities after seasonal hailstorms accompanied by a heavy downpour that pounded the area in preceding mid-April.

The plan and time were finalized, coinciding with the announced closure of the school. All of Azeem's abode were happy, more ecstatic was Shafiq as he took that as the successful attainment of another reflexive desire of their dear Dada-ji. The other reason of gladness was that the proposed visit would coincide with the ripening season of local fruits.

During the postdinner chitchat, while enjoying the customary tea prepared by full attention and expertise of Rukiya, Shafiq unpredictably raised an issue about which the former was totally oblivious while Azeem was inertly nervous.

Shafiq, more directing his oration to Rukiya, said, "Apposite accommodation is always a constraining factor in a setting like Massumpur for guests of your background, and that may be a cause of apprehension in your mind. Fortunately, our revered Dada-ji, in his wisdom and farsightedness, addressed that deficiency before his demise."

Both Azeem and Rukiya were taken aback by such thoughts which undoubtedly would be a discomforting experience for the guests to be. Azeem expressed his comfort with whatever Shafiq would arrange, further commenting, "I am a son of that homestead, born and grew up there. So please don't be concerned about me."

Rukiya, exhibiting her usual prudence, said, "Shafiq Bhai, please don't be bothered about me. Any accommodation that makes your Azeem Bhai comfortable and gives you and Bokul contentment will be okay with me, and I can also speak for son, Fazal. So, please relax. Also, keep in mind that I grew up in the rough and tough surrounding of Margalla hills of Islamabad. If necessary, I will not hesitate to snatch the pillow of Bokul." Uttering those last few words with a sense of prank, she smiled back and urged Shafiq not to worry about those trivial matters.

But the persona of Shafiq was neither to be daunted by any of those views, nor smoothened by the related accommodating words. He had something else up his sleeves, so he recommenced his oration, precisely focusing on that, saying, "My purpose for raising the accommodation matter was not to cause concern on your end but more to assure you about our ability to provide the visiting family with reasonable comforts, and thus to forestall undue angst."

Having said those words of assurance, still withholding the essence of related information, Shafiq finally unbridled what he wanted to share, saying, "Azeem Bhai's departure for Dhaka for higher studies had an unsuspected evocative impact on Dada-ji's thinking. A self-assured man of immense prudence, he somehow, as evident from his words and actions, alluded to the terminal phase of his life. Among many incidents and decisions, one coincidentally was germane to what I am going to detail soon. Azeem Bhai would recall his first, and so far last, visit to Massumpur during the summer break of his first year in college. That was late afternoon of a given Friday. Azeem Bhai, myself, and some other grandchildren were clustered around the easy chair of Dada-ji. While it was normal practice for me and Azeem Bhai to be around Dada-ji most of the time, the presence of the other grandchildren was predictably enthused by the traditional practice of the latter in blessing all present by bequeathing small amounts as token gifts. It was always the happiest moment of the informal Friday gathering in the place of Dada-ji.

That Friday was no different. The assembly was about at its finale as evidenced by the usual gesture of Dada-ji. Being elated by the presence of Azeem Bhai, Dada-ji was in a boisterous mood. Some of the attendees took that as symptomatic of a rather generous gift that evening. That was bounced up when Dada-ji slightly bent to pick up a cash box from his steel trunk. That expectation was further vaulted when he took out coins of varied denominations in his hand as a prelude to a distribution based on simply instinct without looking at the coins. There was no fixed amount. It was always sort of a lottery.

Right at that moment of heightened expectation, Dada-ji suddenly swung his thoughts, and made a revealing tangent. It was more so, considering the absorptive capability of the gathering. He said, 'You see this huge house, something akin to a *haveli* (a townhouse or mansion), as a normal home of a well-to-do person. Your grandfather was not rich to begin with. As prudence, hard work, and luck favored, my wealth multiplied by local standard, and my family enlarged. Allahpak has blessed me with six sons and four daughters. As the family swelled, I went on adding rooms without a plan. Once overcrowded, the house has now become an empty one, with my offspring having their own abodes. In my absence, which is not far away, this house will be a liability, so I decided to demolish this big house and construct a functional three-room brick-cement house for my progenies to come and stay, if they like. Shafiq will have the responsibility of taking care of that abode.'"

Shafiq continued, saying, "So you will have a reasonable place to stay. To keep that abode functional, we most of the time use that house for night and try our best for its proper upkeep, including the regular opening of the doors and the windows. That is not only a house but an *amanath* (upholding in trust) to us."

Emotion laden, Azeem, accompanied by Fazal and Rukiya, commenced their much-desired travel to Massumpur as earlier agreed and reconfirmed in a recent communication to Shafiq. All through initial train travel, Azeem was in a self-questioning mode, lamenting about pursuing the demanding current priorities of life while ignoring the root and link, two vibrant coefficients of existence. After prolonged internal prognosis, Azeem framed his thinking, recalling Rukiya's observation of the ineptness of any postmortem of past actions, and suffering resultant internal stress. Each past action, right or wrong as proven to be so with the passage of time, had its own premise. One is motivated to take the best decision based on the information at the moment. With the passage of time, much of the information may change, but the decision, as acted upon, can't be reversed. This is life. This is the standard behavior pattern of human beings. This is how the social system is framed. No one is immune from that. So instead of lamenting and stressing, the viable option is to see what that experience teaches one so that similar mistakes are avoided in life. With that sort of insinuation, Azeem felt at ease and promised to himself to make the best use of this visit, mitigating prevalent misgivings and frustrations that his long absence might have caused or contributed to. He then exchanged an adoring look with Rukiya and initiated friendly discourse with Fazal, mostly narrating the features of the present journey compared to his last one years back.

After a travel lasting about seven hours, the train reached the Netrokona Railway Station. Azeem and his family got down slickly and asked the porter to proceed to the stand for the bus passing through Massumpur.

The departure of the designated bus encountered a delay of about forty minutes because of an unforeseen mechanical hitch. Azeem took out a small water bottle and gave it to Fazal as he looked thirsty. He then ordered two cups of *garam chai* for him and Rukiya, following most of the other waiting passengers.

But that was not enough of a diversion for Fazal as the station surroundings, even though bearing a semblance of up-keep activities, was in an unexciting status. Noting that, Azeem thought of a diversion. He then started saying, in the discourse style in which he excels, the history of Netrokona. The essence of that impressed even Rukiya as the oration was embedded with dates and details to attract the attention of the inquisitive mind of Fazal. He said, "Until 1826, present Netrakona (commonly called Netrokona in Bangladesh) was known as *Nator kona,* signifying that the family of reigning *Zamindar* (landlord), as a leasehold property holder from the British Crown, was from a place called Natore near Rajshahi district. The Bangla word *Kona* denotes 'corner,' and thus the Bangla words 'Natore Kona' came to be known as 'Natore Corner' in its English rendering.

In between, the leased possession of the territory changed hands a number of times due to the incursions by competing *Zamindars* from nearby places, particularly from Mymensingh. As a consequence, Netrokona territory was also named Kaliganj by one of the reigning Hindu landlord, commemorating the construction of a temple in the name of Hindu Goddess Kali. But the British government preferred the previous name, and hence the territory continues to be known as Netrokona."

The bus was all set to commence its journey after the completion of the needed repair work. That made the sundry passengers happy as it was few minutes earlier than projected. As the bus continued its unexpectedly smooth journey, it was the turn of Azeem to be astounded, observing the phenomenal changes in all the streams of life and living in the surroundings compared to what he could remember.

In the midst of that emotional semblance, Azeem was thrilled hearing the name Massumpur as pronounced by the helper of the bus to alert passengers and indicate the next stop. Excitement notwithstanding, Azeem was apprehensive of the reactions of his relations, whom he would be meeting after about twenty years. He was preparing himself to respond to any probable unfriendly comments and twists.

With that sort of thought, Azeem concentrated in ensuring the safe steps in exiting the bus by himself and his family, and was astounded, seeing hosts of his relations by the side of the bus stand's small office. Shafiq, dressed in attires befitting the occasion, was the first one to greet and embrace him. Azeem and his family was slowly introduced to all present, many of whom were even new to Azeem himself, being born after his last visit.

Shafiq's exhibition of the rheostat in handling diverse family members and sundry gentries of the different age profiles present to greet them overwhelmed Azeem. Being overawed by the unexpected warm welcome, he forgot about his luggage, kept on the top of bus body, having affixed rails to keep luggage stable by tying them up. A few rickshaws were lined up earlier to take the visitors to the ancestral place. Shafiq was meticulous in planning that half-a-mile journey, with himself and Fazal occupying the first one, followed by second one carrying Rukiya and Azeem. The remaining rickshaws were to carry luggage and some elderly persons.

As the rickshaw puller was about to press his foot pedal, Azeem recalled his luggage being on the top of the bus, which had already left for its next destination. Being flabbergasted by his onerous failing in tracking their luggage, Azeem squealed, as an expression of nervousness, though uncharacteristic of a retired major, to draw the attention of Shafiq, telling him about missing luggage.

Shafiq was calm in responding and said, "The two rickshaws immediately behind you have those under care of our two nephews."

Embarrassed as he was, Azeem, in the midst of unbounded happiness, had a pale look at Rukiya and said, "I am sorry. Being taken aback by the reception at the bus stand, I for a moment was lost in a hiatus between expectation and reality, and thus forgot about the luggage."

Before Azeem could continue further in explaining his embarrassment, Rukiya, as usual, quickly retorted, "Since the luggage had been retrieved under the watchful supervision of Shafiq Bhai and now following us under the care of your nephews, let us not be burdened by that. What you experienced is quite normal. The lesson is that it would be unwise to doubt the sense of responsibility of Shafiq Bhai. We should always try to keep that in mind so that no negative inference could be drawn from our words and actions by anyone, and least of all by Shafiq Bhai."

As Azeem and his family stepped in the compound of the ancestral home, the senior members of the family of both genders present showed up to greet them with the youngsters, most of whom met him at the bus stand. That profound welcome brought tears in the eyes of Azeem. He had mixed feelings, missing some because of death and meeting others who grew up in the family or joined the family through matrimony. Everyone was cheerful.

The only exception was Julaikha. Standing below the lone *Sal* (with scientific name *Shorea robusta*) tree, a specimen of trees belonging to the deciduous type and most common in the *Madhupur* area of adjacent Tangail district, fondly planted and nurtured by Dada-ji, she was lost in reminiscing her very precious and happy experiences during her growing-up days on the same property. Totally disengaged from the merriment inside the house of Shafiq centering the guests, Julaikha was cogitating her paces, travels, and events in the growing-up and prewedding periods of life. Unreservedly, she recalled the love and care of dear Dada-ji, more particularly after the sad demise of mother at her early childhood. That was closely matched by the feelings of support, sympathy, and adoration from almost the same-aged cousin Azeem, who was also growing up under the loving parasol of Dada-ji.

Among others, she recalled her past habit of exchanging smiles with most, indulging in emotional libretti and lingos besides enjoying the twist of words and expressions having dual meaning. She was totally oblivious of their ramifications until her husband pointedly advised her from desisting those as it could cause misunderstanding and problems within the family. The husband emphasized it more due to the traditional repute of the house and its current political prominence. Julaikha was glum facing the reality of life, being alone under the much-noted Sal tree thinking all through the moods and motions of the growing up phase in the lone company of her pre-teen daughter. Azeem was enjoying his time with virtually forgotten uncles and cousins in the company of Rukiya and Fazal.

In the midst of such gloom and thwarting feelings, Julaikha could not help but recall some interesting events and exchanges involving Azeem. Though almost of the same age, being senior by a few months, Julaikha, as a teen, was mentally more grown up and emotionally more mature than Azeem. In ruminating the most evocative occurrence of the last summer before Azeem left for college studies in Dhaka, she unknowingly got involved in a self-talking, muttering, "That was the fifth day of my period. My whole body was aching. I experienced a slipshod mood. Because of that and my preference to have a nice bath alone, I deferred the same for the opportune time when most adults were either relaxing or enjoying siesta. With my body submerged chest-deep in the water of the pond, I got engaged nonchalantly in scrubbing the lower and middle sections of the physique. As a preemptive caution, I was surveying the surroundings to monitor unexpected presence or traffic. In that process, I suspected the presence of one on the camouflaged trunk of the *chini am gass*, a favorite mango tree of Azeem. But realizing that any effort to identify the person present and creating undue noise would be more embarrassing for me as I already disinterred my *anchal* to cleanse the body, including my protruding breasts. In order to avoid something akin to public shame, I kept quiet, pretending that nothing was noted by me. I continued the cleansing course as before.

Right at that moment, a tenuous possibility overshadowed my immediate thought. What if it was Azeem, a likelihood I would love to have. My following acts and musings were reflective of that feeling. Even when a mango slipped from the hand of the onlooker and splashed in the pond water with noticeable noise, I did not look to find out the reason. I involuntarily indulged in making my physique visible within the limits of decency, and enjoyed enticing him, more as an emotional density. I continued that process while changing to my replacement saree. My nonchalant way of changing possibly assured him about my not registering the sound of noise the mango caused, and I assumed that he continued his focus on my wet body and its twisting movement.

In taking my steps towards home, I cussed myself for indulging in acts which only could cause a bad name for me if it was not Azeem." She had quickly thought of a strategy to test Azeem: to smile at him impishly on their first encounter and read his reactions. If his response was usual, then it was not he. If his reactions were introspective, then she would assume that it was he. "And that precisely happened sooner than expected. I was coming out of Dada-ji's place and crossed him. As planned, I passed on my puckish look, and he lowered his eyes to avoid eye contact. I was certain that it was he. That was confirmed when Dada-ji advised me about his decision to allow Azeem to study in Dhaka for college-level education as my constant presence of and that encounter with me were causing distractions to him. I was happy."

While Julaikha was enthralled in ruminating her happy memory of years back in this house, early teen daughter was twitchy for being deprived of hilarity as well as the liberal service of treats inside the abode of Shafiq *mama* (as maternal uncle is addressed in Bangla). To calm her down, she passionately placed her hand on the head of daughter and politely said, "Yes, we will join them soon."

Right at the moment, Shafiq showed up with wariness embodied in his facial and physical reflexes. He hurriedly released his anxieties by saying, "What happened to you, Julaikha-Bu? Bokul is eagerly awaiting your helping hand in handling the gathering. Even Azeem Bhai inquired about you twice. So, apprehensive of unknown occurrences with a preteen daughter by your side, I came out."

Embarrassed as Julaikha felt instantly, she took a defensive posture and started saying, "Shafiq, I was conscious of the time indicated to me yesterday by Bokul and started joining her in welcoming Azeem and his family. As I passed by the new house of Dada-ji, mostly constructed and finished after my wedding, a very emotional imprint dazed me. I involuntarily went to the childhood and growing-up phases of our life and got lost in many reflections centering the house, Dada-ji, and all my relations, including you."

The omission of Azeem Bhai, with whom she had a more passionate relationship, did not escape Shafiq's attention, but he opted to bypass that by saying, "Julaikha-Bu, if we get involved in recollections, we can talk for and spend hours, and consequently would miss all the fun inside. It is a very exceptional occasion full of happiness and contentment. Everyone present is happy in getting back Azeem Bhai among us. Dada-ji must be very happy in his own domain. So let us go and be a part of that."

As Shafiq escorted Julaikha and her daughter, the former had a feeling of distress and isolation with steps becoming slower and somewhat viscous. Contrarily, her daughter, on seeing Bokul *Mami* (as Mama's wife is addressed in Bangla) among many, rushed to her embrace, and was affectionately hugged by both Rukiya and Azeem.

The palpable discomfiture of Julaikha in her own parental house and among close and dear family members was for her to sustain as most present were preoccupied with talking with Azeem, recalling the past events, sharing formulated opinions about the present, and partaking authoritative outlooks for the future.

Though Fazal was quiet, he was enjoying the rural practice with respect to conversation—simultaneous and loud opinions crossing each other. He also relished the esteem with which his father was being treated.

Julaikha stepped on the entrance door and got engaged in having ocular exchanges with family members whom she did not meet earlier. In a preferred choice to avoid direct eye contact with Azeem, she focused on Rukiya, more to assess her traits. That was for a while.

Rukiya was not to be mortified. Even in the midst of freshly introduced senior and young relations, she unhesitatingly stood up solely, breaking local traditions, took confident steps toward the door Julaikha was standing on, held her hand, and adoringly said, "We were awaiting so long for your presence. I heard so many things about you from Azeem and Shafiq Bhai, as well as from whispers of Bokul. I was waiting to embrace you. Now standing here at the doorsteps, you are possibly trying to create a space. But that is not to be." With those words, she pulled Julaikha toward the lounge seat she had been sharing with Azeem since their arrival and said, "Now sit here between Azeem and myself and be easy. I may be new to you, but you are known to me for quite a time even though we had no contact with each other."

The ease exhibited and the confidence shown by Rukiya rather baffled Julaikha, as it equally amazed all present. Such an experience was new for her. As a diversion, Julaikha whispered, observing, "You are beautiful."

Rukiya promptly retorted, saying, "You are much more beautiful than I thought of, and equally attractive."

Having said those few words, she took a respite and held one of Julaikha's hand, more to stir a feeling of bonding. To make that setting more casual and relaxing, Rukiya jokingly commented, "You see the oddities of life. A few years back, you were the adored daughter of this house but now a loving visitor. Born in Karachi and growing up in Islamabad with parental roots in Dhaka, I am now the daughter of this house. In that sense, there is no difference between me, Bokul, and others like us. That is the irony of life. That is the vicissitudes of living however frustrating and challenging that could be."

Laying the premise of life's vagaries that she wanted to highlight, Rukiya alluded to the issue of pathos that thunderstruck many human lives, Julaikha's experience being one but not necessarily the only or worst one. Allying herself with the appalling events of Julaikha's life as could be gauged from the guarded observations of Shafiq Bhai in Dhaka but without referring to that directly, Rukiya purposely, but prudently exercising caution, raised the issue of the vagaries from the perspective of her own life.

With soft and sustained pressing of Julaikha's hand in her clasps, Rukiya continued her oration, saying, "Within months of our wedding, and in an unfamiliar surrounding with no kith and kin to share agonies, I almost faced widowhood in Lahore. Azeem's posting as commander of an advance army post near the much sensitive and strategically critical Wagah border crossing was just like a death warrant. That was more fearsome and challenging being a Bengali officer of the Pakistan army and in the backdrop of the raging war of liberation in Bangladesh. The moment he was leaving our cantonment home to join the new post, I looked at him standing on the exit door, being apprehensive of that being our final encounter. I had nothing to say but murmur, 'Fi Amanillah (I leave you in the custody of Allah).'

It was about late October of '71 that two soldiers from his battalion showed up at my residence. Seeing them, I was shaken. The resultant nervousness froze my physique until one of them said, 'Captain sir is safe but injured. He is receiving extensive medical attention in CMH. We have been sent to escort you to CMH to ensure the peace of mind of both of you. We are awaiting outside in the jeep. Please take your time and join us.'

Those were the moments I saw death with all its implications. I was stunned, unsettled, confused, and bewildered in spite of the consoling word 'injury.' I thus feel, with all intensity and sincerity, the grievous dimple, an experience like or similar to my moment of fearfulness as the army jeep stopped at the parking lot of CMH. That impression is preserved in my thoughts and feelings.

That was not the worst I faced. Azeem had his own reflections and frustrations. Handing over his army uniform with his insignias to subordinate personnel of his own battalion and walking in a detention camp were internally the most infuriating experience for Azeem. That shattered him in the prime phase of his professional life, with commitment and ambition unbounded.

We did seldom talk about that with sedentary locale beholding our life. That was a matter of feeling and not talking. However, those shocks and spurns gave me the urge and confidence to face reality without just lamenting. One of my dear college professors taught and encouraged me to accept the quirks of life, encouraging me to be a part of that and not just a silent player."

Observing the tenor of Rukiya's reflections and being petrified by a possible emotional outburst of Julaikha, Azeem started feeling tense. He fretted and was crossing fingers to have the opportunity to intervene without causing any mayhem.

Having said those words, and to divert focus from her emotion-laden avowals, Rukiya, as she always excelled in handling snags and in defying challenges, channeled the discourse to lighter relationship matters. Rukiya stated, "I am conscious of the fact that you are a loved granddaughter of our treasured Dada-ji and the rated cousin of Azeem, Shafiq Bhai, and most cousins present or absent. In that analogy, you are my *nanadini* (sister/cousin of the husband as generally called in Bangla). But I, without contending traditional valued relationship, would like to have you as a friend. We will be here for four days. Let us enjoy these days as friends without any inhibition. That will cement our bond for a long-lasting relationship and familiarity. My proposed offer of friendship is for life—both in happiness and distress."

After those words, Rukiya drew the attention of Fazal and introduced him to Julaikha, saying, "She is your *fuppie* (aunt) and a very dear cousin of your dad, Shafiq uncle, and a host of other cousins."

Julaikha hugged Fazal very dearly, kissed his forehead, and drew him still close, giving a feeling of family bond. She simultaneously looked for her daughter for an identical introduction and was embarrassed not being able to locate her. Shafiq intervened, saying, "Even if you shout, you will not reach her. She is engrossed in helping Bokul in her cooking-related chores."

Responding to what Shafiq said, Rukiya, after passing a signal to Julaikha, stood up and proceeded to Bokul's kitchen. That more than demonstrated Rukiya's aptitude to adjust with unknown settings and be a part of it. Enthralled family members present were all delighted, and complemented Azeem for having such a wonderful life partner.

Azeem was both exultant and gratified but was struggling to have a proper response expressing both thankfulness and exhilaration. At that point of time, Farash *chacha* (paternal uncle), the only living sibling of Azeem's late father, came to his rescue. He initiated his discourse, saying, "There is no doubt that in Rukiya we have the presence of a gem in this house. I was earlier briefed by Shafiq about her manifold qualities and capacities. But the style and depth of her communication a while back that all of us witnessed, along with wisdom and passion in her articulation, captivated me, and I am certain that it had similar bearing on the feeling of all others present. I had some idea about Azeem's unusual absence from the family locale for a very long time and decided to put off any specific query at an appropriate time. But in a wonderful way, she touched based with that and Julaikha's pain without ever mentioning either. I admire her and congratulate Azeem to have such a wonderful life partner."

In that scenery of contentment, Farash *Chacha* all of a sudden proposed a dinner at his home for Azeem and his family the following evening. That caused a mild commotion, but the family's sensitive stance was soon resolved through the intervention of Rukiya.

As a long talk was going on about who would host the guests and when invitations are to be scheduled, Rukiya coincidentally returned to the venue accompanied by Julaikha. She, by design to make relationship casual and normal, got Julaikha seated by one side of Azeem and herself occupying the other side. Rukiya listened joyfully to the irritation caused by Farash *chacha*'s uncoordinated invitation proposal.

With the sanction of Farash Chacha, Rukiya intervened, observing, "I do not see anything wrong with the proposition of *Chacha*. Moreover, as the icon of the family, he has the right to do so. But the schedule of our stay is a fixed one. We are here for four nights to enjoy our stay as you all would prefer. All cousins and nephews cannot be accommodated. So you decide in consultation with Shafiq Bhai and select four families. We will be happy with whatever the outcome is. But I have two suggestions for your consideration: those who wouldn't be hosting meals for us would be invited to planned events by groups; and second, both food and arrangements should be kept simple as the main intent would be to share happy moments and enjoy the event. I assure you that we will have many visits to Massumpur, and any unfulfilled longing to host us could be taken care of at those times."

Everyone was happy, more so was Farash *Chacha*. Most of the assembled families and relatives slowly vacated the congested venue. A sense of serenity abounded the resultant void space.

After dinner, Shafiq guided Azeem and his family to the abode of Dada-ji: their place to take rest and sleep. The neatness of the place and bedding preparations, including the quality and freshness of duvet and the water-filled jug with two glasses on a not-too-distant traditional table, meticulously arranged under the caring guidance of Bokul, impressed both Azeem and Rukiya. Azeem complimented Shafiq for taking care of the house and making all the arrangements for their comfort. As Rukiya was about to add her positive views too, she was flummoxed seeing Bokul entering the room with three cups of *garam chai* for them and a glass of blithely squeezed mango juice sherbet for Fazal.

Seeing that, Rukiya could no more held back her enthusiastic impressions. She observed, saying, "Shafiq Bhai, you are not only a person of immense qualities, but your ability to camouflage a real gem like Bokul in letting us have ideas about your family is just groovy. I am thunderstruck observing Bokul arranging and completing all chores related to our visit singlehandedly and very efficiently. The meticulous service of tea and sherbet epitomizes that. You not only observed our way of life while sharing a few nights with us, but also transmitted that to Bokul, and she is performing all those pedantically. Congratulations for having Bokul as your life partner."

Saying those words, Rukiya pulled Bokul to a nearby sitting position next to her, embraced her, and kissed her forehead as a symbol of sincerity and unreserved bonding.

After those spontaneous acts and in between sipping *garam chai*, Rukiya went through a tangent in her observations while both Shafiq and Azeem were engaged in a preliminary sharing of ideas for next few days at Massumpur.

Rukiya was suffering the impulse of saying her concluding words before Bokul stepped out, so she intervened, saying, "I am sorry for interfering but need to say something. This is the right time. This is more relevant in the context of aptness of this evening."

Continuing her oration, Rukiya said, "Shafiq Bhai, the more I see you, the more my respect for Dada-ji for locating the subsumed gem in you and nourishing that is burgeoned. My adoration for you for living up to his expectations even many years after his demise, including living up to his trust with sustained commitment, is enhanced with multiplicity after each encounter with you. All those feelings within me bolstered my trust and faith in you.

But on one score, you were not fair. When Azeem asked you in Dhaka about your family, you casually mentioned about Bokul just as a cousin from a slightly far-away location, and thus not having much interaction. But this afternoon and evening and in observing her taking care of the divergent needs and demands, we found in her a very wonderful life partner of yours. Thus, I would like to pronounce my feeling, love, and admiration for Bokul without reservation."

Unpredictably, Azeem took over the discourse from that point and said, "Sister Bokul, you might have noted that I mostly prefer to talk less than your *Bhabi* (sister-in-law), who compensates for my resultant shortcomings. But in this case, I just can't help but articulate my feelings too with respect to you. I fully concur with what your Rukiya Bhabi alluded so far with respect to you both, and unhesitatingly agree with all those. But I have two points for you: first, try your best to groom your children imbibing in them the rare qualities of a valued citizen so dearly held by Shafiq. That made him so exceptional; and second, like all mortals, we too love food and comfort. We enjoy those. But the reason of our coming is to have the opportunity to wash away past deficiencies and reconnect with you all. So we would equally look forward to your time, to your companionship, to your togetherness in reinventing the much desired bond that Dada-ji would like us to have."

Overwhelmed by those words and expressions, Bokul stood up and approached Azeem to *salam* him by touching his feet as an expression of gratitude. Azeem was taken aback as he, because of living in different social systems for the last many years, was insensible to this common and simple local form of expressing sincere thanks with respect.

Unguarded, Rukiya was taken aback when Bokul approached her for similar gesture. Both because of the minimal age difference and the friendliness the specific relationship depicts, that sort of gesture was out of thought for Rukiya. She promptly took possession of both shoulders of Bokul and straightened her physique. Drawing her close to own chest, Rukiya affectionately told Bokul, "Your place is here. That is true not only for today but all the days of our lives. Come what may, no one will be able to disrupt this feeling of mine. This is a promise from me."

Very bucolic in growing up in an equally pastoral setting with an exceptional receptive mind and ability to absorb, adjust, and assimilate, Bokul, under the shadow of the words, advice, and guidance of Shafiq, soon carved a place of adoration in the legacy of Dada-ji's family heritage. The way she handled scores of relatives and made arrangements for the care and comfort of Azeem and family manifested that in all its indices.

Bokul was in tears in the cuddle of Rukiya, more as a demonstration of unrestrained happiness. She expressed her simple reaction, saying, "Bhabi, please pray for me so that I can guide my children in growing up to have the paradigms of you both in terms of values, ideals, and stances."

Both Bokul and Shafiq than left for their own abode, allowing their esteemed guests to take a rest.

In their discourse of last night, Azeem expressed his preference to revisit the land to reassess some queries that captivated his thoughts ever since learning about the surprise gift from Dada-ji. Some of them were these: What is the specialty in that land? How could that land be of meaningful relevance in my life? What feeling will overwhelm me once in that land? And so on. But Shafiq politely suggested, "I think that may not be a good idea. Many from the neighborhood and some relations are expected to be in the house to meet you after many years. They will be disappointed not seeing you. They will feel bad. It is my suggestion that we visit the land the day after tomorrow having no other pressures." Azeem gladly accepted the suggestion.

On their way to the site of the gifted land on foot, a preferred choice to rediscover old surroundings, Azeem was taken aback observing diverse and positive changes in life and its supporting facets. Improved communications, enhanced traffic, intense economic activities, the presence of multiple brick-cement houses were some to impress Azeem. But he was more surprised seeing hundreds of girls going to schools without any tension and the absence of bare-breasted men on the roads and fields even in the hot and humid conditions of early May. He, however, kept those within himself, concentrating more on the running commentary of Shafiq about all-round developments.

Once on the field, Azeem exchanged multiple views on social, economic, and political matters. He also met two elderly neighbors who knew Dada-ji well. The ensuing reminiscence was both pleasant and emotional. Azeem kept within himself the inner feeling of his childhood visit which caused a mystical contemplation in Dada-ji's thinking relating that piece of land and his future.

While returning from dinner in a cousin's house, Shafiq, as a general courteousness, accompanied Azeem and his family to their accommodation and started checking their sleeping arrangements. In the process, Shafiq winked at Bokul, who quietly left for her home.

As a contrast from the urban practice, dinner in rural Bangladesh is usually served soon after sunset, so was the dinner in cousin's place. Everything related to that event was completed soon. It was too early for Azeem and his family to retire to bed. At his suggestion, Shafiq stayed back to have diverse discussions on family and other societal issues of common interest, just to kill time.

Everyone was surprised at seeing Bokul walking in with four cups of tea. That made Shafiq happy, Azeem amazed, and Rukiya pleasantly delighted. The whole mood was changed with the follow-on sips of tea.

Rukiya drew the attention of Bokul and suggested she be seated by her side. It so appeared that in that unfamiliar rural backdrop, with Azeem preoccupied with relations and childhood acquaintances, Bokul was her only comforting source of poise. That was more applicable in the context of the issue that was at the top of her thought at the time. She took hold of a hand of Bokul, and initiated the discourse, saying, "Shafiq Bhai, how was trip to the land today?" She had many more queries to raise, but refrained from doing that, realizing it being a matter concerning their family land, and as a daughter-in-law, she should not be overly engaged in the matter.

Contrary to the aforesaid apprehension and predicament, Shafiq immediately availed the opportunity as if he was awaiting for a desirable opening.

In a tranquil tone matched with pleasant facial expressions, Shafiq started saying, "Bhabi, that visit was very nice, and rekindled old memories in our minds with renewed respect and gratitude to Dada-ji. I hope the outcome of today's visit would be very fecund in due course.

But before I respond in more detail, I would like to touch base with some matters for the sake of clarity and good understanding. The first one relates to the need to grasp and appreciate the rationale for Dada-ji's decision to earmark that plot of land in Azeem Bhai's and my favor. On many occasions, I raised this issue with him. As Azeem Bhai would recall, Dada-ji had his own communication style. He used to respond to queries he would consider appropriate at the material time vis-à-vis the query, and the rest would be answered later based on relevance. I followed this feature of his communication over a long time, found merit in that, and tried to enthrall in articulating my own communication panache. I found the imperativeness in providing information based on appropriateness and have a firm conviction as to its effectiveness rather than loosely pronouncing as an auxiliary to other queries.

I did not spell out any defense for not agreeing with Azeem Bhai's proposition to visit the land site immediately the day after arrival. I obviously had a reason and would like to share it tonight. A set of neighbors and relations were always mocking the lack of contact by Bhai with parental roots and relished openly related sardonic comments. They are the people whose children could not make much headway in academic pursuits and are living with them. That was highlighted as symbolic of love and attachment to the lineage to camouflage real frustration. The same group of people, lamenting the lack of contact over many past years in the presence of and to the proclivity of Bhai, would prank, in his absence, about the real intent of visit: not motivated by love for the root but more by attraction for the parcel of land gifted by Dada-ji. I thus mildly disagreed to protect Bhai's name and dignity. I hope Bhai would pardon me."

Emotion laden, Azeem was oblivious of the intricate and complex rural mindset due to his prolonged absence from the scene. The wisdom shown by Shafiq so far in conducting his visit awed him beyond description. He was thinking of an apposite and fulfilling riposte.

There has been a marked change recently in Azeem's responses, especially after opting for voluntary retirement. He was still mentally alert but developed the habit of taking time in formulating rejoinders most of the time. Rukiya remained alert and prompt, and most of the time outdid Azeem. That happened in this setting also.

Though the plea of pardon was aimed differently, Rukiya, embarrassed by the time being taken by Azeem, promptly quipped, "Why are you seeking pardon, Shafiq Bhai? You have done the right thing. We as a family are thankful to you for that and all other ingenuities you and Bokul are demonstrating in making our visit more happy and fulfilling from varied perspectives. You are blessed with the wonderful gift of understanding, commitment, and loyalty. That perhaps was the reason as to why Dada-ji reposed in you that much of trust in spite of you being young at that time."

Premised on that reassurance, Shafiq continued, saying, "On my repeated queries, Dada-ji eventually opened up on his return from Azeem Bahai's wedding, and responded by saying, 'Of all my numerous grandchildren, Azeem is intelligent and progressive, having all the mettle to promote the name and fame of this house. Moreover, I promised to his late father to look after him. This is my special affinity for him. But one dilemma haunts me. It was my inner feeling that notwithstanding his ardent current fancy for the army life, his stability and happiness in his life are intensely tied to land. I can't deviate from my first impression of taking him to that plot of land which changed my life too.

So far as Julaikha is concerned, there is none comparable to her in the family. That is both a reason of pride and a cause of concern. Moreover, she was deprived of a mother's love and care from childhood. So I want you to take care of her all through her life.

Recognizing your honesty and commitment, as well your unmatched love, regard, and respect for me right from childhood, and to help you in the process of living up to my many desires, including the specific one related to Julaikha, I decided to gift a parcel of that land to you. One point of clarity: by gifting that precious land to both of you, I am not tying you to farming per se. You can use it in any way you deem appropriate, but preferably something related to agriculture. This particular land is a gold mine to my inner feeling, and will be of value to both of you.'"

Overwhelmed by what was narrated by Shafiq, Azeem was amazed by the sagacity and farsightedness of Dada-ji. That feeling and that decision of Dada-ji had proven to be most relevant in providing the needed jumping board for Azeem to shape his postmilitary life. Within himself, Azeem was drained and felt thirsty.

On indication, Bokul got up, and Rukiya followed her. Both of them returned with two glasses of water and four cups of tea. Everyone was happy. It was time for a break for all except Rukiya. She was under intense emotional pressure to comprehend how this rural man with an intermediate level educational attainment could hold back so much of information without sharing with anyone, including Bokul. She was bubbling with the thought as to "what next?" So without wasting any time, Rukiya motivated Shafiq to continue his stalled homily.

Shafiq obligingly responded but with a tangent. He diverted his oration to more reality around, and said, "Bhabi, there is no similarity between rural Bangladesh that was familiar to Azeem Bhai than the present one. All embracing developments accompanied by radical changes in social values and priorities engulfed the rural setting. The per capita income manifestly swelled, but the increase in prices of property is phenomenal. I have specific information to share but would like to have an indication of Bhai's interest."

Without waiting for the reactions of others, Rukiya muttered, saying something akin to, "Why not? Interest is the offshoot information, so let us have the information first."

Azeem intuited what Rukiya was aiming at. He consented by nodding his head.

Invigorated, Shafiq then said, "In the recent past, I was involved in helping Jasim bhai and Monzur bhai, sons of our second paternal uncle, in disposing their shares of inherited property. The rationale was simple: both the brothers are government officials, settled more or less permanently in Dhaka, and did not have any desire to be back in Massumpur. So they sought my help. That involvement of mine was an eye-opener for me with respect to real estate deals. I came into contact with a number of intermediaries (termed as *dalals* in Bangla) in the process and became familiar with intricacies of land-related deals, more importantly pricing. After that, I helped a number of family members in land-related deals.

In the process, a number dalals approached me with lucrative proposals for our parcel of land gifted by Dada-ji. Apart from the paucity of a big chunk of land in the vicinity, coupled with rapid developmental activities, land became a prized possession for everyone. In that setting, we enjoy a unique position because of the size and location of our land. But it always had two associated impediments: the lack of contact with Bhai, and clarity about consent to proceed.

I was taking time on one plea or the other without divulging the reason, the co-ownership of land in different proportions and the lack of contact with the other. In the meanwhile, both the demand for that large chunk of land and its price were going up.

On my part, I had to follow a path of care and caution in view of the land size, its location, and the price being offered. A single misstep could cause insurmountable complications, and I could not take the risk single-handedly.

My position became much more untenable when the House of Majmadar (in local expression it is called '*Mojundar Bari*') requested my visit to their abode. It was an invitation from the most renowned and influential house of the surrounding. I was awed being in the midst of the elder Majmadar in the company of his three sons. This family, over the last about two decades, made fabulous achievements in all spheres of economic undertakings, making it a household reference point much beyond the northeastern parts of Bangladesh, with credible presence even in urban locations of Sylhet and Dhaka. The presence of all sons was perhaps due to the occasion of Eid-ul-Adha.

My, that meeting was very brief and to the point. Based on the investigative work the family apparently undertook earlier with care, the eldest son put up a proposal to buy our land at a higher price than the latest offer I had. I had nothing to say as it appeared that they did all preparatory investigations and were familiar with all pertinent information, namely the apportion of the land between Bhai and myself, the absence of contact with Bhai, and the dilemma I have. They, without wasting time, also proposed an alternative, suggesting that I sell my portion to them now, and the rest will be settled when contact is established with Bhai. I had nothing to say, consented to consider it duly, and sought a time of six months for arriving about a decision. They readily agreed with a gentleman rider that any negotiation for the sale of this land to any other party would not be undertaken between now and the end of the stipulated period.

As I was coming back, two points overawed my thoughts: first, the extent of the preparatory work the family had undertaken silently before meeting me. That included information pertaining to co-ownership of the land and the much-guarded information about the name change decided by Azeem at the time of induction in the Pakistan army.

During the final process of induction, Bhai was told that the name Ziyauddin Abbassuddin Azeem was too long for functional use. So without any thought, he dropped *Abbassuddin* from his name and had been officially recorded as Ziyauddin Azeem. We were not aware of that. Perhaps because of a sense of inner adverse guilt for dropping the name of his grandfather from his name, Bhai did not discuss this with anyone subsequently.

The second one was related to pricing. From recent experiences in handling the sale of some lands of the family members, due to increasing migration to Dhaka and other urban locations, I came to realization that while price is important, getting a reliable and sincere buyer is more critical. There are plenty of *dalals* in the booming market representing pseudo buyers who excel in having deals by offering higher prices, and then resort to delays in making payments, after initial ones, premised on a host of excuses and ultimate litigations, compelling the owner to settle for much less. In that context, the proposal of the Majmadar family was reliable and lucrative, including the option of possible staggered deals.

I opted to take time to think through the proposed deal in terms of its manifestation and the trust Dada-ji reposed on me in stipulating that I should always be by the side of Bhai. The most haunting quandary related to its definite impact on Bhai's maneuverability to negotiate based on market dictums in the future once I sell my portion now. This feeling never motivated me even to respond to many earlier offers.

Within about a month of my meeting, I received another call to see Senior Majmadar. During such meeting, I was told that Bhai is popularly known in the army as Azeem ZD, and that he recently opted for voluntary retirement.

With my rural background and exposure, I rushed to Dhaka to locate Bhai. I moved from pillar to post of the most unknown path of the army setting and was bewildered. After a few days, I realized that the armed forces, as an organization unit, has its specific rules and traditions about information sharing, and a person of my background has no access to that. So I decided to leave Dhaka for Massumpur and decided to await for any indication from Bhai.

During my stray walk in between Rajarbagh police line and Gulistan cinema hall location, with Baitul Mukarram in between as the most prominent milestone in mind to be assured of my position and location in the unknown metropolis, the most unanticipated encounter with Bhai took place. The absolute abruptness of that happenstance deadened my immediate feeling, transcending between dream and reality. I was both motionless and speechless for some time. My response faculty returned only when Bhai, holding my shoulders, shook me. That was the moment of enormous relief, exhilaration, and satisfaction for me. As I was sharing tea with him in a restaurant around the stadium area and listening to what Bhai had to say, I was engrossed in thinking about Dada-ji, and ascribed the most unexpected encounter as the charisma of Dada-ji's love and wishes. The rest is known to all.

But before I close, I would like to relieve myself by sharing a few more details. So far, I have meticulously complied with all desires and directives of Dada-ji. I have been taking all the needed care of Julaikha-bu, including sending presents on religious and social occasions besides ensuring her periodical visits to this home. My decision not to opt for the sale of my portion of land was perhaps the best one in life. To be able to stand before you all tall and straight is my ultimate satisfaction.

I have, however, something else to share with you. I had no hunch of that until Dada-ji, two days before his demise, revealed to me surreptitiously my lineage."

PEDIGREE

Shafiq recommenced his discourse with reference to the related backdrop, saying, "In such most depressing lonely setting around, especially against the milieu of his deteriorating health status, I was Dada-ji's constant companion. Others were equally concerned, but their presence, as indicated before, was periodic because of the varied pressures of life.

In such a situation, coinciding with the *Azaan* (call) for *Johor* (afternoon) prayer, Dada-ji desired softly that I be seated near the midportion of his lying body. Though normally that was the time for him to take a nap, he was not in mood that afternoon. He evidently had some unknown pressure within. Observing that, I conformed without dithering.

Dada-ji lovingly took hold of my hands, placed them on his chest, and started saying with a blank bleary look, '*Nati* (grandson), my days are limited. I need a solemn assurance that you would not change your respect, feeling, and love for me albeit what I am going to tell you. The prodigious constraining factor at my end is that my sallied soul will never be at rest if I leave this world without being honest to you.'

The bewildering and precipitous tone of Dada-ji's introduction made me edgy and unmoving. I kept quiet to enable Dada-ji to continue telling what he wanted to, though I had no doubt that it certainly would be something ominous. Still then and to facilitate the colloquy process, I, without any wavering, renewed my pledge that come what may, I would never allow that to have a negative bearing on my respect, love, feeling for, and commitment to him.

That appeared to have the desired mollifying effect. Dada-ji exchanged an ardent look with me, and then diverted his eyes to a large envelope kept on his mundane side table.

His grip on my hand increasingly became firm as if he had an innate trepidation of losing me. The more he showed that sort of anxiety, the more I relaxed my muscles in an effort to create the necessary conducive setting.

Dada-ji then said what he wanted to say for so long, possibly more prodded due to a span of time between *Johor* and *Asar* (late afternoon hours) prayer rituals of Muslims. Focusing directly on me with a relatively stable enunciation for his age, Dada-ji said, 'My initial few months in the land of Hindu land owner was a trying one, even though I was having positive intuitions from the land and surroundings. While taking a break in a nearby *chaer dokan* (rural tea shop), I noticed an apparently distressed person about my age, with both frustration and readiness overwhelming his presence and persona. I started talking to him, contrary to my standard preference and practice, and instantly liked him. To develop cordiality, I offered him tea (served at that time in glasses) and soon, before our tea was finished, I discovered in him someone of my trait in miniature.

One point was at snappy variance with me. He got married against the approval of his family and shared living between his in-law's and his parental houses as the family persistently refused to accept his wife as its daughter-in-law. She continued to stay at her father's dwelling. After a lapse of few months, with the news of wife's pregnancy in common knowledge, he was thrown out of his parental home. His family took that step to force him to divorce the daughter of a *jelley* (fisherman), an assumed low professional identity even in the classless social orientation of Muslims.

The initial few days in his in-law's place were okay. Everyone was consoling him by foreseeing a positive outcome since he was the only son of that relatively well-to-do family. With the passage of time, reality showed up with its ugly face. Mixed signals were trafficked from many of the in-law's family, some seriously and some jestingly, with all the negative implications under the seeming adverse situation. Being under pressure, even the in-laws gave in. Their initial sympathy slowly turned into negative postulations.

The only person with a solid shoulder was the love of his life, the wife. But one observation from that dense corner unnerved him when she precipitately said, "The life of ignominy that we presently are encountering is fine with us, but why should our offspring suffer that shame? We need to do whatever is needed to try for an environment of uprightness and dignity for our offspring to grow up. It does not matter however modest the outcome is. The world is much larger than our families. You should go out and explore it. If nothing happens, we will have the consolation that we tried."

That challenge and the urge to do something for the honor and dignity of his progeny brought him to the present place in the course of peripatetic over the last few days. He was honest and blunt in admitting that "I grew up in a sheltered family devoid of any expertise except the reputation of being a good child. While wandering through the plains in search of a work, it became evident that I lack skills of any relevance. I was at a bay with frustration overwhelming me and spent many past nights in empty mosques. My quest for an employment faced the most frustrating likely end as the little money my wife gave me with a positive wish is almost exhausted. I was in deep thought about the future. Right at the moment, you winked at me and offered me a glass of *chae*, a regular social feature in our home, and which I missed over the last two days."

Being from a well-to-do family with obvious social distinction, one undoubtedly needs a quality of confidence and uprightness to detail the glitches of one's personal life as he unleashed. That impressed me most. I revisited my precarious existence of the immediate past and, for an unknown reason, felt an urge within me to share a small portion of my newly experienced lady luck. I developed an empathy for this remarkable young man who sacrificed life's assured comfort for the sake of love, and was now wandering.

Detailing who I was and my own existence presently experiencing an evident sign of some progression in life, I made some propositions to him. The related understanding that all these were subject to concurrence of the Hindu landlord for whom I am working was made clear upfront. The propositions included the sharing of my modest accommodation, cooking food together and sharing the same, and hard labor for augmenting productivity. I also explained that our job primarily was to augment productivity with a focus on input, such as seeds, fertilizer, water management, proper pruning, and the supervising of other laborers. As a compensation, I proposed giving him 15 percent of my daily earning and 10 percent of the block income that I may expect from the landlord after each farming season.

The above stipulations made him thrilled, and he readily agreed with one caveat. He said, "I have no experience in cooking. Frankly speaking, I never stepped into our kitchen. Prepared food was always served during eating times, so I have no idea how can I be of help. On other matters where hard labor is relevant, I will put my best efforts and can assure you that you would not have anything to complain about."

I affirmatively responded, thanking him for his honest admission. I, however, responded saying two things which, surprisingly, he absorbed unwaveringly. My first comment related to getting rid of nostalgic feelings. "Forget about "prepared food." Face the challenge of your new reality. Commit yourself to mastering the art of preparing food in an earthen cooking facility (locally known as *chulla*). The hardships encountered initially, such as discomfort with smoke, the wetness of the firewood, the divergent flow of fire, etc., soon will be accustomed to, or be over. That possibly is the practical way to handle ordeals. Second, there are many ways to handle challenges. Our initial food intake will be limited to *bhat* (boiled rice) and *dal* (lintel). A properly done boiled rice will be a feast for us. If that becomes soft, we can mix it with dal and pretend to have a *dhila kichuri* (mix of dal and soft rice) and, for local taste, can top it up with green chili and lime. If the boiled rice is hard by normal standard, we can put that in water for overnight and have that soggy rice in the morning as *pantha* (water sogged) *bhat* before going to work. Either of these alternatives may not be perfect but good enough to proceed without anguish. These are the lessons I learned in my journey of life, not very different from you except your wedding."

At this point in time, it dawned on me that we were talking to work and live together impulsively without even a formal introduction, so I broke the ice and introduced myself as Abbasuddin Azeem Mohammad, clarifying that people generally address me as Abbasuddin or Abbas. Assumedly, such a long name of the upper class Muslim families was the consequence of the annulling partition of Bengal in 1911 and a silent but determined effort in Bengal to assert Muslim identity. Equally discomfited, he too shyly said, "I am Motalib Majid. People generally address me as Mutalib."

Very amazingly, our life moved on the charted path with no resistance from the Hindu landlord, who was mostly preoccupied with a possible migration after the disposal of his huge ancestral farm property. The relatively small and isolated parcel of land in which I was committing to put all my efforts to change my destiny was of least interest to the family, as for the last many years, this remained to be mostly barren and unproductive.

On a specific query from Mutalib about the footing of my prognosis concerning the relevant land, I honestly shared with him my stances and motivations, saying, "When I first set my feet on the land, I sensed a vibration, as if the land was countering. There is no basis for this type of postulation, and one can summarily discount such a reasoning. It is a question of faith and belief. I opted for that. The other sensitivity is grounded in my gardening experiences of my student life in the empty land around the periphery of our *Madrassa* (religious school). We had an *ustad* (teacher) who is very learned and farsighted. He told us that being barren for quite a while, this land has attained naturalized enrichment, and as such is suitable for productive uses. With his encouragement, and under his regular guidance, we achieved phenomenal results in vegetable production, to be recognized by Madrassa management and community. So I have some idea about farming. Fortified by that feeling, I visited Massumpur *Thana* (the lowest administrative unit of civil administration) Agricultural Extension Services Office on the following day. That was the most fruitful visit for me. I was received and encouraged by one of the most supportive official in my life. We spent almost half of the day, but what he said finally was the essence. He said, 'Have trust in the pastoral belief that land has enormous potentiality. Its productivity depends on its management. Always remember the following five elements in farming: *mousum* (season), *beez* (seed), *shar* (fertilizer), *jotna* (caring and pruning), and, above all, timely and adequate application of *pani* (water). If a farmer is attentive to all these five, there is little possibility of his failing.'

Encouraged by all these, as well fortified by assurance of Thana Agricultural Extension Officer (TAEO) to undertake periodic visits to the site, I met the landlord, Bijon Nag.

Recapping my assessment and discussions with TAEO, I sought his consent in financing a one-third portion of the slightly elevated land formation with features of dryness. That was to be the slice of barren land to be cultivated on a trial basis for the upcoming vegetable season. I also stated that a positive outcome would mean new cash, and that might help the process of migration, minimizing other pressures.

Not much of discussions followed my proposition. Surprisingly, Babu (akin to Mister) Bijon Mohan Nag consented readily. That took me by surprise, as possibly you too. I had no immediate answer. I pondered inexorably but have never been to the end of that obsession. The question of why a well-to-do Hindu family head would take fancy on an unknown Muslim boy, more so when his eldest son-in-law was the victim of a preceding communal rioting about three years back, remained unanswered.

In the past, the family always downplayed the proposition of migration, but the last experience of losing very dear son-in-law was the turning point. The pressure was mounting on him as all three sons and two unmarried daughters had already migrated to Assam state of India. He was living in Massumpur with wife and widowed daughter, both though supportive of migration, resisted leaving Babu Bijon Nag alone. He also wanted to migrate but only after settling large family properties either way—disposal through outright sale, or exchange, or a combination. His repeated assertion was that he would not migrate from the position of prosperity to a status of poverty. So he was taking time for suitable deals and offers. That was the cause of delay.

In such a disquieting standing of life, Babu Bijon Nag probably saw in me one of his close ones, either by tumult or by coincidence. That remains unanswered. I had reasons not to put any effort to unearth that mystery.

The reason for that was: first, there was no urge within me for such an engagement as I was the beneficiary. The second was my singular focus on launching the project on a timely basis with all the farming preparations and planning of inputs.

I did not know anyone in the vicinity. The little cash I had was needed for my survival. On being appraised, Babu Bijon Nag allowed me to use the abandoned accommodation of the family's *purohit* (priest).

That was a win-win decision for both of us. I had an informal setting and casual slant in sharing with him project-related concerns and glitches. That informality provided the most needed window to share frankly project-related matters. He was happy being updated regularly.

The plus point on his side was my regular voluntary presence when he would be sitting in the open veranda mostly alone and enjoying the puffing of his favorite *huqqa* after dinner. In such a setting, elderly people have the inclinations to share their thoughts and propositions. My presence filled that evident gap in his life since the migration of his children.

During regular discourse, I noticed one aura of his talking. In matters of general interest such as faith, philosophy, and social dictums, Babu Bijon Nag was imprudent and unusually open. But with matters related to family, money, and property, he would switch to a behavior pattern that was quite the opposite. In such matters, he would slow down, listen intently, contain his impulses, and spell out briefly his subtle decisions.

I was amazed while undertaking these discussions with him. He would listen more, talk less, and articulate his decisions in still fewer words, but he would never deflect his eye contact with the party involved. His usually soft but solid articulation impressed me most. I learned a lot from him in the process.

The best feature of my understanding with Babu Bijon Nag was his candid stipulation that if the outcome of this venture is negative, that would be end of the story. If it results into positive outcome, then the net income will be shared equally, fifty for capital—that is, for him—and fifty for labor, for me.

With those understanding and stipulations, the project was launched immediately. The trial project with my hard labor and TAEO's regular guidance was a mega success. Our 50 percent sharing amounted to money beyond conventional comprehension. We were on the verge of launching our second effort covering the whole plot with a focus on paddies. It is no more possible to manage the task single-handedly. I need an additional supervisory hand. And there you fit in. I trust you as Babu Bijon Nag trusted me. I need your sincerity and honesty."

After making a statement that far, Dada-ji appeared to be exhausted and needed some break. I went out with his consent and returned soon with a glass full of green coconut water, a favorite of his. He was evidently delighted and took the first sip with vented easing. He finished the first half of the coconut water with equal relaxation and then made a statement of profound but undefined significance.

Dada-ji recommended his oration by saying, 'My relationship with Babu Bijon Nag was exceptional. His love for me was without any inhibition. During our daily sporadic interactions and random discourses, I learned a lot from him and practiced those in my own life. My liking for you is probably one of numerous replications of what I learned from him. All I absorbed in the process was that one must have exceptional self-confidence before reposing trust on an unknown soul.

There was, however, an exception. Based on ruminations of related observations of Babu Bijon Nag, I had the hunch that the former believed that I was the reincarnation of his very loving *mama* (maternal uncle), who died at a young age. He referred to his *mama* a number of times relating to my physical features, way of expressions, and manners of responding, as well as my age profile.

Initially I liked that supposed association as it warmed up my contact and relationship with Babu Bijon Nag, but I maintained the needed distance without hurting his notion. I never contradicted or confronted the rationale of that thinking. I cautiously navigated through his related inkling premised on the Hindu religion's concept of reincarnation. That paid dividends in many ways on my way forward in life.

In the midst of uncertainties and abstractions, a miracle happened. A deal for the mutual exchange of the properties of Babu Bijon Nag with that of a Muslim family in Assam was negotiated and finalized. That deal inexplicably excluded the parcel of land I was working on and his homestead. The only possible reason was their location far away from the main estate.

Babu Bijon Nag was relieved and relaxed. He achieved the major objective to his satisfaction. Small things did not bother him anymore. While sharing the good news of the exchange deal and, out of blue, he proposed a deal to sell the parcel of land and the homestead to me at an incredibly low price with one caveat. It related to maintaining the secrecy about both the deals (for the ancestral landed property and the parcel of land along with homestead) until he safely landed in Assam.

Guarding the information about the exchange deal and the maintenance of confidentiality were not difficult as Babu Bijon Mohan Nag had neither perceptible interactions in the recent past with the outside world, nor was he visible outside mostly. But it did not take much time for me to conclude that the proposition of the suggested sale of the plot of land left out of the main deal and that of the homestead, besides having all the elements of love and feeling which he bestowed on me without reservations since coming into contact, was grounded on his eagerness to migrate soonest and safely.

That did not bother me at all. I was pensive in assessing my life so far with the unexpected turn it is likely to experience being probable owner of this house. Soon that happy thought became a matter of indescribable concern with no end in sight.

The embryonic anxiety discernibly related to the financing needed to have the deal operational. All other issues could be held in abeyance for the time being. I was confused and nervous thinking about the consequences of failing. I had no idea about the way out.

During the process, I was astounded seeing Babu Bijon Nag entering our interim abode, the abandoned residence of their family puruhit. Exchanging a look with Mutalib with oddity and fixing his focus on me, he, as usual, softly said, "Tomorrow night you will have food in our regular meeting place around our usual meeting time, and the food for your companion will be delivered by household help, Jaggadish." Saying those few words, he quietly left.

As I stepped in, I saw Babu Bijon Nag relaxing in his usual place, with his huqqa emitting smoke of a pleasant aroma. The other noticeable feature was the various covered food services in a corner on a *patti* (local mat made of foliage) laid out at reasonable distance from his relaxing chair.

After finishing dinner, I sat on the usual high-raised stool with my back having the support of a patio post. Babu Bijon Nag opened up soonest, saying, "I intentionally had a separate dinner service for you as I wanted to talk privately about something very important regarding my proposed deal for the land and homestead. My feeling for you and my trust in you predicate the position. I am conscious of the financial impediments you have in acting on my proposition. Thus, I am offering you a way out. We will have the deal as I indicated earlier with three staggered payments to commence with the end of the next paddy harvesting season coinciding with the beginning of this month. With the payment of the last (third) installment, you will automatically become the owner. No new agreement will be needed. There will also be a provision for my successors to implement the agreement as it is should anything happen to me or any of them. If you concur, I will ask my lawyer to draft it, get both of our signatures, and take action for its registration as a valid document, with the principal copy for his law office and a copy each for you and me.

My considered opinion is that this is the best arrangement for both of us. I know that I can get a better price, but it is equally possible that being aware of my migration plan, the likely buyer may resort to other delaying maneuvers, for me losing both property and money.

My selling the property to you will minimize my pain of disposing my ancestral estate as in you I see my revered *Mama*. I only hope that you will live up to my expectation and trust. Keep this understanding as private as possible. That will be beneficial for both of us."

After that dictum, and being relieved of an unventilated pressure, he concentrated on puffing his favorite *huqqa*. But I was suffering an internally sustained burden of poignant stress. Unsure about the tone and type of appropriate response, I stood up with idea of retreat to have independent space to think through a possible rewarding expression that would make Babu Bijon Nag contented beyond a shadow of doubt for his decision. But the reality baffled me. Instead of going back to my temporary abode, I involuntarily moved toward Babu Bijon Nag, bent my physique to touch his feet, and blessed my forehead with the supposed dust on it.

It was Babu's turn to be bewildered. He took time to respond. As I was about to turn toward my place with tears glimmering my cheeks, he stood up, took possession of both my shoulders, and drew me close to his chest, saying, "In my long life, this is the first time that I am embracing a Muslim. That is enough to convey my adoration and inexorable commitment to your well-being for no specific return and no veiled expectation. I understand that it is difficult to rationalize, and I have doubt within me about how my own children would take it. But I am at ease with myself. Until your arrival within my domain, I had a worrisome life experience, with every initiative producing contrary results. That pertained more importantly to the exchange of property and the yields in farming. I was suffering inexplainable bewilderment, more so as my children had already migrated. My most unalike and unexpected contact with you turned the table of that experience. Things started taking a turn for positivity.

Also, during our sudden discourse under the mango tree, in the periphery of the parcel of land you are now involved, I noted your intense interest in farming and what you learned from your Madrassa teacher. You proved to be unalike any local fellow I came into contact in the past. That had a sudden and profound impression within me. I discussed all these with my wife regularly. She encouraged me to trust and support you, more due to multiple similarities with *Mama*. What I stipulated this evening was her suggestion, as she believes in the divine incarnation in you of her late uncle-in-law.

I would like to conclude our present parleys with two notations to avoid surprising squabbles in future. That entails: one, in case any perceivable problem relating to the agreement is anticipated, you should promptly and directly convey that to me, or my designated heirs; and second, until the third payment is completed, no one should use my main house. The identity of that structure would continue to be Babu Bijon Nag's home."

Dada-ji continued his oration saying, 'That was the turn of my life to progression and affluence, with the initial phase having its utmost focus on privacy and hard work. The objective was not to fail in fulfilling the stipulations with Babu Bijon Nag.

We hired a household lady help to prepare our food and take care of other errands. That enabled both of us to have more meaningful and more frequent exchanges pertaining to our project, optimizing yield and income. I exercised care and caution in such exchanges to ensure an unimpaired ability in decision-making and ubiquitous authority in management.

That did not have any uptight impression on Mutalib. He was in his own world of bliss at finally having an assignment, even though the immediate return was modest. His prime root of delight was the trust I reposed on him even in the setting of brief and subtle exchanges. Mutalib promptly wrote a letter to his wife highlighting that, equally emphasizing the genesis of that trust without any reference or documentation.

After finishing, Mutalib handed over the letter to me to read. I was both baffled and disinclined but had to give in at his polite insistence. Our journey together started based simply on good intentions and understanding.

Two immediate decisions of mine had a gargantuan influence in bonding us solidly. Those were: scheduling weekly payment for his daily work and offering him free board and lodging during the initial phase. The rationale for the first was extrapolative respectability to earning, and the second one was aimed at responding to the immediate concern related to living. Mutalib was exuberant, and all we discussed day in and day out was our project, the impediments and the prospects.

It was about a month that Babu Bijon Mohan Nag, his wife, and his widowed daughter's left the ancestral home permanently through a secret and covert arrangement. That was organized by his trusted lawyer friend, who, besides a flourishing law practice, had developed a shady operation involving cross-border transactions involving all sorts of actions. I had no premonition and became aware only when Babu Bijon Nag introduced me to his lawyer friend with a brief reference to their looming travel arrangements to Assam.

From mails addressed to Mutalib under care of my postal address, I was aware of exchange of letters with his wife, Ginni, and was happy about it. Assured of regular communication and her well-being, Mutalib doubled down on his commitment and effort for the project. Meanwhile, he also sent small money to Ginni, and my earlier decisions to make weekly payments and provide free boarding and lodging were very helpful in this regard.

In the locale of such positive setting, Mutalib unexpectedly showed up relatively early from his project work, and handed over a portion of a folded letter from Ginni for my read-through. Even though hesitant to respond favorably to that proposition, I had to yield in the face of the silent and equally passionate persuasion of Mutalib. The portion I was requested to peruse roughly stated, "By loving me, you suffered a lot and sacrificed many gains. With your progeny increasingly kicking my lower belly, I am immensely missing you. I want to be under your shadow enjoying your warm embrace, giving me the needed strength and confidence in this trying period. Is there any way to get me in your place? I am yearning for you. Will you consider raising this possibility with Abbasuddin *Bhaishaheb* (Bangla expression for one revered as elder brother)."

I stopped reading the remaining portion of the letter. My memory impulsively traveled back to my sending years back of a telegram to brother-in-law working in Dhaka. That conveyed a similar message from my elder sister being at an advanced stage of pregnancy. Help happily extended by our English teacher, me being in the ninth grade, in drafting that telegram flashed in mind. Unfortunately, my sister succumbed to maternity-related complications. I was grieved, but my solace all through was that she was in the embrace of my brother-in-law while breathing her last.

That most startling experience of my early youth involving my very dear sister distressed me for a while. A passionate feeling within me riveted since then about women's feeling and vulnerability. I thus consented without second thought to the utter amazement of Mutalib. My related subsequent proposition took him aback. That pertained to two days of absence for him with pay to go to his in-laws' home and to return with Ginni. That proposition also stipulated a little cash from me, as a symbol of love, to defray transport expenses.

Mutalib remained in total darkness about the reason for my impulsive decisions. He was obliged and thrilled.

I had demanding days in the absence of Mutalib, and returned from the field later than usual. Sitting on the usual easy chair of Babu Bijon Nag, I was relaxing. Being late afternoon and in the emptiness pervading the locale except for the occasional trifling noise from the kitchen site, there was a total lull. For some strange reason, I had an impulse for trying his *huqqa*.

Our household lady, who herself was a *huqqa* addict, blithely responded to my request. I started unhurriedly with small puff and slowly started enjoying that. This, but perhaps more the reality of me acting the way Babu Bijon Nag used to do every evening, overwhelmed the ambience. I dozed off with end part of huqqa pipe dangling.

Then there was a small clamor. I opened my eyes to see Mutalib helping his pregnant wife in getting off safely from the rickshaw. I smiled and welcomed them. Shy and tense, Ginni, at the behest of Mutalib, took small steps approaching me. As she was about to bend, a challenging posture at that stage of her pregnancy as well as the travel just endured, I quite lovingly said, "You are not only Mutalib's wife but also my sister. In you I will try to find my deceased senior sibling. There is no need to salam me. You have all my blessings and doa. This is your own home, and you should not try to overexert yourself to please us. Our household lady will help you. More importantly, and as she told me yesterday when I was briefing her about your arrival and health status, she has a natural talent and liking to handle delivery and are aware of the complexities involved. That was a great relieving factor. Also, both Mutalib and myself will be by your side always. So do not worry."

We, by sheer coincidence, followed a social life style akin to what practiced by Babu Bijon Nag. Our social contact was minimal, mostly pertaining to farming and the marketing of produces. Being blessed by an unanticipated turn in the lives of both, we were focused on multiplying the startling gains and were least concerned about the milieus. The contractual obligations with Babu Bijon Nag were always in my head. I shared that selectively with Mutalib based on appositeness—never early and never late—a style of information sharing that I learned and mastered from my revered *ustad* of Madrassa as well as Babu Bijon Mohan Nag. In spite of the presence of Ginni, both of us continued to work very hard.

Ginni conversely was at ease in this unknown place right from the time of our initial interactions. Her observation of Mutalib's occupational commitment and the sense of trust he was able to create in our relationship as well as his visible presence and physical proximity all perhaps had their respective role and influence on Gini's acclimatization process.

We never addressed our household help lady by name. It always was indirect inquisitions and references. But that suddenly was reversed with the arrival of Ginni. We came to know and be accustomed with her name, Ambia. To Ginni, she soon became the very caring *Ambia-bu* (*bu* for sister).

Besides performing all the household errands, Ambia devoted the time and effort to take health- and comfort-related care of Ginni. They bonded very well with mutual trust and respect. I came to know all these occasionally from Mutalib. Far from own home, Ginni found one similar to a mother. That was very reassuring for both of them and myself.

189

Time passed happily. I was observing the conjugal life of Ginni and Mutalib with a wink in my thought for a possible change in the status of my own life. I relished such thought but always kept it away, being conscious of the challenges of life I had vis-à-vis the trust and commitment to Babu Bijon Nag.

That was the early period of ten months of pregnancy of Ginni coinciding with the full moon night cycle of the lunar month. Ginni started feeling discomfort, and soon it was evident to be inchoate delivery pain.

Mutalib, keeping in view earlier advice to keep warm water ready for any eventuality, fired the *chulla* and put a pan full of water on it to boil. He then rushed to fetch Ambia and returned soon with her along with an additional support hand.

Both the ladies got engaged in taking care of Ginni who, with anxiety, was groaning occasionally with pain. There was, however, no doubt in our minds about the expertise and capability of both in handling the pregnancy.

In the very early hours of that night, the associate lady came out with the good news of the birth of a son. She quickly added that mother too was relatively okay.

Both of us were overjoyed. In his excitement, Mutalib proposed the nickname for the boy to be *Chandu* (a derivative of *chand*, the Bangla word for *moon*), his birth coinciding with a full-moon night.

After a while, Ambia-bu came out with the newborn baby boy wrapped in a *katha* (close Bangla word for *baby wrap*, made of used sarees to ensure malleable enfolding). That arrival of Ambia-bu with the baby boy happily coincided with the effervescent utterances of *Azaan* (Islam's mandated call for prayers) for Fazar namaz (early morning prayer) from the far-away *Masjiid* (mosque).

We both were very happy. Mutalib took a step forward to hold the boy but took a step back, being a nervous new father. My elation was more for the reality that out of nowhere and without any link, I was instrumental in enabling the couple to have the best feeling among all odds of the past. But I did not dither in taking the initiative in formally naming the newborn. Without giving any opportunity to the father, I ventured to tell Mutalib that, "You have given him an appropriate nickname. I would like to have the privilege of naming him formally."

Mutalib's response was obsequious. With an uninhibited smile titivating his face, Mutalib was prompt in saying without hesitation, "It will be an honor for us, and a divinely propelled blessing for Chandu. So please go ahead."

Frankly, I was not awaiting his concurrence. My initiation of related discussion was premised on counteracting any negative feeling in his mind based on the unmitigated accommodation by me in the past. Neither I was meandering.

In my mind, I was scouting for a suitable name. In that thought process, I was initially guided by the inclinations demonstrated by Mutalib in choosing the nickname. My knowledge and past Madrassa educational orientation were handy in the process.

I promptly proposed the formal name of "Subha Ibn Mutalib" with supportive narratives. Those are: *subha*, meaning "very early morning," denoting the approximate time of birth and constituting his formal name; *Ibn*, meaning "son of"; and the last part being the father's name as we know of. That made Mutalib very happy.

Ambia continued toddling the baby, and soon left for inside as Chandu started quivering in her lap. That did not bother me. I was entranced in evaluating the depth of love of this young couple as manifested, when in a simple but equally emotion-laden observation, Mutalib stated, "I like the name, more because of its meaning and link. I do not recall naming children in my family, and in our social setting, with such deliberations. But before I fully concur, I would like to discuss with Ginni. After all, he is our child."

Life around me changed unnoticeably. Both Mutalib and Ginni assumed a greater role and responsibility in managing household errands. In addition, Mutalib remained ardently focused in farming-related activities, minimizing my worries as well ensuring a greater inflow of funds, both for me and himself. Ginni became more easy, open, and perceptibly communicable, treating me as an elder brother. Subha started growing up, learning to take small steps. I was very much a part of that process, and started enjoying it.

My immediate priority was fulfilling my contractual obligations with Babu Bijon Nag and ensuring the ownership of the related property by producing more and having rewarding returns. That I accomplished as scheduled.

As luck favored me, I was doing extremely well in life. Whatever I planned and touched became an instant success. I started buying lands of choice and relevance. During all this time, and notwithstanding the happiness and fulfillment, I remained singularly focused in making a life for myself in terms occupation, income, and stability.

I did not have much contact with my family. Possibly being from a large family, they did not miss me either. My father's possible consolation was perhaps by enrolling me in a Madrassa, he had assigned me, and wisely so, to the path of Allahpak, and that He, in His infinite mercy, would take care of me. That was akin to the typical mindset of the time.

Perhaps due to such realities and experiences, I had no feeling for or link with my previous place. The only person I had some contact from my pre-Massumpur life was my revered ustad of the Madrassa I was enrolled in. I strangely suffered an occasional yearning to visualize Ustad's beautiful growing-up daughter, Firoza. I used to think about her and occasionally indulged in mapping up her growing physique. Those were the exceptions in my focused objective of financially establishing myself.

That sort of feeling was an exception initially. It became a more regular pattern after Chandu adorned the life of Ginni and Mutalib. I enjoyed every bit of merriment of their life both as a couple and a family.

My participation in and enjoyment of that joy, though intended to be unqualified, was, as I could sense, always peripheral. That caused emotive unrest, from a healthy perspective, within me. The resultant anguish gradually entombed a very poignant desire for a family of my own.

I quietly started communicating with my ustad to create a notion of positivity in the stalled relationship of my immediate past. That worked well from my perspective. He opened up without hesitation, informing me about loss of his job in the madrassa due to local minutiae, causing an acute economic distress for the family. He also referred to the snapping of an almost certain marriage proposition of Firoza for an inability to fulfill the demands of the groom's side, indirectly referring to the present hardship of the small income of being the Imam (priest) of a local mosque. He, instead of being exasperated, thanked Allahpak for His current blessings.

I always believed in and practiced privacy in sharing information. Hence, my communicating with Ustad was only pithily shared with Mutalib without any specificity. But the last letter where the ustad displayed perspicuous trust in the virtuousness of Allahpak' s decision, even in the backdrop of dominant adversities, cut a deep mark in my mind. My reverence for the ustad multiplied. I shared such exceptional attributes with Mutalib.

It was our practice all along to have food together. That practice was continued with the arrival of Ginni, happily with a relative formal setting for service.

On the night following the receipt of the most prized letter where the ustad showed his unabated trust in the goodness of Allah's decisions, I was late in showing up. On being insisted by Ginni to go and fetch me, Mutalib shared with her the elements of the communication from Ustad that was causing emotional pressure within me. To frame his point more solidly, Mutalib also shared, with hesitation, a little bit of my feeling for and anxiety relating to Firoza and the emotional overload I was suffering to raise the issue with the ustad.

Having been blessed with a sharp mind with an equally strong feminine instinct, Ginni impulsively concluded about the contents of the letter and summarized within herself as that being an anxiety more concerning Firoza, and less about trust in Allahpak's decisions.

During the food service time of that night, Ginni raised the issue of her loneliness in this house. She went on, indicating frequent moments of anxiety as she had none to share life's happiness and agony. Highlighting their indebtedness for my enormous kindness and accommodations in all respects, she took me by surprise, and Mutalib by embarrassment, while stating, "You are treating me as a sister. I am grateful for that. It is clear to me that the moment we are deprived of your love and care, we do not have a place to exist.

193

But receiving love and care cannot be a one-way street. We have also some duty towards you. Premised on that, and being the daughter of a *jelley* (fisherman) accustomed to weathering storms in high water, I just cannot help but suggest your consideration of having Firoza-appa in this abode. That will not only make me happy and address my isolation, but more pertinently enliven your life and living."

That was a bolt out of the blue for both of us. Mutalib's mixing of steamed rice and curry for swelling came to an instant halt. I upraised my face from my dinner plate and had a solid full look at Ginni, more trying to unearth the intrinsic sagacity of her even though reared up in the setting of *jelley* (fisherman) families.

But Ginni's confidence remained unabated. With full self-assurance, she candidly continued, saying, "Whatever little I know of about you from Mutalib, and observing your likings and preferences, I am certain about your pining for a family life of own. Keeping that in mind and identifying myself as your sister, I propose to write a letter to your ustad seeking the hand of dear Firoza *appa* (sister). I will request you to visit the family soon and hand over the letter personally. To my assessment, a potential proposition is being encumbered for lack of confidence on your part and a sense hesitation on the part of revered ustad. Let us handle the future as it unfolds. But I am sure about a positive outcome."

The postdinner rituals were as per previous practices, with the exception of the overall lull pervading. Back in the kitchen, Ginni was panicky about the upshots of her unplanned outburst. Her anxieties related to the possible retorts of both Mutalib and myself. Sitting with the support of one of the posts of the verandah (open extended space of the house, more akin to a patio) space, Mutalib was mortified, and thinking of probable escapes from that. Contrary to all those, Dada-ji was enjoying puffing his *huqqa*, thanking Ginni internally for relieving him of his lumbering impasse.

This should have been an occasion of joy and merriment. But the reality was just opposite. Dada-ji then decided to talk to them and desired Ginni's presence.

Ginni's dithering steps were discernible in her approach toward the setting. Dada-ji promptly injected an aroma of openness and friendliness by saying, "A sister never feels shy in meeting brother, so be at ease and sit on the stool by my side. Your prompt assertion about Firoza was not only appropriate but contributed enormously in confidence building within me. You have spoken what was fretting me internally. I agree with whatever you proposed. So write your letter. I plan to carry that soonest."

Things moved fast, and within the next few days, the treasurable Firoza was in Dada-ji's abode as a family member. Ginni devoted her time and energy to make Firoza feel at ease in the new setting far away from her parents. She meticulously exercised care to keep Firoza away from the errands of daily family life. Firoza found a happy diversion in taking care of Chandu and rearing him up.

With the actualization of his family life and the pervading total happiness around, Dada-ji devoted full attention to farming dares and made progress beyond all expectations. Not only he was free from the obligations to Babu Bijon Mohan Nag, his acquisition of new lands made steady advance. In that process, Firoza delivered their first son, bringing added happiness.'

Dada-ji continued stating, 'This phase of my life was that of unabated success and happiness. In the life to follow, I continued to enjoy success in financial matters, being totally oblivious of other probable happenings in life. That stuck me soon as I started experiencing a series of deaths of near and dear ones. This experience continued to be the greatest puzzle of my life.

A cholera epidemic broke out in our neighborhood with the deaths being quick and common in the absence of medical services. In a span of three days, the family lost both Mutalib and Ginni in succession, leaving Chandu under the care Dada-ji and Dadima (grandmother).

That was very unnerving for me. My immediate reaction was as if I had lost my right hand. With determination and focus, I conditioned myself to stand upright so that we can bequeath some tangible assets to Chandu.

That was not the case with Firoza. She found life to be insufferable in the setting that once was dominated by the words and footsteps of Ginni. Ambia tried to console her from time to time. That aggravated Firoza's grief more.

A new factor textured soon, adding unknown angsts. Being the daughter of an Imam (in a general sense, one who leads worshippers in Muslim prayers), Firoza was not comfortable in accepting a Hindu puruhit's home as her abode. That was upsetting for her from day one, but being new in the hybrid family and made aware of obligations to Babu Bijon Nag, she continued to live with that. It, nevertheless, was troubling her all the time.'

The return of the next harvesting season from previous investments was beyond all expectations. That was the first happy experience in that house since the sad and sudden demise of Ginni and Mutalib. The merriment within the family reflected in totality the imprint of Firoza in every respect. Her wise and dominant presence soon became known to many. A few neighbors who visited the family on happy occasions congratulated Dada-ji for having Firoza as a wife symbolizing opulence and exhilaration.

Firoza, intoned by her family orientation and values as well learning and exchange of opinions with father, developed an immense aptitude of social contacts and conversations. That was briefly eclipsed after the wedding perhaps due to presence of and courteous dominance of Ginni. The latter's sad demise opened up a space for Firoza to blossom without causing family banes. Similarly, the absence of Mutalib increasingly motivated Dada-ji to discuss farming and investment-related matters with Firoza Dadima. That gradually transmuted her as an active participant in decisions pertaining to all family matters.

The first evidence of that related to the decision to buy this homestead. As contractual commitments with Babu Bijon Nag were fulfilled and the family had good liquidity, Dada-ji intended to buy additional farmlands and shared his thinking with Dadima. She was matured enough to convey to him initially a sense of agreement to make Dada-ji happy, only to emphasize later her old liking to move out of Puruhit's house by buying a new home. In the process of floating the idea afresh, Firoza Dadima envisaged a buying farmland by 50 percent of the current liquidity, and to utilize the other 50 percent to buy a home, and just move in. All future needs for development and reconstruction could be taken care of in the future based on need and financial standing.

Apart from formulating substantive other logic in support of her suggestion, Dadima introduced a gullible element highlighting her emotional pressure and burden in beginning their family life in a place which was for ages the residence of *purohit* of a Hindu family. She was also smart enough to link the simultaneous deaths of Ginni and Mutalib to such an apprehension.

Without any inhibition, efforts were directed to locate a homestead. Their reconnaissance visit to the site of this homestead was an instant hit. The relative secluded location, the huge family pond, the big trees all around providing an emblem of privacy, the location of the only modest house at the west wing facing the east, and the wide open south side were all to the liking of Firoza Dadima. A prompt decision was taken to buy this homestead, and the deal closed quickly. The family moved to the new home, renting out the previous residence of Babu Bijon Nag to different parties under segregated tenancy arrangements. That logically included the place of the *purohit* also.

Dada-ji then said, 'The second phase of my conjugal life had a smooth start and flourished along with moving into the new home. As part of tradition and religious practice, we organized a *milad mehfil* (very roughly, the expression connotes gathering Muslims participating in the recitation of Quran and poems in praise of Allah and prophet [*pbuh*], etc.), culminating in joint submission to Allahpak and the distribution of sweets) to commemorate our move to and living in the new abode.

As the milad deliberations were approaching the culminating phase, our new household help entered the venue silently, holding Chandu in his lap. Since we were new in the locality, very few people, especially the Imam Shaheeb conducting the milad, had an idea about our family composition. Just as an expression of genuine intent, or to please me, he directed the household help to bring Chandu to him. Imam Shaheeb held Chandu very cozily, kissed him lovingly, and placed him on the *jai namaj* (a piece of fabric used by Muslims, and some Christians, for performing prayers).

Soon thereafter, Imam Shaheeb raised his two hands, followed by all participants, seeking Allah's mercy and blessings for the family, and in the process referred to Chandu many a times as *Boro Mia* (roughly signifying eldest son of the big man). Since then, everybody assumed Chandu as our eldest son, and he became known as *Boro Mia*. Chandu's name and identity went into oblivion.

We had a very considerate discourse at night focusing on Imam Shaheeb's impetuous assumption of Chandu being our offspring. Firoza, maintaining silence and keeping her eyes closed with total devoutness to the divine resolutions, precipitously observed, saying, "Perhaps, it is the will of Allahpak, and we should accept it unswervingly."'

The family steadily enlarged under related impulses. So were the ramifications in terms of living with an addition of rooms as the number of children increased. That mundane three-room house gradually took the shape of a modest *haveli* (a traditional family house of rich persons in the Indian subcontinent as popularized by Mughals with it root in Arabic word *hawala*, meaning private space) in no time until its demolition years later.

Dada-ji continued his emotional antiphon by saying, 'We always kept in view the incidence of the first Milad in our house related to Chandu, and acted as per the conclusion of that night without any inhibition. The family started addressing son Chandu as *Boro Mia*, and we committed to treating him equally in all matters with the other offspring that followed. That included the prime matter of inheritance.

These developments typified a phase of life encompassing realities based on sustained material progressions and taking turns in uncharted directions with a mix of some frustrations, new hopes, and aspirations. Mutalib and Ginni's omnipresence in our life gradually faded, and so was the name Chandu fondly chosen by Mutalib. The process was sad but ironically reflected realities. I sensed it only at mature age.'

PROCESS

Life in the new abode of Dada-ji, similar to other mortals, followed its own courses, having happiness and sadness sharing spans. The significant difference with others is their nature and symmetry. As said to me, that happened in Dada-ji's life at indefinite times and unmarked places under settings never thought of, or consequences ever comprehended.

Many a times, such happenings in his life have had been unexpected, and many a times were surprises. Life's journey was never as envisaged or projected based on existing realities. More interestingly, some surprising good happenings landed the family to unforeseen disdain later, whereas some tragic events eventually brought solid gains to the family in due course.

Having a pause and a sharp survey of the surroundings, Dada-ji continued, saying, 'I had thus my exertions in pursuing life. But that was largely mitigated by the understanding shown and the support extended by Firoza at all times, and sustained positive returns from extended farmlands-related operations.

Affluence and tragedy alternated in my life which had a specific motivation, with emphasis on stability, as the family was getting enlarged. The highlight of this progression was the unalloyed absorption of *Boro Mia* as one of us, bonded by everything except blood. Firoza was always alert about this sensitivity and eternally referred to Boro Mia as "my son."

Our conjugal life was blessed by seven sons and four daughters, including Boro Mia. Of them, we lost intermittently two sons and three daughters. Some of them were casualties at birth while some others died in the early phase of infancy, or by accident. This impacted on the flavor of our family life, more so in the case of Firoza.

With the passage of time, my material chattels proliferated, and surprisingly my prominence in the social setting burgeoned significantly. An aura of foresightedness and competence increasingly enveloped my social personality. A very popular image was created around my surroundings about my special ability to foresee product outcomes of variable plantation seasons and varied farming undertakings, forecasting reasonably about the possible output.

There was no doubt about my inherent ability to assess the productivity of lands based on site visits. But for farming practices and other related decisions, I used to rely on two sources. One, I used to consult the *Panjika* (Indian astronomical almanac), used mostly by Hindus, and limitedly by Muslims. This is a handy reference book for thousands of years guiding its Hindu followers in determining auspicious moments for important social and family events and activities. Some Muslims also used it for varied nonreligious purposes. I used it to assess forecasts for the weather (heat, humidity, etc.) including rainfall and flood for determining the time of sowing or transplantation.

When I first started farming in the land of Babu Bijon Mohan Nag, I found him always consulting the *panjika* regularly in guiding me in determining the type and variety of crops in assessing rainfall, heat, and humidity, etc. I found that very helpful and followed the practice. For updated information, I continued my regular contacts with TAEO. These helped me enormously in many respects. The attainment of social prominence was an unintended benefit.

My social prominence had a most welcome benefit in augmenting greater social contacts. People slowly started visiting me regularly. Firoza's unceasing efforts to entertain them with snacks and drinks contributed positively. The house and the family quickly earned an unmatched social distinction.

In such background, one of my friends suggested the need to get Boro Mia married as he was twenty years old. Before I could respond, others present in the deliberations supported the proposition.

I also started feeling positively about the suggestion as I too got married at about the same age. But there were two constraining factors. Boro Mia had no interest in farming. In addition, his academic attainments were mediocre. Contrary to my expressed desire, he discontinued didactic pursuits after high school. Though Boro Mia was lazing away time without any meaningful engagement, he exhibited exceptional competence in handling family irritants and social banes. He demonstrated ease, ability, and command while communicating with many at the same time.

I was engrossed in thinking through options for Boro Mia's progression before getting him married. During this phase, I had to visit the Office of Thana Land Registrar, popularly known as *Tashilder*'s office. This is a very prominent government outfit at Thana level. Its importance was magnified by the sheer reason of the paucity of land and overt efforts to register land holdings to establish rights. I was a frequent visitor to that office due to regular land-related transactions and had a good rapport with successive *Tashilders*, more pertinently the current one in position for good number of years.

In the course of the discussion during the latest visit, I was told about a position created in the office due to the increase in land documentation work as the offshoot of the abolition of Zamindari (permanent settlement system introduced by the British government) years back, an evidently high-priority job neglected so far. Taking advantage of my cordial relationship with the *Tashilder*, I requested him to consider Boro Mia for the position. Fortunately for the family and my own prestige, the response was a spontaneous positive one.

To my great delight, Boro Mia joined the position. My social relevance swelled due to twin factors of land holdings and my son being a functionary in a government outfit.

With that backdrop, I raised the issue of Boro Mia's marriage with Firoza. She was more enthusiastic than I ever thought of, and as always, she stressed, referring to her recent weak health, an inner inkling to see and play with a grandchild.

Boro Mia's wedding was done in a manner and a scale unthinkable to his deceased parents and was gregariously gratifying for us.

Firoza was not only ecstatic but also demonstrated, to the happiness of all, steeled demeanors in moves and actions after her protracted ailment.

Happenings causing unceasing happiness were recurring in my life in a routine manner. The capping was the birth of our first grandchild within about eighteen months of Boro Mia's wedding. I did not lose time in naming the newborn to avoid what happened in the case of his father. I fondly named him Ziyauddin Abbassuddin Azeem without giving any chance to anyone. The name that triggered in my mind, always aspiring for a grandson, was Ziauddin Azeem. Sudden embryonic thinking propelled the insertion of my name, Abbassuddin, in between the first and last name. To my mind, there were at least two solid basis for such an insertion. The first one was a sort of selfish desire of mine to be in circulation even after my death. But the second one was very important and genuine, assimilating the newborn to my pedigree, compensating for the lack of blood links.

Everyone was happy. The Muslim religious rite of *Aqeeqa* (consists of giving a name to the newborn and offering a sacrifice) was duly performed to the delight of Azeem's parents and Firoza. Its ramification was much greater and bigger as it was the event marking two Aqeeqas, the other one was for Azeem's marginally elder cousin sister, Julaikha.

Julaikha was the first child of my third son. Her mother was a casualty of childbirth complications and died soon after Julaikha was born. Many in the family casually voiced blame on Julaikha (a superstitious practice) for her mother's death, and she was being referred to as a bad omen.

Firoza acted quickly and determinedly. She was openly critical of near and dear ones suspected of fostering blame on Julaikha for her mother's death. Firoza took all responsibility to rear up baby Julaikha and brought her to our *haveli*. Because of her actions, the murmur died down before gaining any footing.

The house was full of joy and happiness. Momentarily, I lost an inkling of other plausible breadths of life. That did not last long. Soon the inevitable happened. Boro Mia was required to go to the district tehsil office. After finishing the official assignment, he, in eagerness to be with his family, took the last bus for Massumpur even though the weather was bad.

Halfway through, the weather worsened beyond comprehension. Rain was heavy and incessant. The wind velocity was intense. The visibility was very poor. The rudimentary only right headlight, the other one being nonfunctional, was of little help.

The driver was, however, nonchalantly continuing the journey relying on his familiarity with the route and the muddy road. Most bus passengers kept their eyes closed, some to escape the fear and most others praying to Allahpak for safe travel.

There was a huge thunderstorm nearby. That coincided with the fall of a big uprooted tree on the left side of the road. To avoid a disastrous collusion, the driver quickly maneuvered the steering wheel for the right while placing a foot on the brake. And that caused the disaster. Instead of the brake, the driver impetuously pressed the accelerator, and the bus, propelled by the slippery, muddy road condition, hit one the big wayside *korai* tree. Many were injured, but some also succumbed to death. Boro Mia, sitting on the front seat as a privileged passenger being a government functionary, was one of the deceased.

Sadness overwhelmed my surroundings. Within a split second, all joyous reflexes around were frozen, and stillness permeated our thoughts and actions. The only meaningful deviation was the initiative of Firoza in lifting the crawling Azeem and making arrangement to feed him.

A special person was sent early that morning to the place of Boro Mia's in-laws with responsibility to convey the grievous news. The news shocked the family and stunned the relations and neighbors. Close family members closeted themselves in a room to map out the best course of action. There was consensus in no time. It was decided to send a set of senior relations to Boro Mia's house immediately as an appropriate demonstration of sharing the grief and to send a definite message to their daughter in utter distress.

I just could not say anything assuaging to our *Bou-ma* (daughter-in-law) while preparations were afoot for the burial of Boro Mia.

She was standing static, reclining angularly with the support of one of the entry door post. The only perceptible feature was the rolling down of unending tears overflowing the cheeks of her distraught face.

A set of eight family members of Bou-ma arrived just before the burial. Seeing Father stepping in our courtyard, Ayesha, wife of Boro Mia, lost all senses, rushed toward the father with the accompanying howling, and lost her balance in the embrace of Father, shivering incessantly all through.

Shocked and shattered, Father had no words to console Ayesha. Female family members came forward, took charge of Ayesha, and escorted her to inner space of the *haveli*, consoling and nursing her simultaneously.

In my short discourse, I told Ayesha's father that the outburst of Bou-ma was needed very much as she had been keeping mum all through since last night. It should work as a therapy for her.

During subsequent discourses with Ayesha's father and other relations, matters pertaining to her future life came up repeatedly. Finally, her father made a passionate submission to take away Ayesha to her paternal home, emphasizing that "she is too young to lead a life of widow." His final point highlighted the reality. My own feelings had repeated inquisitions as to what I would have done in the circumstances had she been my daughter. Finally, it was agreed that after some days, Ayesha would leave her home for her parental house while we would have the custody of Azeem, being the son of Boro Mia. That is the saga of Azeem, who grew up as one of us.

As Azeem passed the phase of early childhood and growing up under the passionate care of Firoza and the loving company of Julaikha, I was overwhelmed by problems created by our youngest son, Rakib.

Firoza had been a wonderful life companion for me, supporting me in all my endeavors. But when it was a matter involving Rakib, she was sort of blindfolded. She did not see any wrong in the doings of Rakib. More consequentially, she used to funnel little money to Rakib from time to time, assuming that I was unaware of it. In my long married life, I was for the first time in such a situation of discomfort. Any of my mild observation and reference to Rakib's negative or wrongdoing was always matched by a vociferous retort of Firoza. I started withdrawing from and avoiding such discourses. Nevertheless, the inherent discomfort as a consequence of my most promising son's negligence and lack of purpose continued to bother me intensely. My earnest desire of having a prudent offspring with intelligence and discernment has become a mirage for me.

My problem was I had no one to share this agony in an otherwise blissful life of mine. I stopped chasing the desire.

During this time, I was in need to get some legal advice on a proposed land-related deal.

All of a sudden, I recalled the Hindu lawyer of Babu Bijon Mohan Nag who, unlike many Hindu populace, stayed back in Bangladesh.

Though not involved anymore in active law practice, he graciously consented to meet me. At the end of our discussion, I raised the dilemma I was having concerning Firoza's deflectory responses to my occasional queries about Rakib and the latter's unfamiliar reactions typifying stubbornness and arrogance.

The lawyer, Ukil Debnath Bashu, kept quiet for a while, closed his eyes, and had a passionate look at me after opening those. He took his time and observed, saying, "My response has two parts. First, life itself is a uniquely complicated experience. That, among others, also applies to relationships. Our relationships take unpredictable turns at every bend. There is no doubt that your wife continues to love you, but that has a small catch with significant reflective allusions. Your wife's love for you has been overtaken by her concern for your well-being. She perhaps is convinced that your lack of total happiness is due to the erratic behavior pattern of your son, Rakib. Your wife is trying to address that problem by bequeathing unconditional love and support to win the confidence of your son, ultimately to bring him into line. You will discover apparently missed elements of love if you look at reasons for her concerns. Second, it is very common in our social system for a mother to be more tolerant, understanding, and accommodating in the case of a child, more a son, who is relatively less successful in life irrespective of inherent potential.

A mother's frustration and empathy usually are manifested through apparent indulgence without any thinking about implications. Your wife is exactly doing that. And that is not uncommon."

With those eclectic assessment and related feedback, I came back with a consolation assuming the present experience as of temporary occurring. Still I could not help but thinking about life's dealings consequent to Rakib turning the wrong way. That came into prominence the next winter after seasonal harvesting was over.

Visits to productive agricultural areas like Massumpur by popular Jatra (groups presenting open-air melodramatic shows) parties after each harvesting season was a time-honored cultural tradition of Bengal, as it was known before 1947. That continued in Bangladesh in a minuscular fashion against the backdrop of migration major patrons (Hindu landlords and business elites) as well as stiff competition from the movie industry.

Jatra has had its root in the Sanskrit drama performance under the Gupta Empire in fourth century CE. As a performance presentation, Jatras included various forms such as a narrative, a dance and song, a supra-personae, scroll paintings, puppet theater, etc. In some areas, the presentation of processional forms also became a part of Jatra.

The courtyard of rich people, temple areas, sports fields, and annual mela (exhibition) locations are the normal venues for a fixed period.

Though mobile, it was a least cost operation as the presentation is held in flat surface of open space with the audience seating around the stage. Loud music and high-pitch oration by the *Odhikari* (producer/manager-cum-narrator, and also spelled as *Adhikari*) were the highlights to energize the audience. Odhikari's main onus was to link songs and scenes in an attempt to keep interest of the audience alive.

The instruments normally used were *dholak* (two-headed hand-drum), *Mandira* (a pair of metal bowls to enhance rhythm effect), *karatal* (wooden clapper with 'kara' standing for hand and 'tala' meaning clapping), and khol (folk percussion instrument).

Its forms and presentations changed with the passage of time and in response to the need for survival. The important elements were greater female participation, the staging of relative current epics, and the increase in frequency of dances and popular songs.

Like previous years, Massumpur was to host a renowned Jatra party in about two months' time following Dada-ji's discussions with Ukil Debnath Bashu. It transpired in the society soon that the prodigious popularity of this Jatra party was mostly predicated on the presence of a number of young performing girls. The one performing *Bandhana*, a solo dance recital before the actual play by the most attractive and professionally competent dancer of the party, had particular prominence. The dance performance, being a fairly long one with the dancer's competence to communicate with the audience through eye and lip movements, was the center of attraction. That was especially applicable for the younger audience in the accompanying mix of cheery lexes of the elders and the giggles of ladies. Those elements were regular topics drawing the interest and attention of the elderly and young alike but from different perspectives. Dada-ji was aware about the publicity elements of this visiting Jatra party too.

Rakib, young and carefree, was popular among his friends. He was physically attractive, with a very passionate voice adulation, and mostly played a lead role in discussions and negotiations on behalf of his group. His financial liquidity, through the unabated indulgence of Mother, was an additional factor. He was told about hearsay centering the *Bandhana* dancer by his trusted friend Sobhan. The latter subsequently told Dada-ji all that happened.

Sobhan stated that knowing about the budding and sublime interests of Rakib in cultural activities and performances, friends prevailed upon him to be present in the opening show.

The Jatra audience normally sit on spread-out straws for their comfort in the winter while few chairs are placed at the center of the seating place for the important local people and the invited government functionaries. Rakib not only attended the opening show but also managed a seat among the special seating arrangements for local gentries.

Sobhan finished his report by observing casually, "Rakib's friends were ecstatic seeing him in that setting, but to most others, it was discomforting to see a young lad among socially acclaimed gentries."

Rakib was totally indifferent about the surroundings. He was more annoyed due to time being taken to commence the show. By the time Odhikari finished his long oration, all surrounding lights were turned off, to the further annoyance of Rakib.

The preordained was manifested with the focusing of the high-powered electric light on the beautiful ankle and decorated feet of the damsel with the sound and symmetrical rhythm of the *nupur* (musical ornament for the feet). That light focus remained unchanged, the rhythmic sound of the *nupur* continued unabated with the delicate positioning of the feet while other instruments joined, making the accompanying music louder and more pungent. Rakib was stunned seeing the beautiful feet and their musical intuition. Noticing that raptness, I moved close to him and whispered, 'Her name is *Bijli* (lightning).' He just nodded his head. Continuing his unbridled attentiveness on her feet, Rakib was eagerly awaiting to have the full silhouette of the dancer.

And that happened soon but after a lurid narration by the Odhikari grounding the backdrop of the next move of the dancer with a significant mellowing of musical buzzes. This was followed by the gradual enhancement of instrumental intones and the speedier matching moves of the feet. The light was repositioned from the knee to the upper chest, creating beguiled expectations in the surroundings. At this phase, three varied actions mesmerized the audience present. Those were: the brash shaking of the upper body of the dancer with the full focus of light, the blaring pitch of music, and the sudden lifting of light focusing on the face with the synchronized action of the dancer throwing off her facial cover piece, almost like *orna* (similar to mantilla). The audience was exhilarated. Some took a sudden standing posture while clapping incessantly.

That quiet rural setting presumed all imperative syndromes of wild expectations with the coherent deepening of night, enhanced winter coldness, and increased darkness. The main lights surrounding the venue mostly focused on the actors and their movements. Bijli, in that milieu, unleashed herself in a most provocative manner.

But that was not all. Having the light on her full body and shaking all gorgeous and stimulating body features rudimentarily imitating the movement, motion, speed, and pattern of classical Indian *kathak* dance, she engaged herself right from the beginning to allure the audience with suggestive movements of her eyes and lips. That thrilled the male audience while the female attendees were mostly hiding their face with the extended cover of *anchal*, tail end of saree."

In his continuing narration to Dada-ji, Sobhan, however, was as factual and candid as he stated, "Rakib, however, was in a different world and mood. For him, Bijli was an instant hit and the center of his dedicated attraction. Though an adored young man of the surrounding, he became unwittingly vulnerable to her beauty and grace, murmuring within that 'It is you I have had been waiting for so long.'"

Besides being smart and handsome, he was intelligent enough to conclude that any direct approach to Bijli is both improbable, impractical, and futile compounded by time constraint of the party's short stay. Rakib winked to one of his trusted associate and whispered to get the preliminary information about Odhikari.

During the intermission, a movie showing the style practice adopted in the current Jatra staging and schedule to keep it modern, Rakib was briefed about Odhikari: With formal name of Probir Mitra, he was from an influential Hindu family of Comilla and a long-term spinster. Theatrical virtuosities and related activities, especially Jatra, are his passion with an equal liking of and enjoyment for drinks and damsels. That, over time, delinked him from his family, and Jatra became his life's focus and priority. Probir earned successive progression in planning, managing, and directing Jatras and soon became the Odhikari of the now famous Nandita Jatra Party (NJP) staging the show.

Backed by the intrinsic background details obtained through his associates, Rakib spent more time in thinking about the strategy. His priority undoubtedly was Bijli. Being intelligent and smart, he had clear feeling that the way to her was evidently cumbrous and time consuming. He opted for patience in place of speed and decided to focus on Odhikari. Rakib decided that if so warranted in that long-course approach, he would pressurize his mother for more money.

With that sort of mindset, he got a bottle of expensive local drink and then told his friends bye with a frivolous smile. Rakib kept on waiting until the show setting was stabilized and Odhikari took his seat to relax. As always, Sobhan was waiting in a nearby isolated place, keeping an eye on Rakib as per the trust reposed in him by Mother.

Taking cautious but equally courteous steps, Rakib stood in front of Odhikari. Without giving Odhikari any opportunity to react, Rakib promptly bent down, touched feet of the former, and blessed his own forehead with the supposed dust on the feet of Odhikari, a revered practice, known as *podo dhuli*, in Hindu culture.

Bewildered Odhikari, notwithstanding his well-known frivolous characteristics of communication, appeared to have lost his grip for a while. Instead of the usual practice of shrieking in the setting of his Jatra Party, Odhikari politely inquired as to the identity of Rakib and the objective of his presence since the show was over.

Ever vigilant, Rakib availed the opportunity to foster his objective and adroitly formulated a response to achieve Odhikari's trust. He answered, saying, "The fact is, not as vanity, I am the youngest son of most well-to-do Muslim gentry of the area and an ardent admirer of all cultural goings-on. I have seen many events including jatras but never saw something like your one before. Various aspects of your show, including vocalization and articulation of Bandhana and the interweaving of various segments were all well conceived, well coordinated, exquisitely rendered, reflecting a much superior level of planning, directing, and execution. I am so impressed that I just could not leave without personally acknowledging that to you. Hence, I stayed back to have much the desired audience with you in a private setting. As a token of my sincere feeling, I have this small bottle of drink for you. I will be obliged if you would kindly accept this."

Odhikari reacted saying, "In our business of entertainment, we meet many aficionados, but most of them had ulterior motives. You, in spite of your youth, are visibly different to highlight the fundamental attributes of our amusement endeavor. That was more striking as you are being from a Muslim background and an elite local family. It is now my turn to say that I will be honored if you would share a drink with me."

Rakib, upon returning, happily told Sobhan that "perhaps Odhikari has fallen into trap."

That drink sharing went smoothly, with Rakib taking the precautionary approach to limit his participation. Even at that young age, Rakib was certain that any unguarded move might derail him from reaching his ultimate goal of Bijli's embrace. Odhikari, being intoxicated by the successive services and the very high performance rating of the show in its first performance here, was in a mood to continue. Rakib insightfully avoided additional services and left with the promise to come back following evening.

He did so in successive nights with three specific practices: he always brought a new bottle of drink, he never mentioned Bijli in discourses, and he kept his meeting relatively short, focusing the discussions more on Odhikari's talent and competence. That bonded them very tenderly despite their age and occupational deviations.

That had a solid imprint in Odhikari's mind. In occasional exchanges with the jatra party functionaries, he continued to eulogize Rakib's focus on matters contrary to standard ones like access to acting or an association with girls. That impressed all but not Bijli. In her mind, it appeared to be conflicting with what she observed in his reactions on the maiden night of the show. Unlike others, Bijli was more surprised knowing that Odhikari invited Rakib to be with the Jatra Party in the proposed mega show at Lakhsham. She preferred to keep quiet.

Rakib's happiness that night was due to his ability to win over Odhikari, his continuing interest in Bijli, and the rendering of the Jatra party.

Sobhan was cognizant of the fact that as the youngest offspring of an affluent family, Rakib sustainably exhibited an interest and eagerness for activities related to the arts and culture. That brought him back to Massumpur and his discontinuing higher education beyond the intermediate level in Comilla College. That was against the serious persuasion of his close roomie, Mafeez, an ardent activist in student politics. That decision of Rakib did not surprise Sobhan at all, and the latter made all efforts to sincerely mitigate the frustrated feelings of parents.

On his return to Massumpur, Rakib was mostly present in varied local events and performances in multifarious capacities: as a facilitator, as a patron, as a sponsor, and so on. Thus, though unexpected, the invitation from Odhikari to be in Lakhsham as part of the party pleased him enormously.

Thinking about Lakhsham and the super opportunity to be close to Bijli, he accepted the invite without further wavering. He made every effort to squeeze as much money from Mother as he could, putting the additional reason of taking Sobhan with him.

During the journey process, Odhikari was deliberating on the importance of the upcoming show, and linked the same with political ambition of an upcoming local leader by the name Mafeez Mia. The latter sponsored the Jatra performance as pseudo part of his broader political ambition.

Reference of Mafeez Mia triggered old memory in Rakib of his roommate in Comilla College hostel by the same name with the location coincidentally at Lakhsham periphery. He was fondly hoping that it would be the same Mafeez Mia. A possible meeting with the roommate became an additional allure for the trip. The prospect of reuniting with the forgotten friend and roommate thrilled Rakib. In his inner mind, he took that as an ordained opportunity for him in achieving the cherished hidden objective of being close to Bijli. Outwardly, Rakib opted to be cautious and responded, saying, "I too had a college friend by the same name from Lakhsham area. Since it is a very common name, I would refrain from any observation." That was all planned by Rakib to have full tremble and ecstasy to win over Odhikari. And that happened exactly as he thought of.

The reunion was wonderful. The reaction of Mafeez Mia was full of emotions and reminiscence, thanking Odhikari copiously. The one of Rakib was boisterous, expressing gratitude generously. Odhikari was enjoying self-serving pleasure as the mastermind of the event, cementing his relations with Mafeez Mia and having the trust of Rakib. Both of them took the time to settle down while Odhikari was beaming with self-assured confidence.

With snacks served at the behest of Mafeez Mia, all the three got engaged in having them. Both Odikhari and Rakib profusely thanked Mafeez Mia for the elaborate snack arrangement for the Jatra Party as a whole. Odhikari took the chance of the most unexpected congenial setting to highlight his inner feeling. He quipped, saying, "Jatra, though a traditional form of genuine imaginative virtuosity, is struggling for survival in the face technological competition and its facet of market. Patrons like Mafeez Mia and ardent enthusiasts like Rakib can help it to survive."

While tea was served to Rakib and the host, Odhikari was enjoying his locally made alcoholic drink. Rakib had some interesting queries about that drink. Odikhari responded to some of them while for others decided to give a chance to Rakib to have his own answers and conclusions by testing it. That served the intended purpose after initial services. But more importantly, it contributed to the cordial and open interactions between the two, with Mafeez Mia continuing to sip his tea. Ignoring the latter's presence, both started talking about sensory matters with the proliferation of laughter as if they had known each other for a long time.

That did not last long. Life's inexorable reality eclipsed the hilarious ambiance suddenly. The most unexpected thing happened to the utter dismay of all three present. Odhikari's assistant showed up with the catastrophic news of the hero of the play having an attack of cholera. There were hardly eight working hours left before the scheduled maiden staging at Lakhsham. The resultant worries were of equal significance in terms of publicity and goodwill. Implication wise, it was grievous for both Odhikari, the man in charge of Jatra, and that of Mafeez Mia, the local elite who sponsored the Jatra with public relations as priority.

Right at the moment, the golden saying "every dark cloud has a silver lining" came in to rescue. Odhikari's first and major decision was to keep the news secret. Dispatching the assistant with that directive, he continued focusing charismatically on Rakib with newfound attractions premised on latter's smartness, build, skin tone, hairstyle, and theatrical voice articulation.

Spontaneity was the hallmark of Odhikari's next move, to the surprise and shock of other two. Placing his drink glass on the side of the lone table, Odhikari knelt on the ground, held the two hands of Rakib, and repeatedly asked for his consent, help, and cooperation in that hour of tribulations. Being unsure, Mafeez Mia inquired as how they could be of any help.

Odhikari sobbed and said, "What I have in mind not only helps me in staging the play tonight, it would also help you in your long-term political strategy. So you too should join me in requesting Rakib's help." Saying those few words and keeping his focus on Rakib without wavering, Odhikari narrated his game plan, saying, "The sudden cholera ailment of the hero is not known to any. Nor does anyone here know Mr. Rakib. The latter fits in very well in the role of play's hero by all attributes. If he agrees, I would do everything within my competence and capacities to prepare him for the night. We still have some hours. I plan to spend first one hour to explain the play's context and the character, the next four hours for two slots of rehearsals, and the last hour to expose Rakib Shaheeb to the moments of disarray and the ways to handle them related to theatrical performance. I am certain I can prepare him for the role. In my first exchange, he attracted me, but his probable involvement in jatra play was never in my thought. Now I need a decision soonest. Otherwise, I will have to defer staging for an indefinite time depending on variable alternatives. This has major financial implications also."

Mafeez Mia listened intently, exchanged looks with Rakib sporadically, and found merit in whatever was stipulated by Odhikari. He also found good reasons for Rakib to make a try as in real life he was not doing anything meaningful. Mafeez Mia took no time to double down what was proposed by Odhikari.

Rakib, having an interest and involvement in artistic activities, always had subdued and fastidious interests in acting. The lack of self-confidence and absence of opportunity precluded possible induction. Prior to that instant proposition, Rakib had some good discussions on dramatic matters with Odhikari and was convinced about the latter's talent, expertise, competence, and confidence, so after a brief consultation with Sobhan, he readily agreed. The process begun with no loss of time under the enthusiastic guidance of Odhikari.

That initiation was smooth. The preparedness was more than expected. Odikhari said he himself would do prompting, and in case of unexpected inadequacy, Rakib should move around the setting with the immediate past dialogue. The message would be loud and clear, and Odhikari would repeat the missing dialogue forcefully.

In that situation, the piece of guidance Rakib received from Odhikari was incredible in terms of generating a perceptible self-assurance. Odhikari said, "Always bear in mind that once you are on the stage and the screen has either been drawn or lifted, you are the one in charge. Through your articulations and deliberations, you can make your audience giggle and shriek at the same breath. On the stage, you are not acting but depicting reality as visualized in the script. Whatever you say is part of dialogue, and whatever you do is part of acting. So, if you can't get my prompting properly any time, move around the space and murmur but do never look back or side wise for help."

The joining of the Jatra play by Rakib was evidently coincidental. His subsequent appearances in the same play and role at varied locations were conditioned by the unexpected demise of the original actor and the need to allow the Jatra Party to fulfill its contractual obligations for staging the play at various locations during the season. That was the combined outcome of the alluring proposition by Odhikari and the initial sustained persuasion by Mafeez Mia.

Right from night one, Rakib was a success story. He was happily assimilated in the Jatra Party sooner than expected. Fame, recognition, and the sustained flow of money due to enhanced popularity of the play, triggered mainly by his presence and performance, contributed to that outcome. But the inmost equation for Rakib's current immense liking of and commitment to the norms of this jatra party, *based on his attractions for Bijli*, remained absolutely private.

His enhanced popularity made access to drinks and damsels, the unfulfilled longing and weakness so far in life, easy for him. It gave him immense pleasure observing that the usual traffic of desires for companionship with female artists just reversed in his case. Even

215

the one like Bijli, for whom he was initially motivated to join the jatra party, came to join on the second post-play night informal gathering of artists, and sat by his side, nonchalantly placing her one thigh partially on his adjacent thigh. The signal was loud and clear. That made Rakib exalted.

Odhikari was aware of these, and being shrewd and smart, relaxed his own rules pertaining to intra-artist relationship to ensure that Rakib remained happy, enabling the Jatra Party to sail through the season. Indirectly that made everyone happy and contented.

Within a short passage of time, Rakib showed mettle in handling multifarious responsibilities besides being an actor, and started exercising ostensible management and organizational functions.

Having gained confidence and being aware of the need for a prolonged stay, he sent back Sobhan with a good amount of money for Mother. As a prudent young man, he did not fail to reward Sobhan for his time and companionship.

Sobhan did not fail in telling Rakib's mother all that was needed to positively portray Rakib's current accidental involvement and the stupendous success in Jatra. He also marginally referred to Bijli.

Though from a conservative background, Mother did not see anything wrong in Rakib's accidentally getting involved in Jatra. In a sense, she was happy for Rakib being an emerging success story. With that mindset, she did open up before her husband in no time. But the response took her aback.

In her later thought through narration to Sobhan, the mother lamented by saying, "Your uncle's immediate reaction was not a positive one. With frustration mirrored on his face and in eyes, he reacted saying, 'In my contented life, blossomed by your presence and participation, the only frustrating point is my son Rakib. Being outstanding on most counts, he suffers from one pertinent inadequacy—the lack of focus in life. He thus is wasting lot of his potentials. My previous efforts, within the frame of parental love and care, failed to mend those. He is now grown up and emotionally beyond my reach. I do not need his money. You keep them separately to meet the unanticipated challenges in his future life. Pertinently, I am also aware of

Bijli and her background. I only hope she would be able to keep him on track of a meaningful life.'

In a latter conversation, I advised Firoza to consider resending Sobhan to be around Rakib and keep an eye on him so that we have a reliable source to know about Rakib's well-being."

That was done easily as Sobhan's father was the family's share-cropper. In later life, Sobhan became the only continuous source of information pertaining to Rakib and Bijli.

Time passed happily for Rakib. His relationship with the family remained normal even though the warmth was fading and the con-tact gaps were increasing. The Jatra Party became his family and the center of all concerns and actions. Unexpected, and more than the normal turnaround phenomena caused a quick rotation of artists. That made Rakib's involvement in management matters common and, after some time, absolute, more due to gradual slowing down by Odhikari.

Rakib, though he grew up as an unfocused young fellow, showed an extraordinary ability in shaping up his future after joining the Jatra Party and enjoyed a quixotic intimacy with Bijli. Though he had occasional secrecies with other party girls of his choice, Bijli had a permanent impression in his mind and thoughts almost akin to his first impression. With the passage of time, that liking bonded them very firmly.

That was a strange phenomenon. Bijli had loving and warmer relationships with Odhikari and the second son of the owner of the Jatra Party (the investor), besides Rakib. The latter was aware of it as Bijli too was aware of Rakib's sexual indulgences.

The unexpected uncertainties premised on the unsettling recent phenomena of quick artist transition and the helplessness that created made both Odhikari and Rakib dependent on each other. Likewise, it was clear to both Rakib and Bijli that their present prominence in the arena NJP had no foundation of its own except attractiveness, performance, popularity—all finally judged by the inflow of mone-tary returns measured by the whistles, clapping, and screams during the show. The related obsequious elements were pertinent so long one was valued and could draw audience. The inevitable declining reality over the passage of time was familiar to both, but they brushed that off as being too early.

They took refuge within the umbrella of their mutually supportive relationship to remain where they were. With the passage of time, that relationship rapidly turned into quixotic feelings. The base of that emotional feeling was accentuated by a candid impression about the implications of the decisions of Odhikari and the investor's son on the sustenance of their future and success in Jatra world.

But neither of them had any inkling that such apprehensions can unexpectedly become realities too. That happened with the sudden decision to relegate Bijli from the pivotal role of *Bandhana* performer.

Though a shock for Bijli per se, it was a wake-up call for Rakib too. They kept quiet, retreated deep, weighed consequences, and decided, assuring each other about mutual feelings and trust, to keep low. Their consensus was that by playing such a role, Rakib still remains relevant within the management and can influence decisions in some cases. The visible utilization of his skills in planning, organizing, directing the plays, and his ability to assign proper roles to proper artists, besides his proficiency to perfectly carry out the critical role of a prompter, as were done during recent frequent indispositions of Odhikari, made Rakib have renewed belief in himself. He likewise advised Bijli to look for expertise in addition to dancing, and without any wavering, suggested she exploit the area of fashion and costume, for which she had an inborn talent and in which the Jatra Party had explicit deficiency. During this period of irritation and transition, both became emotionally attached to each other and were more open in sharing their hopes and agonies. As a strategy, and with the consent of Rakib, Bijli paid enhanced attention in warming up his relations further with Odhikari and the investor's son without making complaints and exhibiting outward annoyance.

As the time passed, both were of the view that their designed strategy yielded positive results even though short of original expectations. There was no apparent domino effect. Outward peace and happiness were demonstrated by both while concealing persistent anxieties.

That exactly was not symmetrical to the thinking on the other side of the aisle. Both Odhikari and the investor's son met frequently and were discussing options in handling Bijli and Rakib, who could, due to their current popularity and professional competence, challenge management at any opportune time. They were thinking of an appropriate space and opportunity to throw out them off the circuit.

In the midst of such a capricious environment pertaining to professional relationship, Bijli, to the anxiety and surprise of all three close to her, confessed about her unexpected pregnancy. She, with certainty, traced its link to the merriment and drinking on the moon-lit night about two and a half months back, celebrating the successful closing of the party's twenty-fifth solo presentation.

Bijli, without hesitancy, stated that being intoxicated, she had no sense of propriety that night. Enticed with each gulp of drink, she was high in mood and responses. Bijli hazily recounted having sex with all three in different settings and variable times of the night. She elaborated, saying, "Notwithstanding the intoxication, I vividly enjoyed the most exceptional occurrence during those intercourses. I felt like, on all three occasions of that night, being slowly filled with something that caused immense pleasure and prickly feeling beyond stimulation and normal orgasm. That, to my utter joy, traveled from vagina down to lower nerves. Since that experiences, I have not had a period, and the *Mashi* (aunt), the elderly guardian lady of the Jatra party, is certain that I have conceived. I too do not have any doubt from the physiological indications but am uncertain about who of you three is the father."

Shrewd Odhikari, the ultra confident son of the investor, and the amorous actor-partner were all just immobilized at hearing that news, with their unfinished drinks remaining static.

The jatra's organizational frame and practices had outwardly been governed by specific rules and practices to gain the sanctions of its patrons and sponsors. Its operations and presentations had the highest esteem for decorum, more due to the varied nature of its staging as well as the sizeable presence of homely women in shows of Jatras.

But that was an exceptional night, one filled with sustained success, joy, and happiness. Rules and regulations pertaining relationships at various stages and levels of artists and operatives were negligently ignored. Unexpectedly, the domain of traditional requirements and practices was subsumed to be irrelevant due to the nature and setting of the celebration. No one among them had the mindset to contest or interfere. For the first two, Odhikari and the son of investor, it was a game enjoyment, taking advantage of position and power, and, for the third one, Rakib, it was the outcome of a professional relationship having the tint of romance. But the outcome was too gargantuan for each one of them from different perspectives, complicated by the involvement of all three major agents of NJP and the openness that characterized the actions during celebration event. There was no single one to be blamed, and there was nothing to hide. The eventuality, by all considerations, was too arduous to handle.

In a subsequent discussion between the two, Bijli told Rakib candidly that even though she had said so and there was a probability that her conception was due to sex with any of the three, it was her inner feeling that Rakib was the father of the child to be. She went on clarifying that "my interaction with the investor's son was at the height of the intoxication of us both, and he discharged prematurely. Odhikari approached and started playing with my vital physical organs leisurely after enjoying the new Bandhana girl, so he was tired and did not have the capacity and resolve to continue long. He too was off the play sooner than expected. I was totally frustrated, and my intoxication withered away in no time. With my sexual urge at its zenith, I went to you and got you triggered. Whatever I described to all of you earlier about intercourse-related stances was in fact pertained to this phase of sex with you. So I am of the view that it is you."

Bijli continued, saying, "You can, of course, ask me the premise of getting all three involved in the game play in view of my earlier assertion. The answer is very ingenuous and forthright. First, it definitely preempts any unpredictable adverse decision by the management pertaining to both or either of us centering my pregnancy, and second, it keeps them on their toes and shaky for some time. And we need that time."

The subsequent profound pronouncement of Bijli took Rakib by surprise when she said, "We know each other. We like each other. Of late, we started loving each other without reservations. We have a common commitment to sustain that. But always remember that in earthly matters, the female mind is more ingenious and travels much faster so one should not try to underrate that in the journey of life."

Explaining the background, Bijli continued talking to share a vital information in the process. In a remorseless tone, she said, "As the investor's son approached me for having sex against the known impression that I do not have liking for him, he softly touched my breasts and started playing with those. But I maintained a stiff posture even under intoxication. To win me over under that pressing desire, he took me to confidence and advised that I should better be away from you as your future in this Jatra party is tottering. He further assured me about his full support to reinstate me in the position of Bandhana performer."

Instead of sharing that information with Rakib immediately, Bijli pursued the allusion to ascertain its authenticity and gamut. She followed various possibilities in her own way and to the best of her understanding. After being convinced about the authenticity of the plan shared at vulnerable moment, she thought it appropriate to share it with him.

Rakib was not surprised at all for Bijli's pursuing such a critical hint singularly. He recalled that in a related discussion soon after his having the lead role position, and in a mood full of compassion and trust, Bijli said, "I know that I am gorgeous. I am aware about my talent in dancing as well competence in alluring the audience. But it is equally true that I also know and have the ability to protect my chastity under all pressures. This virtue is perhaps bestowed from Allahpak to protect me, who lost my mother while taking the first breath in this world. Allahpak is never that cruel to His creation. He compensates His creation in ways He thinks appropriate. I took note of your initial expressions and advances, but those did not trouble me at all. I have had been used to multilevel and multidimensional signals right from an early age, with my *Dadima* guiding me in every step and phase of life more openly and frankly. I learned the techniques of fortification as I was growing up. That was the reason I did not respond to any of your advances but definitely tried to keep you on the track based on inkling of possibility.

Besides Dadima, there are two additional individuals who taught me to think prudently, judge things pragmatically, and take decision objectively. The mid-aged geography teacher of our local school, popularly known as *Bhugal Sir*, had an avowed interest in music and the associated cultural activities. He was very close to my family and addressed *Dadima* as *Chachi Amma* (paternal aunt). My induction to dancing was at his behest under the earnest training protocol of the dance teacher, Shibnath Bishwash, a very closely associate of *Bhugal Sir*.

The venue of the training was our home. Dadima was always present and sometimes participated with trifling comments and suggestions. That distinguished her as an acclaimed elder compared to others of her age and position.

Our home had a unique background. Two of my *fuppis* (paternal aunt) were married to very deserving young fellows. The elder one was living in Australia with her family, and the second one, after short-lived conjugal living in California, got divorced, moved to Madison of Wisconsin and got married for the second time with an African-American physician.

The first fuppi, being engrossed with her own bulging family, had little time to touch base with her mother, my Dadima. The second Fuppi, since her second marriage with an African-American, a relationship still considered insupportable by most Bangladeshi families, chose a secluded life in the warm embrace of her physician husband. Both the daughters were, however, meticulous in remitting money every month for their mother.

That, however, was not the case with my father and his two junior siblings. My mother died while delivering me. Father got married a second time with the unmarried daughter of his office boss and remained, all his following life, an acquiescent life partner of his new wife, happily playing the role of a house husband. In the process,

Father almost abandoned me with the sweet justification of being looked after by the more compassionate and experienced *Dadima* (his mother). I learnt later that being a house husband and distancing from me were the two conditions he had to agree to get married, and Father did so. I never did blame him for that because he had no attachment to me except being my father. What pained persistently was the way he treated my existence as a disposable element for his future life of hope and expectation.

The other two uncles of mine systematically distanced themselves putting forward a number of excuses: the demands of their jobs, the uncertainties that hinge around, the liquidity factor, and so on. Their consistent position was that by not asking for any share of income from parental properties, they were supporting their mother and orphan niece. They were, however, always critical of Dadima's decision to allow me to learn dancing.

I really enjoyed learning dance. More pertinently, I liked in between commentaries regarding pitfalls that swarm the passage. At every opportune time, both the Bhugal Sir and Babu Shibnath Bishwash, my *guru* (revered dance teacher) made me aware of the slippages inherent in this journey. They always indirectly referred to the associated vulnerability, the emotional blackmail, the unrestrained openness, the propensity to seduction, the heightened dilation of romanticism, and so on to be watched and to be careful of. Those were enhanced very often by Dadima's commentaries, either in conjunction with those pitfalls or a solo rendering.

What, however, beguiled me was sudden statement of Dadima about her unfulfilled desire to learn dancing and her admission of taking advantage of accomplishing that desire through me. I was both charmed and proud. I took dancing as an inherited passion.

Time passed. I was growing up. Both my beauty and associated gossip became a subject of common interest. Dadima was nonchalant about that. With the feeling of bubbling youth, I started enjoying that hearsay.

The abode of my Dadima was her remembrance and pride. That was my identity being left out and forgotten by close ones of the family with varied reasonings. Even in that rural setting and adverse situation, the world just looked beautiful, and I was cautiously stepping in to enjoy that.

Then the most unforeseen thing befell on us. In the dry month of *Choitra* (second month of Bangla Calendar) experiencing unusual elevated heat, the abode of my Dadima was gutted totally.

The whole community showed up in no time. The people sharing distress and showing empathy were many. Corresponding views concerning the cause of the fire and what could have been done to mitigate the damage were as divergent as the onlookers and sympathizers were.

People were prompt in expressing sympathy and left promptly. Not a single soul expressed concern about the living of the revered widow lady and her growing granddaughter.

Upon his return from the indigenous *Maghrib* (evening time Muslim prayer) assembly, Bhugal Sir was taken aback, taking note of continued presence of Dadima's old sharecropper only. Clad in a *lungi* (akin to *sharong*) and covering the upper body with a tottering *gamcha* (hand-woven lengthy material mostly used to wipe the body), the sharecropper unhesitatingly offered his thatched home for the ladies, with him and his wife sleeping in the open outer space of the house as long as necessary.

Bhugal Sir had a real assessment of the community people by and large. Most of them were vocal and loud in articulating options but carefully avoided their own involvement, either physically or materially. To Bhugal Sir, as told later, the apparent destitute sharecropper sitting on the moribund branch of the burnt tree just epitomized an angel in that setting, offering everything he had, though nothing tangible.

Tormented by the community's failure and his inability to be of any help to the distressed family being from another place, Bhugal Sir was struggling for a temporary but satisfactory escape. As a motivating effort, *Bhugal Sir* mustered some courage to look at the sharecropper. In the process, he accidentally exchanged brief look with his loving Chaci Amma. To avoid looming embarrassment, he kept his face positioned down as a getaway.

Right at the moment, Bhugal Sir was dazed seeing the dance teacher Shibnath Bishwash approaching the gutted premise hurriedly with a lantern in his right hand and the clutch of loose dhuti ends in his left hand. Interestingly the lamp was emitting fairly less than the desired light, having more shadows due to the constant movement of hand along with other body parts. But that did not dampen the alertness and deter the speed of Shibnath.

Placing the lantern at a central position, Guru Shibnath Bishwash took his seat on a *mora* (an indigenous cane stool shaped round both at the top and bottom with a clinched midsection, and no back-rest), and requested for a glass of water. He finished that briskly and handed over the glass for retrieval.

That was a major happening in the setting of the community with the relationship being premised on religious differences. Likewise, it was a major variance in the life of Guru Shibnath Bishwash, being an ardent Hindu. Hindus generally considered Muslims as lower than untouchables, and taking food and drink in a Muslim abode was unthinkable.

Bhugal Sir knew all those and was bewildered when Guru Shibnath Bishwash requested water to drink. He refrained from making any query. Rather, in follow-on actions and words, he tried his utmost to deflect such references. Bhugal Sir quietly shared the quandary he was facing in finding a temporary shelter for the two ladies. He lamented the lack of positive response while most present were full of eulogizing expressions and unrestrained sympathy.

Listening to the frustrating narration, and equally burdened by a distraught feeling, Guru Shibnath Bishwash kept quiet for a while. He then unfastened his thoughts, saying hurriedly, 'You know that I was lucky in inheriting some property and a big house. I could not make much headway in life due to my irresistible liking for and bonding with attractions of cultural life.'

He continued saying, 'Dancing to the tune of music always mesmerized me. Even being a *dholak* player of the Jatra Party gave me enormous ecstasy. The combined loud music of popular jatra instruments like *dholak, Mandira,* and *karatal* always enchanted me beyond description. It was the failing health of Roma that eventually brought me back to living a life you all are familiar with. It was too late for me to start a stereotype life afresh. I thus opted for a modest and childless life taking care of Roma and playing *dholak* for my own pleasure. In the midst of that contented life setting, I was asked by you to be the dance teacher of Bijli. From day one, I bonded with Bijli. The eagerness and commitment demonstrated by her from the beginning were rare for even a girl from a Hindu family, forget someone from Muslim family background. I always thought that had I been lucky to have a daughter, she would perhaps be a facsimile of Bijli. So Bijli is my daughter. A fatherly impulse invigorated me.

Observing the lack of a specific response in support of these two ladies and proliferations of gratuitous advice, I just decided to act. We generally use two southern rooms of the house. The central one and three other northern rooms are mostly not used. It clicked in my mind to offer those northern rooms as temporary accommodation for the two distressed ladies with necessary logistic arrangements in place.

That positive desire faced an immediate negative reality: the in-depth and sensitive nature of Hindu and Muslim relationship. With that constraining feeling, I left the venue quietly to talk to Roma. She, all along, even in discourses with me, was relatively more liberal than many due to her upbringing as a child of an affluent family living in a mixed social setting. Her respect for me as a husband was enormous even though I failed on many scores miserably. It is, however, on the question of inter-faith amalgam, she openly criticized my very conformist Hindu views.'

Roma was more than willing to house them. Her quipped comment was that 'if Bijli and her grandma agree for relocation to a Hindu home, this property would get back its adrift vibration and life, even though temporarily.'

Guru Shibnath Bishwash continued, saying, 'With that backdrop, I am here, after completing arrangements for their stay in our shared accommodation, with an open heart and without any faith-related misgivings.'

That took Bhugal Sir by surprise. His relief was absolute and his happiness unbounded. The sharecropper fellow was bemused because of the persistent tension between Hindus and Muslims. It was difficult for him to swallow it.

Bijli and her Dadima had no luxury to think around the proposition. Dadima's immediate relief was in having a secure shelter for her grown up *natni* (granddaughter). Bijli's comfort in moving to the proposed place was her familiarity with the housemaster. The pressing necessity of life and being the only resort, the proposition had no inkling with faith and belief.

Life moved on pleasantly, and the extraordinary flexibility shown by Shibnath's family impressed both Dadima and the granddaughter. Roma inoffensively cemented the new relationship by addressing Dadima as her *Mami-ma* (maternal aunt).

Maintaining the mandated religious requirement of not mingling in respective food preparation and eating disciplines, they had a very warm and friendly living under the same roof. Both the families had a very respectful and responsive attitude to respective prayer practices.

Most of the time, their discussions were on neutral social matters, recounting living as experienced. Discussions in the presence and participation of Shibnath Bishwash were mostly on reminiscing his early life, his affluence and the indulgence he enjoyed, and his boisterous adult and early married life. In all related narrations, Shibnath Bishwash would reiterate unreservedly his gratitude to Roma for not abandoning him even though she had reasons to do so.

Roma, normally a shy and reticent individual, looked inquisitively at her husband, and then addressed Dadima, saying, 'Mami-ma, you please tell me as to the options I, for that matter any Hindu girl respecting religious injunctions and dictates, had in the circumstances. I outwardly maintained a nonreactive attitude but once broke down before Mother.

She implored that 'I should have patience as some men have the tendency to overreact to demonstrate their independence after marriage. That is more for the consumption of their friends and associates. You will see that sooner or later, *Jamai Babu* (son-in-law) will return to your lap. Remember always that for a married man, the ultimate destination is his own home.'

It so happened that the mother proved to be right. Roma continued saying, 'He acted independently but never ignored me. Even after joining the Jatra Party, he would frequently come back, spend nights in my warm embrace, inquired about any predicament, and took actions to make me happy. He astounded me when he left his favorite Jatra Party on being appraised of my twin emotional and physical illnesses and settled down in our abode to take care of me. Whatever normalcy you observe with respect to my health and emotions are the outcome of his efforts, care, and love. So the question of leaving him did never wink in my mind.'

The dance teacher, Shibnath Bishwash, was overwhelmed. Roma was relieved. Dadima was pleased. More importantly, Bijli thought through the experience and prudently internalized a lot of esteemed lessons.

The mutual liking and their bonding were premised on an unconditional feeling and empathy. That was more so due to one party's graceful inclination to have shelter in unknown home and the other party's alacritous to have within the same roof not only unknown but also believers of inimical religious identity.

Their happiness was burgeoned as preliminary work for reconstructing the burnt old house, in a relatively small scale mode made satisfactory progress under the joint efforts and supervision of both Bhugal Sir and the dance teacher as well as needed guidance of Dadima.

In that contented setting, their journey of life took a most bewildering turn, unsettling all assumed and planned equations. Dadima succumbed to a sudden dysentery attack.

The precipitousness of that tragic demise impeded the opportunity to know Dadima's desire and have guidance about the future of Bijli. No concrete and supportive response were received from any of her uncles. The youngest uncle even surprised all by referring to Dadima's recent act of bequeathing all ancestral property and the homestead favoring Bijli. According to him that act relieved them from further responsibility vis-à-vis Bijli.

In a follow-on discussion, it was agreed, as per the suggestion of Roma, to maintain status quo for some reasonable time and then think through options with the active involvement of Bijli. That was considered to be the most prudent arrangement as it would give Bijli time to adjust with reality.

But Roma's act on that night was the most beguiling one, making Shibnath eternally blissed and Bhugal Sir unboundedly obliged. During the long stay with Bijli on the day of Dadima's death, Roma extended all cordiality, giving her company, consoling her, helping her in having little food at night, and made arrangements for her needed sleep at night. Roma then returned to her portion of the home and sat down by the side of Shibnath as he was lying in the bed. He was awake but speechless, waiting for Roma also to lie on the bed for him to get updated.

But that was not what happened. Roma softly lifted her pillow and night spread and quietly left the room. She placed the pillow by the side of Bijli's one and silently slouched by the latter's side, pulling her close to chest and hugging her as if she was a mother helping the daughter to fall asleep. It was too much for Bijli. She started sniveling, thinking about her own mother and the warmth of feeling of the just deceased Dadima. In that embrace, she was overwhelmed, discovering a new bonding beyond blood and faith. That feeling and rapport continued unabated.

Guru Shibnath Bishwash was incessantly thinking about Bijli's future life. He desisted from raising the issue as it could be interpreted as being his unwillingness to house her anymore. Bhugal Sir refrained as he had nothing to suggest. That was aggravated by a lack of tangible responses from all others who mattered in her life. The father discharged his responsibility by stipulating an immediate marriage option for her and did not hesitate to give full authority to both Bhugal Sir and Guru Shibnath to negotiate one. He was nice enough, possibly by his screwed mind frame standard, assuring his presence at the wedding to bless Bijli on being informed timely. The youngest fuppi had encouraging words about her willingness to sponsor Bijli for migration to USA but simultaneously highlighted the time needed for completing the immigration process and her lack of education to be assimilated in the US systems. Roma was nonchalant about Bijli's future as she was enjoying the latter's presence and association. Her comfort level was palpable from the marked improvements in her emotional and physical health conditions. However, one pertinent issue continued to haunt Roma: what would happen to Bijli once she would not be there? Roma internally was in a state of doldrums.

That, however, was contrary to Bijli's fathom. She not only sensed but had a clear impression of reasons of why her well-wishers were encountering sustained tension. Both to remain courteous and clear, she was awaiting for an opportunity when all three would be present. And that happened soon.

Both Bhugal Sir and Guru Shibnath were together in the latter's residence and were engrossed in discussions. Bijli stepped in with eatables made by Roma-ma. Roma followed her soon with cups of tea and took a seat. The setting was ideal. Bijli acted promptly and prudently without thinking of aptness.

She spontaneously said that 'I am certain what is keeping you all unsettled since the demise of Dadima and the receipt of various responses from those who are my supposed blood relations. Irrespective of social imperatives, I would always value your opinions and your suggestions.

When it is discernible for me to take a decision about my life, you three would be the first one to know. Now relax and enjoy the eatables Roma-ma so lovingly prepared.'

Due to the steady migration of Hindu population over time, the social net of Guru Shibnath contact and communication was constrained significantly. That was additionally goaded due to the lack of offspring and his particular involvement in NJP during the youth. So visitors were few and far between.

The unexpected presence of a mid-aged unknown Muslim fellow calling Guru by name startled Roma-ma. Bijli, practicing assigned dance lessons with prominent oral sounds matching *tal* (bit) and *bhol* (rhythm) as well equally rattling sounds of *nupur,* was oblivious of the call outside. Roma-ma, being uncomfortable with unknowns, sent Bijli.

Bijli complied but in her dance outfit. The visiting gentleman was awed and at his wit's end. She met the visitor and received a letter from the Odhikari of visiting NJP after a gap. Bijli went back to her rehearsing after handing over the letter to Roma-ma.

Resuming rehearsal was not that easy for Bijli. She had many stipulations about that letter, but the prominent one was the possibility of an invitation to Guru to rejoin his old but now famous Jatra Party. She was feeling happy as that would allow her to witness jatras regularly.

The letter of Odhikari alluded to old association, and mentioned that his party was in nearby Shariatpur township after a considerable gap. The presence was for staging jatra shows as an added attraction for people to visit the local annual *mela* (exhibition). He then implored, for the sake of old association, that it would be wonderful if Shibnath and his family would be present on the inaugural evening as Odhikari's guests.

Shibnath was happy that an old friend remembered him with an invitation to be present in the opening show of his jatra, and that too with family. But both excitement and thrill were visibly lacking. That disappointed Bijli, her short-lived thought about witnessing the jatra more frequently mislaid.

The scene at Shariatpur was just the opposite. The bearer of the letter enthusiastically narrated his interaction with the girl in Shibnath's house, who, besides being primly young, was exquisitely attractive and appeared to be a good dancer. That was thrilling information for Odhikari. He paused for a while and then decided to visit Shibnath personally.

Odhikari acted on that the following day. In the midst of friendly reminiscing and warm rebonding, he carefully avoided any direct inquisition about the girl, his prime interest at that time as his Jatra Party was suddenly abandoned by their *Bandhana* dancer. Odhikari made his score by getting the commitment of Shibnath for the latter's presence in the opening show with the family. Odhikari did not default in specifically inviting Bhugal Sir, who incidentally was present during the visit. That gesture made a very pleasant impression in the mind of the latter.

Shibnath was hesitant to take Bijli to the jatra opening show. The other dictum was she could neither be alone in the house. In that disarray, Shibnath had unspoken exchanges with Bhugal Sir. After thinking a while, Bhugal Sir suggested that Shibnath should attend the opening show along with Roma *Bou-di* (sister-in-law) and Bijli, and he too would accompany them. His principal reasoning was it would be a desirable diversion at that time for the distressed Bijli.

Odhikari valued his associate's initial assessment about Bijli and harbored a favorable impression within. He was aghast seeing her on the inaugural night with Shibnath and family. The resultant penchant outshined the reality once he exchanged a few welcoming words with her. He was certain that the solution to his most pressing problem was in front of him. The issue was how to convince Shibnath and the family in reaching the goal. He thought of a number of ways forward, such as emphasizing the old friendship, highlighting the commonality in religious root with Shibnath, or stressing the critical need to save this traditional form of art rendering or the imperative need to encourage Muslim girls to get increasingly involved in art and culture, especially the jatra because of its rural setting and patronage. But most of them were rated as disjointed and too synthetic both in content and depth.

As Shibnath and family were awaiting in the private space of Odhikari's retiring room, the sounds of laughter and contentment from outside were overwhelming. Shibnath clarified that all these are signs of the super success of the show, and that Odhikari would be terribly contented.

Contrary to that expectation, all present were taken aback seeing Odhikari entering the space in a dejected mood. That was an outward manifestation of his hidden worries. Internally, he was attuning himself for a jatra type exposition: loud in volume, forceful in expression, and sincere in conveyance.

Odhikari slowly stepped in, stared at all present, remained repellent, and took a seat unexpectedly by the side Bhugal Sir. His follow-on histrionic performance bemused all present. The façade of Odhikari's face was suddenly swamped with tears, a position quite the opposite to the hilarious outside noise a few minutes back.

As baffled and nervous Bhugal Sir was trying to unearth the reason by inquiring and simultaneously consoling Odhikari, the latter burst into a loud swaying cry, stating, 'What many see in today's show as a success, I frightfully rate that as the beginning of the demise of what I built over the years. Besides story, dialogue, sets, costume, and acting, Jatra's success and sustenance mostly depend on entertainment, and *Bandhana* is the essence of that. On this critical point, my NJP is at the lowest ebb presently. The current uproar pertaining tonight's performance is a temporary phenomenon and will be washed away soon. Unless we can address this deficiency on a priority basis, my Jatra Party will be waning away in no time.'

He paused for a while and then resumed, saying, 'Your presence is a God-sent blessing for me. You can help me in this critical hour. I have a special knack and penchant for picking up diamonds out of both mud and sandy particles. Based on experience, I can see a lot of potentiality in the young girl in your company.'

Having said those unexpected words, he astounded all present by getting on his knees down on the floor and holding alternatively the hands of Shibnath and Bhugal Sir with persistent sobbing, begging for an endorsing response.

Shibnath, embarrassed and perturbed, slogged for a way out by assuring a response soonest. All the four politely left the place under the care of an escort provided by Odhikari in view of the hour of the night.

The follow-on discussion was both grim and tensed. Bhugal Sir emphasized the point of trust reposed in them by the late Dadima. Shibnath had his obvious reservations but equally had a compelling inner sympathy being an ex-performing member of the same Jatra Party. His silent sympathy for Odhikari was apparent. Roma-ma was deadly opposed to the propositions and emphasized the need to discuss the proposition with the father of Bijli. Discussions went on centering on aforesaid positions.

Unexpectedly, Bijli showed up and made a statement which was both polite and equally firm. She said, 'You all are discussing my future without my involvement. I respect you all but would like to say what I feel. I too think about my future independently. I do miss Dadima but am presently equally comfortable in the warm embrace of Roma-*ma* (mother), a mother I never had. Dadima groomed me very well. Guru has taught me about challenges of life. Roma-ma showed me the way to win over sensitive life issues. And what to tell about Bhugal Sir! He has taught me, by his words and actions, the value of compassion, love, and fellow feeling with sincerity and commitment. When it is imperative for me to take a decision about my life, you three would be the first one to know. I sincerely reassure you about that.

I treasure my relationship with you all. I am still breathing and have dreams about life though being a daughter abandoned by her father and a child abandoned by the family. I grew up carefree under the shadow of Dadima. I am growing up more carefully since her demise. The persistent concern of Bhugal Sir, the sustained alertness of *Guru-ji* (revered teacher), and the assiduous love and warmth of feeling of Roma-ma are guiding me in all my thoughts and contemplations.

The present issue pertains to a decision needed on the proposition floated by Odhikari last night. I know that you all have been deliberating on that as my well-wishers and guardians by default. I too evaluated the same whole last night. I overheard some of the points you exchanged in this sitting.

Evaluating all those and reflecting my own choice and preference, I urge you all to keep your trust on me and convey affirmatively to Odhikari, having the binding of prudent stipulations that you consider appropriate. Those may include but not necessarily be limited to privacy, security, emoluments, and the periodic access to you all. Your affirmative actions will give me much pleasure and help me in learning to take care of myself in your absence.'

Listening to all these, Bhugal Sir almost closed the discourse, saying, 'What Bijli just said has all imperatives for a thoughtful decision by us. She has grown up. Her just finished words and statements are ample proof of that. We are not her legal guardian but well-wishers only with additional implied responsibility in the absence of near ones. So I think we should shake off all inhibitions, allow her to do what she wants with careful advice and stipulations. I have trust in her ability, but my worries are on different score. Higher level Jatra people like Odhikari are men of art and culture, adored generally by all. But once intoxicated, they lose all senses and find justification for all acts and exploits. In formulating conditions to be complied with by Odhikari, we should keep this in view as well stipulating Bijli's involvement for two years only. That is a good time frame for finding a new Bandhana dancer.'

Having detailed all these, Bijli looked at Rakib with all passion and intensity and continued, stating, 'The rest of the story is simple and short. I landed in Odhikari's Jatra Party (NJP) soon, and brought rejuvenated fame and popularity to the party and its show. And there you met me.

The last point I want to make, and that too for my satis-faction, is about my chastity. I maintained my plainness in the midst of pressure, allurement, and provocation true to my teach-ings and the words I gave to my patrons. The only exception was the night of celebration. I fell prey to the evident evil-de-signed plan to mix orange juice with a trifling helping of vodka to be served during the merriment. I started liking the supposed orange drink service without knowing about the mix of vodka and was oblivious of consequences. That was how I got derailed on that night. And the consequence is my pregnancy.'

After detailing all that needed to be told to put Bijli in her proper pedestal and highlighting Rakib's devotion in alleviating the latter's distress, Dada-ji hit the bottom, saying, 'Bijli delivered on time a striking baby son, and, interestingly, it is you. When you were one year old, your parents decided, based on earlier planning, to join a new Jatra Party named Maharaja Jatra Party(MJP), located in Gaibandha of Rangpur. That undermined possible action taken by Odhikari and the investor's son that they were planning to subvert the couple in one way or the other.'

Jatra as a career and full family life with children are conflict-ing propositions. Moreover, the contract with new company clearly stipulated a no-child policy. Under the aforesaid constraints, Rakib returned to his parents' abode to leave the newborn son until some-thing else could be worked out.

Stunned and bewildered, both Dada-ji and Firoza Dadima were initially almost frozen. But as always, Firoza Dadima rose to the occasion and opted for a positive gesture without risking the possible loss of her dear son and being blamed by posterity for avoiding responsibility. She went on quietly stating that 'any negative stance could be a bad augury for the *haveli* which you so painfully built.' Dada-ji nodded his head and kept quiet.

In the midst of constant sniveling for always causing problems to his parents and not being able to make them happy by any act or deed, Rakib briefly narrated what he wanted to share. Rakib's suo motu admission of his own guilt and failure as well as Bijli's life, as an orphan and abandoned beginning at birth, made a deep mark in the sensation and thought of both Dada-ji and Dadima. Firoza Dadima swapped looks with Dada-ji and extended both her hands to have the *nati* (grandson).

Holding their nati very passionately, she commented impromptu, 'What a beautiful child and what a set of piercing eyes, indicative of super intelligence. Though we have not seen Bijli, we can safely conclude about her beauty and brightness.'

She then asked for the nati's name. Rakib, being sorry and embarrassed, said that 'in the midst of problems and pressures, we could not name him. We always referred to him as *baby*.' Saying so, Rakib intelligently stipulated that 'it would augur well for the baby if his grandma names him.' Firoza was ecstatic, looked again at Dadaji, and pronounced, 'I name him Shafiq. Besides being a popular name with a good meaning (kind, compassionate), it is nice to have a name in close proximity with that of father.'

Dada-ji finally smiled and agreed pronouncedly.

In his two-day extended stay, he told Mother every bit of Bijli's life and his own involvement freely and frankly. Though there were reasons to be dismayed and dejected, his parents eventually found reasons to endorse Rakib's action to be by the side of one who lost her mother at birth and was abandoned by her father and family. They embraced Shafiq with an open mind and full commitment.

Rakib returned to his base, informed Bijli about the most unexpected adoration of her by Dada-ji and Dadima, notwithstanding the convoluted features of her life and even without seeing and meeting her. At the same breath, and relieving apparent pressure on Bijli, he confirmed their unqualified embrace of the baby, whom Dadima fondly named Shafiq. Rakib finally observed to the delight of Bijli that, 'I am so happy thinking of Shafiq growing up in my parental home under the wise care of his Dada-ji and enjoying the love of the ever vigilant and caring Dadima.' Both renewed their commitment to make MJP a success.

MJP, with a top-rated conception, higher level direction, and mindboggling presentation under the able leadership of Rakib and the concurrent gorgeous and responsive Bandhana performance of Bijli, with the accompanying modernity in costume and character-ization, was a roaring success. Bijli soon became well known and popular as *nortoki* (dancer) and *nayika* (heroine), with both being synonymous to MJP.

The commitment of both to Jatra and their determination to uphold its status as an institutional prominence of culture and the source of rural amusement were bizarrely outright. Success was not only limited to patent popularity and the inflow additional money, even though a junior owner. In subsequent private discussions, Bijli complimented Rakib for his earlier decision to negotiate for a share in the ownership of MJP, even though that meant an initial cut in his emoluments. With funds slowly being built up primarily because of part-ownership, they were dreaming to have their own Jatra Party, and Rakib, even at that preliminary stage, had a name for their pro-posed company. That was *Bijlirani Jatra Party (BJP)*.

While BJP was to be a hope and proposition for future, Rakib, being in a lounging position, did not fail to cash the current reality. In an outburst of ecstasy, Rakib precipitously positioned Bijli on top of him and put one of her bulging breasts in his mouth. In an effort to swallow, he reached a discomforting stage of near suffocation. Bijli enjoyed every bit of that and the subsequent merrymaking, dreaming a complete life of contentment.

She recalled every word of her promise to Bhugal Sir and Guru Shibnath to inform them before any life major decision was taken. She was determined not to default on that score. It palpably became imperative for her to visit Guru-ji after knowing about the recent sad demise of Roma-ma. Also, both Rakib and Bijli were conscious of their son being away from them for a long time and felt immeasurable joy for the near possibility of being united soon after having their own company. They, taking advantage of an upcoming lean period due to the Muslim holy month of Ramadan, planned to visit Bhugal Sir and Guru Shibnath and take a side trip to see Shafiq and meet Rakib's parents.

As planning for the synchronized trips to the parental roots were being worked out, the political climate started heating up all over the country due to the upcoming national election after the ensuing holy month of Ramadan. It attained added significance due to the scheduled election for the lowest representative level of governance, known as Union Council, within a month of the national one.

Political slogans by supporters predominated various common social settings, arenas, and even heavily trafficked roads, by-lanes, and marketplaces. Propaganda pamphlets overtook all empty spaces by the sides of structures, offices, electric posts, the railings of bridges, the back of rickshaws, big wayside trees, and so on. There was stiff competition to win over voters. Besides politicking, entertainment attained a relatively significant prominence and role. Jatra thus suddenly got a boost in demand with more shows of shorter durations in different locations, implying more sudden and unplanned travels. That was a unique situation considering the first approaching season change after winter and the ensuing fasting month of Ramadan before the elections.

Both Bijli and Rakib were busy in handling the emerging professional demand in a normally supposed to be lean period. They nevertheless enjoyed having a quick flow of unexpected money which would be a definite plus for launching their proposed BJP.

The MJP team was at Kurigram, staging shows covering five nights. Everything moved as planned, with arrangements being afoot for the return trip. At such point, it received a pressing entreaty from Gaibandha directing the party to proceed to river port Chilmari. Located on the confluence of Tista and Jamuna rivers of Kurigram district at a distance of about twenty miles, Chilmari is an important business place, and the offer was very lucrative. The sponsoring entity, Chilmari Merchant Associates, were very keen to adhere to their proposed schedule in terms of date and days. The only possible way was for the party to leave Kurigram by early morning following the last show to arrive Chilmari by around evening time. That would allow the artists to take a rest and the other staff to initiate preparatory setting work for the premier show the next night as per contract. That was to be the first one of the contracted three.

The distance was nominal, but the time was too tight to move a Jatra party with all its paraphernalia as per the dictate of the schedule. Ordinarily, the said distance of about twenty miles from Kurigram to Chilmari is negotiable both by rails and roads. The train frequency connecting Chilmari was inadequate, one in the morning and the other one at late afternoon, with delays being experienced frequently, so that option was out. The option of travel by road needs three buses, and that became a problem in view of the limited bus availability and their scheduled commitments.

Rakib and Bijli had parleys with staff and artists that early evening and night. The consensus was that the best arrangement would be for artists and other staff to travel by bus leaving following morning. Critical items like tents, gears, musical instruments, microphone and related equipment, mattresses, makeup items and tables, dresses, and so on could loosely be packed and carried by boat in the company of remaining staff.

Rakib exchanged a mischievous look with Bijli but soon diverted his focus on the staff to say, 'I propose that myself and Bijli also travel by boat in the company of other staff. There are two advantages: one, in case of any emergency, we can have a decision on the spot, and the second, frankly, is a personal one. I have not traveled by boat in my life. And that too is true for Bijli. So let us have lifetime experience.'

The resultant decision was to hire three large boats based on availability, pack them with the needed staffs, and try to leave by about midmorning. That was carried out meticulously, and the move from Kurigram to Chilmari commenced as planned. Rakib and Bijli were in the middle boat in the company of three junior staff while the remaining others, except artists and musicians who left early morning by bus, made their way in other two boats.

The sailing was smooth. The flowing river, passing cargo and passenger boats with sails decorated by different colors and canvas looked as a living portraiture. Riverbanks having symbols of erosion and the growth of new vegetation with vast open arenas and the blue sky were amazing for all, especially for Rakib and Bijli. The journey could not be better. Shading all earlier irritations for the directive to proceed to Chilmari, both Bijli and Rakib felt exultant. In expressing such happiness, Rakib stated that, 'It is going to be about five years that we have not seen Shafiq. However, the high point is we are going to be united soon after our proposed BJP is launched. Once that is done, I plan to take out you and Shafiq in a boat journey like this.'

As the journey continued, the gentle breeze got warmer. The resultant humidity was discomforting. Both Rakib and Bijky retreated to the lower space of the boat. As a diversion, and more as a defiance to the emerging signs of bad weather, the accompanying support staff and some crews of the boat started singing traditional *Bhawaiya* (a form of popular folk music originating in Rangpur that normally depicts pains and separation of *mahouts* [elephant trainers], *mahiishals* [buffalo herders], and *gariyals* [cart drivers] from their families) song.

But the signs were ominous. Emerging patches of gray and dark clouds soon covered the blue sky of the sunny day hours back. The boat crews were worried as the boats were sailing in the midstream of water, with the banks far away.

As the clouds became dark and thick fast with its position around the north and northwest horizon, the Serang, headman of the lascar (a term used by Portuguese to describe an assortment of sailors of Indian, Malay, Chinese and Japanese crewmen) communicated with Rakib about the risks apparent in the horizon.

The decision was prompt. The action likewise was fast. Boats were being brought closer to the nearest shoreline by aligning sails with an effort to bring them to line with the wind flow. But the Serang was visibly worried and nervous recalling that it was the last day of the last Bangla calendar month. This period of related Bangla calendar months is associated with heat and humidity. Sporadic and area-specific localized storms, hails, and rains are a common phenomena. They are commonly called

Kal Boishaki. The Serang sensed that one tidying in the northwest horizon could be one of them.

Hardly had Sarang finish his assessment when a sudden upcharge of wind, accompanied by roaring thunderstorms, lightning, rain, and hail, overwhelmed the entire surroundings as could be gauged and seen. The waves of river water were dancing to the tune of the storm flow. That assumed storm soon took the turn of a virulent tornado.

The crews of the first two boats racing for shelter near the shores lost control due to the onslaught of the unexpected tornado with the accompanying whirlwind and belligerent waves generated by the tornado covering a span of few miles. The boat carrying Bijli and Rakib collided with the one tailing behind, and both the boats capsized with the unexpected surge of a sudden tornado splash. Ironically the one carrying Bijli and Rakib went down upside down with no possible recourse for survival.

That was the sudden end of everything related to the treasured desire and dream-centering life of both Bijli and Rakib. Their dream of having own Jatra party, and the desire to have an enjoyable boat ride with their son Shafiq, once reunited, just vanished. Dada-ji and his family were informed about the tragedy in detail by the Odhikari in a passionate letter.

Dada-ji then continued to say that, 'I was advised that Bijli's guardians were also informed about the tragedy. I absorbed the shock, taking it as the latest periodic happening of tragedy in my life beginning with the demise Mutalib and Ginni in quick succession.

It was difficult for your Dadima. Fortunately, she responded initially to my urging to overcome the feeling for your sake. Though she was meticulously discharging her responsibilities of a mother and bestowing love and care of a grandma, it was never the same. She totally surrendered herself to the will of Allahpak. Most of the time while waking up at night, I found her either engrossed in saying optional prayers or in Sajdah (also pronounced as Sujud, entailing a low bowing or prostration to Allahpak facing Kaaba at Mecca).'

After a pause, Dada-ji continued, saying, 'As she started life with me, Firoza proved to be a remarkable lady: emotionally steady, intellectually resuscitated, socially pliable, and materially credible. She tried to recuperate after every tragedy the family suffered, ever vigilant and ever cognizant. However, this time it appeared to be different. Her primary relief in that depressing setting was your presence and the responsibility reposed in her to groom you. She took that responsibility as an esteemed task and you as a precious trust. That worked initially but got weakened over time silently.

Your Dadima did never make her agony and failing health to be a problem for others. She suffered at her end. I was preoccupied with my material accomplishments, and unfortunately did not pay required attention to her health and ailing conditions. I mostly assessed her well-being from outward indicators but never tried to evaluate her agony from stifled physical and emotional indicators. My introvert personality, I believe now, propelled that sort of response.

Notwithstanding silent efforts otherwise, Firoza emotively continued to sustain physical glitches frequently. She gave up all hope of recovering and devoted her time and energy to telling you all that she could about the family and about your parents, your father Rakib and mother Bijli. Among other impacts, that definitely created the most favorable imprint in your mind having pride for the family and love for parents, as I could gather during later discourses with you.

As you are aware, all possible and available medical care were commissioned regularly. Treatments, unfortunately, focused on external symptoms. Local physicians were oblivious of the inherent reasons. Rakib's shocking and sudden death with his wife in that unpredictable mishap was too much for her to reconcile with and live through. Those years she lived after that catastrophe was, to my best assessment, perhaps due to the commitment she gave to Rakib during his last visit and her anxiety related to you.

Your Dadima regularly advised me about my obligations to you once she is gone. I outwardly laughed those away but internally became very concerned. Your Dadima gradually gave in and surrendered to ultimate dictate of life when you were twelve, six years after the sad demise of your parents.'

Taking a break and looking at me with all intensity, Dada-ji narrated his approach in helping me grow up and what he did to charter that for fulfillment of his inner desire of life. He started saying, 'I do not have much expectations from my offspring. Your uncles and their families, due to the sheer dictate of time, opted for an urban life pattern. Their offspring literally, and logically so, have no feelings for and attachments with this abode.

This reality and frequent family tragedies caused a disarray within me about the future of this abode and its legacies, so I focused on my grandchildren and loved you three (Azeem, Julaikha, and you) most with expectations premised on feelings, intelligence, and ability. However, in emphasizing education, I lost Azeem permanently, so it appears. A structured life, like the one of the army, is his growing-up passion. Though he has had been the apple of my eyes, I would never interfere with his preferred way of life for my happiness. I accept the reality of his being far away from this milieus. Having lost her husband too early, Julaikha is a hostage of her own emotions and literally deserted this home. Then you came in our life.

Obsessed with the desire to protect the heritage, I singularly focused in grooming you with an urge to have a life centering this abode notwithstanding your proven astuteness, competence, and prudence. Possibly I have done an injustice to you in the process. I am sorry for doing that but would exercise option now to redress the same to the extent feasible. If at any time in the future your life's choice dictates a relocation, feel free to act on that. The only request is that this accommodation, my bed and attached anteroom, should never be bartered away.'

At the end of his marathon soliloquy, Dada-ji appeared to be at peace with himself. Wearing a smile of contentment, he said, 'I feel lighter. I am happy in being able to convey to you what I wanted so long, and being able to provide a window in your life for a change if flexibility is needed. My only other request is your maintaining effort to touch base with Azeem as possible and taking care of Julaikha.'

That meeting setting was experiencing a total lull, with each one being enthralled in specific thoughts. To obviate that burdensome silence, Rukiya inquired about what happened to Dada-ji. The answer was short and sad as Shafiq said, "He embraced death very easily, and appears to be happily, on the seventh day of our discourse, and in the presence of *Imam* of our Masjid (mosque) reciting Dada-ji's favorite verses from the Quran (the Holy Book)."

The evening started exuberantly, with Shafiq elucidating features of the gillnetting event slated for the following morning. It was planned and arranged by him for the exposure and pleasure of Fazal. That lighter proposition took an unforeseen abstemious turn when Rukiya inquired about his own childhood.

That served the purpose of a much-needed opening that Shafiq himself perhaps was looking for to state the most pertinent life episode of both Azeem and that of his, in the care and love of Dada-ji and Dadima and surroundings of this abode. At the outset, Shafiq clarified, stating, "Bhabi, to appreciate our childhood, one should know about Dada-ji and Dadima. All that I would be stating are word for word what Dada-ji told me. There are some components concerning my father for which Dada-ji relied on what Father told Dadima in detail during his two-day extended stay while leaving me behind in early infancy. Some other aspects of discourse were premised on what he could know from others like Sobhan Chacha (as father's younger brothers and friends are addressed), and the only encounter he had with Bhugal Sir and Guru Shibnath Bishwash."

More pertinently the narration of Shafiq, quoting Dada-ji, was candid about the family's initial hardships, the prominent role of destiny in showering blessings, the rotation of happiness and distress, and the sort of reclusive life pattern. But that was more relevant in articulating who Azeem and Shafiq were, and Dada-ji's love and concern for them along with his adorable *natni* (granddaughter Julaikha).

Azeem was speechless. Shafiq felt relieved. Bokul was pleased that her husband could detail everything candidly. Fazal demonstrated a reclusive aura. It, nevertheless, had multiple ruminations in the thinking of Rukiya. She was at ease in knowing the early life of Azeem; delighted for him being loved and cared by Dada-ji and Dadima; proud to be told about Dada-ji's adoration for his all-embracing qualities, and evidently felt pleased to have his trust and love notwithstanding deviancies in pursuing life. She soon concluded that like many destined opportunities of Dada-ji's life, this one could as well be the germinal of a better life for them, and Shafiq would probably be the main usherer of that.

The following morning was one of merriment with the arrival of *jelleys* (fishermen) carrying longish fishing nets. Under the supervision of Shafiq and having the presence of most elders and children, *jelleys* carried out gillnetting from one end of the big *pukur* to the other end dragging the fish along within. As the nets were close to the contour and there were many fish between the net and the land, the cramped fish pile started to jump out of water, mostly landing in the same water space while a few could escape the dragging fishing net. That was the thrill for the children and elders alike. Rukiya, Bokul, Julaikha-bu, and a host of other ladies also enjoyed that from covered locations, maintaining modesty. Fazal liked it very much as he told his Shafiq Chacha. He equally enjoyed the fresh fish curry at lunch, which he thankfully acknowledged to his Bukul Chachi.

That evening was a somber one, and socially more solemn. In the *kacharikhana* (elders' sitting place as well as visitors' room), Azeem was busy in saying *Khuda Hafiz* (the local style of saying goodbye meaning "God protect you") to local gentries and other visitors while nodding his head in responding to common requests for more frequent visits. Shafiq was busy in ushering visitors, offering them *pan* (betel leaf preparation) and escorting them out while leaving.

Inside the property, the ladies were busy doing their respective errands: Bokul was preoccupied in preparing a sumptuous dinner and arranging other eatables to be taken to Dhaka the following morning; Julaikha-bu was guiding and helping Bokul as well as reminding her of any missing act; and Rukiya was in the midst of packing and piling. The common feature of that going was while Rukiya thoughtfully would discard an item considering capacity and convenience, Julaikha-bu innocently, and as showing love, would appear with three more items. The seesaw continued unabated until a happy compromise could be reached. Fazal, sitting at a distance observing Bokul Chachi's way of cooking and Mother's way of negotiating, enjoyed such rural expression of the warmth of a relationship.

In spite of predominant laughter and warmth among sisters-in-law pertinent in completing various tasks, Rukiya was internally upset and annoyed noting Azeem's lack of reactions and responses. She interred her frustration so that others did not have inkling of that. She decided to give him time to react to what Shafiq said about property until they left for Dhaka, and kept quiet with worry intensifying. The resultant soliloquy was, *If Azeem does not discuss tonight with me about what and how he intends to handle the inherited ancestral property matters, and if he remains silent even at departure time, then I will intervene the way we should, come what may.*

On her part and at the end of the dinner, Rukiya thanked Bokul profusely for her hospitality and Julaikha-bu for her love and compassion. She simultaneously invited both to visit them in Dhaka, quipping, "We do not have a big house, but have a big heart. Myself and Fazal will do everything needed to be done so that you enjoy your visit. That is the only way we can cement our bond and live up to the desires of Dada-ji."

That evening was full of predicable joy and sadness. The dinner was served with apt preparedness in spite of a few close relations' unexpected joining.

The after-dinner discourse that night was brief by choice of all. The light discourse centering on the plan for the following morning's departure ended with all somberness with heightened respect for Dada-ji. More pertinently, the narration of Shafiq, quoting Dada-ji, was candid, clear and adequately sourced and was appreciated by all.

PUSH

ll related arrangements pertaining to the travel back to
Dhaka were accomplished perfectly except that hilarity and exhilaration were missing from the actions and
responses of Rukiya. Azeem took it as an emotional reflex of leaving
her real home for the first time. He remained indifferent and quiet.

Contrarily Rukiya was stunned in observing Azeem bidding the usual and simple goodbye to Shafiq. Without conveying
that contemplation and maintaining due tonal adulation, Rukiya
requested Shafiq for a visit soon to Dhaka to have a definite follow-up conversation to chalk out the consensus as to the future
move and course pertaining to the property and other home-related
stuff.

Azeem and family returned to Dhaka with almost twice the
number of baggage they took to Massumpur. Once settled down in
their own abode, Rukiya was preoccupied in thinking about the lack
of responses from Azeem.

She decided to buy time before raising the issue of Azeem's quiet
attitude in response to what Shafiq Bhai so painstakingly narrated in
clearing what they were and their standing in the family, in explaining the reasons for the various decisions, in articulating the farsightedness of Dada-ji with respect to the present dares, and the future
options for progenies based on need.

Rukiya's mother taught her always to give issues time for proper
reflection, so the day passed without much interaction between the
two while Azeem took that as the pain of leaving Bokul and Julaikha,

a relationship that blossomed fast and was likely to recede soon with physical separation.

Back in school, Fazal was exuberant in explaining to his friends the happy moments and experiences of his visit to his grandpa's place. Taking advantage of the somewhat delayed arrival of the next teacher, he started his narration and said that apart from the unbounded love and affection of every one of relevance, and the hospitality of close ones, the one experience he most enjoyed was the gillnetting operation to catch many fish in one go from a pond.

Logically, gillnetting came into prominence in terms of the interests of the folks. Fazal felt proud in being able to explain something that his friends never saw or experienced even though it was very indigenous. He said, "Gillnetting is a fishing method generally used by fishermen in large-scale fishing efforts in ponds, rivers, and lakes. Gill nets are vertical panels of fishing nets covering the two ends of the water space. Such panels are mostly added to meet the need of the horizontal water space. The related water panels are kept afloat from one end to the other with the help of lighter and spaced floaters while the bottom line panels are weighted to maintain firmness as the net is drawn. Mesh sizes are designed for the head of a midsized fish to pass through but not its body. Facing the obstruction, the stranded fish tends to undertake a bac-off maneuvering, and in the process, their respective gills get tangled with the mesh. When the net reaches the desired end of the pond, the bigger ones started jumping while the crammed others form a pile. That was something to be witnessed."

Fazal was intently describing his experiences. As a debater, he knew the art of talking and exchanged focus with his friends for better communication. He was embarrassed to see the next teacher, who had entered the classroom by its back door and kept standing with a quiet posture.

Calling the class to attention, the teacher took time for the standard roll calls and asked, out of context, his students as to how many of them had seen a pond. He then commenced, stating, "I listened with rapt attention to what Fazal was saying, and honestly am at a bay as what to say in advising you or guiding you. At the initiation of my class of today and keeping in view what Fazal was detailing, I asked how many of you had actually seen a pond. Unfortunately, only two hands went up out of about the forty of you present. Modern education is vital for us, but knowledge about the settings of our rural society and the practices of our predecessors are equally relevant to have a proper feeling and knowledge as to who we are! Unfortunately, we now know more about pools compared to ponds, more about friends compared to families, and more about other countries compared to our own. We tend to prioritize buildings and structures over farmlands and greens, and we waste water and release more arsenic lead and mercury in the nature merrily. Such realities cannot augur well for us, and in the process we run the risk of losing our identity at the behest for modernity. The time is ripe to discuss and assess them at family levels, as a social group, and as a national priority."

Upon return and in the afternoon snack table conversations, Fazal enthusiastically detailed all that he experienced in the school related to the visit to Massumpur. He demonstrated enormous pride and happiness for his visit to ancestral abode. He did not fail to mention that the teacher encouraged others to take such visits, even if of short duration, to their roots for better awareness and assimilation. Azeem was very happy to know all these and responded by smiling and nodding his head.

Taking advantage of that joyful setting, Rukiya politely but with all firmness in tonal expression inquired about Azeem's recent quietness. She commenced, saying, "Shafiq Bhai and your family have done so much to make our visit a success. In return, you only said 'thank you" while departing. The traditional gesture of embracing to convey gladness and thanks was palpably missing. You did not say a single word of appreciation to Bokul and Julaikha-bu. More so, when Shafiq Bhai elaborately detailed all that Dada-ji said about the family, specifically you both, you had no reaction. Your silence about the future of the inherited land obviously frustrated Shafiq Bhai, and I could sense that easily. To me, it appears you are in a different world with no opinions to convey and no emotions to express. That was the reason I invited Shafiq Bhai to

Dhaka for a frank and to-the-point discussion with you in your own environment."

Notwithstanding the provocations, there was no reaction from Azeem. He kept quiet with an apparent indifferent mien and concentrated sipping his favorite coffee. That irritated Rukiya. As learned from Mother in the childhood, she countered with a still colder retort by quietly leaving the space without bothering to look at him or the disorganized paraphernalia on the table. She decided suddenly to have a personal discourse with son but took a preemptive decision to keep the most recent frustrating experience with Azeem absolutely private in effort to an uphold the dignity of the Father. She, with her usual smile, entered the room of Fazal, and started talking more in general terms about their visit to Massumpur. She took the opportunity of that window to convey to Fazal her happiness and thanks for his positive and warm approach in interacting with all and sundries of Massumpur and treating all, based on age, with love and respect. Fazal was happy in noting Mother's silent observations of his etiquette in mannerism and subsequent evaluation. He was even enthralled by Mother's inquisition about the details of what happened in the school and happily shared all that he said and what the teacher subsequently articulated. Fazal felt encouraged.

The ambience around the dinner table of that evening was not that warm. Even though the main curry item was the big fish from the pond of Dada-ji, an item that could normally generate lighter and varied discussions centering the just concluded visit—the taste of fresh fish, the pleasure of having fish from own pond, and the like—that was not the case.

Sensing the emerging uneasiness, Fazal retreated to his room after dinner, taking the plea of homework. Rukiya cleaned the dining table nonchalantly, finished all postdinner errands in the kitchen, and came out of the cooking area with usual cup of coffee for Azeem. She was about to leave the dining area after placing the coffee cup on the table. Azeem suddenly said, "Please take your seat. I have something to talk to you. I am noticing that you have had been, for the first time in our married life, somewhat distressed and agonized, and our resultant conjugal communication is definitely constrained.

Initially, I thought that to be related to the separation with Bokul and Julaikha, both of whom you surprisingly bonded with very quick and very warmly. Then your direct stating of my many genuine failings during the later part of our stay at Massumpur caused an inner awakening within me, compelling to be frank and candid with you. The rest, of course, is up to you.'

Rukiya was thunderstruck debating within as to what he was up to! Nevertheless, she maintained a calm posture with a loving look at Azeem.

Azeem, likewise, exchanged a passionate look and then started saying, "I solemnly assure you that my love and feeling for you are the same as the instant instinct propelled at our first encounter. I adore you as I always did during the course of our journey together beset with challenges and uncertainties. You should not have any misgivings about that. But I would like to take a little more time to explain my unusual predicament.

What Shafiq narrated reflect the later demeanor of Dada-ji. Transiting from a life beset with problems and lack of direction, he was transformed quickly due to the gift of Mother Nature, the unanticipated affection bestowed by Babu Bijon Mohan Nag, and his luck. Such rapid transition achieving success at impulses transformed his life, attitude, and behavioral pattern. He soon came to be known as a rough and tough guy all around, particularly to those who had contact and dealings with him related to farming and land holdings.

Dada-ji practiced a polite way of conduct in dealing with elders both outside and within the family trying to maintain decency and sobriety. Contrary to that, he was very tough with children of the family like me. I, like the other family children of the same age, always dreaded him most. While growing up, I indulged in arguing with myself that perhaps that was the manifestation of his worries, based on own life experiences, about our future, and he wanted to take care of that while we were growing up. Later on in life, I had no doubt about his reasons for worries to ensure a sustained good life for all of us. But many of our uncles could not relate that with good intention. Thus, they mostly preferred separate living in different locations of the country, mostly citing occupational imperatives.

They generally assumed that such separate arrangements of living would offer a better life to their children outside the regimentation of Dada-ji. Being an orphan and a trust, I had to stay back. Later events proved that it worked positively for me.

The successive family tragedies shook Dada-ji enormously. That and influence of Firoza Dadima transformed him rapidly. But for me that was too late even though I tried to understand him better. My inner self always pressed me to be away from the shield of Dada-ji, and living in Dhaka was the first step. Joining the army coincidentally was the culmination of that.

As learnt from Shafiq, the tragic widowhood of Julaikha, the joining of loving son Rakib in a Jatra Party, and the latter's precipitous arrival with an unannounced one-year-old son, named later Shafiq by Dadima, progressively prostrated him from both social and personal life perspectives. He mellowed down unexpectedly. And that was aggravated due to the accidental death of his youngest son Rakib and the subsequent sad demise of Dadima. This is the Dada-ji Shafiq is familiar with and was talking about.

I also enjoyed a bit of that changed zest, but that did not significantly upturn my childhood impression and feeling. The iron twisted Dada-ji that embodied in my childhood mind was always a contemporaneous one. Even with physical distance, I could not get out of that.

Since childhood, and due to extensive exposure to Dada-ji in the absence of my parents, I developed a mindset of always looking for order and directive. I learned to carry out directives but not to think independently except on two counts—the initial yearning for higher academic accomplishment imbibed within me by Julaikha and later to join the armed forces influenced by my exposure and the India-Pakistan war.

My joining the army fit in well with what I am. Strict regulations with axioms of command, control, obedience, and dedication (CCOD) somehow sheared well with my personal traits. I was best in performance wherever there was a defined mission.

Regimentation, training, and commitment with a specific focus on trading simultaneously between life and death, the indelible *mantra* of the army life, did have a major dent on my private mindset even though I was missing Massumpur, Dada-ji, Dadima, and other family members. For some inexplicable reason, and notwithstanding such milieu, I started developing some admiration for Dada-ji during this period. This was propelled perhaps by the stories narrated by some batchmates about their parents and grandparents. In telling my story, I dealt with my childhood status, and the simultaneous roles of grandparents and parents played by Dada-ji and Dadima in the cases of two orphans of the family, Julaikha and myself, of about the same age. The Julaikha information was shared to generate empathy for both of us and glorify the roles played Dadima and Dada-ji.

In a setting of all men, any talk about, forget the presence of, the other gender is sufficient to breed excitement among male friends. One of my batchmate, Tariq Saiyed, referred to the famous Persian romantic poem titled 'Yousuf and Julaikha' (as is written in Bangla but authentically spelled as Zulaikha). Everybody joined him in echoing 'A-Z', a new romantic saga titled "Azeem and Zulaikha." Julaikha's unmarried status added to the speculation and hilarity notwithstanding repeated denials by me.

I started understanding Dada-ji better, but my childhood memory always remained an impediment. It worked so incisively that even though he came to Dhaka to attend our wedding, I just could not be gregarious with him.

In spite of the repeated persuasion of uncles and his close relations, Dada-ji persistently declined to visit Dhaka. But our wedding was so close to his heart, that he ventured to attend that despite knee-joint pain and discomfort. I was a prisoner of my own negative thinking. I increasingly tried to come out of that rumpus attitude, but found that difficult. Notwithstanding all these, and mostly because of knowing about the feelings of other batchmates for their respective grandparent, I started developing love for Dada-ji on the simple justification that no individual is perfect. I fervently acknowledged that Dada-ji tried his best. I started developing admiration for Dada-ji for being what he was and for playing simultaneous roles of father and grandfather."

Azeem further continued, saying, "I was speechless while listening to Shafiq about Dada-ji's oratorical exposition just prior to his death highlighting the elements of the family. Being appraised of his wisdom and sagacity in delineating and the assignment of ancestral properties; his frankness in detailing who I am and who Shafiq is; his extraordinary ability to groom Shafiq as a unique individual capable of handling the load of the varied trusts reposed in him; and, more significantly, the flexibility envisaged by him for us in handling the issues of life in the future, convinced me about the attributes of his persona that made him what he was. I now not only love him but respect him enormously even though divergent earlier premises beset my current thinking. And that caused an insurmountable challenge within me in formulating a proximate response in that setting, positively reacting to what Shafiq so far said.

On one point, however, I have a bug in mind when Dada-ji alluded to Shafiq about receiving vibrations from the land, enabling him to take decisions at various stages of life. I thought through it but do not find a rationale to accept that proposition in decision taking. He met Babu Bijon Mohan Nag at a bend in life when the challenges both faced needed to be tackled earnestly to shape up the life of each, which appeared to be mirages from their respective perspective. I think all good attainments in that bend of his life were due to sheer his hard and honest work with the aim to make a break for him and his progeny's future. The coincidental liking and love of Babu Bijon Mohan Nag, premised largely on the religious belief in reincarnation, had all the elements of lady luck."

Azeem momentarily paused. Rukiya maintained her silence. She was certain that he ought to have something more pertinent to talk to and divulge, and that could as well be drastically the opposite of what she has in mind. Rukiya would not, however, like to create a dent in their happy and quixotic conjugal relationship to be beset by ups and downs in unanticipated bends. Internally she was struggling both to weather her emotions and keep her expectations low.

Azeem's follow-on action bemused Rukiya. He quietly got up from the chair, took slow steps, unlike an ardent army personnel, approached the family's midsize refrigerator, opened the door to fetch

254

cold water, and came back to his sitting place. Maintaining calmness notwithstanding pressing qualms, he started sipping his cold water serenely.

Rukiya was stunned as this was the first time since their marriage that Azeem took water to drink with his own effort. Normally, even if the water jug is on the table and he is sitting nearby, he would always ask Rukiya to serve him water, for that matter anything desired by him. Some of his friends used to riposte him for giving Rukiya so much trouble. Even their son Fazal observed that and conveyed his dissent. In reply to Fazal, Azeem once lightly responded saying, "This has a special piquancy. Once you grow up and will get married, you will appreciate it." As an obedient son, he did not respond but kept his head straight, indicative of dissonance.

In that elusive conversation trajectory, Azeem, as internally thought through by Rukiya earlier, opened up, saying, "Life is a mix of strange and inexact portents. In view of this and unexpected turn of events, one's dream of life mostly remains disjointed and unfulfilled. As you know, that precisely happened to me. There is a saying that 'once beaten twice shy.' I am a live example of that. My self-confidence has been shattered.

I was determined to be away from *Dada-ji's* area of influence, and joining the army was an immediate option enabling me to be away from him and to have a good life, simultaneously exceling in my military career. My short-lived army commitment in Pakistan was exceptional with two challenging engagements. In one I even risked leaving you behind as a widow within months of our marriage.

Back in Bangladesh, I kept my expectations low and tried to do best what I was tasked to do, always believing performance is the criteria for recognition and progression. I valued performance over politics. With your support, I overcame my initial frustration, but then the system appeared to succumb to freestanding pressures. I lost all confidence in myself and the *mantra* of CCOD that I engrossed in the Kakul Military Academy of Pakistan.

I took that precarious life journey to avoid Dada-ji's demanding discipline regime, which was distasted by me with sadistic pleasure. On hindsight and as a tragedy reflective of absolute churlishness, I harbored a strategy and plan to escape that soon and manipulated my interactions with him to earn his love, care, and accommodation in ensuring my life's progression. In that process, I lost all sense of civility and decency, and worse, lost too all considerations of respect and gratitude due to this remarkable man. I was totally oblivious of his love, care, and accommodation in my life's progression. His every accommodation to my desires and wishes was taken by me as my inherited right without any clue of not having one legally.

With that backdrop, I landed in the army. The coarseness of the training protocol and the rigorousness of life did not disturb me much as I was familiar with those due to UOTC exposure, and the prospect of a possible structured life it held for me. That blushing expectation has blessed me with one like you while other elements were overshadowed and mostly overtaken by the silent penetration of influence peddling and outside pressures. Those were against the values with which I grew up. Those were against the ethos that I assimilated while reading various books of relevance. Those absolutely conflicted with the frame of mind I have had in my upbringing. That was aggravated by the trauma I suffered immediate after retirement from the social contacts I developed during my professional life. I saw the ugly face of many of my so-called well-wishers.

With that setting and a frustrating future looming in the horizon, I lost all confidence in self and started considering myself a misfit. I gradually withdrew myself from talking and acting while taking shelter in listening and thinking, more to avoid responsibility. That is the me you are alluding to since Shafiq surfaced in our life with fresh positivity and opportunity. The outcome so far has been so positive that it enhanced many a times my nervousness.

Coming to the bottom line, you have full freedom and authority to act on any family matters in consultation with and the support of Shafiq. You are just to tell me what I need to do, and I will act accordingly. This decision of mine is irrevocable and covers all aspects of our life."

Having said so, Azeem felt relieved and at ease. He looked at Rukiya with passion. She moved closer to Azeem, hugged him, and went to kitchen to make tea for both.

Rukiya smilingly returned with tea and positioned her chair facing Azeem. After having a few sips, Rukiya, with a mix of wit and intelligence, premised her narration, saying, "In the cricket game's parlance, Shafiq Bhai scored a century in piloting us back to the family track. In elucidating that, you scored a half century. So I can only play a sixer.

I am thankful for your frankness, for having trust in my judgement, and for showing unabated confidence in my understanding of related issues. In the process, I will have my ideas, discuss that with Shafiq Bhai from time to time, and then share the same with you for the final decision. Nothing will be done behind you, nor will I be keeping you in the darkness. I solemnly assure you that I will not fail in my duties to you and in discharging my obligations to the family. You are the best gift of Allahpak for me. I will always be by your side, with you and the family, enjoying each day as a *niamat* (gift) from Allahpak, and would endeavor to sail through all storms."

Rukiya took a break and outwardly devoted time to sip slowly, her tea being very warm by her standard. Internally she was scanning the parameters of the issues to delineate a broad frame of initiatives to tentatively lay the ground rules for the needed discourses with Shafiq.

On his part, Azeem bemused himself with varied thoughts of the divergent implications in zeroing on what Rukiya was going to articulate more. He had not to wait longer. Placing her empty cup on the table, Rukiya opened up, saying, "Our immediate priorities are two: to refocus priority on land and land-related activities, and to consolidate the family's living status in Dhaka, taking prudent advantage of the present structure and unexpected liquidity. In addition, we need to prioritize decisions about options in managing the inherited land at Massumpur; concentrate future landholdings near Dhaka, as Massumpur is too far away; and needed consolidation of future acquisitions, as feasible."

Rukiya took a small break before resuming her statement, saying, "Besides these material things, we need to focus on other aspects of life: guiding Fazal to become a good human being. We need to motivate and inspire him further for imbibing within him a strong

257

urge to be an excellent army professional achieving the unfulfilled objective of his father. This is more relevant, notwithstanding the exceptional maturity shown by him so far, as sailing successfully through the rough waters of life, as Bangladesh is currently passing through, has unforeseen negative possibilities. We should also try to align Fazal's unqualified endorsement of Shafiq as an important member of our family and to value his opinion on family matters, particularly on property-related ones."

After pronouncing weighty life-related stipulations like those, Rukiya felt suddenly exhausted and wanted a break. She went to the kitchen area to fetch cold water, but that was more to create a space to absorb what she just said. There was something that was worrying Rukiya about the turn her life was taking! At about this stage, most of her friends were enjoying the lighter aspects of their conjugal lives while she was occupied with the hard realities in pursuing life. Besides, she had to silently handle the most unexpected emotional problem of Azeem, depressed and dejected due to successive career setbacks. Even though she refrained from discussing this outwardly or showing any public concern so far, she had been monitoring these for the last few months internally. Azeem's latest reference to his emotional problem this evening was his first admission. She was relieved but equally very worried, noting his deteriorating symptoms. That compelled her to articulate her views on property and other matters as her history teacher, Ms. Rashida Anjum, always insisted that her students be proactive in life and actions. Her very favorite saying was "hit the iron when it is hot." She was certain that between one-to-one, that was the best time and opportunity to convey what she wanted to.

Oblivious of what going in the mind of Rukiya, Azeem was sort of in a relaxed mood for being able to convey his emotional quandary straightforward, and was pleased, noting Rukiya's substantive responses. The impulse associated with the redolent smile of Azeem was momentarily confusing for Rukiya until Azeem burst into laughter, affirming all what she mentioned earlier.

That made her happy. Rukiya never wanted or wished to navigate alone in conducting their family life. However, the latest discourse was good for her as she was getting the needed clearance as to how to guide the family in case anything unfortunate happened to Azeem.

That was early midnight of late summer. The neighborhood was unusually quiet even though it was still warm, made worse due to the waning humidity spell. Both were quiet from their respective vantage points, a state of silence more indicative of the elements of vagueness after realizing and sharing the pressing concerns of life.

Azeem broke the silence due to an acute thirst he suddenly felt and desired to have his favorite *sherbet* (a local cooling drink of pressed lime juices with a service of the desired level of sugar). Of late, Azeem occasionally mentioned having the feel of being dehydrated. Because of that experience, Rukiya always had some stock of lime. That proved to be handy that midnight. She rushed and made a big glass of sherbet putting good number of ice cubes in the glass. That was very helpful and soothing for Azeem.

Exchanging a look, Rukiya profusely thanked Azeem for all the clarity enunciated and the flexibility provided by him in enabling her to discharge her responsibility. She then quipped, saying, "We have discussed whatever we needed to. That is by connotation is not absolute. Both of us have the flexibility to revisit any of them, and as warranted, any new issues. But there is a matter which we have not as yet discussed. I want to do that now with a caveat that we would not revisit it anymore, showing respect to the person who not only did so much for us but is also helping us even now in moving forward with honor and dignity."

The sherbet of a few minutes back had cooled Azeem down unexpectedly. The new stipulation of Rukiya caused just the reverse, causing a strange anxiety within Azeem.

In response to Azeem's blank and nervous look, Rukiya clarified, saying, "In your narration and at its end, you did cast a definite doubt about Dada-ji's 'receiving vibrations from the land, enabling him to take decisions at various stages of life.' I thought it through but do not find a rationale to outright discount that from being a common enabling position in taking numerous decisions in life.

My observation and response related to that are, 'It is not that something was fundamentally wrong with that statement. The root problem is how we look at. Even with learning and progression, mankind is often prone to make suggestive statements. When we go to buy something special, we often comment, 'I have a feeling that it will be good.' Dada-ji's quoted statement could be treated as one such like that uttered by a senior rural person having firm belief in divinity. Also, we are committing an err by considering the statement in isolation.

Dada-ji also mentioned his visits to the '*Thana* Agricultural Extension Services Office (TAEO)' on the following and successive days throughout. Those advice and guidance were very useful for Dada-ji in ensuring better farming practices and marketing. In one of such visits, Dada-ji was told by TAEO, 'Remember that land has enormous potentiality. Always keep in view the following five elements in farming: *mousum* (season), *beez* (seed), *shar* (fertilizer), *jotna* (caring and pruning), and, above all, is the timely and adequate application of *pani* (water). If a farmer is attentive to all these five, there is little possibility of his failing.'

All these are of universal application and use. There is nothing wrong with those. Moreover, though an ardent Muslim practicing an Islam's tenets in its totality, Dada-ji did not default in consulting the *Panjika* on a regular basis as used to be done by Babu Bijon Mohan Nag, another devout Hindu."

Azeem was amazed by the pragmatisms shown by Rukiya, the practical orientation of her thought, the farsightedness of her vision, and her ability to link loose ends to make needed sense. He felt assured afresh about the family's future lest anything untoward happens to him. He felt himself relax but did not fail to convey his full appreciation for all her soft understanding and firm conviction of calling a spade a spade.

After a few days, Shafiq showed up, this time with different eatable items as per Rukiya's liking that Bokul could recall. Among others, Bokul did not forget to send the homegrown tamarind that Rukiya like so much. She also did not forget to send a properly packed fresh big Ruhu fish from the family pond, which Fazal liked.

The trouble undertaken by Shafiq in carrying all these during the most arduous travel from Massumpur had a deep mark in the thinking of Fazal and cemented his bond with Dad's root and kinsfolk, particularly Shafiq uncle.

After a rest day, all three, Azeem, Rukiya and Shafiq, sat together with the most welcome intermittent participation of Fazal.

As earlier agreed between them, Azeem kept quiet while Rukiya made the stipulations articulating future steps and moves. The essence was to sell the inherited Massumpur land to the preferred customer based on a single payment option, buying fresh farmlands about the vicinity of Dhaka, such as near the Kashimpur and Azimpur areas. Most of the separation money for early retirement was also to be invested in appropriate and innovative farming initiatives and practices, based on market demand and opportunity. On this, what Rukiya said took both Azeem and Shafiq by awe. She said, "My premise for buying farmland near Dhaka was the outcome of my assessment of what Shafiq Bhai earlier said in helping cousins Manzoor Bhai and Jasim Bhai to buy similar land parcels. Considering farming attributes, especially soil conditions and access to water, those lands proved to be very productive. So Shafiq Bhai has the necessary exposure about the availability and suitability of the farming land, the water availability in and around, the pattern of present farming practices, the necessary contacts at local levees, and the prospect and efficiency of marketing opportunities of the produce.

I gave a lot of thought in proposing this investment. Moreover, Dhaka is not only growing. Its demand for farm produce is outstripping the current availability. This is going to accentuate rapidly. Second, this proposition is aimed at fulfilling Dada-ji's preferred wish. If his hunch about land has served him so well, there is every feeling within me that it will work likewise in the case of his *natis*. But more seriously, Azeem's overall health condition is not conducive to taking regular long journeys to Massumpur. He needs care and rest. So Kashimpur and Azimpur are better options from supervision and marketing perspectives, with, as required, the likely help of Fazal from time to time. Based on my discussions with the vegetable vendors of Cantonment Bazar and Karwan Bazar, I have a reasonable idea about the emerging demand.

That does not mean that I am alluding to delink from Massumpur. That is not the case. We will always use it as a sort of vacation home. We will keep track of Julaikha-bu too on a regular basis. These are what we have in mind. The rest depends on you, Shafiq Bhai. I fully understand that our propositions have a huge element of imposition on you and your time.

Our blood relationship remains as it is. You have outlived the trust reposed in you by Dada-ji. There will seldom be another person like you, so honest, sincere, meticulous, and trustworthy. Your involvement and participation in our planned farming endeavor will be critical. I envisage that you would be inclined to spend at least fifteen days a month on the farm, two days with us in Dhaka exchanging plans, finance, and other matters and activities. The rest of the month is to attend to Massumpur family-related errands and share time with and support the family. If things work out, you may eventually think about the option to relocate your family in Kashimpur or near a place in between Dhaka and Kashimpur. Your daughters will soon grow up. We are to think for them also."

As both Azeem and Shafiq were maintaining absolute reticence, Rukiya took a break to make tea for all. She was very clear as what she was going to say next but preferred to give the other two space to digest what she had said so far.

Silence was all pervasive. Though the couple had discussed and shared earlier what Rukiya would be telling Shafiq, Azeem had no inkling about the depth of those. He was both amazed and astounded, with a blend of unmixed exhilaration, for the prudence and insight shown so far by Rukiya.

That was totally a different experience for Shafiq compared to the notion he had about Rukiya Bhabi, besides being smart. The cautiousness and farsightedness exhibited by her in delineating options pertaining to the land, her full endorsement of Dada-ji's conviction as to the feeling of stepping into the land, and her indication to pursue farming as an occupation of success made him overawed. He was in a totally different world of thought.

Serving tea to both and lifting her own cup for sipping, Rukiya resumed, saying, "All I said are propositions from my own perspective. I, and for that matter, both of us, will be guided by your opinion and suggestion. However, before that opening is availed, I will like to conclude by making a point.

All that you have done so far for us and the family are just beyond any debt to be repaid. To be respectful to your sincerity and honesty, we should not even try to do so. Any contrary action will be an insult to you. So I am not looking back. However, I have a specific proposition as to the future.

Since we presently are stipulating substantial amount of your time, commitment, and effort, we would like to give that the shape of a formal structure, doing justice to all concerned. We will title that as Azeem-Shafiq Associates (Asha), symbolizing our joint involvement and aspirations. The partnership will have 80 percent holding by Azeem, for capital, ownership, risk, and 20 percent holding by Shafiq Bhai for labor and time, with an additional initial monthly allowance of taka 5,000 for travels and incidentals. This will be reviewed in the third year based on performance and progress. Your consent is the prime pillar of my proposition. But it also serves you, your commitment to Dada-ji to be by the side of Azeem. I have made my points after thorough premeditation. It is now up to you and your brother."

As earlier agreed, Azeem made a brief statement, saying, "Whatever Rukiya stipulated reflects our understandings earlier agreed to. So I am on board. It is now Shafiq's turn." He went on clarifying that "If everything is in the affirmative, I can easily request my lawyer associate to reflect it in a simple deed and get that registered. That friend of mine once told me that if I am in need of any legal services, he would be glad to help me without charge."

Shafiq was nervous thinking of a new relationship proposed to be documented in a deed even though he had no qualms with the broad stipulations of the proposed association. In conveying his agreement per se, Shafiq did not hesitate in mentioning his discomfort with the deed. Azeem fully understood the inherent reason of

Shafiq's disquiet and explained, "That agreement alluded to earlier is not for us. The business world is much larger and complex. Because of health reasons, it may not always be feasible for me to go to every place. That deed would serve the purpose of a legal backup for you and the firm."

That relieved Shafiq. He came out of the prevalent tense feelings, moved forward, and salam Rukiya by touching her feet, to the utter astonishment of Azeem, and then said, "Whatever you proposed was on my mind too, except my apparent shyness precluded its communication. Apart from everything else, I have learned a great lesson from you. That was the premise of performing salam by touching your feet, a first in our relationship. By interacting with you, I have learned the value of girls' education and will endeavor in every way to impart proper education to my daughters."

Everyone was jovial of the outcome. Fazal was called in and briefed. He was also told about the new resolution of Shafiq uncle to impart proper education to his daughters.

As Fazal was moving toward Shafiq uncle, apparently to salam him for his pragmatic decision, the latter took steps forward, held both shoulders of Fazal, and drew him close to his chest. Tears of joy popped out of Rukiya's eyes while Azeem was beaming with smile of pleasure.

VENTURE

—

Asha was launched with simultaneous actions on all fronts: the reconnaissance of the land and the prices in and around the Kashimpur and Azimpur areas as well as the Rupganj and Chappaigonj areas in Savar periphery, more as a fall-back option; contacting TAEOs of respective jurisdictions; the availability of committed labor; the conditions of farm-to-market roads; the availability of reliable transportations; and the size and nature of weekly bazaars nearby. Shafiq simultaneously commenced guarded contact with *Mojundar Baree* for the disposal of the inherited plot based on past interest.

On another front, Fazal returned home with an excellent performance card for his ninth class final examination, topping the class for the first time. Besides marks in various subjects, what pleased Azeem the most was the assessment of the individual teachers about his commitment and performance in both academic and extracurricular activities. His inner dream of having Fazal in the military academy for a professional army career appeared to be within reach. Azeem could not conceal his exuberance and started talking incessantly with Rukiya. The latter, to the surprise of Azeem, was quite reticent, urging him to be quiet and cautious. She believed in possible bad omens when excessive happiness is pronouncedly exhibited. Azeem was in no mood to listen. He concluded, saying, "You'll see, nothing can stop our son now from fulfilling my dream."

To Rukiya's happiness, there was a forced relief from talking continuously about Fazal's proposed military life. A number of imperatives made Azeem visit the Massumpur, Kashimpur, and

Azimpur areas a number of times within months. Azeem felt tired after every such trip, necessitating rest. Thus, the blooming phase of Asha took more time than anticipated. Except the time that was taken to finalize the deal involving that large patch of land located in a commercially important location, the other negotiating element was the price.

There had been a steady hike in the price of land all over Bangladesh during the period, and Massumpur was no exception. Even small plots of land were selling at five to seven times the price prevalent years back. Demographic pressures, remittances from contract workers, the general increase in productivity in varied sectors, the employment boom for the female workforce in the ready-made garment sector were some of the many supposed reasons.

Those were relevant for Shafiq in determining the proper price benchmark for negotiation, and not of immediate relevance to Azeem. The latter was more concerned with his worsening heath status, and thus wanted to have the deal soonest. The latter was pressing Shafiq to finalize the deal early at whatever the offered price was, so long as the would-be buyer had a reputation for straight deals and prompt payment. Shafiq was conducting the negotiations under the close guidance and supervision of Rukiya, so he was comfortable with the time being taken.

Eventually, the much-desired deal was agreed to, with 20 percent Ushul (advance payment) money being paid on initialing the contact and the final payment of the balance full amount to be paid at signing.

The venue of signing was to be the Tehsil Office (land registrar's office) of Massumpur at the behest of the Mojundar family to avoid any unintended time gap between full payment and registering the deed. All the three sons of the House of Mojundar icon were to be present. The presence of some local luminaries, including the local bank manager, were also agreed to give the deal a public and social endorsement.

Everything moved as planned. Bokul, on her own initiative, brought Julaikha-bu and her daughter to be a part of the happy process, culminating the desire of Dada-ji. Azeem and Shafiq were there days earlier, for Azeem to take rest and for Shafiq to ensure the smooth supervision of the event.

Most of the time, things do not move as planned in spite of care and preparations. And that is the vagary of life. One can try, but to avoid that in entirety is well nigh impossible. What happened in this case epitomized that.

Out of the blue, the most unexpected snag developed in carrying out the plan. The arrival of the eldest son was unpredictably delayed by a day due to the sudden tour plan of his boss from the headquarters. At his request, the signing was delayed by two more days.

Everything was done in a time-efficient manner and accomplished as per the revised scheduled. Happiness was all pervasive: for the Thesil Office being the venue of such a big deal; for the House of Mojundar for being successful in having the land they wanted so much; for Shafiq being able to put a seal of closure to what Dada-ji wanted so much and what he'd promised; and for Azeem having the unexpected bounty and blessings from the most thoughtful decision of Dada-ji, whom he had always misjudged.

As the event was coming to a close, a commotion was observed, seeing some people approaching the venue with food and paraphernalia. The icon of the House of Mojundar took the opportunity to thank all present and concluded by saying, "The postponement of the signing event caused possible discomfort to many. As a token of our gratitude, we have arranged some food for all present today. I would be delighted if you would kindly join me in this happy sharing, more so as we are not from Massumpur."

Toward the end of food intake, Azeem started feeling feverish, begged to be excused, and retreated to his home being escorted by two staffs of Tehsil office. He stipulated, after expressing his sincere apology, that if anything needs to be done, he would be ready to do it, if necessary even at home.

Seeing Azeem returning and being aware of his unstable health status, Bokul called Julaikha-bu. Both of them accompanied him to bed where he softly complained of fever.

Julaikha took out Bokul and said, "I am familiar with it. I need a rubber cloth, a bucket of water, and an empty bucket and a towel. Then both of us will help him to lie down, and I will pour water in his head."

That was done as planned. Azeem closed his eyes and sort of dozed off. Bokul went to the kitchen to make hot tea. Around that time, Azeem quietly opened his eyes, had a passionate look at Julaikha, and placed his hand on one of her hands engaged in applying the wet cloth on his forehead while water was being piped in by another.

@Momentarily, Julaikha was momentarily rendered motionless, varied emotions flooding her—anxiety, nervousness, embarrassment, and so on. Her eyes were voluntarily closed. She recovered soon, opened her eyes, disengaged her hand from the grip of Azeem, looked outside while observing, "I am presently a trustee of an amanath (safekeeping) of my late husband. You have a wonderful son besides a very talented and smart life partner. Please do not spoil it."

Saying those words and with an agonized mind, Julaikha went back to kitchen. Bokul looked at her and was taken aback, noting the facial changes in about a few minutes' time. She sensed something but kept quiet.

After a while, Bokul was on her way out near the family pond side looking for Julaikha-bu. She was taken back, locating her under the *chini am gass* (sugar mango tree). Before she could inquire about anything, her attention was drawn to about ten people approaching their home, with Shafiq leading them. They quickly retreated.

After escorting them to the sprawled sitting arrangements of Dada-ji, maintained as such, Shafiq went in and came back with Azeem after a briefing. Azeem was relieved to know that everything was done as needed, except two signatures and three initials in identified segments. The eldest son of the Mojundar family took the chance to interact, saying, "I am here at the behest of Father to thank you for doing everything needed in spite of your poor health. Since you left suddenly, we did not have the chance to convey that earlier."

Azeem beamed with happiness and nodded his head, drawing the attention of Shafiq, who went inside and helped Bokul and

Julaikha-bu to make the required glasses of lime-sugar *sherbet*. He reentered with a tray full of them and served those to the guests present.

The paperwork was completed promptly, but the assembly was in the mood to disengage. Both the relative wellness of Azeem and his presence were sort of boosters for the gathering, more to know about their life in Pakistan after Bangladesh became a reality.

Back inside, Bokul had not much to do as the Mojundar family earlier sent plenty of food. Julaikha-bu was obviously overladen by revisiting the site of *chini am gass* from where Azeem had his secret look of her bathing and the back view of her physique without any clue of her being aware of his presence. Bokul availed the opportunity and frankly, with all candidness, shot out the most delicate query, saying, "Would I be wrong in saying that you still have a soft and warm feeling for Azeem Bhai shaheeb?"

Julaikha-bu was in a vulnerable mental frame after many years. She thus spontaneously narrated what happened many years back in the setting of *chinni am gass*. She said, "I went to take a bath past noontime at a locale of quietness, removed my top, and went to the chest-deep water with a mixed uneasiness about the presence of a second person around. Then there was the sound of a mango dropping in the water, preceded by total silence. That convinced me it was Azeem. We, both of the same age, were growing up together, but being a girl, my intuition level was much deeper and pungent. I knew for certain that he had a liking for me, but due to social impediments, they could not be expressed. Knowing fully well Dada-ji's liking for him and his soft attitude toward fulfilling any desire of Azeem's, I decided to entice him by baring my back while changing to my dry replacement saree. I just thought that this rare experience would revitalize an insoluble urge within him to talk to Dada-ji about our liking. Every time Azeem went inside to meet Dada-ji, I had the hope of his talking to him about our mutual feelings. That did not happen. As super intelligent Dada-ji was, he noticed my frequent presence outside. Finally, he called me in, and without any pretentiousness or feeling otherwise started saying, 'Take your seat, my dear sister. I am quite aware and fully understand your feeling for

Azeem. But he is a different individual, far divergent than the locale of Massumpur, and is not for you. I promise I will get someone to be your life partner who would love you more than you would expect and make you happy.'

Even during the tumultuous days of the liberation war, he fulfilled his promise in getting me married with a wonderful young man of Gobindapur, a nominal distance of five miles but quite far at the time, considering the lack of roads and availability of transports. The outcome of that marriage was a prodigious expression of love and the warmth of unconditional feelings in spite of his periodic absence due to his study requirements in Dhaka. Out of about five years of married life, we were together for about nineteen months, which gave me the happiness and satisfaction of ninety years. That is the capital of my love, and I sustain that having an endearing look at our daughter, the trust I am holding. Yes, I still have growing-up nostalgic recalls, but that has nothing to do with sustaining earlier romance.' Julaikha-bu continued, saying she could still vividly remember Dada-ji's last credence, "He is not for you. Ardently, he is not for this periphery."

Bokul was pretty certain about the authenticity of Julaikha-bu's avowals. She moved her stool closer and embraced her very warmly without any space for doubt to pass through.

That was the end of the romantic feeling nurtured by a rural damsel in the growing-up phase of her life. With her mother deceased and her father opting for a life abandoning her, she grew up under the unconstrained leniency, care, and love of Dada-ji. Being an orphan and blessed by the unrestrained love of her grandpa, she continued to nurture her dreams and desires with frustration and desolation omnipresent in every turn of the corner.

DARE

Azeem returned to Dhaka to the joy and happiness of both Rukiya and Fazal. His safe return in good health was very relieving both for mother and son. The update about the successful conclusion of the much-desired land deal with *Mojundar Baree* and the price settled were all icing on the cake that made both Rukiya and Fazal ecstatic. The inner contemplation of Fazal was significant and did not escape the notice of his parents. He was unusually joyous and animated. Fazal made the parents all the more happier by sharing his school's conducted test examination result prior to appearing in the High School Board Certificate examination. That continued to be the same: topping the class. With mutual exchanges of looks, both Rukiya and Azeem too were floating in their world of opportunity and challenge.

While Azeem was engaged in reexperiencing himself and reassessing his prospect in the shades of evident affluence, Rukiya slowly vacated the place to his qualms. She complied with required *Wudu* (ablution) and performed a few *nafal* (voluntary) *rakats* (a rakat comprises of reciting optional suras [verses] with prescribed body movements) of *Salah*.

Any quick transition from professional disengagement and the resultant financial worries to the unanticipated affluence is a difficult one, with an equal chance of squandering the opportunity. Rukiya was sound and practical in thinking through the challenge. That, however, was not the case with Azeem. Not having good health of late and being run down by experiences due to his recent professional setbacks, he was constantly preoccupied thinking through quick options to ensure that the family would continue to enjoy steady financial standing even if something happened to him prematurely. Unguardedly, and being provoked by his so-called well-wishers, he was inclining to business options afresh. His consistent response to the uneasiness expressed by Fazal from time to time and to the sustained objections of Rukiya, was that, "my current position is quite different from the earlier one. At that time, I did not have capital. Now with capital and being the prime investor, I will exercise command and control. That gives me the option to walk out anytime."

Rukiya could not take such persistence anymore. She took their son Fazal into confidence, weighed different options, and decided to have a candid and final exchange with Azeem, exercising her choice not to hurt feelings in any way. Both of them also took cognizance of Azeem's not very positive heath conditions.

Life continues to be the most unpredictable journey, with the most unexpected bend having its own challenges and charms. Both mother and son had intermittent preliminary exchanges as to the way forward in conducting the current sensitive topic of the family investing in business options. Time passed, with misgivings and apprehensions dominating the thought of both without outward repercussions. Azeem noted that but remained nonchalant.

That was late noontime of a Friday. Surprisingly two gentlemen came and requested an audience with Major Azeem. In that social setting, no one addressed him as Major Azeem. They were unknown to Fazal and probably equally unknown to his father. With his hesitancy ubiquitous, Fazal just succumbed to the dictates of social niceties and welcomed them to the porch while going inside to inform his father.

Azeem quickly came out, had some hush-hush talk with the visitors, changed outfits, and left with them promptly with no backup indication.

That was alarming for mother and son. They promptly decided to raise the issue for final resolution during tonight's traditional post-dinner discourse. They also exchanged ideas of formulating talking points with civility. Fazal observed, saying, "We need to highlight the earlier premise of naming and launching *Asha*, generating enthusi-

272

asm and ushering commitment in Shafiq *chacha*. To deflect from that and now deciding on business investment would be a total betrayal to a person who so meticulously and sincerely protected the asset and its returns when we had no idea about it."

Rukiya was impressed and agreed, suggesting, however, that "Dada-ji's preference for involvement in the activity directly and indirectly related to land should be an important determining factor in our decision-making process. All our current affordability is due to his pragmatic decision. We need to respect that." Fazal agreed and rehearsed with mother his oration to highlight the point.

Concerning Azeem's newfound optimism about a business venture premised on capital and control, Rukiya formulated her position. She shared with Fazal her counters, having formulation akin to, "We fully agree with your strong position as the prime investor and your likely command and control on the company affairs. But I also listened to the occasional discussions some business contacts in Islamabad used to have with my father either to off-load them, or seek his help or suggestions. The real problem is that what you have in mind could be good enough for the first few months. Sooner or later, the capital is just an entry number in the accounts book and is no more liquid. It gradually fuses in stocks and stores (inventories), working capital, work-in-progress, credits, and debts. It is no more a capital at call. So one just can't get out with his or her capital at will. It is just a myth.

Further, your choice of construction-related business investment is contrary to what Dada-ji envisaged and tasked Shafiq Bhai to take care of. Can you bear the burden of the associated guilt inherent in that decision?

Both mother and son were tense about the upcoming discourse. Their principal worry was how Azeem would take it and possible impact of that on their affable relationships nurtured over so many years.

Rukiya was more concerned about the likely offshoot of the proposed discourse. She enjoyed so far an excellent conjugal life even though it had plenty of bounces of varied types—the lack of liquidity being the major one since retirement. It was reversed presently. The cause of present tension was the unexpected liquidity impeding the making of a rational decision acceptable to the family. She talked to herself, susurrating, "What an irony of life this experience is! The lack of liquidity is an all-encompassing explicit problem. Sudden liquidity beyond expectation is a greater challenge in life, destabilizing rationality and treasured rapports."

Azeem returned home with the same two gentleman but appeared to continue unfinished conversations, positioning themselves in front of the house. The innate affability during that discourse of Azeem and his associates caused concern to Rukiya. She called Fazal to witness that, expressing an apprehension of something going very wrong and contrary to their strong preference.

Apprehensions in any negative situation breeds miscalculations, causing a misdirection in thoughts and actions. The specific setting of Rukiya and Fazal was no different. Both were worried and stressed, obviously less talkative.

That was not the case with Azeem. He entered their home with a happy face and jubilation in his expressions and words. But the responses of both wife and son were just the reverse. He ignored that, concluding that his game plan was yielding results.

Azeem earlier took note of his wife and son's strong and sustained opposition to his business investment proposition. He thought through the premise of their objections and gradually decided not to get involved in business but, as a strategy, refrained from revealing that presently. On the other hand, Azeem was desperately looking for a family discussion afresh at their initiation but the persistent reluctance of the mother and son to open up was the bottleneck.

He was thinking about a probable game plan to induce a discussion on the subject at their initiative. That would be the proper setting for a much-desired revelation being dependent upon fulfilling two of his latent strong desires. He had good reason to harbor those desires. That was accentuated due to the recent bulging anxiety in terms of health and life.

Azeem was having a feeling of weakness and uncertainty in terms of life. He was having regular consultations with the designated physicians of CMH but kept many of the findings private, so a clever idea dawned on his mind. He decided to create a scene in which the family would be compelled to open up.

Accidentally Azeem met those two gentleman after a long gap while stepping out of CMH. These two gentlemen were very supportive associates in his endeavor to keep the detainees of Bangladesh origin in the Charsharda camp emotionally steady and physically fit.

Pleased by the accidental meeting, Azeem invited them for tea for late afternoon next Friday with the clear understanding of sharing that outside as he would have visiting family guests that evening. Azeem shared his residence address with them with the indication that they would go to the preferred tea stall together.

That was a wonderful afternoon for those two being able to spend quality time with the Major Sir. The whole game plan was played perfectly from Azeem's perspective. The icing of the game was the voluntary return of those two with Major Sir while recalling old days. This was the milieu when Rukiya saw them joyfully exchanging happy notes with Azeem. She had no doubt about those two being his likely business associates and thus called Fazal to witness that.

Both mother and son were tense throughout the evening while Azeem was outwardly glancing at some retirement papers with ease and comfort. He was certain about the probable outbursts as he monitored the home casually while talking with his associates and after observing the physical and emotional symptoms since his return.

That precisely happened after dinner. Fazal stayed back, requesting Mother, as a very exceptional act, for a cup of coffee for him too. Outwardly Azeem showed surprise, and was happy inside. To Azeem, that uncommon request was something like the repercussion of a likely brewing storm in the mind of Fazal while the coffee itself was being brewed by Rukiya in the kitchen.

Serving Azeem and their son their desired coffee and placing her teacup on the table, Rukiya took her seat, making a light observation about the assiduous silence around the dining table.

Azeem uncaringly exchanged a look with his wife and son but refrained from making any comment. Fazal took the first sip of his coffee and without any direct exchange of glance, said, "Dad, we have something to talk to you about, and that should be tonight."

Without allowing any scope to Fazal as to what he wanted to convey eventually, Azeem pointedly asked whether it was related to his proposition for investment in construction-related business.

Fazal not only confirmed that but also referred to trepidation being evident due to the presence of unknown visitors and his prolonged discussions with them.

Azeem took two quick sips of coffee, clarified who the visitors were, and then observed, stating, "I have pondered on the apprehensions you both have and am wedging toward an acceptable decision. How that decision is routed depends on both of your unqualified willingness to comply with two innermost cherished desires of mine. Rest assured that both of them are independent of the money factor."

Azeem paused for a while, and then continued, saying, "I would not like to argue with you both on the investment-related issue anymore. I was feeling poorly for the last few months. I am gradually and markedly deteriorating. I had the same feeling while in Massumpur, so I was relatively quiet and reserved. Upon my return from Massumpur, I have been having varied health-related symptoms and visiting CMH regularly for various types of tests and investigations. Even though no concrete outcome is in the horizon, I am increasingly feeling weak and uncertain about life. I did not share that with you both as nothing concrete was identified and the investigation continues. Moreover, sharing incomplete information often causes undue stress and anxiety. I thus opted to bear it alone.

In this agonizing time and preferred lonely space, two very selfish ideas dawned in my thinking. Both of them entail understanding and sacrifice on the part of you both, but would egoistically make me very happy at the tail end of my life."

The setting of the discussion turned precipitously to one of anguish and ambiguity from the premise of skirmish. Fazal was concerned but preferred to park that to be a transient mindset premised on possible deception. Rukiya was not only dumbfounded but blamed herself for ignoring the well-being of her beloved husband, a reaction engulfed by anxiety concerning money and related security. She was speechless and ashamed but had the most simple and genuine query when she asked for his reasons for not sharing the innate health concerns that took him to CMH often. She apologized to Azeem, saying, "I am so sorry. My anxiety with the possible impairment of the unexpected financial liquidity was so overwhelming that I ignored the years of trust, faith, and love that enriched our conjugal life. I even had misgivings about your frequent absence from home as time being spent on business propositions. I was wrong, but how could you hide your health concerns from me, or your going to CMH regularly?"

Azeem had a very innocuous exchange of eye contact with Rukiya. Involuntary tears plunging her cheeks were the ultimate testament of Rukiya's regret and shame. Azeem, being blessed with cavernous thought about life and living, preferred to keep quiet. Fazal's predicament continued, worsened by indication as to the "two innate desires" mentioned earlier by Father. He could not wait anymore and shot out a direct query about Father's hidden desires.

As a rare act, Rukiya was visibly upset by such direct questioning of Father by Fazal, especially when the former was not having good health. She had an unusual hardy look at Fazal, more to shut him up.

Having noted the same, Azeem stated his liking of the direct query of Fazal and expressed his willingness to share those but cautioned that "by nature and implication, they require a lot of understanding and involve unquestioned nonfinancial sacrifice."

Azeem paused, and then, with glumness and angst overpowering, slowly and softly started saying, "It is a fact that my health condition is not good and, as I feel, is deteriorating rather fast though a proper diagnosis is still to be completed. There are frequent disquieting indicators causing problems in the diagnosis. Broadly speaking, the variables relate to hemoglobin, platelet counts, triglyceride, and uric acid, and so on.

I spent a significant time pondering about the way I should behave and act. All these were trying thoughts and hours, the related resolutions being as elusive as the diagnosis is. That is the impasse I was encountering.

Before I reveal my innate two desires, I would like to tell you both about my intrinsic bizarre feeling concerning longevity, something which is just my sensitivity, and there is no basis to argue for that. To my mind, such feeling is usually normal when an individual is shaken by physical weakness and uncertain investigation status.

I always had a robust feeling about my health and a clear view of what I want to achieve in life, but those have since been shaken by successive professional setbacks, and now by an undiagnosed health status. When I first started to sail in the current rough water of life's boat, a thinking about the longevity of my immediate forerunners ordained in me. As far as I know, none of them had reasonable longevity. As you know, my father too died very young in a bus accident. All such thoughts gradually are engulfing my life, and I am shaken day by day. These are the premises of my very selfish hidden desires.

To put it simply, if you both agree to act on my intentions, my remaining life will be a happy one. If you are unable, I will not have any complaint, but the dark stain of ache in my inner self will persists and perhaps hasten the process of my journey to the other world."

This prolongation was too much for Fazal to bear. Rukiya, through an exchange of looks and expressions, restrained him from reacting while the thrashing within her own heart was evident. The relief came when Azeem asked for a glass of cold water to calm down his own impulses.

Azeem finished the water in one gulp, put the glass back on the table, repositioned his chair to deflect direct eye contact, looked outside in the darkness to the lone street light outside his abode, and started saying with an elfin smile, "My inner urges are to see Fazal getting married soon after his military academy graduation and to see the loving face of my first grandchild soon thereafter." He continued, saying, "That, in essence, entails that I would be totally out of the earlier preferred business investment option. I also assure you both of my full involvement and support, in spite of my health status, in buying new land strips near Dhaka with the help and involvement of Shafiq, consistent with Dada-ji's desire."

Rukiya demonstrably was relieved, but her disquiet related to Fazal's reactions persisted. Fazal was motionless, as he never expected to face such a situation. But the apparent adverse health conditions of Father motivated him to take a supportive stance. He desired to have a sheltered milieu to give further thought as to the propositions of his father and quietly left the dining table for his own room.

Both Azeem and Rukiya were surprised. The former was pondering in silence, and the latter was at the edge of her thwarting. In a soliloquy, she started talking to herself, saying, "What is wrong about your proposition? You are not desiring Fazal's getting married now. It is still about three years down the line. About that age, you got married at the behest of family. So there was nothing so unusual to induce him to leave our discourse."

Azeem surprisingly was more abstemious and empathetic. He consoled Rukiya by saying, "Nothing is wrong with Fazal. First, he belongs to a different generation. The views of his generation about marriage are evolving with free and sustained inflow of and exposure to other cultures and practices. Moreover, it is the age of dreaming with unlimited horizons. So, and very normally, the sudden proposition of marriage has shaken Fazal. But we should be thankful that he left the place quietly without creating any scene."

Fazal returned a few minutes later with his face down but having the semblance of certitude in his physical expressions. He took his previous seat, looked at parents penetratingly, and tenderly said, "I am your only child, born at the dry setting of Charsharda in a very challenging context. Since then, you have bestowed unqualified love and care in rearing me up. All your focus and attention was on me. That intimacy, love, and care enabled me to understand who I am and cement my bond with you both sturdily. The last visit to Massumpur was an eye opener, listening to the reproduced version of Dada-ji's statements and the stipulations that Shafiq uncle painstakingly narrated ensuring my presence.

In knowing all family-related details and in interacting with relations of different generations, I understood the value of relationships and the significance of family commitments. Julaikha Fuppi's decision in rearing up her only daughter in her late husband's home was an eye opener for me.

I also had the apposite inkling about the love a single child gets often but became very conscious of his obligations to the family as epitomized by Shafiq uncle. The related acumen to the instinctive reality that engulfs the single-child and parents moving relationships and obligations came into my thought prominently when you articulated your two desires.

I needed time and space to assess them. Both your desires are obviously very dear to you, and you are emotionally attuned to those. Contrarily, I have opposite views. But because of all that I detailed earlier, I came to the quick conclusion to agree with your proposition if that makes you elated. So you have my word whatever the consequences of that be in my life. Rest assured that I will never blame you for any misgivings in my future life. But being the son of a determined father, I have also a nonnegotiable proposition, and you need to concur with that.

You would recall that when we were back from Bogra ending your military career, you discussed with me your raging frustration and got my promise that I would also opt for a military career and would strive to at least reach the rank of lieutenant colonel. I remember that and renew that pledge tonight. But once I reach that level, I would opt for voluntary retirement, and concentrate on farming, a strong desire of Dada-ji which he could not get done through you in spite of his strong desire. I want to test his hypothesis with the sustained support of Shafiq chacha. I want to make his soul happy. That would be my dream to chase."

Pleasantly surprised, and with the nodding of Rukiya, Azeem happily agreed, saying, "If you succeed, Dada-ji will undoubtedly be happy in the other world, but that simultaneously would release me from the burden of guilt that I carry. If you succeed, you would have a single-handed double plus, and that would make us enormously happy."

Being pleased with affirmative decision, Fazal said, "Now please be rest assured, relax, and enjoy your life. Do not pressure yourself with the thought of death anymore. As there are illnesses, so there are cures also. Have faith in Allahpak and take stable steps in pursuing life. Please always bear in mind that these two souls are always by your side and will do every plausible thing to make you happy."

Fazal took slow steps forward to wipe involuntary tears flowing from the eyes of Azeem. As Rukiya stepped forward to share the happiest moment of her life, Fazal extended his hand, got Mother close, and hugged both parents intensely, showering kisses alternately on the foreheads of parents. On eventually getting disengaged, Azeem cheerfully commented, "Those were tears of joy."

WAGER

---

heir sudden financial buoyance shook the premise of a solid conjugal setting, but the family soon overcame the irritants through frank deliberations and pragmatic understandings. That imbibed within Azeem's family a strong desire and determination to succeed in life, leaving the past behind.

An anxiety, however, cropped within the mind of Azeem was the time being taken by Shafiq to show up. The agreed plan before leaving Massumpur was for Shafiq to follow Azeem with a detour of the Kashimpur and Azimpur areas after next harvesting season. The objective was to ascertain land availability in terms of blocks, productivity, and prices.

Shafiq was seldom away from Massumpur for too long at one go. Hence, he was lacking experience of and assessment concerning the related challenges. Shafiq was also certain that he could not ignore his truncated farming activities. Thus the planning, focusing, and assigning related responsibilities to his trusted associates took longer than expected time. He also needed time to appraise and prepare Bokul, who never experienced living without Shafiq for a relatively long time. Shafiq thought through the likely issues the family per se and farming in general may encounter and clearly detailed possible actions to redress them, with advice to contact him, if considered necessary, through his close friend Ali Karim.

Things were evidently behind schedule compared to the indicative time frame agreed subsequently. Shafiq left home later than planned, but the main reason of the delay was the unexpected need to spend additional days to take a detour of Kaliakair Upazila (subdistrict) in addition to the Kashimpur area. The Kaliakair visit was suggested by Assistant Tehsil Dar (assistant Tehsil officer) of the Massumpur Tehsil office with whom Shafiq became very friendly since the time of selling the inherited land to the House of Majmadar. That Assistant Tehsil Dar was posted in Kaliakair Tehsil office before his transfer to Massumpur. He, in detail, explained the highlights and potentiality of Kaliakair as being bounded by fast-emerging growth centers like Mirzapur, Sakhipur, Savar, Dhamrai, and Ghazipur upazilas besides being crisscrossed by some major waterways like the rivers Turag, Bangshi, Salda, and others. Shafiq's first impression of Kaliakair was very favorable. He spent a few unanticipated days deliberately to have a real feel of the place and to assess its farming potentiality. Based on such effort, he concluded that Kaliakair may be the place at the moment, but it would soon succumb to the urbanization and industrialization pressures liquidating the farms, so he refocused his attention on the Kashimpur-Azimpur areas and visited a number of farm plots with the help of his contacts developed during the deals Shafiq negotiated on behalf of Manzoor Bhai and Jaseem Bhai some years back. He had full trust in those *dalals* (brokers), and most of the exploratory visits Shafiq undertook were at their behest.

Fortunately, Shafiq identified a major chunk of farmland with a big pond in about the middle, with large coconut trees surrounding that mostly. The plot's specific location near Turag river, but at a sufficient safe distance not to be affected by seasonal vagaries like floods and likely erosions, were additional points noted by Shafiq.

Armed with those findings and assessments, Shafiq happily showed up, to the relief of Azeem, the delight of Rukiya, and the pleasure of Fazal. Initial discussions were mostly related to the impediments Shafiq encountered in leaving the family for relatively long time. Other farming-related hurdles were, of course, there but were relatively easy to handle.

Rukiya insisted, "Let Shafiq Bhai take some rest now. We can have a detailed briefing after our dinner." She left the sitting area, additionally saying, "I also need time to prepare dinner, definitely in a modest scale compared to that we had in Shafiq Bhai's place."

The discourse resumed after dinner with usual coffee for Azeem and tea for other three. The setting was obviously a happy one even though the anxiety about the uncertain future concerning the type, nature, and sustainability of future investments was assiduous in Azeem's mind because of health conditions. Rukiya was relatively quiet and more confident, having full faith in Allahpak and the assiduousness of Shafiq Bhai. Fazal maintained a discreet posture.

Being from a rural background, Shafiq finished his tea fast and put the cup on the table. While doing so deliberately for drawing the attention of all, Shafiq detailed the backdrop of his unplanned visit to Kaliakair, his experiences and assessments of the place, the reasons for his preference of Kashimpur based on his findings from earlier visits, and the identification of the plot that he preferred. He said, "The plot I have in mind is fortunately a remarkable one, with diluted landscape, water accessibility, and a big pond at about the middle surrounded by greeneries around."

In stating so, he alluded those as the reasons for the delay in coming. He further said, "I just did not like to discuss and get unspecified direction. I believe in concrete propositions to move forward. Even though I spent more time than expected in the field, I am convinced that it was worth it. I am of the judgment that the specificity we have would now make it easy for Azeem Bhai to indicate his preference."

On hearing all these, specially the pond location, Rukiya readily consented to initiate the negotiation. That was the outer shade of her feeling. Her real feeling was to have a quick and solid investment decision with the full endorsement and consent of Azeem before his health deteriorated.

Shafiq, evidently happy, reacted with a cautious indication. He observed, "*Bhabi*, different eyes see the same thing differently. Similarly, liking depends on inner feeling which varies from person to person. So it is very important that all four of us see that, evaluate the suitability, and assess the price depending on information available locally. If necessary, we can also visit the local tehsil office for related information. If agreed, it would be a day trip."

Fazal made a query before articulating his position. He said, "Chacha, everything you said sound so positive, but I have query—why the plot was not sold so far?"

Shafiq joyfully responded, saying, "First, the size of the plot is relatively large compared to local demand, and second, the related factor of price being beyond local capacity."

Very unusually, Azeem reacted promptly, giving an affirmative decision. The family visited the site in the company of two trusted *dalals* (brockers). Everyone was serious in making a proper evaluation within. Rukiya could not hold that anymore after seeing the pond and the surroundings. She whispered to Azeem and Fazal about her liking. It was not Rukiya alone. Fazal also liked it. So did Azeem.

Shafiq spent a few days shuttling between Dhaka and Kashimpur, successfully negotiated the deal with the full involvement and consent of the family. The family and Shafiq visited Kashimpur Tehsil office to sign the deed, and that was done promptly.

Overtaken by the joy of the successful culmination of the land deal, Azeem was temporarily oblivious of his health status, particularly the current illness pertaining to muscle cramps and weakness. He tried suddenly to stand up to shake hands with the tehsildar as a prelude to say goodbye, lost his balance, and fell on the floor. Fortunately, the chair on which he was sitting came to his immediate rescue, the fall was mild, and Azeem recovered quickly.

While commencing the drive back home, and at Shafiq's suggestion, the family took a slight detour to pass by the farmland they just bought. Everyone was both surprised and equally ecstatic in seeing a big billboard with the writing, "Azeem-Shafiq Associates (Asha) Agricultural Farm, owned by Major (Rtd) Azeem Abbas."

But the quip came from Rukiya, saying, "Shafiq Bhai, you are a very special person, always ahead of us in thinking and action taking." Shafiq took that as a spontaneous and equally genuine observation being that, as he observed earlier, she was emotionally preoccupied thinking apparently about the health of Azeem since his slipshod fall.

In subsequent discussions, it was agreed that the main focus of the current farming would be paddy and seasonal vegetables.

Changes in farming protocol would depend on experience, feedback, and the emerging market scenario.

Among others, the presence of Fazal in many of such discussions was aimed at ensuring his listening to and being familiar with relevant decisions. And that was ensured at the behest of Shafiq.

But Fazal often startled his parents and uncle with comments and observations pertaining to the arrangements being worked out. And that happened in this setting too. As the seniors were busy in detailing the farming practices envisaged, Fazal jested, saying, "You all are talking as if Shafiq Chacha is a native of Kashimpur. The reality is, he has no footing in the area enabling him to stay even for a short time, forget about a long duration, so we should think about that now before we take other decisions."

Azeem was impressed by the practicality of Fazal's concern and thinking. Rukiya was thrilled by the astuteness so demonstrated by him. But most happy was Shafiq as Fazal's intervention relieved him of his quandary in raising an issue that was related to him.

Everyone was conscious of the need that Fazal highlighted. Shafiq's presence and involvement was needed by the family. It was primarily for their benefit. The swath of Shafiq in this regard was his words given to Dada-ji, but the latter never stipulated that at the cost of Shafiq's family.

With that realization in his thinking, Azeem exchanged confirmatory glints with Rukiya and Fazal before saying, "I vividly recall each word your Bhabi uttered in Massumpur for compensating you for your time, commitment, and effort. I stand by those with little upward revision of monthly payment to Tk. 7,000, and a one-time grant of Tk 25,000 for you to build a two-roomed modest structure near any suitable edge of the land. If that is not feasible, you may opt to buy a small residential plot nearby and build the structure. We can discuss details of financing the purchase of that piece of land in due course."

He continued saying, "I am thankful to Fazal for raising the issue and would request you not to treat it as a charity. You are needed by us more than you need us. This is just to keep your immediate anxiety away and to enable you to commit yourself copiously for our conjoint benefit.

Before concluding, I have one more suggestion. In looking for such a plot and in constructing your own place, please keep in view that you may be required to move the family to Kashimpur some time in future for the sake of family tranquility and to enable you to fulfill your desire to educate your daughters. Do you recall your firm desire to educate your daughters when you said to your Bhabi, 'By interacting with you, I have learned the value of girls' education and will endeavor in every way to impart proper education to my daughters.' I remember those words. Kashimpur, being in the vicinity of Dhaka, is likely to have better learning facilities and access compared to Massumpur, so that could as well be a strong possibility and keeping that in your thinking and plan will be helpful."

The innate enthusiasm of Azeem was multiplied by the recent developments in spite of the concerns related to his health. Against the expressed position of Rukiya, Azeem, along with Shafiq, undertook a consultation visit to both the Bangladesh Rice Research Institute (BIRRI) and the Bangladesh Agricultural Research Institute (BARI) to acquaint the latter with the latest progress in related fields to make him up to date with the latest development and thinking. That was possible as Azeem happened to know a senior functionary of BARI who started his career in Lyallpur Agricultural Research Institute of Pakistan very late in the 1960s.

Armed with new insight and information, Shafiq returned to Kashimpur and wholeheartedly devoted his time and energy first to get some reliable people on board. Once that was achieved, he took a short break for visiting Massumpur as he was missing the company and hugs of his daughters.

The family got happily reunited, seeing Shafiq stepping in his compound. The girls screamed and Bokul, to hide her pleasure, put the *anchal* (tail end of a saree) on her head to form a *ghomta* (head cover). Time just flew in the midst of the diversified updates by Bokul and girls.

Bokul observed a meaningful change in Shafiq's homily as he showed greater concern and interest in matters related to learning, the school atmosphere, and the general upbringing compared to his earlier interest to know about the *Munshi Mar* parable, a locally popular didactic story dealing with instructive lessons.

The dinner tasted splendid to Shafiq after eating in rudimentary restaurants of Kashimpur for the last few days. Unlike most men of the society, Shafiq had no postdinner preferences such as *pan* (traditional betel leaf service) service.

Prevalent traditions have sort of an embargo on wives to express longing for physical intimacy. Wives are generally subservient to men's desires and initiatives. To overcome that impediment, Bokul, through practice and repetition, worked out a sublime protocol. That related to service of a postdinner *pan* as an indication of desire for physical intimacy. As Bokul was stepping forward, having *pan* in her hand, Shafiq unwittingly took the time in detailing the way of living in Azeem Bhai's house and how Rukiya Bhabi manages things. That erroneously wedged on the thinking of Bokul. She retorted, saying, "Bhabi is an educated woman. I am not. You can't expect same ability from me."

Shafiq realized his blunder. He quietly took the pan, held that in his left hand, and suddenly pulled Bokul toward him. Having her on his chest, he passionately inquired, saying, "You don't hear anything? The vibration and zest of my heart do not convey anything to you?' Having said those words, Shafiq pressed Bokul toward his chest once again with kisses abound in all the sensitive parts of her upper physique, including her neck and ears. Those were preludes to immersed physical rapport to the fulfillment of Bokul and pleasure of Shafiq.

Shafiq then put the thrashed out pan in his mouth, to the happiness of Bokul. As she exchanged a fulfilling look with him, Shafiq positioned her opposite him and said, "You misread my reference to Rukiya Bhabi's management capacity. That was never meant to compare you with her. You have many adorable attributes that many lack. That was aimed at the renewal of my realization about the value of the girls' learning and its impact on family upbringing. I just wanted to renew my pledge to do everything to impart proper education to our daughters. I need your help and support in their grooming." Bokul was pleased as well relaxed more to know about Shafiq's earnestness to educate their daughters. Observing that, Shafiq was happy too.

That happiness, however, was suddenly marred by Bokul's response to Shafiq's query as to how she passed her time during his absence. Bokul said, "After a few days of your leaving, Julaikha-bu suddenly showed up. She was stressed and distressed, no more the previous Julaikha-bu. What she told me was very disturbing. On my specific query, Julaikha-bu, with obvious reluctance, said, 'Even though my in-laws' family is no more involved in active politics, their past association with Majlis-e-Islam is still haunting them. They lost most of their properties and a part of household to emerging power brokers. My daughter and me are now to share a bed and room with my mother-in-law with no privacy for my growing-up daughter and me. I can't bear it anymore. I always wondered why I have such a life while my blooming youth was full of admiration and possibilities with associated dreams. I came to you just to escape from that temporarily.' Having quoted Julaikha-bu, I felt bad for making your joyful evening a dejected one."

Shafiq was really glum. He rearranged his pillow, turned himself to the other side, and pretended to fall asleep. On his part, he thought of a solution of Julaikha-bu's agony, but kept it to himself for the time being. Bokul felt bad and fell asleep in due course.

Before leaving Massumpur, and as an exception, Shafiq indicated to Bokul his plan to be home after two weeks for a short visit. He also desired that Bokul manage to get Julaikha-bu to come and spend time together. The objective palpably was to discuss Julaikha-bu's current constrictions in order to find a solution.

Part of the sloped plan that Shafiq quickly thought through that night was within his domain. He was comfortable with that. The other part would need Azeem Bhai's consent. Obviously he was uncertain about that, though he was hopeful. He revisited that plan in the context of what Dada-ji would have liked him to do under the circumstance and what would constitute keeping his promise to him concerning looking after Julaikha-bu.

Shafiq returned home as per earlier plan and was pleased to meet Julaikha-bu and her daughter. The plan in mind was emotionally very delicate, and the time was short. So while having tea on arrival, Shafiq was amazed seeing *pua pitha* (oil fried rice-based snack) and *patishapta pitha* (Bangladeshi rice crepes), both snack items of his preference.

Noting his wonderment, Bokul promptly said that those were brought by Julaikha-bu. As Shafiq reacted with both penchant and hesitancy, Julaikha-bu stated, "I could not bring anything when I came last time and felt miserable before my nieces. So I opted for these two mundane items. Bokul prepares much better pithas. But those pithas enabled me to look straight at my nieces and offer them something."

Shafiq remarked, saying, "Yes, Bokul makes nice pithas. But in these two prepared by you, I am having the flavor of Dadi-ma's touch."

Both the girls took Julaikha-bu's daughter to the surroundings to make her familiar with different households. All the adults were sipping their tea, each one having his/her divergent mental pressures: Shafiq had his in opening up with his part of the solution in mind; Julaikha-bu was at her wit's end, agonizing about the reasons for their asking her to visit on specific date; and Bokul was confused, having no clue of why they had called Julaikha-bu to come.

Shafiq had no plan to discuss the current living scenarios of Julaikha-bu so soon after his arrival, but considered the current locale as the most appropriate one. So without wasting any time but avoiding what she shared with Bokul during her last visit, he went forward, suggesting, "This is Dada-ji's house. We are presently using two rooms only, and other rooms are generally empty. So respecting your earlier choice of staying back in your in-laws' place, I suggest you move to this house, on which you have equal right. I will take full care of your needs as I promised to Dada-ji on his death bed. Everyone would like to have you back, and so does Bokul. You and your daughter will have a new identity and will be respected. That could even help future matrimonial propositions for our loving niece."

As Shafiq paused, Bokul promptly said, "That will be wonderful. Me and our daughters will be delighted. Even, and very selfishly, our niece would be a good guide to our daughters."

Shafiq was pleased. Julaikha-bu started sobbing, saying, "What you suggested is acceptable to me, especially for proper upbringing and the future life of my daughter. I stayed back in my in-laws' family at my will. I can decide to move back to my own abode, and perhaps that would relieve them too."

Unlike others who expressed their thanks in lexes and looks, Julaikha's ultimate response reflected the residue of influence of Dada-ji on her too. She observed, saying, "Shafiq, what you have detailed is normally done by the elder brother for his widowed sister in distress. You are many years younger than me. In spite of that, you elevated yourself to the position of the highest esteem by all consideration. I am equally beholden to Bokul for her effort in shadowing my organic conditions."

Enthralled and relieved equally, Shafiq shared with her about the near-term possibility of moving the family to Kashimpur to have better access to learning for their daughters. He continued, saying, "There would not be a cause of concern even if that happens. The family is here. We have a host of cousins, nephews, and nieces. You will never be alone. Further, I would be visiting you from time to time. You can move at any time of your choosing. Just keep Bokul informed."

He completed his avowal by saying, "Azeem Bhai too would be happy to know about it. When he was here, he lamented to me for your living in your in-laws' place in an apparent shabby condition. He gathered that from discussions with the family elders."

Shafiq left Massumpur as per earlier plan. He stopped in Kashimpur for a few days to oversee progress and label other pending preparatory actions for the first farming event under Asha's management.

While awaiting the after-dinner routine tea and coffee service, Shafiq appraised Azeem about the progress being made at Kashimpur for launching Asha's maiden farming in the next season. Labor, water, seed, fertilizer, and so on were all matters of relative minor interests on that evening to Fazal as he was holding back sharing exciting information which came to his knowledge just before dinner while slouching through much-neglected daily postal mails. Keeping his father's health condition in view, and to ensure that he had a proper meal without distraction, Fazal opted to share it after dinner.

Noting that his mother was taking more than the normal time in appearing with the tea and coffee, he moved to kitchen to find Rukiya busy in cleaning the kitchen while water was boiling in the kettle with the respective mugs in tidy condition. Rukiya stated, "As the daughter of Fatima (household help) is ailing, she had to leave early. The sudden arrival of Shafiq has compounded the problem. Hence, the delay."

With all four sitting and sipping their respective stimulating drinks, Fazal opened up, saying, "Dad, I have something to share with you. Ammu will be excited, and Chacha would likewise be proud."

Azeem, in spite of his prolonged affliction, got back his military life's jocularity and said, "It cannot be related to the military academy as you would only apply next year. So I am at a bay in my thinking. I do not see anything else except our son has fallen in love."

The affirmative answer of Fazal caused bewilderment among the others present. He took a sip and then said with a pause, "It is a fact that I am in love. That is not with any person but a passion. Both of you are aware about my liking of debate. I just received this letter from the Ministry of Education informing and congratulating me for my selection as a core member of the Bangladesh Debate Team for contesting in the SARC (South Asian Regional Countries) Debate Forum to be held in Goa of India."

Rukiya could not help herself. She sprang up from her chair, rushed toward Fazal, hugged him warmly, and kissed him profusely. Azeem's reaction was more uplifting, with a broad smile of contentment and bliss, politely saying what he had in mind, "That ought to be. He is my son. It paves the way for his cherished admission to the military academy in chasing my dream."

Shafiq observed happily, "I have discreetly seen Fazal from day one and have no hesitation in saying that he is one in the family having the most of the positive attributes of Dada-ji. I am so proud of that. In my next visit to Massumpur, I will specifically visit the necropolis of Dada-ji, pray for his noble soul, and convey the news of this exceptional achievement by Fazal."

Of late, Azeem preferred an early retirement to bed after dinner, but, to the surprise of both Rukiya and Fazal, he desired to have a second service of favorite drinks. That was happily complied with.

Availing that opportunity, Shafiq recounted the understandings agreed with Julaikha-bu concerning her relocation to Massumpur and his assurances to look after her and the niece. He took advantage of the situation to appraise all about the future plan he had in mind for relocating the family to Kashimpur for the benefit of daughters' education.

To both father and son, that was a significant news but not to Rukiya. She induced that idea in every one-on-one talk with Shafiq and impressed upon the imperative need for a father to be around daughters when they are growing up. In recounting her own growing up in Islamabad, Rukiya profoundly observed, "This relationship between a father and his daughter is unique, belying articulation by words and description. The care is predominant. The love is sublime. The affection is swarming The apprehension is ubiquitous. A mutual feeling between the two evolves and flourishes, preparing the daughter to leave her father's abode and for the father to be happy seeing his daughter settled in unfamiliar milieu which she'll soon refer to as her home."

Fazal congratulated Shafiq Chacha for the arrangements made for Julaikha fuppi's relocation and indicated his desire to contribute as per ability once he gets his commission in the army. He also conveyed his unrestrained happiness for the decision to relocate the family to Kashimpur. Apart from others, he further observed, "This decision will foster a unique bond between our generations which I never thought of. Of course, having Bokul chachi near us is just a much-desired plus point for me."

The subsequent queries of Fazal took all by amazement. He said, "Chacha, among others, there are two points on which I am very unclear. Hence, I am asking you directly, and I beg to be excused: first, how you can, most of the time remain, so calm, and second, how you can think through the tasks to be undertaken before even the party concerned could think of them?"

Shafiq smiled with pride and glee and exchanged deep-rooted admiring looks with Azeem and Rukiya. He then said, "On your first query, it is perhaps precise to say that unlike the shorter period of association that Azeem Bhai and Julaikha-bu had with Dada-ji, I was the sole beneficiary of being blessed by a positive and intimate long association with him. He seldom allowed me to be away from him. He was my animation and the world. I not only observed him intimately but tried my best to internalize and assimilate all that was good in him by my assessment. This particular trait impressed me most, and I knowingly practiced it constantly. You will note a replica of the same both in your father and fuppi, maybe in a small scale because of their shorter association. My answer to your second point is very easy. Years back and coincidentally, I asked the same question to Dada-ji. His pragmatic response was, 'Never treat a situation necessarily as a problem, per se. Treat it as something relevant and relate it with you and think through the process of a way out. You will get your answer. Further, the best response to human behavior is to love and that too unconditionally. Unfortunately we behave differently: we tend to demean people when they are alive but lament for them when they are dead. This is the real problem. One must try to reverse it.' Those are my responses to your queries."

Fazal left thereafter with ease and exhilaration. Rukiya picked up cups and saucers and went to the kitchen. Shafiq stood up to follow others when Azeem requested him to stay back for a while.

Seeing both cousins closeted together, sensible Rukiya sidestepped them and retreated to her bedroom, always sure that Azeem would tell her in due course the substance of present discussions.

Desiring that Shafiq pull his chair close to his, Azeem took hold of both hands of Shafiq and in an emotion-laden avowal started saying, "Your Bhabi does not believe that I am very sick and my physique is slowly giving in. She thinks it to be a mental state, being battered a number of times in life. But trust me, brother. I am a military man, never being bothered by possibility of death. I faced superior military opposition immediately after my marriage in which three of my comrades embraced *shahdat* (martyrdom) in obeying my command. The reason of calling you, however, is different. You have proved more than the trust reposed in you by your sincerity, commitment, and honesty in preserving and carrying out what Dada-ji desired. With that backdrop, I have an earnest request to you. If anything happens to me, please be by the side of your Bhabi and Fazal in good or bad times, whatever it is. And second, Rukiya, as a person does not like surprises, so keep her always informed and get her valued opinion. Finally, I have two known desires, and I want their fruition before anything happens to me. You know those, and I remember that you politely dissented on the first occasion you came to know about them. I respect your opinion, but pardon me, and treat those as my death wish. I had a lot of dreams in life, but destiny was always hostile. I only chased my dreams but never enjoyed the fulfillment of many of those. The happiest moments of my life are minimal two: meeting you in the outer stadium area and visiting Massumpur with family. I am thankful to you, but please support me in respect of those two desires and give me the word that you will always be by side of my family."

Clasping both hands of Shafiq, he pressed them very hard in military style but soon succumbed to tears, saying, "This is my contract with you. As you promised to Dada-ji, you must pledge your word to me. I will be happy even in my death with at least one desire as being set to be fulfilled."

Shafiq passionately responded, saying, "I am aligned with the known position of Bhabi and firmly believe that, InshaAllah, you will recover and live long. Besides your known two desires, you must live to see that Asha (also meaning hope) lives up to your name and succeeds in all respects. You have my word in complying with all your desires, but you must dream to live."

APOGEE

---

ime passed. Years rolled over. Shafiq worked diligently to plan and launch allied farm activities. Though not highly educated, he had ordained "gifts of God" in assessing the future better, in identifying the qualities of individuals, and in creating trust and common feeling among coworkers besides his own ability to work hard and relentlessly. His prioritization with respect to farm activities was unrivaled. That resulted, in consultation with Azeem and Rukiya, in the setting up of a rudimentary field office and the construction of a modest residential facility for himself with the provisions for need-based expansion in future. In the year third, an internet communication system was set up for efficient recording and periodic communication with Azeem and Rukiya.

Compared to the bare break-even performance of the first year, *Asha* made significant headway in the subsequent years both in production and marketing. Crop diversification efforts, the adoption of improved production technologies, including greater attention to HYVs, prudent plant protection works under the close guidance of and collaboration with the local agricultural extension services office and that of BARI and BIRRI resulted in outcomes never thought of. The performance was outstanding. Part of the seasonal income was invested in acquiring additional farmlands in the vicinity. There was no irresolute centering the decision to relocate farm activities from Massumpur to Kashimpur.

Overall, both Rukiya and Azeem were ecstatic. Their sensitivity of being euphoric was magnified many a times with the news that Fazal was recommended for the award of Chief of Staff Gold

Medal for excellence in military subjects at the time of the upcoming "President Parade" on the occasion of the "Awarding Commission."

Even though not in a good health, the positivity centering Fazal's success and sustained gains in farm outcomes had a discernible good impact on Azeem. That was strengthened due to establishment of the internet link with the field office of *Asha*. For a little while, it appeared that Major Azeem insistently progressing for a rejuvenated future.

As an unofficial routine, Shafiq used to report personally every fortnight, and get guidance. It was one of such days. In postafternoon tea conversation, Shafiq updated the couple with all field and account details. Both Azeem and Rukiya were very happy. The news of Fazal's achievement was an unexpected bonus and a facilitator to Shafiq.

As he was awaiting a suitable opening to highlight what he wanted to say, Azeem took a tangent, being unable to hold his happiness only to positive outcomes of *Asha*'s farm operations. He was, at that point in time, more thrilled by the news of Fazal's success and wanted to have a happy conversation with the participation of both Rukiya and Shafiq. Azeem maintained that Fazal's achievement was a definite stepping-stone in his pursuance of the dream to become a lieutenant colonel eventually, an aspiration that remained a dream for the father in spite of credibility otherwise. Happiness overwhelmed Shafiq too knowing about achievement of Fazal. But that was not his main objective.

Noting the improved health status of Azeem Bhai and seeking the consent of Rukiya Bhabi, Shafiq updated the couple with his ideas and suggestions about a new strategy and innovative approach. He emphasized the imperative need for new thinking and took the opportunity to detail his own thinking and suggestions for the enlarged operations of *Asha*. Shafiq emphasized that traditional farming practices had signs of evident constraints, and those were likely to affect productivity and the cost of production. Besides, the unpredictable market price phenomena and the predictable shortage of labor in the future due to rapid urbanization around were other constraining factors at this stage. Kashimpur bazar people were also worried about the likelihood of paddy markets being flooded by other sources' supplies. "So we need to think proactively now. Our stake is significant. Our possibilities are enormous, provided we are on a progressive track."

Keeping all these in view, Shafiq said, "I had a number of exploratory visits to adjoining growth centers, the relevant government agricultural offices and facilities, including the extension services. I also maintained my contacts with BARI and BIRRI through sources introduced by Azeem Bhai. Based on the series of recent exchanges with relevant and experienced officials, I am toying with the idea of a major redesign of farm activities, redirecting the focus from a hundred percent traditional paddy cultivation to designed priorities focusing on vegetable, fruits, and herbal plants in organic modes. As a side operation, I am also thinking of taking advantage of grazing options in *Asha*'s considerable farmland. It would perhaps, subject to your consent, be prudent and economic to get involved in dairy farming. The location of Kashimpur is ideal in this respect, being in the close vicinity of emerging growth centers, with Savar being the most prominent one. Savar traditionally has high demand for milk being, among others, popular as one of the centers of milk-based sweets. Savar is also easily approachable by road and the tributaries of the Old Brahmaputra river. My last visit to the facilities of the Animal Husbandry Department in Savar and discussions with the officials concerned convinced me about yield-related productive results of artificial insemination and the emerging need of new types of fodder for cattle to enhance productivity."

The discussions continued during postdinner settings. Unlike other occasions, Rukiya was relatively quiet. That drew the attention of Shafiq. He realized that to be a consequence of her brooding anxiety concerning the health of Azeem Bhai. As a diversion, he initiated discussions on his plan to relocate his family to Kashimpur soon. Shafiq also informed both that Julaikha-bu was well settled, mingled with all happily, and was comfortable with the arrangements made. Rukiya spontaneously welcomed the plan with an expressed desire that Bokul and daughters would visit them in Dhaka immediately after relocation.

Azeem seemed tired and maintained relative quietness. With hope and anxiety preoccupying his thought, Azeem observed, saying, "I get your assessment concerning the future challenge that traditional farming will face soon, but I do not subscribe to idea that paddy cultivation would have a negative experience. With the bulging population, the demand for paddy will continue to be significant. I nevertheless agree with the rising cost of production, minimizing the margin of return. So we have a very delicate path to choose. Agreeing with whatever you articulated earlier, I suggest that we move cautiously and in phases, and adjust our plan based on experience."

Shafiq was delighted as the decision of Azeem Bhai was just what he had in mind. That happiness swamped the thought and expressions of Shafiq. He instantly made a proposition, saying, "If your health permits, and InshaAllah that will be so, I propose to arrange a thanks-offering lunch in honor of our workers and notable local gentries. Though *Asha* will complete four years of its operation on the next *pohela Baishak* (first day of first Bangla calendar month Baishak), I have in mind to plan that, subject to your endorsement, coinciding with *Nabaanna* (literally signifying harvesting of new rice with a festival of food) festival in June as that is more appropriate and weather friendly after the onslaught of *Kalboishaki* (scary Boishak)."

That proposition thrilled Rukiya, and she reacted very sportingly and supportively deviating from her mute participation. What she said subsequently alerted both Azeem and Shafiq.

Rukiya went back to her days of growing up in Islamabad, stating, "The Punjab province of Pakistan has the tradition of celebrating Boyishaki (on the first day of Boishak) by merrymaking, flying kites, and, for those who could afford, by having drinks, rather privately. They were very proud of that traditional legacy.

In response to one of my growing-up stage inquisitions, Mother referred to '*Nabanna* festible in East Pakistan (now Bangladesh).' Her related portrayal was so glowing that even at that stage of life, and notwithstanding apparent deviances in setting, I had a firm imprint in my mind enabling me to explain to my class fellows about the *nabanna* festival. That perhaps is the reason for me to remember *nabanna* festival even after so many years."

Her euphoria was not limited to that. She, after an exchange of looks with Azeem, indicated going to Kashimpur in the company of her younger sister and some of her cousins and nieces to attend the *Nabanna* lunch and suggested that Bokul and daughters be relocated soonest.

In one response, Rukiya, demonstrating her prudence and ability, tackled affirmatively both the issues Shafiq floated: the relocation of family by Shafiq and consent for *Nabanna* lunch. Azeem ceremoniously conveyed his approval by nodding head.

Preparatory actions were taken by all concerned. All arrangements were made for the travel, including a helping hand for Azeem. Surprisingly, and belying related apprehensions, Azeem appeared to be in a stable health condition and more eager to see the farm. The only disappointing trigger was Fazal's inability to join the joyous family event due to his commitment related to the "President Parade" in October on the occasion of annual commissioning event.

Shafiq made all preparatory arrangements. The family was relocated well ahead of time. Shafiq was beaming in happiness for another reason. His daughters got into the respective classes of Kashimpur school, and they liked both the change and school environment. That made Shafiq and Bokul happy even though the latter initial settling days were challenging and exhausting.

Azeem and his family joyously arrived in Kashimpur with expressed delight, having noted the new billboard of Asha in the outer periphery with Azeem's portrait prominently on one side. Azeem was pleased and thanked Shafiq silently.

But occasionally one happiness is overtaken by another surprise, adding flare and flavor to the experience. That happened in the case of Azeem's family too. The rented vehicle with Azeem and his family on board was guided by an escort in motorbike detailed by Shafiq from the main road intersection to the farm site. As the vehicle slowly moved into the compound of half brick- cement construction with another half with CI sheet extension, everyone was taken aback. The frontage of the cement-brick half construction had the name

"Rukiya House." The happiness of all present was irresistible while Rukiya succumbed to emotions with tears in her eyes.

Shafiq escorted Azeem to introduce him to the workers and guests present, prefixing that "Bhai Shaheeb is not feeling well. In spite of that, he took the trouble to meet you all." As Azeem was being introduced, he shook hands with most, embraced the elderly and respectable guests, and thanked farm workers for their sincerity and commitment. The guests and workers were entertained under a *shamiana* (a flat tent/canopy), and Azeem left the venue in between to take rest.

With a hectic day behind and considering the health condition of Azeem, preparations were undertaken to leave earlier than planned. Rukiya embraced Bokul and thanked her profusely for everything done to make the visit a memorable one. Holding Bokul's two hands and drawing her close to self, Rukiya whispered with all firmness, "You are my sister. Visit me whenever you feel like it. Do not await for an invite. Our house is always open for you and your daughters." Rukiya hugged the daughters before boarding the vehicle.

The return trip seemingly was tiring for Azeem, but the other occupants were very cheerful. Rukiya maintained monitoring Azeem and casually participated in the joyous commentary of others.

Back to Dhaka, Rukiya took things easy to give space to Azeem to recover from the stress of travel as well to enable him to ruminate about his dream in the light of current progression. In casual exchanges, both of them voiced renewed trust in Shafiq and confidence in his candor, commitment, initiatives, and visions. Rukiya further observed that "he has tremendous ability to foresee the future and never took any steps without our approval. I have monitored it carefully."

Azeem responded, saying, "In that perspective, our family appears to be an unique one. Dada-ji was, most of the time under, influence of Babu Bijon Mohan Nag, and the recipient of his unending trust, compassion, and love in spite of the prevailing conditions and constraints related to the partition of India and the bitter communal feelings across the board. Likewise, Shafiq, in a different situation, is a blessing for us in all perspectives. Besides his adorable honesty and sincerity, I believe he has inherited some of the qualities of Dada-ji in sensing potential, besides having a real-world mind blessed with broader vision and goals. I am not worried about my health. If anything happens, he would always be by Fazal and your side."

Azeem was feeling better since their return from Kashimpur. However, in one of the following nights, he suddenly started having multiple complaints, including muscle weakness and breathing problems. Azeem was immediately rushed to CMH. He stabilized after a few hours' stay and was sent back home in spite of Rukiya's plea otherwise.

Rukiya became really apprehensive for the first time. She always assumed past complaints of indisposition as a more emotive reverberation, but the previous night's experience was sufficient to cause fretfulness and trepidation in her mind. Consequently, the ambience in Azeem's place suddenly changed. Despair and nerviness swiftly overtook the exhilaration surrounding the farming-related dream, especially after the *Nabanna* visit.

Upon hearing from Rukiya, Shafiq rushed in. As he was about to enter the house, Shafiq encountered the mailman and took possession of the incoming mail.

Keeping the mail on the dining table, Shafiq rushed to the bedroom of Azeem, where he was resting. Azeem welcomed Shafiq with a broad smile and jokingly commented, "Your Bhabi presumably asked you to come. You see I am fine. There is no reason for concern. It was something exceptional that night. I am now relaxed."

Shafiq commented, saying, "It is nice to see you in such good spirits. My coming was worth seeing that."

After some time, they got engaged in discussions about the farm-related matters. Complying with the call of Rukiya, both of them moved to the dining table area and took their respective seats. Rukiya soon served snacks, tea, and coffee. Finally, she came with her cup of tea and joined the cousins. While chomping on snacks, Rukiya's attention was drawn to a decorative invitation envelop in the mails. She pulled it out and screamed, saying, "Oh, it is from the military academy." Having uttered those, the envelop involuntarily tumbled from her grips.

Observing the decorative envelop, Azeem was sure that, first, it was not ordinary mail from the military academy, and second, it must be carrying some positive news. He opened it with all love and reverence and said, "This is formal invitation to both of us and for two additional guests to witness the Commissioning of Fazal as part of the President Parade under advance indication for which the form and a self-addressed envelope have been enclosed."

A glimpse of exhilaration just sparked in Rukiya's reaction. Shafiq was thrilled at the success of Fazal, and said, "Had he been alive, Dada-ji would have enjoyed it most." But the follow-on reaction of Azeem stalled both. He said, "This is the occasion and that is the day I have had been longing for. When fortunately everything is in place to fulfill that dream of mine, my health lamentably is not in good shape. Illness is one thing, but the unstable nature of illness is most disturbing. Still I will try."

Having said so, Azeem requested Rukiya to fill up the form with their names, and that of Shafiq and Rajib, the younger brother of Rukiya. Shafiq promptly said that, "I will myself visit the general post office and will post the letter before returning to Kashimpur. Also, I would keep the receipt with me until its handing over to Bhabi."

His immediate departure was necessitated due to some urgent pending actions at Kashimpur.

There is a social belief that positive thinking crowns upbeat outcomes. In Bangla, it is called "*shuv shuv chinta*." So Rukiya and Shafiq committed themselves to praying for the good health of Azeem so that they all could enjoy the happy event together.

But destiny charted it the other way. Five days prior to the journey schedule, Azeem started feeling unwell. Doctors advised him not to travel at all. Because of such definite prognosis, his hands were tied. Azeem thought of options and then stipulated, proposing, "You should not miss the event. For a soldier's mother, this is the moment of pride and happiness. You can travel by taking a commercial flight both ways. It would mean you leaving Dhaka by the early morning flight and returning the same day by the evening flight after attending the event. That will make me happy as I am sure you would witness the whole event through my eyes. Also consider I am envisaging your absence for twelve hours only, and I can manage myself. As a safety step, you can hire my regular caretaker for an additional day. Shafiq and Rajib would leave two days early by train to make the necessary arrangements."

That sounded infelicitous to Rukiya, and she felt dejected. She vehemently opposed Azeem's proposition for her to attend the event leaving him behind.

Shafiq showed up in response to the urgent message from Rukiya, and for the first time found himself in an obdurate situation. He was caught in a dilemma between the candid craving of Azeem Bhai and the ever-pressing spousal responsibility of Rukiya Bhabi.

Shafiq knew what he would say but was taking time to validate his neutrality in this emotional discourse of the most compatible couple. Eventually, he opened up, saying, "I assessed your respective positions and am glad to be convinced about the authenticity of both. There could be no other better decision than what is articulated by Bhai shaheeb. But ultimately that will be symbolic of the physical presence of Bhabi only. Once there and in the midst of preparations, including the occasional martial tune of the military band, Bhabi's mind and thinking will have focus on Dhaka and all perceived concerns related to you. She will likely not have the mind and eyes to capture those as you were hoping for. I also thought of getting Bokul and my daughters here for two days, but that would not be an adequate arrangement due to the formality-focused relationship and total unawareness of her with Dhaka.

So I suggest that both Rajib and myself leave for Chittagong days earlier than scheduled and hire a reputable photographer to graphically capture moments and actions. That will be something for your personal possession, with access at will. The only obstacle I see is having access permission for the photographer. That is why I needed an extra day."

Azeem, as habitual, exchanged looks with Rukiya and said, "I think what you stipulated makes sense, and both of us agree. I am planning to write a letter to the commandant of the academy and in that would request his favor of allowing permission to a family photographer. That possibly would ease your angst."

Everything thereafter moved as planned. Shafiq and Rajib returned to Dhaka with a bundle of photographs and surprisingly, a videotape too. Both of them availed alternative openings to explain the backdrop of each photograph, from the décor of *shamiana* and the sitting arrangements, the graduates' march past, and the award of Chief of Staff Gold Medal by the president of the republic to Fazal. While those photographs captured symbolic moments of relevance, the videotape was reflective of the seriatim projection of the event. The other good news they carried was posting of Fazal.

Azeem took the photographs and looked at them individually with emotion-laden expressions. Rukiya's reaction was identical, but her countenance was different. She went on putting photographs serially on every conceivable space in the house to capture the reality as feasible after carefully placing the tape temporarily on the top of family TV.

Rajib was very happy observing his sister and brother-in-law exultant with efforts made by them for the participation and bringing back substantiation of what they witnessed. But that was not the end. He then shared the exciting news of Fazal being assigned to a popular and well respected armored battalion, presently positioned in Moinamoti Cantonment. Azeem was evidently happy. Rukiya felt relieved as Fazal, being nearer, would be at her beck and call based on urgency.

And she had not to wait long. The recurrence of Azeem's illness happened soon, with additional symptoms necessitating a short admission to CMH. On being informed, Fazal met his Battalion CO (commanding officer) and got two days of special leave prefixing the weekend.

Fazal spent most of his time with his parents during the present visit. He finished preparations by early noontime of the weekend in order to be certain to leave by late afternoon. As a bonus, he was having an out-of-turn coffee with Father while Mother was preoccupied preparing snacks on time.

In that setting and right at that time, the just retired major general Akram Shafi showed up with his wife and daughter. Apologizing for banging on the door without advance indication, General Shafi stated, "I was in a lunch in the Army Gymkhana Club, celebrating the happy return of one of my junior colleague, Colonel Mukhtadeer, from a Peace Mission in Congo. In that lunch, one of the doctors of CMH was discussing the dilemma they were having in treating a patient. He exercised due caution in guarding the name of the patient but on query from me, suddenly defaulted and uttered your name.

There was another guest in our table who identified you easily, saying, 'We live in the same community and have vague ideas about his health status. Today it is clear to me.'

As the doctor accidentally mentioned your name, my memory lane traveled back to my very warm interaction in your place with one Captain Riaz. Being a fresh lieutenant, I was at the receiving end of the sizzling tattler of that evening. Notwithstanding rank and status, I clicked warmly with Captain Riaz and promised to maintain contact with him. He also shared with me his native home address of Nowshera.

That was mid-November of 1971. I was posted in Kohat Cantonment and was surprised to receive an invitation from Captain Riaz to have lunch with him in his Nowshera home the following weekend. The question of acceptance was not relevant. I showed up slightly late on the appointed day. That did not cause any problem as Pakistanis, like most suncontinental people, are used to have a late lunch.

After the lunch, we were having green tea sitting in the open courtyard of his home. Suddenly Capt. Riaz inquired about me, saying, 'You are not the same Shafi I met in Azeem's place months back. Is something bothering you?'

I was having a heavy heart and unguardedly alluded to the ongoing political convolutions and military tensions. I also said, 'I joined the army to serve Pakistan, and it now appears to be a mirage. I am in doldrums.'

He then straightaway asked me whether I had other options in mind! Having opened myself that far, I decided not to play dubious game, so I frankly said yes.

Taking his time, he then said, 'I know very intimately a tribal Sardar (Chief) from Darra Adam Khel, commonly known as Darra, a place notoriously famous for replicating guns of all types and make without any license or other government authorization. The government does not dare to intervene. That is just west-north of the Kohat mountain range, dividing the terrain into civilian Kohat at the southeast and the rough and ungovernable Darra Khel at the northwest with up and down zigzag road having sharp turns.'

Having said so, Captain Riaz appeared to be very tensed. He was persistently monitoring the surroundings and whispered, 'If you want to escape, that Sardar may help you. You can rely on him as I am relying on you in proposing it. You need to tell me now. But, remember that the decision is absolute, and there is no turning back. We do not have much time, so I am giving you about fifteen minutes to think and decide."

Upon return and getting clarity as to the option I had in mind, he thought for a while, had an intense look at me, and elaborated, saying, 'From now on, we will not have any contact. My agent will always introduce himself as one from CRN, standing for "Captain Riaz from Nowshera." You are never to utter my name or refer to Nowshera.'

He further clarified that, 'As a standard procedure, the agents contacting you will be different from occasion to occasion but will introduce themselves identically as earlier mentioned. But once you leave my home, you are to forget everything, including myself. Possibly you are carrying my letter for address. Please hand over the letter to me, and you enjoy my burning that, more as an abundant caution, and not of trust.'

Everything was worked out meticulously, and I reached Kabul on the fifth of December, took flights to Dubai, and then routed to Agartala of East India. I reported for duty and was positioned around the end of second week of December with Mukti Bahini (liberation force) of the Akhaura sector. The rest is part of history.

But those few days made my life. I made steady progression in my army career with a mukti bahini identity and, honestly speaking forgot about my Pakistani days, and unfortunately you too. As I heard your name today, I was determined to meet you, and requested the other guest from your surrounding helping me to identify your home. So I am here with the family. I apologize for not giving you advance notice."

As Azeem was not well, he was not very enthusiastic in gossiping like the early days but apparently was happy for being remembered by an admirer and colleague, even after prolonged disassociation. He listened intently to Shafi's narration and noted his regret for not keeping a track before. But Azeem's eyes were following Shafi's daughter as a hidden desire preoccupied his thought. Azeem, based on his hidden thought, diverted the discussion about the family life of General Shafi.

In responding to that query, General Shafi started saying, "Once the initial euphoria relating to the liberation somewhat settled, my parents got serious in getting me married. I got married with Reba, the daughter of a renowned family of our area, in 1974. Due to two unfortunate miscarriages compounded by monthly period-related disorder, the doctors advised us to delay our attempts for a child. We were blessed with Faria in early 1978."

As he was about to continue, Fazal, being ready to leave for Comilla, showed up. Azeem introduced him to General Shafi, saying, "Here is, like yours, our only son, Lieutenant Fazal, a fresh graduate from the military academy with the Chief of Staff Gold Medal."

Shafi instantly liked Fazal and congratulated him for his recent attainment.

In the midst of nice and encouraging chats they were having on professional life, Rukiya came and requested that all of them move to the dining table to have tea and refreshments.

Fazal was introduced to Faria at the behest of Reba. Not only that. She even suggested that after snacks and tea, Fazal takes out Faria to show the surroundings around as otherwise she would get bored and edgy. Fazal's quick response was in the affirmative. The youngsters left the dining space, enabling the parents to talk freely.

Azeem observed Shafi's liking of Fazal during their initial discourse. He concluded affirmatively about Reba's penchant for Fazal, keeping in view her suggestion to take out Faria for a stroll. Azeem monitored Rukiya too and had an exchange of looks with her, which mostly had the indication of neutrality.

Azeem made up his mind. With emotional prelude dating life and experience in Lahore and the warmth of their mutual bonding, Azeem just proposed what he had in mind. Drawing the attention of both Shafi and Reba, he said, "You have done a major injustice to feelings that bonded us. You are to pay a price!"

Saying that, he observed their immediate reaction. Shafi then said, "I have always treated you as an elder brother, and your aspiration is an order to me." Saying this, he looked at Azeem.

Taking his turn, Azeem said. "My health condition is not good at all. You have heard from the horse's mouth in your lunch today. I have two dreams: one, to be able to bless my daughter-in-law and to kiss my grandchild. Fazal has grown up as a very responsible and compassionate individual. I am more than certain any girl would long to have him as her life partner. Whatever I could observe, and to my best judgment, Faria is the girl I have been looking for. So I most humbly ask you for the hands of Faria for Fazal to fulfill my dreams." Saying those words with coped effort, Azeem lounged on the nearby couch and looked at Shafi for a response.

Looking at Azeem, the once confident and committed army captain holding a high vision championing the high values of life, and sharing tenderness and empathy without hesitation, it was distressing for Shafi to see him now lying on the couch, shedding hopes of a vibrant life and asking him for a favor involving his dearest possession. He had reservations in saying "yes" but had hesitation in saying "no" also.

In that vacillating situation, he suddenly indicated to his wife to come out for a discussion. They conferred mellifluously. He observed that "the young man is a very solid person, has vision like his father, and is destined to go high. He could be a good match for our hypersensitive daughter. My concern is even being at the end of teens, Faria has not yet shaped up well."

Reba could sense Shafi's willingness to concur with what Major Azeem proposed, but unforeseen fearfulness was holding him back. As a supporting wife, and more driven by her own assessment of the family, particularly Rukiya as the would be mother-in-law of Faria, she agreed without hesitation. In response to Shafi's observation about "shaping up enough," Reba pragmatically explained women's physiology, stating, "A girl's transition to youth, to marriage, and to motherhood have physical symptoms, but all those are accompanied by silent but significant emotional changes. I am certain Faria would follow the nature's dictate and would settle down soon after marriage." With that broad understanding, the couple walked back under the glare of the vague look of Rukiya and the eager expectation of Major Azeem.

General Shafi emotionally stated, "Azeem Bhai, your dream of having Faria as a daughter of this house honored us. We unhesitatingly convey our consent with one caveat: she is too young and has not so far exhibited stable growing-up stance."

Fazal initially objected but gave in to his father's desire.

As progression for the proposed wedding was being made, the saneness showed its ugly face notwithstanding the love and care with which a child is raised. Faria, sensing reality for the first time, openly dissented. But Shafi, being an army personnel, said, "I may be retired but I am still head of the family, responsible for everything. I have given my word to Azeem Bhai, and that will be honored."

On being aware of Faria's disarray, some of her close but blatant friends showed up by rotation. Most of them were devious characters, congratulating Reba aunt publicly and discouraging Faria privately. As nothing was being changed, three of Faria's brazen friends decided to meet Faria's dad with a final plea. He listened to them, and in a very dense voice said, "To me, all of you are like Faria. But daughters, remember, I am a general. My word carries a lot of weight. This wedding will go ahead as planned. As a father, I am requesting you all to help me in the process."

Returning to Faria's room, they reported the outcome verbatim quoting her father. Faria's rage was noticeable in her facial expressions. Her follow-on words were still harsher. She loudly said, "This is my age to go to parties, dance on the floor, know various types of characters, emotionally play with young guys before I settle on anyone. Now my parents have decided that I should have a life fretting about my so-called husband, demanding in-laws, and soon carrying a baby in my lap. But that will not happen. If my father is a general, I am too a general's daughter. I give my word to you all that I will make the life of my so-called husband untenable and my in-laws' lives miserable from day one."

Traditionally, the *bashar rath* (the wedding night) is the most exciting one in an arranged marriage for a new couple—exchanging a glamorous look, getting intimated in the warm embrace of each other, and starting to know one another. But that was not the paradigm for Fazal. He was greeted by the insensitive utterances of Faria saying, "I am going to sleep and will get up late in the morning. All of you should finish your breakfast. I will have mine when I desire to have it."

When Fazal joined the others for breakfast, Rukiya astonishingly inquired, "Where is *Bou-ma* (daughter-in-law)?"

Fazal calmly said, "She will have her breakfast after getting up."

Everyone was upset internally but externally showed as nothing to worry. Rukiya could not hide her worries and shared her concerns with Bokul. The latter responded by saying, "Bhabi, have trust. It may be that Fazal did not allow her to sleep until the early hours, and she is now making up."

But that was not the case with Azeem. At his request, Shafiq assisted his adorable *Bhai Shaheeb* to move to the living area. As Shafiq was moving out, Azeem held his hand and asked him to be seated next to him. Azeem closed his eyes for a while holding one of the hands of Shafiq and lamented, saying, "Perhaps I have spoiled the life of my dearest son, who never complained about anything or caused me any worry or embarrassment." He started shedding tears relentlessly.

Shafiq had a perspicuous feeling about what his dear *Bhai Shaheeb* was alluding to and going through. He opted to hide that and opined, "It may as well be so that our *Bou-ma* is not mentally ready for marriage so soon. Also, being a lonely child and because of her pampered upbringing, she might have been spoiled. You please bear with it. This restlessness in her will probably wither away as time passes and she becomes a mother."

Azeem listened to what Shafiq envisioned, thought through it, and argued with self. He nevertheless had no justification to console himself. With a sober tone full of frustration, he said, "Bhai Shafiq, I will keep in view what you articulated. But bear in mind that I had a command role in my army engagement. I can read the minds of people. I do not see any hope."

Rukiya felt frustrated, more thinking about the dismay of Azeem and what was in store for Fazal. Life's tyranny was like that: What one dreams of and what would be reality may, at times, be completely different and many a times frustrating. During that agonizing veracity, Bokul took pains to solace her dear Rukiya Bhabi the way Shafiq tried to give comfort to his dear Bhai Shaheeb.

Fazal was nonchalant. He was behaving as if everything is normal. That was a topic of discussions among parents and his *chacha* and *chachi.* The consensus was that it would not be appropriate to raise it with Fazal, but have more focus in monitoring their embryonic relationship.

Fazal had not much of an interest in getting married so soon. In a sense, he was reluctant but gave in due to the promise made to Father while settling the issue of business investment. That was done in all seriousness. The question of backing off from that solemn promise does not arise. He was happy that he could at least fulfill one of the promises, the other one remaining unstated.

Many of the times, events happen in life causing surprise and satisfaction, the magnitude of any or both of them depends on the recipient's reaction. That happened on the evening of the seventh postwedding day. The couple and her parents were invited by *Boro Mama* (big maternal uncle) of Faria living in Uttara township.

As Fazal was about to put on his favorite blue striped tie, semi-attired Faria moved in, chose a bright burgundy tie, and put that around his neck with a subtle smile. Fazal, though apparently happy, took that easily, and silently complied.

That was a night of incredulity for Fazal. They as yet had not exchanged any word of romanticism or adoration. But as the night advanced, surprise and amazement dazed Fazal. Laying by his side, Faria had all the signs of restiveness. Eventually, she put her one leg on the lower body of Fazal, still pretending that it was involuntary.

Fazal's excitement and urge surged impulsively. He pulled her positioned leg on his body, and suddenly the whole frame of Faria was on the top of his physique. The rest continued unabated with mutual groaning, but no word of adoration was expressed.

Faria remained engaged with her cluster of friends during most part of the daytime, besides socially interacting with other visiting guests. She did not sit by the side of Azeem, nor did she ever visit her mother-in-law in her kitchen. Rukiya showed extraordinary patience, more considering that any expression of open displeasure would hurt Azeem more than anyone else and would damage the life of her loving son.

News soon spread about the pregnancy of Faria. Azeem was thrilled and silently pardoned Faria for all her negativity of the past. Rukiya forgot every grumble and started taking preparatory activities. Faria's parents were jubilant and visited Azeem and Rukiya with plenty of sweets and fruits. Fazal internally had the kick of being a father-to-be and was happy, feeling that he was on his way to fulfill his second promise to Father.

In nattering with visiting friends, Faria started asserting that her marriage did not materially change anything in her life. She insisted, saying, "I still wake up when I want. I continue to have my own breakfast. I am not to be in the kitchen. I am not required to sit by the side of my father-in-law as an ideal Bou-ma. On the top of that, I have access to nightly pleasure at my will."

One of her friends took those comments rather negatively and commented about her pregnancy. Faria, instead of being embarrassed, laughed merrily and said, "Wait and see. The play just started."

Except Major Azeem, most of the relations were in CMH at the time of delivery. When the nurse came with the baby boy, everyone was ecstatic. Observing that, the nurse quipped, saying, "Such a beautiful baby! But the mother refused to hold him and even look at him." That subtle observation was overlooked by all present in the milieu of their overwhelming happiness. Fazal took the baby, went to Rukiya, saying, "*Ammi* (mother), here is my amanath for you to keep him safe and take care of." Rukiya tenderly held the baby, kissed him with passion, and uttered Quranic verses before handing him over to Reba. She then handed him over to *nana* (maternal grandfather) with joy and happiness. The nurse took the baby back, and all dispersed in due course.

Faria was escorted by Fazal on her return travel home with the baby boy. The ambience of the house was full of cheerfulness and fulfillment. Rukiya was serving coffee to Azeem, who was lounging on the bed.

Right at that moment, Faria stepped in and handed over the baby to Rukiya and said, contrary to decency and norms, "You wanted a grandchild, and here he is. Fazal already attributed him as *amanath* to you. I am not going to be engaged in rearing him up. I am not going to spoil my life at this beautiful stage. It is your responsibility. So take care of him."

Both Rukiya and Azeem were equally stunned by this turn of events. Rukiya looked at Azeem and was scared observing his suppressed angst. To divert his attention and to ease up the situation, Rukiya smiled and said, "What a miracle! I was scouting for a way out to indicate to Faria about my earnest desire to take responsibility of rearing up our *nati* (grandchild). Here she shows up and proposes the same. I am so happy."

Azeem did not contest. He knew what motivated Rukiya to stipulate that. He preferred to let that go. But he lamented within, thinking, *How fortunate I am having a life partner like Rukiya and how unfortunate my son is in having one like Faria, who is unable to think of anything else except herself.*

To escape from that agony, he momentarily closed his eyes, and Rukiya left the space warmly holding the *nati*.

On the following day, Faria's parents showed up with flowers, dresses, and sweets to formally greet dearest *nati*. They were equally surprised not seeing Faria. Rukiya stated, "Since Fazal is not here and I am taking care of nati, she was feeling bored. She thus stepped out to spend some time with friends"

Azeem marveled about the wittiness of Rukiya in hiding reality. Azeem and Akram Shafi were busy in visiting their respective lives during the last twenty-five years. At this point, Azeem made a very candid observation by saying, "I fully understand your position. Career priorities and challenges, especially in the context of the turbulent game play going in the arena of the army, kept yourself preoccupied and focused. I knew about your headway, but preferred to keep myself away, having backlashes in my own career path. My courageous performance in the Wagah encounter became my most haunting episode. I was disheartened but not bested. Rukiya's support and encouragement opened up new vistas of opportunity for me, and I am relishing that now in tandem with Fazal's accomplishments. The only current bad feeling is due to my health status.' After off-loading those emotional librettos, Azeem looked outside and kept gazing.

Akram, being overwhelmed, kept quiet. Reba was holding the baby. Rukiya was engaged in preparatory chores in entertaining her most esteemed relations.

In the follow-on dining table discourse, Azeem opportunely made a stipulation. He said, "I want to refer to our *nati* by a name. I am conscious of the fact that it is the privilege of parents. But he is our first nati, and yours. We should logically have an edge over this society-mandated privilege."

Akram Shafi readily agreed. He fervidly opined, "We are their fathers. And we definitely have a right. If they have other thoughts, they can change the name during *Akika* ceremony." Reba readily consented. Rukiya suggested time to get the endorsement of at least Faria but was overruled.

At Shafi's insistence, Azeem cooked up a name instantly. He proposed that the baby be named as "Ameen Akram Azeem." He hilariously added that "the name proposed has his own identity, a nexus to Shafi and an allusion to me. The other brighter side is, we can always refer to him as 'Triple A.' Every one chuckled and relished. Faria had no visible reaction, but Fazal was happy in having a name that will carry the legacy.

Faria was reluctant to move to Comilla even though pressed by her father. Fazal consoled his father-in-law, saying, "Give her some time. Once her so-called friends get married and start their own lives, she will have a sense of reality and is bound to change. As you are aware, she is resistant to orders and command. So let us handle this with care and compassion. In the meantime, I will continue to rotate between Dhaka and Comilla on a weekend basis."

Meanwhile, Azeem was having a rough time healthwise, so he desired Shafiq's presence on an urgent basis.

As Shafiq showed up, Azeem apparently felt very relieved. He took Shafiq by his side and started talking in a way he never did. Requesting Rukiya's presence and unusually holding his hand, Azeem, to the utter dismay of Rukiya, said, "Brother, whether one likes it or not, it is certain that my days are limited. You must give me your word that you would always be by the side of your Bhabi and Fazal."

With tears swamping his eyes, Azeem continued saying, "My life is a mix of strange phenomena. Sometimes luck betrayed me, but some other times I grassed myself. The worst example of that was my decision to choose Faria as our daughter-in-law. I know the agony beholding the feelings of both Rukiya and Fazal, though they are endeavoring to demonstrate that everything is okay. I can't undo what happened, but I need to be careful for the future.

So I requested my lawyer friend to register Asha as a private limited company, with Rukiya as managing director, with 80 percent shareholding, and you as operations general manager, with 20 percent holdings. In a separate deed being prepared, the plot of land on which you built your home was assigned to you irrevocably. It is just to guard our common assets against false claims and possible litigations. Your presence is needed to sign the deeds and other documents."

That was done. Both Rukiya and Shafiq complied reluctantly, notwithstanding the recent multiple symptoms which were definite indications of the aggravated status of Azeem's illness. Rukiya always concluded that it was the feeling of despair and guilt for his role and responsibility of getting Fazal married to Faria and utterly spoiling the life of a fine soul that Fazal replicates. Azeem's pain was greater seeing Fazal behaving contrarily to make the former happy. One good thing, however, happened during the phase: Fazal was promoted to the rank of captain.

Soon thereafter, Azeem succumbed to his illness. Doctors came out of ICU and told Captain Fazal, General Shafi, and Shafiq, "After two successive cardiac arrests and an additional one after putting the ventilator, he has gone beyond us. We tried our best. Sorry."

Shafiq rushed to Azeem's abode with the sad news. General Shafi was preoccupied with complying with the prerequisites for delivery of the dead body while Fazal was busy in informing friends and relations as well as making arrangements for *Janaza* (community prayer) prior to eventual burial.

In the midst of this unfortunate tragedy, Fazal was transferred to the Jessore cantonment.

That coincided with an unanticipated fretfulness as it was the turn of General Shafi to be sad and sick. He was frustrated observing obvious the foibles in his daughter. He inexorably blamed himself for not being able to properly guide Faria while growing up, mostly due to being the only child. He equally blamed himself for the death of a brother like Azeem and for spoiling the life of Fazal. Frustrated and disjointed, General Shafi started suffering from a combined as well acute causes of a breathing problem and the recurrence of a high level of blood cholesterol. He died within three months.

The unexpected consecutive demises of both father-in-law and father had a fleeting impact on the thinking and behavior pattern of Faria. She eventually decided to move to Jessore. And that was good for a few months initially. Faria than started feeling bored and missing Dhaka, including pleasurable outings, walking in the malls, gossips and sharing coffee and other drinks with friends, and the well-wishers of both genders. She started rotating between Jessore and Dhaka as she queerly started missing Fazal once in Dhaka. Her feeling oddly accentuated on hearing the news of Fazal's promotion to the rank of major. Her behavior pattern did not change much. She was enjoying her life happily as goaded by friends and as per her coherent enigmatic sensitivities.

Her mother, Reba, always had mumbled health conditions. She had no expertise in handling babies. Faria had grown up under the care of ever-changing *Ayias* (lady baby seaters).

Fazal's upbringing was just the opposite. He thus continued to miss the adoration of his dearest Amma (Muslims' common reference to mother) and started missing his precious son, Ameen. Each update from Amma about his smiling, crying, crawling, and taking steps thrilled Fazal. He thought of requesting Amma to be with him along with Ameen, but desisted due to her engagement with and commitment to *Asha*. Fazal compensated for that by making short trips to Dhaka.

During the period, the lax border situation was causing concern at the policy level of the government. The border control and administration policies have had experienced routine changes. The government in power in early twenty-first century was zealous in curtailing smuggling across about 2,200 km of land border and approximately 260 kilometers of riverine ones. The problem was huge, as most of it was unfenced and artificially drawn in 1946–47 at the time of the partition of India. That caused such the porous border to become seamlessly popular in cross-border trafficking in varied things, from persons to animals and drugs to fake currencies. So the government in power decided to be tough and curtail smuggling and supported BBR with additional resources and manpower. Authorities identified the three western civil divisions of Bangladesh (i.e., Khulna, Rajshahi, and Rangpur) as the most vulnerable ones and decided to augment their capacities.

As a consequential decision, Major Fazal was deputed to BBR and was assigned to a sensitive outpost corresponding to North 24 Parganas district of West Bengal, a prominent and popular corridor of smuggling with Bangladesh.

Fazal performed outstandingly in that outpost and earned a name. He was also an unspecified beneficiary of the sublime identity of being known as the son of a major and son-in-law of a major general, besides the recipient of the Chief of Staff's Gold Medal.

Apart from the impact, the significant difference between good and bad news was that the latter travels first and had many recipients. That happened in the case of Fazal too. While Fazal's reputation of being a very efficient and dedicated officer had professional circulation and acknowledgment, the news concerning his family life and patterns had a much wider circulation, and some of the senior functionaries were also aware of that even though they did not want to be.

Amma, in that phase of her life, had only two but very focused priorities: one was the rearing up of Ameen with all the love of a mother and the care-cum-consideration of a grandmother; and two, to pursue Azeem's dream of making *Asha* a total success, upholding his bequest. That was facilitated by the utmost loyalty and continued support of Shafiq. Any prolonged absence of Amma from Dhaka may send a wrong signal to him, and thus Fazal refrained from proposing that any time before. Alternatively, he took time to visit Amma and Ameen periodically.

During the political upheaval 2008 causing a military coup with a civilian face, Fazal got the most exciting news of his transfer to BBR headquarter in Dhaka. Everyone in the families was happy, and, as an exception, Faria too.

Faria was socially popular, and a very polished floor dancer. There was no one to match her. Officers, both senior and junior, used to aspire to dance with her. She was equally skillful and alert as a "housie" (crossing numbers of sheets purchased to hit the jackpot) player. Playing with luck and numbers, Faria used to add luster and joy to the surroundings. To those who did not know who Fazal was, his interim identity was "husband of Faria."

Fazal had mixed feelings. The social prominence of Faria made him happy, but the continued foot-dragging of the former in acquiring norms and practices of a housewife and that of a mother pained him always.

Ameen did not bond with Faria at all. To him, she was "a third person singular number" in the periphery. Other than going to school, Ameen's attraction and preference was playing games, spending time with his friends and father, and returning to the loving company of *Dadi-Amma* (similar to *Dadi-ma*) while his mother was mostly not visible.

Ameen very surprisingly bonded very warmly with Shafiq-dada. He used to look forward to his periodical visits to know more about his Dada and the family in Massumpur. That made Fazal very exultant.

Neither Fazal nor Dadi-Amma made any specific effort to help Ameen bond with the mother, being fearful of a sudden mood change of Faria. In that event, she could decide to leave her home for that of her mother or any of her friends. That definitely would be a trauma to handle, having an adverse impact on the psyche of Ameen.

Fazal was still hoping for the best outcome for the sake of their son and related congeniality. Against his will, he sustained that life as a testament of respect to Father and for the sake of his son's future life.

CLIMAX

As per notification, Fazal was one of the 33 NCOs, JCOs, and commissioned officers deputed from army as well belonging to BBR, being recognized and recommended for commendation/promotion, to receive their respective citation, rank insignia, and batches from the president of the country (being BBR's patron) during the annual *durbar* (convocation).

The *durbar* was scheduled for the next day following the carousing arranged by Faria. That was the premise of blast in Fazal's quarter within the Bilkhana location of the BBR headquarters. Most of the participants were Faria's friends and associates. Shafiq Chacha was invited but obviously a misfit in that backdrop. He was by himself most of the time.

So was the position of Rukiya. Standing alone in the open verandah, she was reminiscing life, both spent cheerfully with Azeem for about twenty-seven years and the current life of about eleven years without him. In summation, she consoled herself that it was perhaps better that Azeem died rather early as both the behavior pattern and lifestyle of Faria would have pained him much. Rukiya's loneliness was more palpable as Reba, Faria's mother, conveyed her inability to join at the last moment.

Fazal showed up a number of times to give company to his mother. Being caught in between his mother and wife, he made efforts to explain to Mother the vagaries, the changes in norms, and the priorities of life of the present generation, contending nevertheless that "I have no liking for this sort of life. Notwithstanding that, I can't deviate as that may impact on my professional progression being identified as a conservative. Further, it is likely to adversely affect my conjugal life with severe repercussions on the psyche of Ameen, being in his early teens."

Earlier, being felt uneasy with the high-tuned sound of music and screams and garish laughter of that overcrowded assembly, Ameen quietly retired to his room and closed the door. He soon had the thought about the likely discomfort his beloved Dadi-Amma was suffering. He came out to join her and give her company.

In between occasional commentary, Dadi-Amma and her grandson exchanged looks with each other. Ameen then went to be by the side of his loving Shafiq Dadu, initially pretending as giving company, and then escorted him to the room of Dadi-Amma. At that very early phase of life, he astoundingly uttered, "We do not fit in, in that setting. Let me have some quality time with you, with the participation of Dadi-Amma, and have some more detail about Massumpur, Dada-ji, Julaikha Dadi-Amma, and my Dada's growing up."

Keeping quiet for some time, Ameen then said, "Dadi-Amma and Shafiq Dadu, I promise to both of you that having no interest in army life, I will carry the legacy of this family and would endeavor honestly to pass that on to the next generation. I hope and pray that the said promise and subsequent effort of mine would put to rest the souls of my revered Dada and his Dada-ji."

The eyes of both Rukiya and Shafiq were moist with overflowing tears. Efforts were made by both to contain that, but suddenly Dadi-Amma started sobbing. Both Ameen and Shafiq came to her rescue and consoled her. Rukiya happily said, "Ameen, this is the best gift in my life. May AllahPak bless you always."

The following morning started as joyously as last night was. Dressed in the standard officers' uniform having the insignia and batch of a major for the last time, he came to salam his beloved mother before going to *durbar*. He then saluted the photograph of his adorable late father, saying, "When I return having the insignia and batch of lieutenant colonel, I will salute you again, sir." Exchanging looks with Ameen, he jokingly said, "Beta (son), if you want, I will salute you too."

The durbar venue, nicely decorated with scrupulous arrangements for the reception and the sitting provisions, was something to be admired, and colleagues were congratulating each other. Equal focus was dedicated to ensure that the nicety of the arrangements were maintained for early afternoon session when the president of the republic would grace the occasion.

By the designated hour, all invitees were seated. Upon arrival, the director general (DG) was received with honor and grandeur and escorted to the upraised section of the pavilion to grace his seat. The *durbar* proceeding started with the *tilwat* (recitation of verses) from the Holy Quran. Thereafter, the formal *durbar* was called in order.

Right at that moment, a group of lethally armed NCOs, JCOs, and BBR sepoys appeared from nowhere and created a mutinous situation by resorting to brushfire. Everyone was taken aback and momentarily wondered about the failure of intelligence operations. Besides others, sixty-five senior deputed army officers, including the DG, were brutally killed. Fazal was one of them.

It took the government about two days to have a footing in the sprawled Bilkhana surroundings, sufficient time for the miscreants to change outfits or flee from the locale.

The bewilderment and gloom persisted. The initial focus of the government machinery was to contain the situation, rather than taking immediate action to find out what caused the catastrophe That conveniently provided the space and time for meaningful evidence to wither away.

Pulsating and engaged Bilkhana immediately became a ghost place. One could hear *tilwat* (recitation) of Holy Quran from most of the houses while the fragrant smoke of *Agarbatti* (incense made of aromatic biotic material) was be noticeable when burned, especially at night. Fazal's house was no exception.

With Fazal no more relevant and no emotional attachment for their son Ameen, Faria decided to relocate to her parental home. In a sense, Rukiya was relieved. Shafiq and Bokul alternately visited and stayed with them to help the process of healing.

With amorous care and the consideration of the ever-vigilant Bokul Dadi and the intermittent interactions with her daughters, the guidance of Shafiq Dadu, and goaded by the unbounded love, care, and emotional support of Dadi-Amma, Ameen slowly and steadily recovered and focused on his educational pursuit.

Faria initially settled down in her parental home but soon started taking shots at friends and adversaries alike. Unexpectedly, she started missing the ever calm and quiet Fazal, and with a queer mindset opted for a riposte to life ahead. Encouraged by a few friends, she slowly started attending parties and gatherings, initially as an attendee with gradual induction in merrymaking.

Her agonizing life was too onerous and shocking from own perspective, but she was somehow oblivious of the fact that there were scores of others who were victims of that massacre with a more challenging and uncharted future.

The whole nation was shell-shocked. Uncertainty, confusion, and the dragged inactions of authorities gave rise to rumors and related conspiracy theories. There was a strong view in circulation that the whole rebellion was engineered to eviscerate an important segment of Bangladesh's border strategy.

As pressures mounted, authorities created a one-man inquiry commission. That produced a lengthy report with not much specific findings and conclusions. The report was treated as somewhat a classified one, and very few had real access to it.

Time passed. People, very bizarrely and briskly, bypassed the major Bilkhana tragedy. Rukiya once lamented, saying, "What happened to this nation? One Assad, a protester against Ayub Khan's military rule, was killed by army fire in 1969 near the Ayub gate of Dhaka, and people by and large revolted and renamed the gate as 'Assad Gate' within days when Ayub Khan was still in power. Now, hundreds of BBR personnel and about sixty-five senior army officers were killed in a mutinous exploit, but the nation is preoccupied with making money." She further hinted, while exchanging with Shafiq and Ameen concerning prevalent conspiracy theories, to an evolving mindset in which the emerging psyche was "so long as one and his children are okay and making money, it is fine for the nation to be where it is heading irrespective of consequences."

In the midst of the subdued commotion, authorities announced a package of benefits for the affected of officers and sepoys (as GIs were identified by the British administration referring to soldiers of Indian origin). Among others, the package for the officers included official recognition for those who were recommended for promotion, a one-time cash compensation, and gratis allotment of an apartment in the cantonment area for each of the officers assassinated.

That was a master stroke. Pressing demands so far for revealing the truth became subservient to the allure of cash and apartment.

Faria was one to opt for that at the earliest, with most others following the suit. She, without notice, showed up to claim her son, Ameen, and to get consent to accept the package on behalf of the family.

Rukiya was dumbfounded. Ameen intensely listened, and the rage of his facial expressions were fretting Rukiya. Nevertheless, and following his late father's footsteps, he calmly, and mastering all decisiveness, said, "You may see a son in me, but I do not know you ever as a mother. In about last seventeen years, you never cared about me, nor hugged me. I see my mother in the person of Dadi-Amma, and that is absolute. Also, I am not interested in the apartment. I do not know as yet why my father was killed, who engineered the plot, and who executed it. An apartment is no substitute for his life and my being deprived of his love."

Rukiya listened carefully and with equal firmness said, "Your claim of Ameen as your son is a mockery and premised on an apparent interest. You have heard the decision of Ameen without any provocation on my part. I also agree with him that we do not have any interest in the compensation package. You can act as you deem appropriate, but remember that this would be our final settlement and nothing new will be entertained." Saying those words and without leaving any option for Faria to counteract, both Dadi-Amma and her *nati* left the venue.

Rukiya, as a scape from surroundings, wanted to be engaged more actively in *Asha*'s management and operations. In consultation with Shafiq and Ameen, a manageable office outfit was set up in one room of her home, and a reconditioned Toyota vehicle was bought. She also started visiting Kashimpur more regularly, often with Ameen, along with need-based incremental visits to banks and other government offices, minimizing pressure on Shafiq.

With sadness and despair behind, recalling her college history teacher's advice always to focus on the future irrespective of the enormity of past gloom, Rukiya envisaged her future concentrating on her *nati* Ameen. She argued with herself, saying, "A mother's pain of losing a child is enormous. In her case, losing a vibrant son is irreparable." But leaving everything to destiny is a self-defeating decision, so she decided not to give in to the dictate of destiny. To her, and as the fact stands, Ameen was Fazal's amanath, and no emotive heaviness should deviate her from keeping up to that trust.

Ameen not only excelled in his board-conducted secondary school certificate examination attaining 5 GPAs, but he soon, to the happiness of Shafiq and Bokul, proved to be a vigilant associate of Dadi-Amma concerning *Asha*. In a chat alluding to the future of *Asha*, Shafiq, with pride, observed, "In spite of the negativities and dismay behind us, we definitely are fortunate to have a *nati* with the aptitude of Ameen. His attachment with and sensitivity for you are irrefutable; his interest in *Asha* is unpretentious; his commitment to *Asha* is beyond any qualms. So Dada-ji's desire, Azeem Bhai's dream, and your dedication will not lose track. I am so happy for that."

Rukiya looked at Shafiq and pointedly asked, "Shafiq Bhai, are you a man or an angel? I crossed life's pathway so far interacting with many, mostly under adverse settings. Among those, I can honestly count two persons, Captain Riaz of the Pakistan Army and the history professor of my college in Dhaka, as genuine ones. I have heard about the magnanimity of Babu Bijon Mohan Nag, the unreserved noncommunal musings of Guru Shibnath Bishwash, and the love and farsightedness of Dada-ji. I respect them likewise, even though I had no chance to interact with any of them. To me, and most genuinely, you are a combination of all their good qualities and a God-sent angel to be by our side. Whatever we are discussing today is the fruit of your commitment, honesty, sincerity, and unbiased feeling for us. You can't deny that. You appeared in our life at a critical moment and have had been by our side with complete dedication. I do not have any means to repay you, but I am aware of your keenness and desire to give a proper education to your daughters. Keeping that in view, I have a proposal for your consideration. Please relocate your family to this humble abode. We will construct two additional rooms. Besides getting Bokul as a companion, I will be able to guide your daughters and help them in growing up in an urban environment. Please do not hesitate. You can supervise *Asha* by having frequent visits and short-term stays, with your Rukiya House being used partially more as barn."

Right at that moment, Ameen jubilantly entered the house and sat by the side of his favorite Dadi-Amma. Rukiya promptly shared with Ameen the substance of her instant discourses with his Shafiq Dada. Ameen was excited to know that Dadi-Amma already suggested the relocation of the family of Shafiq Dada to Dhaka. In his exuberance, he commented, "It will be wonderful for me. I am tired of being among seniors all the time. Now I will have growing-up aunts to play with, to taunt, and to guide also. I am so happy as I will logically have a position of authority."

Ameen did not like to dampen that pleasure of his Dadi-Amma and Dada but equally was unable to hold back a pleasant surprise awaiting them. As he was noticeably shuffling a piece of paper in his hand, Shafiq Dada inquired, "What is in that piece of paper?"

Ameen gave in and just said, "It is about my HSC result," and handed over that piece of paper to Dada.

Ameen stood up and then bent to *salam* Dadi-Amma by touching her feet. She was astounded and engulfed by an unmatched joy when Shafiq said, "He has the twentieth merit position in the entire Dhaka Board." Hearing that, he drew Ameen closer to him and kissed him generously. With Dadi-Amma, the inevitable happened. With a heavy tone and weepy eyes, she was recounting the unfortunate absence of his father and that of his grandfather on this blissful occasion.

Shafiq immediately stood up and left the room to return soon with two packets of Bangladeshi sweets and two fruit cakes. Ameen was evidently happy and asked, "Why two of each?"

Shafiq Dadu responded by saying, "I will celebrate it twice: once here with you both and later in Kashimpur with the family tomorrow."

Ameen was jubilant. Rukiya quickly commented, "Such pro-active thinking is only possible by one of your sagacity and mettle. Please bless our *nati*."

Everyone, nevertheless, missed Azeem and Fazal, Rukiya more intensely.

Ameen was scouting the related departments of Dhaka University to have a stable decision about the subject in which he would like to pursue his future study. The conflicting fields were economics, English, and history.

As he was sipping tea sitting in *Modhur canteen* (popular and very traditional eatery from early 1950s, and commonly identified by the name of the first owner, Modhu) of the university, he overheard exciting conversations going on in the adjacent table. A fellow student was referring to a recruiting team's visit and a planned event for sharing the comparative advantage of pursuing higher education in Cyprus. The end objective was to motivate Bangladeshi students of merit for admission in various Cyprus universities. On hearing those, Ameen too got interested and decided to visit the related hotel right at that time to get additional information.

With sketchy information that he could have on his maiden visit, Ameen felt content and enthusiastically shared some of that with Dadi-Amma. Ameen's objective was to ensure that surprise and shock due to his desire to pursue higher education abroad did not impact her on physical health and cause mental agony.

But he was taken aback by noticing the sudden dispiriting change in her facial expressions, though she refrained from making any immediate comment. Ameen thought it to be normal and took that easy. He had all the trust in the erudition of Dadi-Amma.

While lounging in his room, he thanked his luck for being at the right place, at the right time, and at the right table, unintendedly enabling him to overhear encouraging information pertaining the education options abroad that was being shared among some senior fellows.

Believing in the "instinct" that Dada-ji always emphasized, he got the motivation to pursue the hint. That took him to the hotel the next day where the recruiting team from Cyprus was to have a workshop following day. He enlisted himself as a participant-to-be. The fellow at the registration counter observed, "Registration for this workshop is not necessary, but it is helpful, being indicative of staid interest." Ameen complimented himself for taking the right decision.

But the pallid face of Dadi-Amma precipitously came to his thought. Ameen assessed her immediate but somber reaction. He concluded that her depressing reflex had a solid premise having lost her husband and grown-up son in succession. At this moment, he was the apple of her eyes and the reasons to pursue life. She maintained a number of times earlier, saying, "I gave my word to your dad and took your custody when he said, 'This is an amanath.' Do not worry. I would not leave you without getting you settled in life."

Ameen was somewhat certain of being able to convince Dadi-Amma premised on all the supporting points he had. His only dismay was the absence of Shafiq Dada at this critical time. Had he been here this evening, the process would have been easier.

As Ameen was about to leave the following morning with papers and backup documents, he encountered Dadi-Amma with *Tajbee* (Muslim prayer beads) in her hand. Without saying anything, she drew him close and blessed him by reciting some Quranic verses. That was taken by Ameen as her clearance and blessings.

Ameen was very impressed in knowing about the reputation and recognition enjoyed by most universities of Cyprus, both in Europe and North America. Not only were credits transferable but degrees obtained were also treated as qualifying educational standards for pursuing still higher level education also in Europe and the USA. And all these were possible at one-third of the undergrad education cost in reputable US schools. Another advantage was that being a student in Cyprus with a valid resident visa, one could move around EU countries freely.

At the end of the workshop and his one-to-one discussions with head of the team sharing the background details and results, he was assured of an affirmative communication soon.

He was excited and enthusiastically shared the relevant information with Dadi-Amma. Rukiya, camouflaging her inner anxiety, maintained a poised posture to keep her dearest *nati* cheerful.

At Ameen's end, the itching impasse was fortunately settled quickly when Shafiq Dada came and all the three had a discussion. Ameen explained the rationale for pursuing higher studies abroad and stated that if he went to the USA, communication would be limited to telephone calls and e-mails. The Cyprus option helped one to have the same standard of learning at about one-third the cost and the possibility of frequent short visits to Dhaka, as Cyprus was not that far off. Shafiq Dada articulated his viewpoints and delineated his thoughtful affirmation.

On his part, Ameen renewed his vow to be back to Bangladesh after finishing his educational pursuits and concentrate on work pertaining to *Asha*. He further said, "There will be no compromise on that. This is my pledge."

As indicated earlier, Ameen got his acceptance letter from the University of Cyprus, located in Southern part of Nicosia, the erstwhile segment of the capital city of Cyprus. He, at the same, received a favorable response from the college he applied in Massachusetts. Though he was eager earlier for study in USA, the practicality in terms cost and family obligations made him opt for Cyprus.

Among the many related information to help and motivate accredited applicants in taking an affirmative decision, the acceptance letter had along with it all related information about Cyprus. The objective was to make one familiar with Cyprus beforehand.

Among the many interesting details, Ameen was excited to know about the division of the island country in 1974 based on ethnicity, with the southern part being Christian dominated and the northern part being primarily Muslim inhabited. What pained him most, however, was the nonrecognition of the north as a state by any country of the world except Turkey, and its lagging behind in all spheres of life, especially in economic development and social progression.

As a UN-backed interim arrangement, Cyprus, and similarly Nicosia, were partitioned as Greek Cyprus of south and Turk Cyprus of north. Similar to the notoriously famous erstwhile Berlin Wall, this divided capital, like rest of the island, is well-known for its Green Line of about 180 kilometers monitored by UN peacekeepers.

Ameen was thrilled and focused all attention to comply with the related requirements. Among many others, he was occupied with visa-processing matters and opening a foreign exchange account in his favor. He was very much visible in the Cyprus Consulate area of Dhaka. and his bank in the Karwan Bazar area with need-based visits to the Bangladesh Bank (the Central Bank).

Ameen's gladdened movement, apparent liquidity, and joyful comportment fortuitously drew the attention of a gangster group, locally known as "*Malam* Party" (for using specific ointment to dope victims and then rob them of their mobile phones, cash, and other valuables). Their main activities were hijacking for resale in black market and kidnapping for ransom. To their local group, Ameen appeared to be a good candidate for immediate kidnapping. They touched base with the leader of the Malam party and got the approval to undertake the operation.

Ameen attended his final call in the Cyprus Consulate, merrily came out, and boarded an auto rickshaw to go home. Unexpectedly, two other persons boarded the same transport from its two sides and pointed a pistol and a big knife with instructions to keep quiet. After a while, they applied their *malam*, and Ameen was senseless.

Ameen regained his senses around midnight to see two strangers sitting on a long bench happily looking at him while exhaling smoke with an obnoxious smell. Ameen asked for a glass of water. That was given effortlessly with the brief commentary that "It is all. Until the boss decides otherwise, there will be no food. He will meet you tomorrow morning."

Ameen's repeated attempts to know his fault did no impact on those two guards. They were engaged in their own world.

Isolated and hungry, Ameen did not have much of a recourse. He spontaneously started thinking of the family icon, Dada-ji, and recalled the struggle and hardships in his initial life. Ameen just thought that perhaps, as Dada-ji's nexus, he was going through the rough time of life. He ardently recalled each word that Shafiq Dada told him about Dada-ji and passionately prayed for his blessings. In the process, and while lying on the floor, Ameen dozed off.

Weary and fatigued, Ameen woke up late, seeing a young man sitting on a chair with a mysterious look at him. He was surprised also to see the semblance of some food on the side table.

The young man introduced himself, saying, "People here know me as *Badsha*." On his clapping, two associates showed up. He asked one to accompany Ameen for morning cleansing, and the other fellow was asked to fetch a chair.

Badsha asked him to take a seat on the chair and to have food. That was diametrically the opposite of the experiences of the kidnapping and the night before. Ameen could not hold the feeling to himself. He started sniffling and inquiring as to what his fault was.

Badsha was straight and candid and said, "Your fault is that you palpably are from a rich family. No bodily harm will be inflicted if your family pays us taka five hundred thousand clandestinely. They can easily afford this if they really care about your life and well-being."

On hearing that, Ameen stopped eating and in a soaked voice, observed, "There must be something wrong with the information that predicated my kidnapping. If my family was that rich, then why I should go to Cyprus for higher studies instead of the USA, with my admission from a prestigious institution located in Massachusetts?"

He then took Badsha by surprise, saying, "You referred to physical harm. Nothing, including death, bothers me. I come from a family that in chasing dreams, frequently experienced shattering setbacks. My grandfather, Major Azeem, was a victim of a conspiracy and injustice depriving him from becoming a colonel. My father, Major Fazal, was brutally murdered in a Bilkhana massacre just hours before he was to be decorated with the rank and batch of a colonel. Now perhaps it is my turn to go. So be it. I only feel sad for my Dadi-Amma, who all through her life, chased frustrating dreams, and now to have the final shock."

It was now the turn of Badsha to be in tears. He observed, saying, "What a coincidence. My father, Raju Ahmed, was a subed-ar-major in BBR too and died in that massacre while on duty. We, as yet, have no credible information about the massacre. We did not get any justice, so I opted for this life. I understand your situation and will talk with the Party Leader. In the meanwhile, you will have to be our guest. I will make possible arrangements for your comfort and food."

Badsha showed up after two days and handed over his mobile, saying in a low voice, "The chief is at the other end. Talk to him."

As Ameen said "hello," the husky voice at the other end said, "Look, normally I do not talk to captives. It is because of insistence of Badsha, I agreed to talk to you. I know your points of argument. That are not enough. But because of your family's past sacrifice and Dadi-Amma's present sufferings, I am willing to let you go. But be careful. Always have a low profile and do not travel alone. Since you were picked once, there is a chance of being picked up by another group again." He snapped the call, saying those words of reflection, empathy, care, and prudence.

On hearing the news of the kidnapping of Ameen, Shafiq and the family rushed in. Badsha, using the mobile of Ameen, communicated with Rukiya and conveyed the demand of ransom giving an ultimatum of five days to act.

That was the afternoon of the fourth day. Dadi-Amma became restless and ordered Shafiq to go out and arrange the money by mortgaging the properties she owned. Even though assured by Shafiq that the money would be delivered to her tomorrow by banks, Rukiya was continuously screaming and blaming all for the lack of timely actions.

Right at that moment of disarray and depression, one part of the entrance door opened, with the passionate address of "Dadi-Amma." Rukiya instantly opened her eyes, looked at the door, and was stunned seeing Ameen standing there. She impetuously stood up and started running toward the door with most of her saree dusting the trail.

Rukiya put both her hands on the face of Ameen, having a look, and then asked, "Are you my nati, really?" As Ameen answered affirmatively, Dadi-Amma collapsed on his chest and momentarily lost consciousness.

In their subsequent exchanges, Ameen detailed everything related to his hostage experience, but what he narrated about the thought of and link with Dada-ji dazed all. He said, "In that hours of trauma and insecurity, I started having a queer feeling, as if Dada-ji was guarding me from the other world. I felt relaxed and prayed silently, seeking his blessings and the *raham* of Allahpak. I also concluded that accidental access to Cyprus option is perhaps an ordained one coming to my rescue in placing a convincing plea to Badsha that my family is not that rich."

Having said so, he further observed, "Finishing all related requirements and paperwork, I soon plan to go to Massumpur to visit the grave of Dada-ji, thank him for taking care of me, and asking for his continued love, care, and guidance."

Everyone present was delighted, especially Shafiq uncle, who had the renewed conviction that this *nati* was a special progeny.

Rukiya Dadi-Amma, being in a perennial emotive condition, instantaneously laid out her positions, stipulating, "From now on, Shafiq Bhai will always be with you in your going out. You will only travel in our family vehicle, and I would go with you when you visit Massumpur."

Ameen jokingly commented, "For the first time this afternoon, my Dadi-Amma returned to her old-self: concise, confident, and clear. Being her *nati*, I have my position too. In these two months' time, Shafiq uncle should complete all actions to relocate the family to Dhaka before I go."

That was happily agreed to, and Ameen visited Dada-ji's grave in Massumpur, complied with the formalities related to travel, and took other steps socially warranted. But he declined to meet his mother in spite of the insistence of Dadi-Amma.

The whole family accompanied Ameen in his travel to the airport en route Nicosia. Dadi-Amma was constantly reciting Quranic *suras* (verses) for her *nati*'s safe travel but outwardly maintained a steady posture.

Rukiya recalled that during her travel times, both passengers and well-wishers could see each other until going inside the aircraft. But that was no more possible with development all around—terminals enlarged and remodeled, the number of flights registering phenomenal growth, and the enforcement of security-related restrictions.

Though steady and smart outside, sadness and irritating intramural feelings bothered Ameen very much. After saying *Khuda Hafeez* (akin to goodbye) to Shafiq Dadu, Bokul Dadi, and bestowing kisses on the forehead of his tender aunts, he took Dadi-Amma to the side and whispered, "Be careful about my pseudo mother. She lost all money and was divorced by her second husband recently. I came to know all these from the cousin of her husband who is known to me. She might show up with excuses. Please remain alert to protect yourself and me too, your *nati*."

After sharing his final thoughts, he went inside for immigration check-in and security compliance before boarding.

The family moved to the open parking lot, and Bokul and her two daughters already took seats in the car as Dadi-Amma, gawking the endless clear blue sky, continued reciting Quranic verses. Her gazing was reflective of the deep thrashing feelings within her inner self.

Rukiya, reclining by the door of the front passenger seat, her preferred one, was engrossed about life per se. She recognized that life essentially was a journey propelled by desire triggering dreams in its horizon. But the reality was that many of those were shattered in the process, activating distress, solitude, and uncertainties. But the magnificence of that soon turns to by-product dreams, bringing back contentment and gratification in life. Chasing dreams was a life reality, and accepting that can only help the journey of life.

Armed with that musing, and with no regret behind for her life, she boarded the vehicle followed by Shafiq.

The vehicle moved on, and so did life, illuminating a reality of paramount relevance.

ABOUT THE AUTHOR

Born in the Noakhali civil district of undivided Bengal, Jahed Rahman grew up in its urban locale known as Sonapur. That was the place for the residences of the higher-level district management team. Their clustered presence ushered a better social interaction milieu and quality of learning. Majority Muslims and minority Hindus shared and enjoyed life and happiness equally. Upon his retirement from government service and international financial institutions, Jahed Rahman opted to settle in Vancouver, Canada, and then relocated to Chicago, USA. Loneliness in a totally new setting of Chicago rekindled his boyhood yearning to write. Jahed Rahman's first publication dates to 2014. *Chasing Dreams* is his fifth publication since then.

CPSIA information can be obtained
at www.ICGtesting.com
Printed in the USA
LVHW090001120921
697633LV00001B/6